SWIMMING

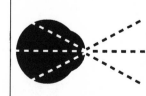

This Large Print Book carries the
Seal of Approval of N.A.V.H.

SWIMMING

JOANNA HERSHON

Thorndike Press • Waterville, Maine

Published in 2001 by arrangement with The Ballantine
Publishing Group, a division of Random House, Inc.

Thorndike Press Large Print Basic Series.

The tree indicium is a trademark of Thorndike Press.

The text of this Large Print edition is unabridged.
Other aspects of the book may vary from the original edition.

Set in 16 pt. Plantin by Rick Gundberg.

Printed in the United States on permanent paper.

Library of Congress Cataloging-in-Publication Data

Hershon, Joanna.
    Swimming / Joanna Hershon.
        p. cm.
    ISBN 0-7862-3368-0 (lg. print : hc : alk. paper)
        1. Brothers and sisters — Fiction. 2. Sibling rivalry —
Fiction. 3. New Hampshire — Fiction. 4. Fratricide —
Fiction. 5. Large type books. I. Title.
PS3558.E788 S9 2001b
813'.6—dc21   2001027460

9|01

For Derek

ACKNOWLEDGMENTS

First things first: for their encouragement, enthusiasm and, above all, love, thanks to my parents Judy and Stuart Hershon and to my brother Jordan.

For years of constant support, wit, and care, thank you Caroline Wallace, Sallie Sills, Jennifer Moorefield, Allison Frazier, and Tanya Larkin.

Thanks to Victoria Campbell and Andrea Gager; and thank you Florence Phillips, for pointing out the green lights.

I'm grateful to both the Edward F. Albee Foundation and the Bread Loaf Writers' Conference — serious blessings along the road toward taking my writing seriously.

This book was nurtured and kicked into being, beginning in Columbia University's Writing Division. My teachers Helen Schulman, Michael Cunningham, Stephen Koch, and Alan Ziegler helped me tremendously. Thanks to all of you and your very distinct forms of wisdom.

I also want to thank my classmates at Columbia for their generosity and creativity, particularly: Heather Clay, Halle Eaton, Matthew Rooney, Meg Giles, David Hopson, and Victor D. LaValle. I'm especially indebted to Robin Epstein, Merrill B. Feitell (patron saint of *Swimming*), and the fabulous Ellen Umansky, who all read the first completed draft and left me dizzy with insight and good faith.

Thanks to Tim Carroll and Mary Davis for their offerings on violence and the law (respectively), and to Amanda Davis for all kinds of great advice.

Elizabeth Sheinkman, I thank you over and over not only for your belief in me and your exquisite guidance as an agent but also for your important friendship.

Immense gratitude to Dan Smetanka, my remarkably talented editor: your vision and patience have amazed me each and every step of the way.

And finally, for his careful readings, inspiring paintings, general hilarity, and excellent love: thank you Derek Buckner.

PROLOGUE
1966

There is no such thing as silence in the woods. Vivian Silver trusted this, as she followed the man she'd met only hours ago down the pine-dark path of his property. She watched his lean figure and became hypnotized by his uneven gait, the majesty of his long narrow back. He hadn't once turned around to make sure that she'd kept up, and this did not surprise her. Just as she knew that there was no such thing as silence in the woods, she also somehow trusted that as carefully as she was watching him, he was listening even more carefully for her quick footfalls and the high-pitched swish of her navy blue windbreaker. She could feel him listening, and that was good enough.

She walked on and heard skitters of invisible creatures, the wind through the thinning pines. There was a sense of clarity that accompanied the quiet, and this was something Vivian already knew to look for in a man. When one held back from her, she couldn't help but pay attention.

The path finally opened up into a clearing, and because the sun had just set, the land — his land — was the darkest of greens, a shade brought on by October in New Hampshire when the day holds on to the richness of color even when light is gone.

There in the distance, just as he'd promised, was a pond.

She couldn't quite see the water. He was blocking her view with his body, but she could smell the wet sand and fallen leaves, the swampy, reedy darkness. And although it was unquestionably autumn, Vivian could feel the brazen heat of summer, the lovely shock of a dive. She could also hear the slice of blades on ice, the scrape and shriek of skating. On sensing this body of water, she briefly forgot why she was here. Then a distinct shift took place inside of her as he placed his hand — as if he'd done so countless times — under her long tangled hair. He still hadn't said a word. Here was a feeling both thrilling and disappointing, as if someone had just informed her that the world was about to end. Her neck was cold and his hand was warm. It was the first time they had touched.

Vivian was saving money to sail away to Spain. She was substitute teaching and writing poetry while staying with her brother Aaron. That night Aaron sent her to Cal's Bar, where he knew the bartender. Aaron knew a lot of bartenders for someone who didn't drink. He knew everybody in Portsmouth. Only months later, having decided not to go to Canada, he would die a reluctant private in a Vietnam helicopter accident; the funeral in their Massachusetts hometown would be so crowded that his pregnant sister wouldn't recognize half of the people there. Her first son would be his namesake. She would name him Aaron and pray, like any mother, that he would not die young.

But she knew none of this that evening, when she sat alone at Cal's Bar, drinking a bottle of beer. She had been aware of Jeb Wheeler's presence since he'd walked through the door in worn jeans, a workshirt, and a red down vest. She guessed he was at least thirty-five. He was very tall and thin with a long crooked nose, full lips, and arresting green eyes. It was his eyes that she noticed first. There was something wrong with them. She tried not to stare as he sat down beside her and ordered a rare hamburger. She tried not to stare but soon became acutely aware that he was the one who was staring. And he wasn't shy about it either.

"Hello," he said.

"Oh, hi." She smiled and looked into his eyes that were strange. As one moved normally in the socket, the other stayed quite still. While his pupils were the same light green color and were framed by the same long dark lashes, the left eye appeared to be made of glass. It was foreign and would stay foreign. She'd never quite get used to it.

"I've never been here," she said, just to say something.

But he wasn't like that. He kept on looking at her and smiling. Finally he said, "Well, I'm glad you're here now."

She told him what there was to tell about herself, how she'd graduated from college and was leaving for Spain in the springtime. She tried to keep it brief and ended up drinking her beer too quickly. He didn't ask many questions and the ones he did ask were blunt: *Why Spain? What will you do for money once you're there? Have you noticed my eye yet?*

He had lived in New York City and worked as a chemist. In a slightly suspect explanation of how he'd ended up here — looking like a lumberjack or possibly a carpenter — Vivian learned that he had sold something, a patent of sorts, and that he had quit his job.

"What do you do now?" she asked, leaning into him, not completely aware she was doing

12

so. She could smell woodsmoke on his clothes, the faint toxic smell of varnish.

"Well," he said, smiling, as if he somehow wasn't quite sure what to say, "I bought land. I bought some fine land, and I've been building myself a house."

"Where is it?" Vivian asked. She pictured herself on top of him on a spare iron bed, being cold and even lonely and asking him to build a fire. She didn't bother trying to stop fantasizing. She knew herself better than that.

"It's about forty-five minutes from here," he said, and raised his eyebrows. "Kind of out there." He gave her a look as if to say, *I dare you.*

When he was through with his burger, they left together. He opened the passenger door of his truck for her.

He said, "You don't need to worry; I'm not very dangerous."

Until that moment, the thought hadn't crossed her mind.

And now they were in a forest clearing between his half-built house and the pond. Pine needles covered the loamy ground, and sycamores framed the sky. They weren't looking at each other. As he moved his hand very gently along the back of her pale neck, she found she was straining to see the pond —

13

over his shoulder, beyond the trees — as if to see the black-green water would be to inhabit the sense of certainty that she knew water created. But from where she stood, the water was not much more than a ghost in the trees watching and assessing this union.

Vivian reached out to touch him, letting him know right away where she stood. Under the down vest, his denim shirt was hot. She rested her hand there as if it were the most normal thing in the world.

"Beautiful," she finally said. The trees moved so slightly. The sky was full of stars.

"You are," he told her, and, taking her pale face in his two rough hands, he kissed her.

A kiss can be as minuscule as a moth or the tiny flame it craves, a torn fingernail or an eyelash; and yet a kiss can be huge. It can be as expansive and dangerous as this one was. It can be the origin of a family.

They kissed softly and tenderly at first, and then things got rougher. As the clear sky became clearer and darker, they grabbed hold of each other's clothing. They kissed hard, almost bitterly, as if they resented their mutual attraction.

They were both impatient people. They'd wage battles against impatience all their lives, but not tonight. Tonight they did exactly what they wanted.

They didn't even make it to the house. Without any debate, she lay down on the cold damp grass. She wasn't taking birth control pills and he didn't use a rubber, and — as if it were a dream and she was using dream logic — she found she knew exactly what she was doing without any fear of consequences. Vivian watched for the pond over his shoulder but couldn't see a thing; the *promise* of a pond sat under the moon and stared at her boldly, watching her gasp for breath. She thought of Spain with a kind of nostalgia: it seemed smaller than before and awfully far away. She said goodbye to Cordoba and Sevilla, adios to flamenco and paella.

He breathed in her ear and she kissed his long, stubbled neck.

"I can't believe we just did that," he told her. But she knew that he was lying.

"Let me show you the house," Jeb said, after gently taking her hand in his and heading for the path. When he kissed her again, she felt a surge of greed and strained to see the water. "What?" he asked.

He was close to her, leaning down to see her face. She could smell the varnish and the brackish smell of his sweat. It was purely carnal and she backed away from him — head tilted, coy — as if she had a secret.

"What?" he repeated.

She retreated some more — a come-and-catch-me set of eyes, an attempt at a wicked smile. The water was so close just beyond the stand of trees and weeds, and — with a toss of her hair, having barely a notion of what she was doing — she ran.

As she expected, he did not run after her. Vivian was now free to get as near to the water as possible, to trample over the fallen wet reeds and feel her boots sink into the sand. The wind blew and the pond came to her, slowly lapped at her boot toes in a lazy, ancient rhythm. The moon shone down in a harsh slant, casting the pond as particularly separate from the soil and the trees and from her. She felt younger out here in this untamed space, and — as if she were being watched, as if the pond itself were judging her — she stood up straighter as she surveyed the landscape. She took a deep clean breath.

Jagged rocks began a few yards to her left. Smooth slabs framed the water, flat as if they'd been carefully beaten down. Dried-out grass stood tall, interspersed with endless weeds.

She wouldn't have changed a thing.

The pond wore its surroundings like careless attire, as if to protect its luminous beauty. Its surface shimmered, innocent of the forest's tall shadows or the mountains' cranky terrain. The water divulged nothing, and she couldn't help but bend down and touch it with her fingertips. It felt brutally cold, and she put her fingers in her mouth at once, sucking back some comfort from herself. Vivian gazed at the water and there it was — her reflected self, round as an infant but twice the size. Then, quick as lightning, the distorted shape was gone as a dark cloud shrouded the moon.

Here was where she would make her life. Over years to come she would swim and sunbathe, take walks with Jeb and the children, take time alone with her thoughts. She would eat potluck meals here, engaging in terrific conversations with neighbors who would move away. And later in life, after drinking too much, she would come straight to the slabs of rock by the water's edge and she would sit — her mouth parted, too tired for wonder — staring at the water for hours.

This was where her future would unfold. Later she'd say she knew it right then and without a single doubt. She would tell her sons and daughter that she just knew it, the same way she knew that Spain was only a single country on so many maps of the world.

"Why are you crying?" Jeb asked her.

Vivian looked from him to the pond and back again. She shook her head and wiped tears from her eyes. She was only twenty-two. She placed her hand, still wet from the water, on his warm and solid chest.

He looked at her strangely, as if she'd done something wrong.

1987

PART ONE

AARON AND SUZANNE

The force behind the movement of time
is a mourning that will not be comforted.
        — *Marilynne Robinson*

CHAPTER ONE

The house was waiting.

This was how it looked to Aaron Wheeler as he drove the last stretch of gravel driveway, up past the compost shed, and through the overgrown passage of trees. The house itself looked aglow, so much so that it was almost difficult for Aaron to picture his family inside of it. And because his girlfriend Suzanne — willowy, pale — had yet to meet the rest of the Wheelers, Aaron knew that she wasn't picturing anyone either. Aaron watched how she sat beside him, her knobby knees together, her feet on the littered floor of the car. He knew all she could see through the evening rain was the yellow light from within the house — the house that really was so tiny, especially against the backdrop of pine trees, hemlocks, and the darkening sky.

Aaron's judgment was cloudy, and colored with the pink and white and saffron and brown colors of Suzanne's flesh. His judgment was so clouded that, gazing at the house, as the skies rained and rained, he could not really conjure up the hostility that had infused his last visit home.

Why had he left? Jack. It was his brother that he couldn't vividly recall. Aaron hadn't spoken to Jack since one awkward conversation in late February (his initiative, his phone bill). But with the way the house looked after driving five hours, all aglow and everything, Aaron knew he could get Jack to come around, the way he always could in the past. Aaron knew this, but he also realized the rain was buying him time, blocking out the sound of the tires on the gravel, so his family wouldn't necessarily be aware that he and Suzanne had arrived. He wasn't in any hurry to get out of the car. The clean smell of pine and rain filtered into the silver station wagon, and Suzanne, following his lead, sat immobile. When they each looked back on the weekend, neither Aaron nor Suzanne would remember how they sat in a kind of preliminary state, watching the house in the rain. Neither of them would remember this moment, this wisdom of hesitation.

They held hands, or rather Aaron held on to Suzanne's fingers, one by one, as loosely as if they were dandelion stems. They talked. They talked as if they had not been driving through traffic and had finally arrived, hungry, at their destination.

Suzanne asked about Lila, the precious little accident, born in 1979, the year the United Nations declared the year of the child. She was born exactly on time and immediately following the county's biggest blizzard since the early 1800s. Her first day on earth was white and hot, a freakish rise in temperature that he still remembered. Was the little girl spoiled? No, Aaron responded, never having considered it before. No, he didn't think so. If anything, his sister was independent. She was an imaginative kid, a bit of a performer, a kid who liked to stare. They didn't talk about Jack. Aaron did not babble on about how Jack didn't talk to him much anymore (since throwing a rock at Aaron's head last summer), didn't repeat what he'd already told her, how Jack was unpredictable in every way, and how (though he'd probably screwed most waitresses in town and tried with all the others) the last Aaron had heard, his brother was dating a girl who won first prize for marksmanship at a nearby county fair. How Jack was, no doubt, one of the most confused people ever.

That Friday evening sitting in the car, the world around Aaron a blurred silver and green, the absence of Jack's name was no accident. He wondered how much he should explain, as he put his hand on Suzanne's neck, where she was always warm and slightly damp, no matter what the weather. He held on to her fingers more tightly.

"I always wanted older brothers," Suzanne said suddenly, while tracing a raindrop down the glass. "If I were your sister's age, I'd be so jealous of her."

"I wanted older brothers too," Aaron said. But as soon as he said it, he knew it wasn't true. He always liked the idea of being the eldest; he only wanted to be treated as if he were older, as if he had some answers worth knowing. Aaron waited for questions that never came. He wanted to advise.

Suzanne rolled down the window a crack; the humidity felt like a familiar day, as if this had all happened before. She said, "Why are we sitting in the car?"

Aaron looked at Suzanne as they both laughed at an unidentifiable absurdity, one that Aaron knew they both only recognized in each other — a shared skewed vision that again and again precluded the need for explanation. He thought that this feeling was particular to him. It never occurred to him that there might have been sculpture studio mates and study partners, people from the computer lab where she pulled all-nighters, who had that very same feeling around Suzanne. It never occurred to Aaron that she might be simply that way — charming — and he was unduly affected.

"Are you nervous?" she asked him, with an unmistakable tone of delight.

"Am I?"

"I don't know, that's why I ask. Are you afraid I'll say the wrong things?" She meant it, he knew, but she was also smiling broadly, as if they were acting out a routine, and that both of them knew their real story was nothing like this nervous hesitance, but one of making SpaghettiOs in a hot pot, of watching the reflection of headlights pass across the ceiling of Suzanne's messy darkened room. Her smile was a smirk, as if she knew him, and Aaron felt blessed under this flicker of understanding.

"Are you nervous?" she repeated.

"Just terrified," he said, smiling back at her. She had a chipped front tooth that reminded him of black coffee in teacups, cream, saucers, cats.

"Do I look okay?" Suzanne asked him. Suzanne, who looked good to him when she was nauseous and green, when she was covered with bright red hives. Suzanne who'd look good bald and toothless.

"Fine," he said. He even added a shrug. He knew, by now, that his appreciation was excessive, and that she needed a dose of self-doubt every now and then to keep her interest keen.

"Seriously, do I? Are you nervous they'll think I'm . . . you know, whatever I am?" She started giggling. "What am I, anyway?"

He kissed her before he said something dumb, something about how important she was, how, well, *too* important this felt, how he knew they were young, but . . . Aaron closed his eyes and felt her touch his dick, above the worn crotch of his jeans, felt her trace the outline not too lightly, not too roughly. Of course it felt good, but that wasn't really the point, was it? They were in his family driveway. Any second someone could have come running outside. But her hand felt good, didn't it? And didn't he want to show Suzanne that he wasn't nearly as tense as he so often seemed? He kept quiet and couldn't help thinking that maybe this would be the weekend when fun alone wouldn't be enough for her.

Aaron opened his eyes. As Suzanne kissed his neck, he looked toward the house again and caught sight of his brother Jack with his hand out the upstairs window, feeling the rain on his skin. His brother's hand was thin and pale, and with his fingers cupped as if to catch the rain, it was more like a claw than a hand. Aaron figured there was a fifty-fifty chance he

26

would have made it tonight for dinner, or for that matter, home this weekend at all. Suzanne must have sensed Aaron's distraction, for she pulled away slightly and must have also noticed Jack, with his shaved head and oversize sleeve hanging loosely from his arm. Jack may or may not have even noticed the car in the driveway, had Suzanne not pulled her hand away from Aaron and placed it on the car horn, pressing down briefly and hard. Aaron couldn't help jumping from the abrupt blast of sound. "Why did you do that?" Aaron demanded, his voice a reluctant reprimand.

Suzanne said, "I don't know," as if she were equally surprised. And then the smile. "Sorry," she added.

Aaron looked up for Jack's response to the horn but his younger brother had disappeared, perhaps just behind the curtains, perhaps out of the room. Before Aaron could tell Suzanne it was okay, not to worry, he saw his eight-year-old sister emerge from the front door, running in boots far too big, out into the downpour. It took a second to recognize her, so greatly was she changed. Lila was a chameleon, one visit chubby and bubbly, and another time slim and serious. This time, with summer starting, she was quite skinny and a little tan. Lila was a great deal taller, and her hair was longer and blonder than he recalled.

He was always surprised by her unadulterated excitement, how genuinely happy she was to see him.

When Lila began knocking on the car window, getting soaked with rain, Aaron realized that he was still not moving. Aaron had a vision of driving away right then and there, perhaps leaving his sister puzzled in the driveway, perhaps pulling her inside before wildly speeding away. She would love that, Lila would; she loved getting lost, then making suggestions. She loved everything about driving.

"Plan on getting out anytime soon?" Suzanne said. She popped three spearmint Tic Tacs into her mouth.

Aaron saw his mother Vivian calling from the doorway. Lila waited outside the car — smiling, and wet as if she'd dived into the pond fully clothed. He couldn't see Jack but Aaron could still feel him watching.

"Aaron!" Suzanne said, impatient yet cheerful, as she unlocked the passenger door and stepped out into the rain.

But when Aaron tried to open his car door, it somehow wouldn't open. Through the rain-speckled window, his mother and Lila and Suzanne looked at him quizzically, as he tried to fiddle with the lock. Minutes passed as Aaron attempted to force the car door open, as his heart set to pounding, and his palms began sweating, along with the rest of his body. The inside of the car felt like a separate planet from the outside of the car, which was, he told himself, New Hampshire. Home. His family. Suzanne. It was where he was supposed to be.

What felt like minutes was, of course, only a moment, but when he emerged from the car, he was oddly choked up. He could barely say hello as the sky bleated a shot of thunder, and Suzanne, Aaron, and Lila dashed into the house.

"Hello, Noodle," his mother Vivian cried, frizzy-haired and frantic. "Lila, I swear to God, you'd better not get sick — what were you thinking?"

Lila shrugged, and Vivian smiled at Aaron and Suzanne. Vivian's smile was expansive; it filled the space around them. She kissed Aaron, kissed Suzanne, saying, "It's so nice to meet you, sweetie," and to Aaron, "Welcome home, darling." *Darling?* It took Aaron an extra beat to realize she was speaking to him. She called him *Noodle. Darling.* Her endearments seemed self-conscious, overly motherly, and she seemed smaller, more delicate than ever. She had maintained a particular elegance after all her years of living in the woods; her presence was no less than opulent.

This evening her eyes were lined with dark green liner and she wore copper lipstick. The blue glass beads around her long neck were dotted with raindrops. Water was dripping everywhere, onto the hand-planed floors and the Turkish rugs. It seemed important to Aaron to stop the dripping, to stop the wood from soaking. His mother was so pretty and careless. It seemed a certainty that the floors, the walls, were bound to warp.

"You're late," Lila said disapprovingly. "You said you'd be here by four."

"The rain," Aaron replied, as he swooped his sister on top of his back, grateful for something to do. "Lila, this is Suzanne."

Suzanne was luminescent. She'd smelled like rain long before rain came. She placed her hand on Lila's knee and gave a small squeeze. But Lila watched Suzanne from the vantage of Aaron's back, giving a definite once-over, doing her best not to look impressed. Aaron could hear Suzanne mutter, "Well, excuse me."

"Don't mind her," Aaron whispered, but Suzanne merely raised an eyebrow as Jack came down the creaky stairs and into the living room where Suzanne and Vivian smiled and nodded. Jack said hello. Aaron wondered, though it had been years since acne had conquered Jack's face, why he still pictured his brother's face spread with it, and why he also thought of Jack as small, skinny. But small and skinny had turned into lanky years ago, and Jack's face was what Aaron supposed one would call craggy: each feature separately a disaster, but taken in all at once, his was a look of impressive disproportion. Aaron had to admit Jack was no longer quite funny-looking. In fact, there was nothing funny about him.

Aaron lifted Lila securely onto his shoulders. He kissed his mother's cheek. He nodded at Jack. Aaron put his hand, casually, on the small of Suzanne's back. He noticed Jack's feet were bare with toenails polished navy blue. There was a slap of thunder and Lila screamed. Aaron held her ankles tightly but she screamed more, and so he put her down. Aaron Wheeler did things step by step, the only way he knew how, when he was nervous, when he was beginning, when he was unaware that in days to come, even this capacity to be gradual would seem as impossible and strange as blue toenails on his only brother, the honk of a car horn blaring through the humid air, strange as the hand that had sounded the horn, the fair freckled hand of Suzanne.

Aaron's father wasn't home yet. The rain

had stopped and night had gently fallen. Everyone sat at the cherry-wood table and proceeded (including Lila, who sipped from their mother's wineglass) to become tipsy. Suzanne had excused herself to the bathroom minutes ago, and Aaron was trying, against his own wishes, to gauge how impressed his family was with Suzanne. As much as he wanted not to care, he did care, a lot. But no one acknowledged his girlfriend's absence as a time to give Aaron the thumbs-up, or to mouth, *Wow.* He felt panicked and doubtful, as if he didn't know his mother and his siblings very well at all. He tried to take a closer look at them. He watched how Jack and Lila both seemed a little off center, as if gravity were somehow slightly different for both of them, how Vivian was opposingly sturdy, in her small, elongated way. They each came into focus again as people to whom he was somehow bound.

His mother's green eyeliner had predictably smudged. By the candlelight, she looked exhausted and young, as if she'd done her eyes dramatically, with intention. Jack kept his hand either on top of his newly shaved head or deep in a bag of Doritos, which Lila continued to tell him were full of additives. Lila was a recent vegetarian and proponent of health food, which made his mother amused but not necessarily happy. Vivian liked indulgence. Rural life, as she called it, was spartan enough without dietary restrictions. In the kitchen, the chicken simmered in white wine, butter, capers, and three kinds of olives; chive mashed potatoes were long ago whipped into a buttery slope of a mountain. Slivered almonds lay — waiting for their string beans — oiled and salted, fixed as closed eyes. The hot food sat hot; the cold food — on ceramic platters, in a subzero refrigerator — stayed perfectly cold.

Suzanne — he tried not to notice — had been in the bathroom a long time.

When he got up from the table, Aaron knew Jack would watch where he went. He was only getting some water, he thought, and then, once up, he might as well give a listen at the door. Maybe Suzanne was sick. Maybe she drank too fast. He had to check on her. He waited at the door for a few seconds, and when he was about to knock, she stepped right out, looking just fine. "You okay?" he asked.

"I just got really involved in an article in *Country Living*." The tips of her ears flushed. "I'm a little nervous, actually. Just getting my bearings."

Aaron felt fulfilled and ashamed. "You have nothing to be nervous about."

"Thank you," she said, and Suzanne kissed him on the neck, where her lips naturally reached without his leaning down. "I know."

They returned and joined the conversation, and Suzanne kept her feet entwined with his underneath the table. *Maybe,* a small voice said in the very back of Aaron's mind, *maybe you shouldn't have brought her.*

When Jeb came home everyone stopped talking. He smiled, grabbed Aaron in a powerful hug, and shook Suzanne's hand. Aaron's father's deep physical affection always came as a surprise. He said no more than a few words (none of which being "Sorry, I'm late") before going upstairs to wash his hands. He hummed: *It's only a paper moon floating over a cardboard sea, but it wouldn't be make-believe if you believed in me.* Aaron was accustomed to his father — his limited use of words and limited array of songs to hum — but now, somewhere between being irritated at Jeb's lateness and being thrilled to see him, Aaron was struck with the question of how his father knew that particular song. As Jeb came back down the stairs, and Aaron looked at his father's glass eye, he wondered if Suzanne had already noticed how spooky and sightless it was.

At the dinner table, Aaron could barely

concentrate. He listened to his right, where Suzanne asked Jack questions about his many jobs, seemingly through with her bout of nerves. She asked about house painting — had he ever fallen from a ladder? Did he ever paint the wrong color? She asked Jack about his current job as a sous-chef. She even made him laugh. Suzanne had the uncanny ability to ask nonsensical questions and still sound extremely intelligent. Jack was obliging her with the story of how once, on a construction job, a chain saw sliced his neck. He told the story lightly, punching up the absurdity, a maniacal gleam in his eyes.

Lila said, "You drove yourself to the hospital."

"That's right," Jack said. "I didn't even feel anything until I was on the highway, halfway there."

"I thought the paramedics took you," Aaron said, as though he wasn't sure if he wanted to take part in the conversation.

"No," Jack said, and shot him a look. "No, I drove myself."

"He was in shock," Lila explained.

"He was an idiot," Jeb said dryly.

"That's right," Jack said, taking a sip of water, "I was."

There was a silence, and his mother said, "Lila, why don't you help me clear the table."

"I'll help," said Suzanne, and everyone but Jeb ended up bringing dishes into the kitchen. Jack slipped out the kitchen door. Jeb was already out on the front porch — with a joint, Aaron knew — looking out at the starless sky, keeping quiet.

The table was covered with cloth napkins, and the cherry wood dipped in places from years of holding up heavy platters. A scratchy recording of Bob Dylan singing with Johnny Cash played softly; his father must have put it on. Vivian brought a bowl of walnuts and a nutcracker to the table. Lila took a nut from the bowl, and Aaron made to catch it, but Lila only passed it back and forth between her hands, having her own game of hot potato. Aaron noticed Suzanne fumble with the prongs and give his mother a helpless grin.

"You've never cracked a nut open?" Vivian asked Suzanne gently, as Suzanne hesitated, with one hand holding a walnut, one the silver. Aaron couldn't tell if his mother was trying to intimidate Suzanne. Vivian was as charming as ever but also just as elusive, watching Suzanne with an expression that Aaron found difficult to read. It was, at this point, impossible for him to understand why someone might not be positively drawn to Suzanne. Bringing Suzanne home seemed to be one way of showing her how strongly he felt, because he loved the *idea* of home — a full refrigerator, walks in the woods, late nights with his storytelling mother — but now that he was here, he was still craving the idea of it. The evening headache he'd begun to associate with New York had arrived right on time. His mother, though animated, looked exhausted, like someone who stayed up all night turning lights on and off. Lila chewed a walnut and then, instead of swallowing it, squished the softened meat with her fingers.

"Lila, honey," Vivian said, nodding to the mess in the little girl's hands. "Eat it or don't."

"I'm not eating it," she said confidently, sitting up straighter and continuing to finger the transformed walnut. "I just softened it up." Her expression was one that he'd seen countless times and photographed years ago. Her eyes and mouth were absolutely set, determined in their stare. Sometimes he wondered if photographing her so often at such a young age hadn't constructed a border — however delicate — between them. He couldn't help notice that while Lila gave Jack straightforward adoration, she was more hot and cold with her eldest brother — not unlike a celebrity out on the town, someone who knew in her bones, all the time, that she was being watched.

Just then she made a fish face at him, undoing his worry by degrees. Lila, he didn't doubt, would always get what she needed from this world. After the fish face, after his smile, her own face went deadpan. The kid possessed eyes like deep water, the lazy stealth of a tiger.

"Do you have any brothers or sisters?" his mother asked Suzanne, who shook her head and said evenly:

"It was really just my mom and me, for the most part. My dad moved away when I was about Lila's age." She laughed, not quite nervously.

Aaron pulled his chair away from the table. Suzanne seemed comfortable with his mother and sister, so he went into the kitchen for a beer. In the bright kitchen, the only bright room in the house, dishes covered the countertop, and the aluminum trash can was filled to the brim. He could hear the lazy thump of Jack dribbling a basketball on the tar patch out back, betting against himself, over and over again. Aaron grabbed two Molsons from the fridge as he thought about Suzanne's affinity for questions, how she loved any games that involved difficult questions. She always insisted on answers. He remembered one question in particular: *What kind of life do you think your brother will lead?*

More exciting and more miserable than mine, was what Aaron had thought.

"You don't have any predictions?" she'd asked, and he'd felt her waiting. She was usually waiting for him to say something. Sometimes her expectation was exhausting.

"No," Aaron had said, feigning disinterest. *He'll move through cities like a shadow,* is what he could have told her; *Jack will laugh hard and make no sound.*

Paused in the kitchen, beers in hand, Aaron heard his mother send Lila to bed. Lila said she wasn't going to bed. She wasn't hysterical, his sister, and Aaron smiled at Lila's matter-of-fact tone, which she maintained even when she was beat and finally agreed to go to sleep. He made a silent promise to pay her more attention; he could learn a thing or two from Lila about maintaining a sense of control.

Out the back door, the cool ripe smell of almost-summer lightened his mood, and the Molsons in his hands gave him the props he needed in order to deal with Jack. Aaron watched Jack swish five in a row, the ball flying through the tattered net with the sound of wings flapping. Jack's lower jaw, always prominent, was exaggerated because he was concentrating. "You look like a marine," Aaron said, offering Jack a beer.

"No, thanks," Jack said, referring to the Molson. Aaron popped one open and put the other down in the grass, watching as the ball bounced fiercely off the backboard. Aaron attempted a rebound with his one free hand, but Jack swiped the ball away.

As Aaron watched his brother's lanky shape twist its way into a layup, he couldn't help but say it: "Thrown any rocks lately?"

"Oh, all the time," Jack tossed off without bothering to stop his rapid-fire dribbling, without so much as looking up. "I might just be a danger to society," he said, and sent another shot toward the aging net, which barely hung together anymore.

"I doubt that very much," Aaron managed. He fought himself not to console his brother, not to say, *It's okay that you hurled a rock at my head for no apparent reason. Hey, buddy? Let's just forget about it. Forget that you never explained.* Aaron knew this was a tricky business, the business of Jack's fucking up. The rules of the business went like this: if Aaron stayed angry, that meant he felt unsettled at best. All the time. He simply didn't have the temperament to carry that kind of fight around with him, to incorporate that night with Jack as normal behavior, no more than a part of their filial history.

As he watched his brother's cocky hands

cradling the basketball, Aaron wanted to grab the ball from Jack and rage about what a mistake it is to throw a sharp rock at your own brother's head. But more than that, to his keen disappointment, Aaron wanted only to make up. This was not only disappointing because he was always making the first move to clear the air, but because Jack was doing nothing more than pounding a basketball into the ground, aiming to beat some personal record he'd never think to share.

Aaron watched the ball and fought the nagging image of Jack hurling a rock at his head. He had to fight bringing it up, because as unsettled as he was, he needed to save some degree of face. He'd learned at least this by now: even if Jack never intended to apologize, it would piss Jack off to no end if Aaron were to treat him with any more fairness than Jack thought he deserved.

Aaron took a step away from the court and looked up at the blue-black sky. Nothing ever changed. Here he was, armed with nothing but beer and shared unpleasant memories, waiting for Jack to say something that could come only from Jack. It was Jack who could remove this heavy feeling, because he was pretty sure that Jack lacked any of it. *Some of us*, he thought, as he watched Jack dribble, *are free. And some of us are not. That's not to say that the free are necessarily any better off. They can become selfish and cold of heart. They can be cowards.* For here was his brother only months after behaving downright absurdly, not to mention violently. Here was Jack involved and engaged with only his game. Jack seemed as if he couldn't possibly care less whether the whole incident was ever mentioned again.

"Don't be an asshole," Aaron finally blurted. "Pass me the goddamn ball." And something relaxed inside him.

"Let's just play," Jack muttered. "Put your beer down."

"Fine."

"But you want to *talk*, don't you," Jack said with a smile, while swinging his long, skinny arms in a dribble. "You don't really care about playing."

"And what would I want to talk about?" Aaron stole the ball, took a shot, and the ball swished beautifully.

"All my bad behavior."

"It just wouldn't kill you to apologize," Aaron said louder than he'd intended, dodging Jack and using his height and weight to full advantage.

A voice came out of the darkness: "Apologize for what?"

Upon seeing Lila seated in the grass, Aaron

42

stopped dribbling and Jack stole the ball, went for a wicked layup. "Shit! You scared me," Aaron said. "Did you know she was sitting there?"

"Don't talk about me like I'm not here. And you shouldn't curse, asshole," Lila said. "Did you see me, Jack?"

Jack shrugged almost playfully.

"Apologize for what?" Lila said. She wore a white cotton nightgown with a bit of lace at the sleeves, but with her messy hair and bare dirty feet outstretched on the ground, she looked unfamiliar with the life of girls. She stood up and asked again.

"Last summer," Aaron said, pointing at his forehead. "Remember?"

She looked at him almost blankly. "He already did apologize."

"I can't believe this," Aaron said. "He already did *not*."

"Lyle bug," Jack said to her, "I kinda didn't."

"Oh." She shrugged. "Well, do it then. Just say you're sorry."

"He'll never let it go, even if I say it. Even if I say it a thousand times. That's just the way he is."

"Oh, fuck you, Jack," Aaron said.

"You're being shitheads," Lila said. "Shithead one and shithead two."

"Great," Jack said, looking at Aaron, and both of them had to laugh. "Way to go."

"Who's winning?" Lila asked, pointing to the basketball between Jack's hand and hip.

"Nobody," Aaron said, and offered his shoulders for Lila to climb on, but she ignored the offer. "Aren't you supposed to be in bed?"

"I couldn't go to sleep," she said, and then, "Jack, pass!"

Jack passed to Lila, but the ball slipped through her grasp right into Aaron's hands. He immediately threw the ball in the air, and she caught it then. "Nice catch," Aaron said.

"I didn't even," she said in exasperation. "You helped." Lila bounced the ball a few times with both hands, stopping to look at Jack. "What do you think of Aaron's *girlfriend?*"

Aaron could feel his nerves climbing up his stomach, climbing into his neck, could feel himself not wanting Jack to answer.

"Phony," was what Jack said. Lila bounced him the ball.

"Phony?" Aaron said, hot in the face. "No."

"Okay," Jack said. "What did you think, Lyle?"

"Phony," she said, laughing, as if this all meant no more than a game.

"I think Lila likes her," Jack said, and Aaron couldn't tell if Jack's voice was creeping toward contrition.

"No," Lila said.

"This bug stared at your girlfriend all through dinner."

"I did not!" she yelled too loudly, but kept a trace of a smile.

Inside, the music stopped and the lamplight switched off, leaving the very faint glow of yellow candles. Lila ran off toward her ground-floor bedroom window, climbing through it expertly, without so much as a wave.

Suzanne appeared in the kitchen doorway, backlit by candles, her hands snug in her jeans' soft pockets. Aaron fought the urge to unzip her zipper and pull, right then, on the fraying denim. "Hey," Jack said loudly. He threw the ball hard, too hard, at Suzanne. She caught it anyway.

"You're too cool," Aaron said, attempting to hide how impressed he genuinely was. Suzanne stepped out of the doorway, gave him the purest of smiles, and passed the ball back to Jack.

"Hey, yourself," she said to his brother.

Aaron looked at him.

"*What?*" Jack said.

"Nothing at all," Aaron said. "Nothing whatsoever."

His mother approached the doorway, detangling her curly hair with nail-bitten fingers. Vivian's hooded eyes and flushed face revealed just how much she'd had to drink. "Good night, all," she said with a yawn, and made her way toward the stairs. And just as Aaron knew Jack would soon disappear, he also knew that his father was already in bed, not having seen the purpose in a formal conclusion to the evening.

"Zander's swinging by any minute," Jack said, as if he were trying to get them to leave him alone.

Aaron nodded, mumbled something to the effect of "Have a ball," and, taking Suzanne's hand, moved inside the dark house, leaving Jack to wait. *Let him wait,* Aaron thought. *Let him wait all night.*

In the kitchen, the house was peppered with the sounds of nighttime in an old, poorly insulated house, where concentration was required to believe in silence, to ignore the occasional noisy floorboards and the sound of running water coursing through silt-covered pipes. Water ran, right then, upstairs in his parents' bathroom. Aaron recognized the familiar pattern of his mother washing her face; he could almost see the smudge of green eyeliner swirling down the cracked porcelain sink into the oxidized drain. Suzanne leaned him up against the refrigerator and Aaron closed his eyes. Suzanne began to kiss him, holding his face the way she did, the way she held a thing and made it beautiful. The sound of water stopped but was replaced by the refrigerator hum. He placed his hands on the cool metallic surface for balance. Suzanne pressed against him, lips at his ear, all breath and skin and hips. Suzanne undid his belt, his pants. He swore the green glass bottles on the windowsill were floating, hovering above the sill — then flew to the floor and crashed. They crashed like the ocean in his ear, the tip of her tongue, the broken glass. "Suzanne." He stopped her, broke free of her grasp. The bottles stood upright in their place on the sill. "Suzanne!" he whispered, and the caution in his voice disgusted him.

"Okay," she said, much louder than his whisper, and pulled him back out the door. It was his turn to find a place to do this, he knew, if he had such a problem with the kitchen. Without much thought, he wandered toward the willow tree between the tar patch and Lila's window. He thought they could find a space under the hanging branches, but the grass there was terribly overgrown and the ground was a puddle of mud. They were kissing sloppily on the lawn, and for a second Aaron opened his eyes and caught a glimpse of his brother waiting in the driveway, staring out toward the highway. Aaron knew that Jack couldn't see them, that they were obscured by the corner of the house, and right then, before Suzanne pulled him down to the chilly ground, before he was taken up in her scent, in the moment before he forgot exactly where he was, Aaron saw his brother looking straight ahead with a completely expressionless gaze. Aaron had always felt that Jack preferred being alone, but that night, as Aaron watched his brother lit up by the lights of an oncoming car, he felt distinctly like a spy. It seemed that Jack was not only alone, but also always would be. It was hard to believe that Jack was a younger brother, let alone his own younger brother. Jack seemed older, even *old*, standing in the hard light. Aaron could feel Jack mocking him as he touched and kissed Suzanne. Aaron sensed the night had ended in a way he did not understand. He was awake, he was turned on, he was with the only girl he wanted, he was home. Yet, as he tried to lose himself completely within Suzanne's tenderness, he could not shake the sense that something was over, and, without understanding how, Aaron knew with the same conviction that it was Jack who had made it so.

CHAPTER TWO

Suzanne found herself holding her breath, something she knew she did more and more often whenever she and her boyfriend Aaron fooled around. She held her breath in his dorm room and in hers, at the movies when they kissed, when they met on the corner of 118th Street, after she'd had a late class. She held her breath that Friday night, on the grass between Aaron's family's house and a low-hanging willow tree. Suzanne waited for something to happen — some reckless, greedy feeling like love. Aaron's palms pressed against her back; he pulled her toward him as they knelt. He took off his sweater, placed it on the damp ground, and she sat on it, waiting. She closed her eyes and found herself wanting to release the breath but somehow unable to do so. Aaron began to kiss her neck, and she finally exhaled. When she opened her eyes, she noticed something new.

The ground-floor window of the house was

open, the blue curtains parted, and Aaron's sister Lila was watching them. She was supposed to be asleep, but here she was, elbows on the wide sill, apparently sitting up in her bed. Suzanne's hands were on Aaron's neck and when she saw Lila — matted curls, white nightgown — she instinctively tugged his hair. But he pressed on, kissing her collarbone, her shoulder, and Suzanne didn't say anything. She watched the girl through half-closed eyes. She didn't tell Aaron to stop. As he lowered himself on top of her — his jeans on her jeans, his chest and shoulders — she kissed him hard and promised herself that if the kid was still watching when she pulled away, she'd call the whole thing off. But he felt good, the weight of him, and the way he held back some of his body. She forgot to open her eyes. When she remembered, moments later, and when she saw that Lila still watched, she figured it was too late to do much about it.

There was something about the way the kid leaned on her hand, with her head slightly cocked, that was oddly grounding. *Here I am,* Suzanne thought to herself. *I'm separate from everyone else in the world. I am eleven years older than Lila; Aaron's one year older than me. When this little girl was born, I was living with both of my parents and I was not pretty at all.* Lila's hair was wild and honey-colored, extending over her small shoulders, and her tiny lavender-painted fingertips touched together, then briefly rubbed her eyes. Suzanne didn't imagine Lila would want to be caught looking. To be acknowledged would only cause the kid embarrassment. Suzanne had an urge to grin at her, to mouth the words, *Our secret.*

Suzanne knew Lila wouldn't tell anyone what she saw; she could already glean that much about her. This kid was all about impressing her elders — her sexy elder brothers — and this was something Suzanne respected. She had been the same kind of little girl — not coy but not quite tough either — needing the high opinion of others. But Suzanne didn't want to go too far in front of the little girl — that would be just *low,* but who knew? Suzanne thought, a dose of heavy petting might not be so bad for Lila to see. Suzanne found herself shaking out her hair, arching her back just that much further. She couldn't help but perform a little, knowing she was being observed; she began to wonder what she looked like as she kissed, and suspected her lips looked swallowed. She focused on her hands — spread her fingers on Aaron's back, pressing hard. She tried to feel adored. They should've been down by water. It just seemed like the thing to do. She imagined her mother's nasal voice: *There was a pond there? A private pond?* She'd describe it as no big deal. She imagined summers by water, swimming whenever she felt like it. It was impossible to see the pond from the house — it was too far away, eclipsed by forest — but since it was there, and they'd driven all the way from Manhattan, and it was the first night after exams, she didn't see a reason why she and Aaron shouldn't just go swimming.

Earlier, when she and Aaron had arrived, Suzanne was surprised not to see the pond, but Aaron assured her it was behind the stand of trees at the end of the sloping lawn. He rarely talked about the house where he grew up without mentioning swimming, and she'd pictured the house on the banks of the water. What she hadn't imagined was the extent of the forest, the almost creepy substantiality of woods. She hadn't really envisioned his parents either, and that aside from refined speech and heavy silver picture frames, the basic dynamic between Aaron's parents boiled down to a talkative, high-strung mother and a father who didn't listen. Suzanne hadn't banked on the cold stares from the little sister, or that the younger brother Jack would have a low voice and tawny skin and not a trace of a smile. She'd expected a younger version of Aaron, but Jack looked nothing like Aaron and older somehow. He just looked older.

She heard Aaron breathing in that way he did, like he was suffering. Aaron had progressed to tugging her shirt off, and Suzanne saw his little sister out of the corner of her eye. It was enough already. They could do this down there, by the water. "Please, Aaron," she whispered. She kissed his ear. "Let's go swimming."

Aaron's breath was sugary and hot as he gave her the lightest of kisses. Everything was so quiet and dark — only beeswax candles burned inside on the dining room table; there were no lights out here, out back. But because they were right outside Lila's bedroom, Suzanne could see her all too well. Lila's bed was right under the big window, trimmed with lemon yellow paint. The sill looked perfect for sitting on. It was an ideal bedroom — easily escapable. Lila could climb out of bed, crawl out the window, and keep rolling down the sloping lawn.

"Aaron," Suzanne repeated.

"Okay," he said and pulled her up. "Follow me."

As they rose, Suzanne couldn't help looking toward Lila. But the kid was clever. She'd disappeared, and all Suzanne saw was a pale blue curtain faintly stirring.

★ ★ ★

Down the lawn and through the wooded path, Suzanne tried to keep in synch behind him. Aaron was best like this, silent and moving; he was more comfortable, she could tell. He stopped at intervals to pull back overgrown branches. Once in a while the branches nicked her arms, but it felt good instead of bad; the scent of soil and pine filled her up, and she focused on what exactly she was smelling — what was somewhat minty and what was slightly burnt — so she didn't stray too far in her mind. She rendered each detail more vibrant than the next and omitted every messy patch — like how she sometimes got annoyed with Aaron when he told her he loved her, how when he said it, she sometimes felt like he was dumbing down. He was the brainiest guy she knew, so why was it that when he said *I love you,* or when he used the rare endearment, he sounded like a fool? But no one, she chastened herself, could ever love her as fully as Aaron. Suzanne had never felt more a part of this world. Only sometimes did she question his devotion, because she knew it hadn't been earned. She thought: *He should move through rooms the way he moves through this forest; he should throw things far into the air, then catch them without looking; he shouldn't always answer me, not immediately, anyway.*

54

The path gave way to grass and sand, which the rain had turned to muck. Suzanne imagined a summer day, a red-and-white beach towel. She stood with Aaron, her sandaled feet sinking in the mud, and noticed the slabs of rock that surrounded the pond and, in the distance, rose toward the moon. There was no ring of clouds, and the promise of tomorrow's sun was a comforting thought, as an afternoon in that house with rainy-day activities was not what she'd had in mind.

Aaron stripped and dove in first, swimming fast until he had to breathe, with a burst of shout from the cold.

"Is it cold?" she asked, and she loved him now, she did.

"Take off your clothes!"

"How cold?" She took off her jeans, and the underwear, took off the light green shirt. The air was icy and then almost warm as she began jumping from foot to foot, shifting her weight and trying not to feel self-conscious about her breasts bobbing up and down. Out here she felt much more aware of her body than usual. She could sense her lower back, the backs of her knees, the very tip of her nose. Everything was slimmer. Everything except her stomach, which looked round and white. She looked out and up and there were stars now, and the stars moved, and there was nowhere to go but toward Aaron, to dive right on in.

Suzanne dipped her foot in the water and cried out, "It's fucking freezing!" She saw twigs and wet grass lying dead in the dark, along with clumps of weeds. What she hadn't told Aaron was that she hadn't been swimming in years. Beaches, at least the crowded ones she knew, made her claustrophobic, and then, at some point, the idea of being in the water — just the idea of floating — was somehow frightening. But she'd imagined this moment for weeks, ever since Aaron had asked her here. She knew it was time to get on with it.

"Come to me," Aaron yelled back, the most relaxed he'd sounded in weeks. "Come with me, to the sea. . . ."

"It's not a sea; it's a pond! With pond scum!"

And it was the thought of Lila that pushed her underwater, how she just kept watching — the shadow of curls and curtain in the dark. Maybe she waited up on purpose, having previously seen her brother in action beneath the willow tree. It was possible Lila wouldn't even remember what happened — that Suzanne or anything about this weekend would not make any impact upon Lila at all.

The water was cutting, the chill was what she wanted, and she did a clumsy crawl toward Aaron. It was like speaking another language, as her hands and legs scissored in a breaststroke, and she grabbed him too hard. It was too deep to stand, and they both coughed a bit, treading water. Aaron lifted her legs and wrapped them around him, but they sank as they kissed, so they moved to a shallower depth. She unwrapped her legs and stood, pressing up against him, her toes gripping the pond's slimy bottom. Aaron held her wet hair in one hand, her left thigh in the other.

"This isn't going to work," she told him with a smile; then she pushed his wet hair over his forehead. " 'Cause you're all shriveled." She still smiled as she lowered herself in the water and forced herself to go under. Down below, she held his legs, almost hugged them, and felt the strange heavy softness of her hair swishing over her shoulders, her face and chest. It was warmer underwater, and she remembered holding her breath in the bathtub as a child, swimming from end to end.

When she came up for air, Aaron was watching her; he looked tired. "Take me to bed, okay?" she said. "Let's get out. Sex in the water never works anyway."

She waded to shore. He waded right behind her, splashing her briefly with his hair as he whipped it out of his eyes. It felt like rain.

On the shore, she dressed quickly. She held out Aaron's pants so he could step right in, the cold no longer funny. "Thanks," he said, and again, "thanks," one step after another. He picked up his shirt, and, rather than putting it on, rubbed her hair between his shirt-covered hands. It was cold, but he massaged her temples, and she unraveled inside; her shoulders felt unburdened. She let her head fall into his grasp.

"Mmm," she managed. "Thank you."

He didn't respond, only deepened the pressure on her scalp.

"You know something?" she asked as he held her head firmly; her eyes were closed, and she couldn't believe how good it felt. "I haven't gone swimming in five years."

"Why so long?" Aaron said quietly, his hands continuing.

"I was scared," she said, and as soon as she said it, she started to giggle, her shoulders spreading with tension. Opening her eyes, she saw Aaron watching over her, along with the vivid stars. "I was afraid of the water."

And he didn't ask why, didn't respond. Aaron shook his head and viewed her askance, his eyes unconcerned and oblique. It was exactly the right response.

Aaron's bed was no smaller than either of

their beds back at the dorm, but somehow they felt closer in it. "I feel like I grew a couple of inches since last night," Aaron said. "This room makes me feel huge."

"You are huge," she said. "You're a very big boy."

"Okay, okay."

"You want me to move over?" she whispered, and she loved him now, saying nothing, pulling his legs closer, her back pressing into his stomach. It was a ritual that developed, this telling herself, *I love him now, and now I don't, and now I couldn't care less.* Here, in the warm very soft bed, with Aaron smelling like pond, she loved him.

He said, "Do you like my family?" And she turned and as she kissed him, started to laugh.

"What?" Aaron said. "Why are you laughing?"

"I was just remembering what you said about your brother liking girls with guns. Did you mean shotguns or tits?"

Aaron laughed, but only said, "Not really your type then?"

"Shh," she said, and of course Jack was her type. He was everyone's and no one's type. He was impolite and dirty, but his eyes were dark and flinty, his fingers were long, and he had probably made a number of terrible mistakes. He wasn't good-looking enough to be yelling *"Stella"* at the top of his lungs in a sweaty undershirt, but if he did it, if he yelled outside a window, you could bet no one would laugh. He wasn't good-looking, but he made you want to look.

Aaron kissed her chest, and buried himself below her breasts. She didn't hold her breath, didn't need to. Instead of telling him, *Thank you for bringing me here, you are who I've always wanted,* she gave him what she could. Her legs snaked around his, unruly vines, her fingers smoothed the knobby course of his spine. He moved inside her, and encircled her in his arms. And Suzanne went where he took her, where she held nothing back but her voice. Her breath was heavy and drunk on silence. She was an underwater guide in the dead of night, pointing out things that glowed.

As Suzanne couldn't sleep, she watched Aaron. His hair was dark and wavy and he kept it cut short. He never let it get long enough to draw attention to how beautifully thick it was. A Roman nose lent an appealing swarthiness, while his upturned lip kept him looking blameless, even childlike. Suzanne watched how his full lips slightly parted, easing out breath — heavy and gentle — like a page turning slowly. His breath was so trusting; it barely changed as she wriggled out of bed.

60

Suzanne stood in the center of the room, looking around the small space, and wondered how many other girls he'd brought up here. She knew about the one high school sweetheart, but she couldn't believe there weren't others — handsome as he was, handsome and kind. She wanted to believe she was not so much more experienced, that — and this was more important — Aaron had secrets, dark secrets involving other girls of whom she could make herself jealous.

The walls in Aaron's room were dark brown wood, and she imagined if she rubbed up against one, she'd come away with a splinter or two. There was a print of men scraping or scrubbing a floor, a few unframed photographs tacked to the wood. And of course music equipment — a guitar in the corner, an amp that looked like it was used more as a shelf, cassettes piled in a crate. But most striking of all was a framed black-and-white shot of Lila — unmistakably Lila — probably from Aaron's project in high school. She was crouched down on the sand, the very sand where she and Aaron had just dried off. The photograph was taken from above and Lila was looking right into the camera, her eyes light and enormous, her hair thin and wild. Aaron's sister wasn't smiling, and somehow Suzanne doubted she was instructed to pose this way. It looked chilly in the picture, murky and poetic, free of any cute trappings.

But beyond being struck with Aaron's talents as a photographer, it was the intimacy of the image, the way a small child's face wasn't petulant or sad nor was it cheerfully sweet. There was a sense of who she was, who she was going to be. Did her candidness have anything to do with her brother there behind the lens? It had to. She was showing him something with her posture and eyes and it was something irrefutable: a first inchworm dug up from the dewy earth, an extracted tooth on a finger. *Here I am,* the girl's eyes conveyed. *Look.*

A mirror hung on the back of the door, where Suzanne glimpsed her reflection but wouldn't look any longer than a moment. It felt peculiar seeing herself in this boy room, being awake, when all of this family was sleeping or worse — awake and silent, thinking private thoughts behind unfinished wood walls.

After putting on a pair of sweatpants and one of Aaron's shirts, she padded barefoot down the stairs, where the refrigerator hummed steadily and the candle on the heavy table cast a woozy light from the dining area to the living room, blending into a dim gray at the foot of the stairs. There was a faint scent of burnt onions and vanilla, the dying African daisies on the stone mantel, a sea of ash where the fire was, and the faint wet of old wood, saying: This is New England, these are trees, there is dampness in the undergrowth outside.

Suzanne went into the kitchen, where the dinner dishes still sat in the sink. She left the kitchen, passed the table — bare feet on linoleum, dusty wood — then the scratchy-smooth of the Turkish rug as she arrived among the couches and pillows of the living room. Up above, wood beams crossed in the dark, and she imagined bats making flustered flight patterns. She had never seen a bat.

She sat carefully on the couch and heard a toilet flushing, a creaking floorboard overhead. If someone were to come downstairs — his mother, his father, if Jack were to come downstairs . . . *I couldn't sleep,* she would say. *I have trouble sleeping sometimes.* She wasn't even tired, not really, and it was three-fifteen on the clock in the kitchen and she was chilly, so she pulled her arms inside the long-sleeved T-shirt, and spied a sweater draped on a chair. She touched the sweater, a burgundy V-necked cashmere sweater that most likely belonged to Aaron's mother. She put it on. Then Suzanne went out the front door onto the porch, where the light shone too yellow and she sat on a rocking chair, on a washed-out weather-beaten pillow.

A car — if she hadn't totally lost her mind — seemed to be pulling up the driveway. It was about three-thirty when a car arrived and Jack got out, waving to a figure with long hair, whose sex she couldn't determine. She took her arms out of her shirt. It was three-thirty when the car drove away and her first reaction was relief — *I'm not the only one awake!*

"What are you doing out here?" Jack said, approaching the porch. He looked a lot like his father.

"What am I doing?"

"Yeah."

"I don't know." She sighed. "I'm not sure." She gave him a smile, the one that she knew worked. "Where have you been?"

He turned around as if he heard something in the woods — she noticed him buying time before he looked back at her. "Nowhere," he said. He made a circle with his foot in the gravel.

"Nowhere?"

"I've just been out with friends. We go to a place on a hiking trail. The top of a mountain, but it's more like a hill. Just a fire and some beers. I'm pretty beat."

Suzanne nodded, and he looked awkward as he sat on the porch swing, his head too big for his body. She could smell the soil on Jack's brown leather boots. The red laces were double-knotted. A sharp pain briefly declared itself in her chest, and she couldn't help but wince.

"What's wrong?" Jack said, unperturbed.

"Nothing."

"You just made a really weird face."

Suzanne felt herself blush, anger rising at how coarse and flustered she was. What she wanted to feel: detachment, nonchalance. "I'm fine," she said, and as she watched him swing back and forth, she couldn't help wondering if he got it on, tonight, if he rolled around in the woods with some earthy, woodsy sexpot.

"What did you and Aaron do?" he asked, and Suzanne couldn't tell if Jack thought it strange that she was sitting out here, on his family's porch, in the middle of the night. He asked a perfectly normal question but it somehow felt like a trick.

"Oh, it was great; we went swimming in the pond. It's beautiful."

Jack looked at her and nodded. "Yeah," he said. "How long have you and Aaron been, you know, all boyfriend and girlfriend?"

It seemed unlikely he wouldn't know this, and she was torn between feeling hurt that Aaron hadn't told him and irritated at Jack for asking. "About eight months," she said, and it felt good to say it, the way it rolled off her tongue. The time gone by felt real, like something she could touch. "Eight months."

"Wow," Jack said, and put a hand to his head, which was shorn closely, the skin eggshell brown through the stubble.

"Didn't you used to have long hair?" she asked him, and he took his hand down. "I thought Aaron had told me that."

"Oh, yeah, I did. I always do until summer. Every year I shave it once. First of May."

"How regimented," Suzanne said, with a little too much bite.

"Well, that's me." He smiled with one half of his mouth, looking remarkably young. "I've been thinking about joining the marines."

"Very funny."

"No, I'm actually not kidding. I'm" — he paused to crack a knuckle — "I'm sick of restaurant work. I've kind of had it."

"So you're joining the marines? You can't just sign up, you know."

"I know."

"You've got to be accepted. Major physical fitness."

"You don't think I'll cut it?"

Suzanne laughed and looked away.

"I don't know," Jack said. "I hated the one year of college I did, and . . . it's just an idea."

When Suzanne didn't respond with much more than a nod, Jack stood and laced his hands together, stretched out his arms. "Well, good night," he said, and grinned. "I'll probably find you out here tomorrow morning."

Suzanne touched her shoulder, felt the sweater's soft wool. "Oh, I'll go to sleep eventually, I'm sure. I don't really need a lot of sleep."

"Me neither," he said, and he crossed in front of Suzanne, put his hand on the doorknob. "See ya," he said.

And she gave a small wave as Jack went inside, taking his loose arms and unmistakable smell of woodsmoke with him. The door didn't creak; it was a clean, even shut, and she didn't turn around to watch him. She didn't turn around until long after he'd gone upstairs. But still, she didn't go inside. She stepped down off the porch and went around back, to where the willow tree hung low. She was cold now, shivering, her bare feet moving quickly.

It was the little girl she wanted to see.

Suzanne peered in through Lila's window, and there was the bed, right beneath the sill. Lila was sleeping on top of the covers, not curled tight but flat on her back. Suzanne could see the rise and fall of Lila's small body, the occasional double breath. She touched the open curtain, and it was thinner than it looked. Suzanne tried to close the curtain so the sun, when it soon rose, wouldn't just stream right in. Lila's eyes opened and Suzanne was stunned, but neither of them made a sound. Overhead, the stars bit down on the sky and Lila's eyes closed again. Her small body turned on its side and she looked as if she were sound asleep. Suzanne watched Lila, and each new second seemed farther from the one that preceded; the details of the day were a blur. Suzanne really wasn't sure if Lila's eyes had just opened. She wasn't sure that the little girl had been awake at all.

CHAPTER THREE

For a few minutes between sleeping and waking, Aaron listened to the bird pecking the roof and thought the rain had begun again. Floorboards creaked and a teakettle whistled; voices blurred outside. Warmth on his skin meant there was no rain, that the sun must be high in the sky. Suzanne was gone.

He rolled over, drew the thin cotton curtains aside, and looked out the window. Lila did cartwheels down the lawn; it was amazing how many she did without stopping. He was sweating. It was disorienting waking late — no Suzanne, and the house already busy without him. It was hotter than it should've been and he hurled off the covers. Standing, his feet felt not quite on the floor, and the breeze through the window licked his skin. In the mirror — the one his mother hung on the back of the door after abandoning the marking of his height each year — he saw himself as dark and blurred. His eyesight was fine, he could see clearly, but his reflection — it was as if he'd been punched too many times. He saw himself as full of protrusions, not as sharp or sleek as usual. His father and Jack, they may have been skinny, but they had a way in which they were noticed not for their bodies but for the way they moved. Aaron's chest was covered with hair, arms and legs not particularly long. He was feral, and he had always been puzzled by this.

His watch said eleven — too late — and as he padded down the stairs, he heard them laughing in the kitchen before he even stepped in the room. Suzanne's laugh was the one he really heard, but he knew that Jack was with her. He fought the urge to stay a moment behind the door, in the small space that smelled like cedar. He stepped in the doorway as they were laughing and immediately said, "Hello."

"Oh, hey there, sleepyhead." Suzanne didn't get up. She said with a laugh, "What are you doing in the doorway?"

Aaron came in the kitchen and went for the coffeepot on the counter. Jack slouched and Suzanne crossed her legs beneath her. They were both in chairs at the small table where no one usually sat.

"Why are you sitting in here?" He leaned against the counter and sipped the strong French roast.

"What do you mean?" Jack said.

"I haven't seen anyone sit at that table in years. It's always covered with stuff."

"Didn't really think about it."

Suzanne spread strawberry jam on an English muffin. The room was too hot and smelled like bacon. He opened the window above the sink, and watched the green glass bottles as a breeze came in.

"Who cooked?"

"Jack did."

"Where are Mom and Jeb?"

"They went to get stuff for tonight. They left about an hour ago."

Suzanne stifled a giggle.

"What?" Aaron said, and he should've kissed her, he'd feel better, he knew that, but there was something about the air, he felt like glue. *What?* She started laughing harder, and Jack was sort of grinning, and out the door, beyond the deck, Lila spun and fell and got up again.

"Jack was just telling me this story." Her voice was high, as if she'd just about die laughing if she didn't try to control herself. "I mean, it's not even that funny, but —"

"What's the story?" he asked Jack. He wanted to laugh, but he knew he wouldn't. He tried to make himself smile but he couldn't.

"It's nothing, it's a stupid story."

"So what is it?"

Suzanne laughed, sipped juice, nodded her head in agreement that whatever was making her laugh uproariously was really not funny at all.

"Forget it," she said in the chair that no one sat in. She held her English muffin toward him, offering a bite.

"I don't mean to be too persistent about this. I mean, I just woke up, I'm drinking my coffee, but what" — he made himself smile; he took a bite of her strawberry-slathered bread — "what's the story?" He looked at Jack. "Tell it again."

Jack sat up straight and said, "Okay, so, okay, I was cleaning out my drawers when I moved some stuff from here to my place in Portsmouth and I found this slip of paper in my drawer. Had a phone number on it. It was really late at night, no one was here, so I thought — what the fuck — I'll call and figure out who it is, without, you know, telling the person who I am. So I dial, it rings, and this girl answers the phone — 'Hello,' she says, and I speak in a thick Southern drawl, I give her this whole story about how I moved into a new place and this number was on the refrigerator, just right there under a magnet, a butterfly magnet."

Suzanne bit her lip and smiled at the same time, played with her eggs with a fork. She didn't look up at Jack, but she didn't quite look down either.

"So she says, *'a butterfly magnet?'* and I say, 'Yeah, a butterfly,' and then I realize it's my ex-girlfriend, Emily, and instead of hanging up or telling her it's me, I keep on going — I hadn't heard from her in a year; I thought she'd moved — I wanted her to say something, something funny, I guess, but she seemed to be most concerned with the magnet design. Anyway, I'm going on and on about Georgia, which is where I said I was calling from, and she's kind of spacey; she just *listens*, which I thought was weird. I wanted her to say *something*, anything about anything, but she didn't, so I said —"

Suzanne started laughing loudly, and Aaron felt like spitting coffee onto the white wall. "So he said —" Suzanne, interrupting, didn't understand that Jack needed no encouragement to go on.

"I said, I asked, 'Why did the feminist cross the road?'" Jack was very nonchalant now. "And she says, 'Tell me why,' kind of provocatively, and I can't believe she's talking like this because, you know, she was really militant when we were together, really reactionary, and so she asks why and I say, 'To suck my dick!'"

73

"She didn't even hang up!" Suzanne told Aaron. "She stayed on the line after that."

"Yeah, she kept talking. She laughed and wanted to know how old I was, what my job was, if I had any *siblings!* She just stayed on the line with a stranger."

"But you weren't a stranger," Aaron said.

"But she didn't know that," Suzanne said back. "She had no idea."

"How do you know?" Aaron asked Jack, who put his hands above his head, surrendering.

"Since when are you the emotional police?" Jack laughed. "I was speaking totally differently. She didn't know. Emily obviously wanted to talk to a stranger. She could have hung up at any moment. She wanted to hear my joke, and she wanted to keep talking."

"See," Suzanne said, "I told you it wasn't that funny." She was still smiling though, and if she were a different kind of girl she would have winked.

The sunlight was cutting up the room, closing them into this conversation, and the coffee was too muddy, and Aaron thought about Emily, someone he'd never even heard of. He turned away from Jack and Suzanne and ran hot water from the faucet. He cleaned the mug too intensely, he knew this, and he felt her hand at his back. He kept the water running, kept looking out the window, because it was this effort to be casual that was important. It was important not to turn and stare at the freckle on her neck or her thin upper lip. Jack was still there, slouched in the chair, probably reading the paper. He felt her hand there, just like that, and only when it rested there for ten seconds or so did he turn off the water, begin to look toward her.

"Your sister doesn't stop," Suzanne said, quieter now, watching Lila through the glass.

"Oh, yes, she does, and when she does, watch out," Aaron said. "How long has she been out there spinning?"

Jack brought the dishes up to the sink, handed them to Aaron, scraped and stacked. "She's been up forever. She's been out there landing on her ass for a couple of hours now, since she woke me up."

"She woke you? What time?"

"I don't know," Jack said, "eight or so."

Suzanne said, "I'm gonna go talk to her," and she headed out the door, down the lawn.

"Not much sleep." Aaron finished drying the plates, left them in the wooden rack.

"What?"

"I said you didn't sleep much. I didn't hear you come in."

"And?"

"And nothing. Nothing. I wondered where

you were, that's all."

"You're getting weird," Jack said. "You should lighten up."

"So where were you?"

"Out in the woods with some people. No one you know."

"Okay. Doing?"

"Doing ritual sacrifice. Killing small animals. What do you think?"

"Jesus, Jack. How would I know?" The few plants on the sill were all nearly brown. Aaron filled a glass and dribbled water in the soil.

"Would you just relax? She's relaxed, at least. Look." Jack pointed outside, where Suzanne and Lila were doing handstands, both landing clumsily. Suzanne brushed grass from Lila's back, put a hand on her hair. Aaron couldn't believe Suzanne could do that, just touch, not worry a person might mind, might want to be left alone.

Jack gathered the sections of the paper, walked out of the room, and told Aaron he was going back to bed. If Aaron could name this feeling, the one he had now — standing alone in a sunny kitchen, somewhere between smashing things and cleaning them — he'd somehow feel better about the *nowhere* that encroached when he was in close proximity to Jack. Naming this would make him feel like the nowhere was just a feeling, something that could transform. This sense only lingered and altered in size, refusing to be identified.

Aaron walked out through the living room and out the front door, circling around toward a row of pines. He walked in the shade, pulling the damp grass with his toes. He told himself he was behind these trees to do push-ups because it was cooler here in the shade, but he was sitting still, and really, he wanted to listen to Suzanne and his sister, and this was the perfect spot. He wasn't ready to join another conversation, and within hours the house would be nothing but talking. In this quiet, here, with the breeze through heavy pines, he watched and he listened.

Lila was holding Suzanne's pale arm, chanting something about rain. Aaron remembered a game, something about a rose garden: scratching skin red until it swelled, then tiny pricks of pain that looked like flowers. A rose garden made of skin. Suzanne laughed.

"Now you," said Lila, "now you're the gardener."

Lila gave over her arm, and Suzanne began, "First we have to rake, rake, rake the dirt, and rake, rake, rake —"

"Ow," Lila cried, delighted. "You're good at this."

"I am? What are you good at?"

"Wait, you have to finish. Then we have to smooth the dirt and smooth the dirt. . . ."

Suzanne, with her legs extended, repeated what Lila told her. Lila sat in lotus position. Lately she was a little yogi, taught by a woman who taught most of the pond kids at their new private school. Lila sat with a straight back, looking anything but placid. Suzanne was scratching and smoothing Lila's skin, laughing when Lila did, then declaring the rose garden complete. Lila lay back, face toward the sky in mock pain.

"So," Suzanne said, lying back beside her, "what else are you good at? What do you like to do?"

"I don't know, what do you mean? Like school?"

"Like anything."

"I'm good at finding things. Christina, that's my best friend? We find things, and find out things about people. Like detectives."

Suzanne turned over, head propped on her hands. "Really? Like what? What do you find out?"

"I can't tell you," Lila said flatly. "That's why I'm good at it. I can keep secrets."

"Well," Suzanne said, "I can too."

"Do you like my brother?"

"Jack?"

"No. Aaron. Do you?"

78

"Oh, yeah. He's my boyfriend. You know that, right? I thought you meant Jack. Do you have a boyfriend?"

"I hate the boys in my grade."

"Yeah, well, that's how it usually is."

"Aaron's so nice."

Suzanne sat up, and said, "Yes, yeah, he is, isn't he? What about Jack?"

"Jack has girlfriends, but I never met any of them."

Suzanne — she was curious now — Aaron could feel her rising toward questions, spilling her questions all over the lawn. She said, "How about Aaron's other girlfriends? Did you meet them?"

Lila looked at her, and instead of answering right away, Lila touched Suzanne's straight hair. "I like your hair. I want mine long," she said.

"Thanks," Suzanne said, and Aaron made himself emerge from the trees. He was afraid of hearing something he didn't want to hear.

"Can I play?" he called out, coming toward them from the trees.

"We're not playing anything," said Lila. "We're just talking."

"That's right, we're talking." Suzanne looked at him quizzically, then reached for his hand, brought him down to the ground. "You can talk with us if you wish. Right, Lila?"

"He's gonna ask about my dreams."

"No, I won't. No dream questions this morning, I swear."

"The one last night wasn't about you," Lila said, and then she looked at Suzanne.

"What?" Suzanne said, a little nervous, Aaron could tell. "Was it about *me?*"

"I don't really remember," Lila replied.

Suzanne pulsed his hand she was holding. Her soft palm felt damp and dirty.

"Well," Aaron said, "I hate when you have nightmares about me."

"It's not like I do it on purpose. You're too *sensitive.*"

"Ha ha," he said to Lila, "I won't even ask you who told you that."

"No one told me. You think 'sensitive' is a big word for me? It's not. I know a lot of words."

"I know you do. You're right, I am. Thanks for sharing. I'm Mr. Sensitive."

"Shut up!" she said, but she jumped on his back, hung on as he rose from the grass.

"Is there something on my back? Is there a bird on my back? Suzanne, do you see a bird on my back?"

Lila squealed and shouted his name, and Suzanne shifted her gaze beyond them. He turned around, and they all watched the low roof over the laundry room, where Jack was standing. He waved, then sat again, obscured by a clay pot of geraniums.

"Okay," Lila said, "let me down now."

He turned away from the house. "Only if you tell me something."

"Tell you what?"

"Tell me *something*."

"Jack's gonna jump off the roof!"

He let her down as he turned to see his brother, standing on the low surface as if it were high enough to matter.

"Tell me something else. Tell me something good," Aaron said.

"Don't jump!" Lila cried, hands clenched tightly at her sides.

"Why not?" Jack yelled back, a game-show host, prompting all the right cues.

"Think of all you have to live for!"

"And?" he yelled, smiling now.

"You're just having a bad day!"

"So?" He inched forward on the roof.

"Don't do it! Don't break my heart!"

"Oh, okay, if you really don't think it's a good idea . . ."

Lila looked up, glittering, ready for the jump, and Jack landed, ever safely — bend at the knees, drop and roll — calling out her name.

CHAPTER FOUR

If there was one place Suzanne felt most comfortable in the whole weirdly beautiful house, it was here, in the laundry room. Aaron had gone running, his parents were taking a drive with Lila, and Jack was in his room, doing whatever it was Jack did. Her laundry spun in the dryer, and she could have been anywhere she'd ever done her laundry; all of the houses and Laundromats and apartment building basements of her childhood could've been this room. There was not enough light; everything smelled dusty and bleachy, not exactly bad, but not terribly good. Her clothes were spinning and she was sweating already.

It was exhausting being sweet for this many people. Soft as she could feel for moments at a time, she wasn't soft, not sweet like she knew Aaron imagined. It wasn't as if she faked being sweet, but no matter how she yelled or looked at him in a way he didn't know quite what to do with, he seemed to ignore all her obstacles. He forgave too easily. Sometimes she felt like giving him advice on how to keep her interested.

But it wasn't always like this. Sometimes she couldn't believe how much she wanted to be around him, keep him up all night long and listen for hours after having sex, when he was blissed out and felt like telling stories. He took longer to articulate things than anyone she'd known well, and this tease could be enticing because often he revealed something good. He was really into small details — the way his roommate's salamander moved, the colored lights in the window across the street from her dorm room — and this felt masculine somehow, how he cared about these inhuman things. He also happened to tell her a lot of small, detailed things about herself, which of course kept her interest piqued.

There were moments she wanted Aaron closer, and it wasn't just because he looked like he did. It was bizarre how unaware of his physical presence he seemed to be. She still wasn't certain if he really was oblivious or if he was somehow embarrassed to be so attractive. Suzanne didn't think she could ever handle having a boyfriend prettier than she. But then she met Aaron at a party. She talked and talked, and to her surprise, he kissed her in the middle of a sentence. He wanted to sleep with her and stay through the next morning and the next. She realized — only a week or so later, when he told her she snored and he was smiling — that he was hers. He wasn't pretty, that wasn't the right word, but there he was, he was right *there*, the minute he walked in a room. Suzanne blended, at least at first, she knew she did. But she also knew that with a little effort, she could sometimes make the right person think she was more confident, more beautiful, than anyone at first glance would expect.

Suzanne sat on the washing machine, nervous about getting the laundry done and back to Aaron's room before the house filled up again. This was a bad time to do laundry, a stupid idea, and if she owned anything she liked besides that one pale green shirt she wouldn't have had to do her laundry at all. If she didn't lose things, if she didn't stain her jeans, spill all over her dresses; and if she'd found time to do laundry before they left the city, she could've been sitting by the pond, reading by the water, memorizing good lines. When his parents asked what she did this afternoon, she could then say, "I went down to the pond and read," instead of, "I did my laundry."

The problem was that she was always asking, asking for too much, and couldn't help it.

Borrowing money, taking bites of everyone else's meals — requests flew out of her mouth like ugly birds, before she had time to think. The plums and grapes she ate an hour ago swirled in her stomach like her laundry in the dryer, and though the room was cool, she was damp with sweat. Aaron was out there running; she imagined him moving, his eyes straight ahead and searching the woods. He was moving and his brother was sleeping, sleeping or reading or it didn't matter what, but she guessed that Jack wasn't moving.

Jack was like her, the her that no one ever cared to find out about, and really, who could blame anyone for not wanting to know? She had recognized this when she saw him sneer in the doorway last night, when he looked away after asking where she was from. It was the one question he asked, and she had seen he couldn't decide if he wanted to ask more or if he couldn't care less. He hadn't known how to talk to her because he was afraid of sounding too eager. She could barely help him last night, and that was what she knew she was good at. She could talk to a wall, she knew she could, but when she met Aaron's brother, she found herself smiling as if he were far away, on a ship sailing out of port, when there's no point in trying to shout.

The laundry room was too dark and Suzanne yanked the door open. With a lurch, the door shifted and one of its hinges came apart and broke. The screech of hinges in desperate need of oil cried out into the day. It was a mystery how this large wooden door had come unhinged at the top, but there it was, the door on a diagonal, and her fucking laundry was through drying, so everything was quiet. Suzanne tried to right the door, align it in its hinge, but it was difficult even lifting the thing an inch.

"Hello," she heard. She let go of the door, gasped, and turned.

Jack was there.

"Oh, God, you scared me!"

"You broke the door?"

"It just kind of undid itself."

Jack tried to put it in place. Surprisingly notable biceps shifted under the skin of his rangy arms. "Not happening," he said.

"Please don't tell anyone it was me."

Jack laughed, and his shoulders rose and fell. "Oh, man," he said.

"What?"

"It's just funny, that's all. You broke the door." He started to cough, then cleared his throat. "You broke the door of the latest addition to Jeb's precious house."

"You're not making me feel better."

"I'm not trying to. There's no reason to

86

comfort you, for christsake. It's no big deal." He jumped up and sat on the dryer. "Look, I'll try to fix it, if you want, but it's not a problem. It gives Jeb something to do."

"Why do you call him that?"

"What, you mean his first name? I don't know. I don't always. They taught us to. It didn't stick with our mom, because she's, you know, she's a mom, but with him, it fits."

The door tilted out, left a slim triangle of day, and Suzanne wondered how far Aaron was running, how it was he never got bored.

"Will you try to fix it?" she said.

"To tell you the truth, I don't think I can. I'll just say I did it, if you really want me to. It doesn't matter."

"Thanks. I just —"

"No problem. You want to get high?"

She felt her eyebrows rise and her head tilt, and she told herself to stop being demure. "No way."

"Why?"

"Why? Your entire family is about to interview me, they'll be back any minute, and I just broke a door."

"No, *I* broke the door," he said, taking a bag of weed from his army pants pocket.

"Could you move for a second? Off the dryer? I need to —"

He jumped down and she could smell the

sweet musk of weed and his sour sweat. He smelled bad. His forearms were spread with veins and very little hair. The laundry filled her arms and she held it close; she inhaled the warm, powdery scent before letting the clothes drop into the brown plastic basket; then she rose and turned around. Jack lit a joint, eclipsing the inculpable scent of clean clothes.

"Let's fold," he said right before exhaling, and surprisingly, he didn't smile. "Do you ball your socks, or keep them loose?" He didn't cough.

"*What?*" she said, and it was she who was grinning a stupid grin, afraid to show her teeth.

"What do you do?"

"With my socks?"

He picked up a tube sock with one green stripe and one yellow. He offered her the joint. His fingernails were bitten down to the quicks. She inhaled and watched the cloudless sky through the triangle of the broken door. In her lungs, a burn, the soothing kind. She exhaled and found the other green-and-yellow sock and gave it to Jack, who tucked them into a ball. She smoked some more — the wet paper where both of their mouths had been, the small orange tip and gray-white ash. She drew in — small and precise — then watched Jack finish it off.

The clothes lay in a pile on the teetering table and Suzanne folded a white T-shirt.

"Jack?"

"Yeah?"

"Are you really joining the marines?" She watched as he smiled and shook his head.

"No, I'm not." He flicked the ashen paper in the garbage basket in the corner, pivoting away from her, then back again. "I thought it was a good idea for about a minute."

"I can't really picture you in the marines."

"Yeah, well, I suppose that's why I wanted to go. Because I couldn't picture it either. Then I thought about all the other things I couldn't picture doing."

"I want to be an artist," she heard herself saying. "Isn't that embarrassing?"

"Are you any good?" he asked. He had a bit of a lazy eye. She hadn't noticed it before, and now she couldn't stop looking, worrying about how to make eye contact.

"You have a lazy eye." She let it slip out.

"Yes, I do."

"Yeah, I am pretty good," Suzanne told him. "I won a scholarship to go study in Italy with a famous sculptor."

"Do you work with industrial pipes or some shit like that?"

"No," she said, and fought back a smile. "Stone."

"Well, well." He sorted through the clothes as if he were at a flea market. "Hey, this is my shirt!" he said.

"What do you mean?"

He picked up the blue-and-green shirt she slept in, the one she had appropriated from Aaron after their first night in his room. "This," Jack said, "is mine."

"Well, I've been sleeping in it for about a year."

He touched the sleeve's edge, where the flannel was frayed and the button had come loose. "I love this shirt," he said.

"Me too. But it's yours. Here you go, it's even clean and everything."

He took the shirt from her and put it on — one long arm after the other. He buttoned two buttons and smiled. "You can have it," he said, and he didn't make a move to return it. "It's officially yours."

They didn't talk. He folded a pair of yellow sweatpants carelessly. Then his hands touched a pair of gray bikini underwear — a pair she must have missed when she subtly gathered her undergarments — and he started in with those too. She found herself watching him create delicate folds — his thin, long fingers now remarkably exacting — then she handed over another pair and continued to observe. When her laundry sat neatly in a folded stack, Jack sat on top of the dryer again, and Suzanne could feel him now watching her as she put the clothes in the plastic basket.

It was quiet for a long time. She stared through the triangle, the breeze came in, and the sky glowed so she closed her eyes and saw spots of light. When she opened her eyes again, she felt like they'd been quiet for a whole day.

"Boo," Jack said. "Hey, what time is it?"

Suzanne looked at her watch and it said one-thirty. "I think my watch stopped." He leaned over to look. He was taller than Aaron, but seemed less substantial, probably a good fifteen pounds lighter. She held her arm out but he didn't touch the watch. He just glanced at the time that had stopped about four hours before.

"I feel good," Jack said. Suzanne couldn't look at him because if she did, she knew she'd say something back, something like "Me too," and then — with the sky so blue and the chill of evening creeping on — then where would they be?

When she picked up the basket and they both stepped out the door, the grass was colder than it should've been, and the air was somehow warmer. "Thanks for breaking the door," she said.

"Where's Aaron?" Jack replied, as if he'd just now thought of it.

"Running," she said, which suddenly seemed ridiculous.

At twilight, their mother Vivian leaned against the deck rail, a glass of white wine in her hand. She wore large tortoise earrings, white jeans, and a loose brown blouse. His mother oversaw the conversation, did a lot of nodding. Jeb sat in front of her, looking too tall for the low chair. Vivian kept putting her hand on his shoulder, then taking it back and placing it on her collarbone, her neck.

Suzanne and Aaron sat across from them, each in wooden deck chairs. Suzanne could smell Aaron's clean smell, his fresh cotton shirt. He was already beginning to tan. As he shifted his body in the chair, he reached for her hand, resting on its armrest. He looked great. He looked like he was holding in the heat of the day, and she had a strange desire to pull her hand away. There was something awkward about the moment. Suzanne was aware she didn't really know this family, that they were all just getting used to her, but she couldn't pin down what was making her keep her hands away from Aaron. Something was making her want to tell dirty jokes, to make them all laugh until they spit out their drinks, to start yelling obscenities, yell anything.

Jeb looked at her, and she wanted to say something intelligent and subtle, but she smiled instead, her warmest smile, tried not to be self-conscious about her chipped tooth. Jeb waited a beat and then smiled back. His glass eye looked *almost* real, almost but not quite. Each second she thought about making conversation, she flipped through her mental file of all Aaron had ever told her about his father during those late-night whispered stories of subtle intimidations.

Jeb's money was a topic that interested her, the cash and how it evolved. The sum of the money was apparently a family mystery, but Aaron's father apparently made a substantial amount on a patent and retired at the age of thirty-five.

Finally Suzanne spoke up: "I'd love to see some of your work," she said to Jeb. "You sculpt, right?"

"In a fashion," he replied. "Mostly I make furniture. I'm more along the lines of a pretentious carpenter," he said. She didn't know whether or not she should laugh.

"Right," Aaron said. The vein in his forehead bulged.

"He's an artist," Vivian said, her hand in his thick hair. "You are."

"Well, I did my one thing, I guess," Jeb

93

muttered, saving the moment with a smile. "What are your life's plans?" he asked Suzanne.

"My one thing?" she asked him, meeting both of his eyes, "or in general?"

"Either."

"I'd like to sculpt," she said. "That's what I'd like to do."

Jeb nodded, as though he may or may not have been listening. "Good for you," he said.

Suzanne realized she was being patronized, but she didn't really care. He presented, if anything, a challenge.

"Vivian," Jeb said, "do we have any of that dark beer left?" His voice was quietly resonant.

"I would have brought it out, if you'd mentioned it."

"Well, I just got the idea."

"I'll get it for you," Suzanne said brightly. *Bastard.* She even gave her best grin. "I'll get it." She took his empty wineglass. She felt young and promising, as she made her way to the kitchen, wondering where Jack and Lila were.

The air was soft, its scent different and dizzying. Who cared what their pretentious father thought? She was free of any identity besides that of the better-looking, smarter son's girlfriend, and she was uplifted, excited,

94

aroused by this. She wanted to have a wedding. She'd dance with Jeb — why didn't they just call him Dad? It seemed creepy, the first names; what was the point of everyone being the same? She could hear the muffled conversation as she walked away from the deck, but there didn't seem to be a lot of it. Vivian was definitely quieter than she had been last night.

The kitchen smelled like garlic and fresh bread. They couldn't see her in here, so Suzanne looked under one of the pot lids and stuck her finger in the sauce. It was tomato based, delicious, and after licking her finger she dipped again. Suzanne opened the fridge, where the green bottles were easy to miss, scattered throughout the crowded refrigerator. But she saw *Beer* written in purple script on each bottle, she saw they were homemade, and they may as well have said *Drink Me*, they looked so good. She wanted one. She wanted to taste this beer more than anything, but she somehow didn't want to ask. So she took one, then thought better of it and took two. Suzanne quickly ran up the stairs and put the bottles in her bag, rolling them in her freshly washed yellow sweatpants. Her heart beat hard as she returned to the kitchen.

Outside, the volume of voices rose. When she looked again, she saw Jack and Lila. Jack leaned, just like Vivian, on the opposite rail, and Lila jumped up and down, until Aaron pulled her onto his lap. It was getting darker quickly. The lawn choked in shadow and the greens looked gray. A violet light led up to an early moon.

She grabbed another beer from the fridge and a glass from the cabinet. She pushed the door open too forcefully, and they all looked at her. "Here, Jeb," she said, "Hi, Lila."

"Great," Jeb said. As she leaned toward him, handing over the beer and glass, she smelled wet paint and shaving cream, the inside of someone's van.

"We went to see the birds," Lila told Suzanne as she scratched an itch on her shoulder. "A lot came."

"The sanctuary," said Jack. He took a sip from Jeb's beer. "Man," he said, "this is good."

Suzanne turned to give Vivian a smile before sitting back down next to Aaron, who took her hand and held on. Feeling expansive, she smiled at Jack, who didn't seem to notice.

"The place looks terrific," Aaron said. He raised his glass of water as he said this. "You've made some changes."

"That's right," Jeb said. "Little by little."

"Little by little by little . . ." Jack said.

"That's right," Jeb said, with a markedly clipped tone.

"The process is all," Jack said, as if he were reciting.

"Why do you let him mock you like that?" Aaron said quietly, not looking at his father.

"Is that what you're doing, Jack?" Jeb asked in a straight manner, no lurking sarcasm anywhere. "Are you mocking me?" he asked, as if he merely wanted to know.

Suzanne looked to Lila in order to appraise the situation, but Lila was simply paying attention, while swinging her legs back and forth.

"Of course he is," Aaron said.

"No," Jack said, in a voice that said *I'm bored,* "no, I'm not." He looked toward the forest, and awkward silence expanded.

"Stop it," Lila said, yawning.

"We will," Aaron said, looking at his brother. But Jack, perhaps embarrassed, did not look back.

"Are you getting cold, Lila?" Vivian brightly asked, while picking up the cheese plate, gesturing to Jack to get the rest. "Why don't we all move inside?"

"What's wrong?" was the first thing Aaron said after dinner, when they escaped upstairs for a minute before dessert was served. He stood in front of the closed door of his room, and she sat on the bed.

"Nothing," she said, "C'mere."

"Why?"

"Oh, gee, I don't know," she said.

"You're not going to push me away?"

"Aaron," she said, leaning to pick up her hairbrush from the bedside table, "come on." The brush bristles yanked her fine hair, nicked her collarbone on the downward stroke. "Shit," she said.

He looked at her. Then he turned toward the door, where the mirror hung, and he backed up toward the bed, watching her in the mirror.

She said, "I hate when you do that."

"Do what? Look at you in the mirror? Well, I don't like when you lie."

"Mm."

"What?"

"You think I lie a lot?" She felt herself getting interested, wondering what he knew.

"Forget it," he said. "We should go downstairs."

"Look, I don't know why I'm being like I'm being. Maybe families make me nervous."

He came toward the bed and took her face in his hands. She closed her eyes and pictured Jack swinging his legs, sitting on top of the dryer. The low din of voices murmured downstairs. With Aaron, it was about getting to the other side of a day, when she could fall away from herself and into his idea of her. "You have some kind of idea of me," she said, not so ready to let go.

"That's not true," he said, "Come on. Now, will you please come downstairs before my mother has a fit?"

"She's nervous tonight, huh?"

"Yeah. I'm not sure why. You never know."

There was a knock at the door.

"Yeah?" Aaron said.

"I've been sent to retrieve you," Jack said in a barely audible voice.

"Come in," Aaron said, and Jack was in the open doorway. "How's it going down there?"

"A lot of Lila," Jack said, biting his nails, leaning on the door frame. He was a leaner, a sloucher. "She's telling them about yoga. Jeb and I are in competition to stay awake."

"Who's winning?" Suzanne asked. Jack looked at her as if to say hi. He had pink, soft lips, the kind prone to cold sores. He had a long and delicate neck.

"Tough to say. Come see for yourself."

She heard Lila's laugh from the stairwell. It was hysterical, as if she was being tickled, but it trailed off when Suzanne and Jack and Aaron came into the living room. Lila fled her mother's lap to sit on a cushion by the fire-place. "There's dessert," Vivian said.

"I've got a party to go to," Jack said, looking at Aaron. "You want to come?"

"You mean do I want to give you a ride?" Aaron said. Suzanne didn't know where to look.

"Do you want to go to a party?" Jack looked right at her, and she nodded without thinking. She wanted to. She wanted to get out of this house.

"That's nice, Jack, put her on the spot. What is she supposed to say?"

"I want to," Suzanne said to Aaron, keeping it light.

"Have fun," Vivian said.

Jeb excused himself and went out on the porch, and Jack pulled Lila up from the floor. He lifted Lila's hair off her neck. "You want to go to a party, Lyle?" Jack said.

"C'mon," Suzanne said to Aaron, "how bad can it be?"

Aaron drove the silver wagon slowly on the dark and narrow road. Suzanne sat next to him, and Jack sat in back. They all managed to escape, after Lila's brief tantrum, saying she wasn't ready for bed, that she wanted Jack to stay in her room. Now the three of them, the big kids, were headed for a party thrown by some older woman Jack knew.

"Her name is Pria," Jack said, cracking a

window. "You'll like her house, and if you don't, oh, well, because I do, and we're not leaving for a while. I'm not bumming another ride. You'll like her," he said, lighting a joint. He tapped his hands on his knees to the "Jumping Jack Flash" blasting on the radio. He tapped it out on the back of Suzanne's seat.

"Quit it," Aaron said, and Jack stopped tapping and opened the window wider.

"How do you know her?" Aaron asked, speeding through the arc of low-hanging elms.

"She's a stripper," Jack said. Suzanne couldn't tell if he was joking. "I slept with her a few times while I was at UNH."

"Busy semester," Suzanne spit out.

"Not busy enough, I'm afraid," Jack said, leaning forward in his seat, his shaved head almost touching her elbow. Suzanne leaned forward too; she changed the music.

As they hit the highway and the car gathered speed, she played games with herself like this: *You have no peripheral vision; you may only look straight on. Right now, no matter what you think or feel, you may not turn around.*

CHAPTER FIVE

Once off the highway, Jack presented a joint. Instead of saying no, as Aaron usually did when Jack offered him anything, he accepted, and the remainder of the drive was mellow. There were no other cars around, so he eased along the dirt road as they approached the house. He hadn't wanted to go to this party but now, with the music blasting and the light shining from inside Pria's house, Aaron felt good. Suzanne took his hand moments ago, and she was here with him, he really felt that now, that she'd come all that way, from New York City. And it wasn't bad having Jack around like this, a leader toward the other side of town, the side that was still awake; people renting houses cheaply, tenants coming and going with the seasons. Aaron laid his hand on the small of Suzanne's back as Jack went ahead, leading the way to the party. Jack was about to knock on the door when it swung open and a dark-haired woman — probably late twenties —

said hello, laughing like their arrival was the punchline to a joke.

Jack slunk forward, all but ignoring the woman, and then turned and kissed her casually on the lips. "Pria," he said, "this is Suzanne." Suzanne gave a nod and a mumble. "This is Aaron," he continued, and then, as if he almost forgot to mention it: "my *brother*."

Pria extended her long fingers toward Aaron, shook his hand, and smiled. Behind her, people lounged on two couches; a few hands waved hello. Guns n' Roses came on the stereo as Aaron shouted, "Are we early or late?"

"Somewhere in the middle, I guess. We're all still awake. Let's get you a drink," Pria said, and made her way toward the kitchen. Her feet were bare and Aaron noticed two silver toe rings. Her toenails weren't polished. "You in school?" she asked them, and Aaron cleared his throat.

"Yeah," Suzanne said.

"Jack told me all about you. The Very Bright Brother, right, Jack?"

"That's right," Jack said, grabbing a six-pack and heading for the back door. "He's a fucking genius."

"Shut up," Aaron said instinctively, ready for something to turn.

But Jack smiled, a real one, and patted Aaron's back with his free hand. "He's shy, but it's true. He is."

Aaron tried to look at no one in particular. Suzanne peeked out the back door, which Jack opened.

"You should check out the yard," Pria told her. "There's sangria. Aaron, can you reach up there?" She pointed above the sink to a stack of plastic cups. Jack and Suzanne went out the door.

"Here you go," Aaron told her, reaching for the cups and handing them to her. "Here." Pria smiled, folding her hair over one shoulder. The kitchen was empty of people and full of trash and Aaron wanted to move out of the enclosed space. "Have you known my brother a long time?"

"He didn't tell you?"

"No — I mean he said he knew you from Portsmouth."

"We had a thing, I guess. Friends with a *sparkle*. Something like that."

"Right."

"Don't you want a beer?"

"Didn't you say there was sangria outside?"

"Oh, right," she said, opening the refrigerator and taking a beer for herself. "We can go get some, if you want." She stood close to him as she opened the beer, a lick of cold curling up from the bottle. "You're sure you don't want one anyway?"

And just as Aaron was about to turn the doorknob and go out, Suzanne opened the door, with a Styrofoam cup of sangria for him. "Thanks," he said. It was difficult not to thank her too hard.

"Nice gazebo," Suzanne told Pria.

"You like it?" Pria asked.

"I love it," Suzanne said with altogether too much emotion. What was strange was how genuine she sounded. Aaron realized she looked happy. He wondered where Jack was. Pria led them into the living room, where the music had changed to Led Zeppelin. The bodies on the couches were sitting up instead of lounging, and they were listening to Jack, who was sitting on the arm of a couch. Pria interrupted and made introductions — Ramon, Jenny, Guy, Kira, and Tom. Jack presented a bottle of vodka, as if he'd been hiding it with him all along. Aaron didn't even wonder where he got it. Jack had produced bottles and bags of every variety for so many years, stealing from Jeb's stash of weed in the coffee can above the refrigerator, his girlfriends' parents' liquor cabinets, various schools' reception supplies, it didn't seem worth wondering about anymore. "*Wodka*," he said. Murmurs of approval circulated, from a group too lazy

to think about going out into the night to pro-
cure more of anything. "Catch," Jack called
to Jenny, and "Catch," he told Ramon, as he
threw lemons quickly. Kira saw that he was
bringing them from beneath the couch, where
Jack must have quickly stashed them, and she
dug there as well and came up with a box of
cheery Domino sugar.

"Lemon drops," Kira said. "Yes!"

"I love lemon drops," Jenny said, and
looked at Aaron and Suzanne, standing, at
Pria leaning in the doorway. "Sit down," she
said, "we'll make room."

Aaron saw the new circle forming, the unraveling and raveling of limbs. Soon, secrets
between these friends, whatever they were,
would spill. Someone would say something
surprising and there'd be a burst of laughter.
It was comforting being around people he
didn't know. The weed hadn't worn off, and
he felt tingly in his legs and hands. It would be
easy to tell a story now, to meet almost anyone. He felt himself smile, and it was good.
He pushed a laugh.

"A knife," Jack said. "We need a knife."

"I'll get it," Pria said. And she lightly
touched Aaron's arm as she went. Jack set the
vodka, the lemons, the sugar, neatly on the
low coffee table.

"And glasses," he called after her. "Aaron,

why don't you help her bring in some glasses."

Do it yourself, Aaron wanted to say, but everyone was looking, Suzanne was looking, so he didn't sit down, but instead went to the kitchen. As he left, he could hear Jack telling someone that they'd better cut the lemons in eighths, not quarters. And a girl laughed — not Suzanne — someone said good, we'll all have plenty to suck.

In the kitchen, Pria was nowhere to be found. Aaron saw a half-empty bottle of scotch on the counter, and he swigged it right from the bottle, a long, strong pull. Then he looked out the window and saw Pria under the crude outdoor light, stirring the sangria. Aaron tapped the window, and she looked up and smiled as if to say, *It's nicer out here.* He stayed where he was and waved back, a folding and unfolding of his hand, and he set about finding a knife and glasses. If he got on with all this, if he stayed buoyant, things would work out fine. Suzanne would be with him in his small bed tonight, and they'd find their way toward one another. She'd whisper about how she'd been distant, how she knew they needed to be closer. She'd apologize.

"They're in here," Pria said, after a fast entrance from outside. She swung open a drawer, and took out a knife. "This one should do."

When he entered the living room and handed over the utensils, Jack said, "Finally! All right, let's get going. And here's Pria with more kitchenware."

Aaron noticed Suzanne had situated herself on the floor, Indian style, looking up at Jack, who was seated on a footrest. Ramon was on the other side of Suzanne, but he seemed gay, at least enough not to worry about, even with the way his leg nearly touched hers. Jenny and Guy were on one couch, Kira and Tom on the other. Suzanne was snug in there, very cozy. To sit with her, he'd have to plow his way through, tell Ramon to move over or Jack to take a walk, and what with Jack being king of the room right now, the party monarch, his departure seemed out of the question. Aaron turned from Suzanne and glanced at Pria, right next to him, who wasn't smiling any longer.

"Have you ever done a lemon drop before?" Pria asked him, and he nodded, still standing. Jack's sous-chef work had really paid off. He chopped the lemons into even wedges, and, in keeping with his style of restaurant work, he swigged the vodka as he chopped.

"They're like tequila shots, right?" Jenny asked.

"Yeah," Suzanne said, "vodka, lick of sugar, suck of lemon. But you really should lick the sugar off of another person's arm — or wherever — and if you're doing it right, another person holds the lemon for you — in their mouth."

She didn't look at Aaron. She poured herself a preliminary shot of vodka, and drank it as Guy and Jenny began. Guy and Jenny laughed as Jenny licked sugar from Guy's neck, as the sugar apparently went down Guy's T-shirt. Their round faces pressed together as Jenny sucked the lemon from Guy's mouth, which turned into a kiss. And then Suzanne looked up, smiling at Aaron — her face red, her teeth white — and she made no motion to move. She gave Aaron a lazy grin, even blew him a little kiss. He'd knock over glasses and step on people if he attempted to get to her now. He was this close to trying it when Pria said, "Your turn, Aaron."

"My turn?"

"Go on," Suzanne said, and handed him a glass, the bottle, the sugar, the lemon, then sat back down on the other side of the table.

His fingers became sticky from the sugared Domino box, and the lemon wedge stung the scratch on his finger from the branches last night. He set down the box on a small table and said, "Okay. Pria?" Suzanne was nodding, from her spot on the floor. She looked thrilled.

Pria moved close to him, and his heart was racing. Out of the corner of his eye, Suzanne watched him approvingly; the knife's blade on the coffee table glinted in the lamplight, Tom had two silver hoops in his ear. Pria gathered all her hair on one side of her neck and offered him the other side, the long almond-colored slope of it. Pria licked her finger and wet her neck so that the sugar would stick. Aaron poured a shot and then felt the box of sugar in his hand — it was as if it had come to him; he didn't remember accepting it. And he poured it on, for a little too long, and the metal music played: *Let me cut your cake with my knife.* Aaron downed the vodka, and, holding the lemon wedge in his hand, licked Pria's neck, which tasted of sugar of course, but also faintly of salt and cherries. Then he shoved the lemon into his mouth and sucked as hard as possible.

The group cheered and his nose ran slightly from the sweet and the tart. He wanted more; he smiled at Suzanne, who raised her eyebrows and gave another grin. "Next?" he offered to her, but Pria took the bottle. He knew when something could feel like too much and this was one of those times. If Pria licked his neck right now . . . he thought he should quit while he still felt on the lighter side of things. *I'll take a breather,* he thought, *and I'll come back in a minute. Maybe then I'll be ready for the rules of this game, for a stranger to lick my neck and have Suzanne watch, and have that be okay.*

Aaron went straight out to the backyard. He could breathe out here; the air felt good. The kiddie pool of sangria sat waiting for revelers, and he assumed Pria had made this ridiculous amount of sweet wine — chopped all the fruit and stirred in the sugar; he hadn't thought of that when he downed it earlier. He could hear the odd car passing on the highway and the crickets too, the music's insistent bass.

Aaron went to the gazebo, but didn't make it past the first step. He sat on the step and watched the house. It was a cheap house, though he'd never have said this out loud. It was a house that hadn't had the same tenant for more than three years at a time. He didn't imagine Pria came from around here, and he wondered where she was from, where her parents were. He couldn't imagine living here. He couldn't imagine living anywhere. Jeb had built his family's house with his own hands, not out of necessity but out of principle — or fashion — depending on what sort of mood Jeb was in when he talked about the past. Aaron couldn't imagine living in that house again, and not in any New York apartment after college, no matter how quiet the neighborhood. Aaron imagined Alaska, working on a fishing boat, alone in the middle of nothing.

Aaron tried to recall the way their house looked when he was Lila's age. He pictured potted pink geraniums on the low laundry roof, the flagstone fireplace. When Lila was born, the deck was completed, but it, too, still felt new. He'd stood outside his own house many nights just like this, looking to see how the logs blended into the smooth wood, how the top-floor bedrooms all had different windows, yet somehow appeared to belong side by side. He'd watched his family inside the house, trying to imagine if he didn't know them, what would he guess just by watching?

Out here on Pria's square of lawn, the wood of the gazebo looked like the wood of the jungle gym Lila wanted last year but Jeb wouldn't agree to buy. If he closed his eyes he could see Suzanne asleep on a rainy Sunday or laughing in a darkened theater, feeding him Junior mints. But when his eyes opened, the bass of the music still softly pulsed from the house. He heard people laughing inside.

Their volume rose and drew Aaron inside, with the door closed behind him. In the living room, the game was going strong.

"You're back," Pria said.

Aaron looked at Suzanne but she was talking to Ramon, downing a glass of vodka, no sugar, no lemon. And then Suzanne looked around, catching Aaron's eye.

"Suzanne," Jack said, over the music. He lifted the bottle, handed her a lemon.

And it was in that moment when Aaron felt something starting or ending, he wasn't sure which. Because when Jack invited Suzanne to take her turn, she looked at Jack for an instant before turning from him, before saying, "Ramon." This voice was mild, not having so much fun, and Aaron didn't even pay close attention as Suzanne drank and licked sugar off Ramon's wrist and modestly held the lemon wedge herself, offering no show. Aaron was stuck in that moment before Suzanne turned from his brother, in what it was that made her turn away with no giggle, no smile, nothing.

He wanted to turn to Pria, to say, *Please bring this to a close. Help me, okay? Please help me out here.* But even if he wanted to, Aaron didn't see Pria around. He couldn't reach Suzanne. She was drunk now, and likely to tell him to lighten up. The last time they went to a party they had fought and he promised — he did — to give her a little room the next time they went out together. And it was normal that she was off having fun; she was entitled to let loose. But what he saw was a certain looseness in Suzanne, the slippery privilege of someone who didn't feel the need to acknowledge more than one person at a time. She didn't seem aware of his gaze, or that she was, in fact, torturing him.

He wanted to go outside again, because the only other option would be to grab Suzanne, carry her out to the car, and say, *It's time to go.* He knew how far that would get him. So he returned to the kitchen, found a cheap bottle of scotch. He took a long drink from the bottle, closing his eyes. He brought the scotch with him and returned outside, walking instead of sitting, reaching as high as he could to touch the leaves on the one tree. He took another swig and ran his hand along the low shrubbery that divided this house from the property next door, where there were no cars in sight. He heard the screech of the screen door, and he looked up to see Pria closing it. "Wait," he called out to her, and she looked startled, in the doorway. He walked toward her.

"Hi there," she said.

"I'm coming in," Aaron said, avoiding her eyes.

"You don't have to."

"Is the game still going?"

"You mean Let's Get Drunk Quickly? I'm not sure. It's changed. Everyone's just passing the bottle." Pria was quiet. They stood in the doorway, and since she was a step up, in the kitchen, they were exactly eye-to-eye.

"This is a nice house," Aaron said.

"Thanks," Pria said, and then she took his hand.

He didn't swat it away but he did let it go, and felt his face redden. "I have a girlfriend," he heard himself say. "I'm with her."

"Sorry," Pria said as she stepped into the kitchen. She gave him a look that said he could come inside, but he didn't.

"Couldn't you tell?" he asked her, "that I am?"

Pria didn't respond — at least not with words — but her eyes flashed with something that looked like intention and she let the door shut between them.

CHAPTER SIX

There's a space between Jack's eyes that wrinkles in a V when he smiles or frowns. When he's older it will be wrinkled there even when his face is in repose. This was what Suzanne was thinking as she sat on Pria's bathroom floor, wondering if she was going to throw up. As the waves in her stomach rose and fell, she pictured how his chest sank on one side, how one bottom rib stuck out farther than the rest. He was hit by a car when he was seven, he told her breezily, when they began talking this morning in the kitchen. He died and came back and it didn't make him believe in God and it didn't convince him of a beautiful afterlife. Suzanne imagined putting her head in the place between the rib and stomach, all hushed and warm with her small breath on his sloping skin — rib to stomach — breathe in, breathe out. *Do not throw up in this woman's bathroom.*

Pria was calling to her from what seemed like awfully far away, asking if Suzanne was okay, but it was difficult to lift her head to speak. The bathroom was carpeted in dark pink, and that was pretty weird and wonderful as well because it was a soft place instead of a hard one. She forced herself not to lie down and sleep because, more than anything, Pria was intimidating. Pria was calling to her and she had to answer and answer fast.

"I'll be right out," Suzanne heard herself say.

"It's okay," Pria said — her voice muffled through the door — and even though the sound was far away, Suzanne could tell she was impatient.

If she could just lose the waves. Yes, she'd had too much to drink. Jack's pot hadn't helped, but it was more than either of these reasons. It was Jack: the wrinkle between his eyes, the chest and stomach, the smell of sweat and the cotton of his shirt, how he lit a match and put it out, the surprising anger that seemed to come and go.

She had been crying for about an hour. The crying felt good; it felt better than unleashing this feeling on Aaron, frightening him with bitter kisses. And she was a crier by nature. She could even cry on cue, a talent she saved for professors who didn't normally accept extensions on papers.

Pria was raising her voice, telling Suzanne it

was okay to be drunk, as if being drunk were the problem. The problem was a lack of control, and a notion that she just might grab Jack's long-fingered hand in the car ride back, grab it and not let go. If Pria would just go away for five minutes she could pull it together enough to emerge, but just the thought of her standing by the door and waiting for it to open was delaying her exit. The fact that Jack slept with this woman made Pria both interesting and dreaded. Suzanne couldn't help but imagine him enjoying himself, letting go and getting loose, long limbs tense and hands grabbing Pria's enviable hair and breasts — dark and exotic and everything Suzanne wasn't.

"Can you just leave me alone?" Suzanne said, her head clearing and her throat swallowing, her knees pressed to her chest. "I don't mean to be rude, but I just need a second or two." As soon as she said it, she knew she had gone too far. She just wanted to be away from here, away from the Suzanne that was beginning to bore her. She stood and her body felt like a children's toy she saw in a store once — hollow and bamboo and turning over while something inside slowly fell.

Suzanne turned on the water, ran it cold on her hands and splashed her face. It was amazing how much better she felt. She looked in

the mirror and smacked herself on each cheek. Color rose immediately and she forced herself to go out into the house again. She swung the door open. "Sorry," was all the armor she had. "Sorry," she said, and coughed. "I'm having a hard time."

"Feel free to tell me to shut up, but why are you having a hard time?" Pria asked. "You looked like you were having a fine time."

"What is that supposed to mean?"

"It means" — Pria sighed — "it means it seemed like you were having a good time. It meant nothing. Forget it." She turned from Suzanne and went to her bed, sat with her back against the pillows and eggshell-colored wall. She ignored Suzanne's stare while opening the bedside table drawer and pulling out a pack of cigarettes. Pria took out one cigarette slowly; her long-nailed fingers closed the box. "What?" she asked Suzanne. "What?" she repeated, this time looking at her. "Do you want a smoke?"

"No," Suzanne said. "No, thanks."

Pria's room smelled like Suzanne's mother — a little cheap and overly scented but very, very comforting. That same pink carpet covered the floor, and the bedclothes looked incredibly soft from many washings. Above Pria's bed hung an art nouveau poster of a small-breasted plump pink nymph. Staying here, Suzanne thought, and talking to Pria seemed, suddenly, like a smart thing to do; at least it felt smarter than facing Jack and Aaron. She blurted out, "You've got a great house here. What do you do?" She could swear Pria was about to laugh, but she answered in a pleasant enough tone.

"I make jewelry."

"Really?"

"Yes, really. Why —"

"Jack said —"

"Jack says a lot of things. If Jack told you something else, then why did you ask?"

"I was trying to make conversation." Suzanne's heartbeat was puzzlingly fast, as if this conversation really mattered. "Okay, Jack said you're a stripper. Are you?"

"Jesus."

"What?"

"Why?" Pria asked with the beginning of a smile. "You thinking of trying it?"

That shut Suzanne up. She still felt dizzy, though the nausea had subsided, and she let herself sink to Pria's bedroom floor. On her bed, Pria loomed above her, and as Suzanne's legs sank heavier onto the carpet, it was difficult to imagine being anywhere but here. There was music playing downstairs; there was a peach smell through the cigarette smoke, and somewhere in this house Jack's eyes were brown and gold and maybe looking for her. It was embarrassing to feel it, but desire — it had swallowed her now, and it was too soon for any of this. It wasn't even three days into summer vacation; the air was still cold through the window. "I'm sorry," Suzanne said.

"What are you sorry about?"

Suzanne didn't answer, because there was too much to explain. There was so much distance between herself and her voice, and each time she spoke the space inched wider and there was that much more to say. *I'm sorry for using your upstairs bathroom,* she could say; *I'm sorry for coming to this party, for wanting too much, for wanting Jack and thinking it's important.* The faint bass from the downstairs music grew a little louder, the drum that much stronger, a few notes on a horn. "What's this music?" she asked.

"You don't like it?"

"I didn't say that. I think Aaron has this album."

"Oh," Pria said, and her face softened. She sank her head onto a pillow and turned on her side, looking down at Suzanne. "What's it like to have a guy like that?"

"Like what? Like Aaron?" Suzanne began laughing, and realized it was Aaron whom Pria had been watching since they arrived hours ago. She had what Pria wanted. How odd that was, and she heard her own laughter, low and breathy. The laugh rose in her chest and reversed, creating the swollen place where the tears began. "I'm the worst," she said, and stopped laughing.

"Why?" Pria asked, and then surprised her by reaching out and touching the ends of Suzanne's hair. There was an awkward silence. "You've got great hair," Pria said almost dejectedly. "Is this your natural color?"

Suzanne nodded, lying.

"So tell me, why are you the worst?" Pria asked with a smile. "I bet I'm more worse. The *worstest*." She laughed, still fingering Suzanne's hair, laying the ends out on the bed like a fan.

"I just met Aaron's family for the first time yesterday. I met them all just yesterday. And it's bad, it's really bad. He's so sweet. He . . . you should see him with his little sister —"

"Aaron?"

"He . . . I'm going to ruin everything." It was back to crying again, to the sniffling and coughing, and she could feel Pria's dislike. "I shouldn't have drunk so much just now." Now was when she should have mustered up the guts to retreat to Aaron's car and wait patiently for the end of the night. She knew that Aaron was worth it. But she felt propelled to-

122

ward the next sentence. "You know Jack, right?"

Pria blurted out. "What about Jack?"

"I don't know. How well do you know him?"

"What are you saying?"

"Have you ever *really* wanted something or . . . someone you just aren't supposed to want?"

"Oh, Jesus, you mean Jack!"

"As soon as I met him, I knew I was going to ruin everything."

Pria put out her cigarette and began to laugh. "You sure put a lot of stock between your legs."

"What?" Suzanne asked.

"I mean, Christ, you're what, nineteen? You've known Aaron how long? A year? There are other girls," she said, looking right at Suzanne's puffy eyes. "You're not the only one who'll shift the air for him when you walk into a room. I'm sorry, but if you don't want him, I'm sure someone else will. I'm sure someone else will make it their business to teach him to forget you."

"You don't know Aaron."

"Unfortunately, no."

"It would be the worst."

"The worst thing you can do is lie to yourself," Pria said, her arms folded against her chest. "Not that this is any of my business."

"I know I sound ridiculous. You don't think I know how dumb I sound? Oh, God, the room is spinning a little." She tried to focus on the nymph in the poster who looked so complete and serene.

Pria said, "You don't sound ridiculous. Do you want to sit up here?" She motioned Suzanne up onto the bed. "Come, sit."

As she rose, the room tilted, but the bed was comforting. She sat back next to Pria, who asked, "What about Aaron?"

"It's confusing. I can't tell how much I might love him because of how much he loves me. I should just leave tomorrow morning. I can't even look at his brother without feeling I'm doing something enormously wrong."

"So do it," Pria said.

"Leave?"

"That or the other thing, the thing you really want to do." Pria was so calm. Everything about her looked smooth, from her cuticle beds to her elbows to her eyebrows. Suzanne closed her eyes and pictured Pria's voice — a low flame tearing off the wall. Suzanne wanted this conversation to evaporate into the night, a night that wasn't even summer yet, that barely had a sliver of moon. She didn't want this talk to be more than talk. "Maybe you'll be doing Aaron a favor. You'll be honest. You want to be honest. Don't you?"

"Of course." The pillows smelled like powder, cool as an autumn day. She dared to put her head on one, and Pria watched her do so.

"You tired?"

"No," Suzanne said. "How long have you lived here?"

"A couple years. But I'm leaving soon."

"Hmm . . ." She closed her eyes and wished for fingers through her hair, palms on the small of her back; she wished for her open spaces to be covered, her awkward silences filled. "I wonder what everyone's doing down there."

"What do you think they're doing?" Pria said softly.

"Wondering where you are." Suzanne opened her eyes and Pria was watching her.

"Guess again," Pria said. "You know, I had a feeling for someone once, really bad, like you do now for Jack."

"You did?"

"Someone I wasn't supposed to want, but I wanted him anyway. Same old story. I thought I loved him, but I convinced myself I was just being selfish."

"So what happened?" Suzanne didn't sit up. She had a feeling that if she did, Pria would stop talking, and she didn't want Pria to stop, even if she was making this up. It was late, and any second someone would come through the door, or knock loudly, or call them away. Pria looked at Suzanne intently, almost tenderly. "What happened with this person?" Suzanne asked again.

"Well, nothing. I knew it was up to me to do something, and I didn't do it. I let it pass, which was the wrong thing to do." Pria looked away, toward the closet. "I thought I was being respectful of someone, when that person, my boyfriend" — Pria looked back at Suzanne, and her voice wasn't as soft anymore — "was actually just as confused as I was. He was young too."

"Are you saying Aaron's not sure about me?"

"I'm not talking about Aaron. I'm talking about missed opportunities." Pria's voice was hard and sure. When someone knocked on the door, only Suzanne gasped.

"It's not Jack," Pria muttered. "Jack would have just walked right in."

The day after Suzanne had sex with Aaron for the first time, he sent her a dozen yellow roses. On her birthday, they ate dinner at a restaurant where green apples sat in a basket in the ladies' room and the waiters brought her a cake with ginger icing. He never noticed when other girls stared at him, or if he did, he wondered if there was something wrong with his clothes. He lived with a kind of focus that reminded her of no one she knew. Aaron didn't have many friends — she was pretty sure there was no one in these woods that he wanted her to meet — but everyone she noticed seemed to like him very much from a distance. She enjoyed pretending, if only to others, that when they were alone it was all about something better than whatever a crowd was doing. If she felt lonely with him sometimes she also felt important, wholly convinced that no one could possibly love her as much, that certainly no one ever had, not even her parents, who were never very strong contenders to begin with. She had somehow tricked Aaron well; this was how she couldn't help but see it. She had him and knew it was a fluke, but she also had a feeling she would never get another to look at her quite that way.

Jack hadn't looked at her in any particular way. But she felt him in her teeth, in the arch of her foot, and it wasn't subsiding.

Pria's party was ending, and after throwing up some alcohol and anxiety, Suzanne had made her way downstairs, where she sat in the small yard, nibbling oranges from the pool of sangria. Aaron sat behind her on the steps of a plywood gazebo. He leaned forward, his broad shoulders slouched, waiting for her to speak. Suzanne could hear Pria saying goodbye to someone, her voice — a good octave higher — different from before when they were alone, talking in the bedroom. Jack was inside smoking with the two guys; she could see him laughing through the window.

"What were you talking to her about?" Aaron finally asked.

"Just conversation, you know — good party, where are you from, like that."

"Sorry we had to come here."

"What are you talking about? I'm glad we came."

"Oh, okay."

"What?"

"No, you're glad we're here. That's good, I guess. You probably couldn't wait to leave the house."

"Aaron."

"I guess it's a lot. My whole family, all of it. I'm sorry."

She should have gone and touched him, started making him feel right, but she couldn't touch. Through the window, she saw Jack look up, and even though she knew he couldn't see her, she felt watched. "Aaron, I'm having a good time. I'm sorry I'm drunk.

I'm sorry I'm high. I'm sorry sorry sorry."

"No, I just wish you wouldn't run off every time you get wasted at some party, and make me wonder if you're okay, if you're —"

"If I'm what?"

"I just get worried."

She should've told him that he had no reason to worry. She should have put her arms around his back, her hands through his hands, which were now tapping on the gazebo wood. "You act like a father," she said. "Not mine, and not yours from what I can see. You worry more than anyone."

Aaron stood up and began to crack his back. The mass beneath his shirt twisted and she closed her eyes and listened to the release of sinew and bone. There were faint cricket noises and a now-and-then rush of cars passing on the highway. He looked at her and she didn't know what to say. She wanted . . . she didn't know what exactly, but to stop looking through the window and to end this agitation would've definitely been a start.

"Did you talk to Pria?" Suzanne heard herself ask.

"Some."

"What about?"

"I don't know," he said, clearing his throat. "School. This house."

"She likes you, you know."

"What are you talking about?"

"Pria. She does. Do you think she's pretty?"

"What are you doing?" The vein on his neck flexed, the one right above his collar.

Suzanne sat on the steps with one knee up, leaned back on a wooden frame. Her nausea had stopped and the cool air was starting to really kick in; the breaths she took were deep and round. She couldn't help but smile. "I'm just asking if you find her attractive. I'm curious."

"I find you attractive."

"Well, thanks, but that's not what I'm asking. If I weren't here —"

"But you *are* here." He leaned down and reached his hand toward her; she grabbed it and grinned.

"But if I weren't, come on, if I weren't here —"

"I'm not doing this. I'm not," he said. "You are here. You're here with me, and I want to leave this place with you now. Okay? Can you get up? Can we please just go?" He was angry now, and his anger felt good to her. It just did.

"Go where?"

"Home."

"Home?"

"Where do you want to go, Suzanne? Where?" He started to yell.

130

"Where do you want?" she asked him. "Anywhere. If you could take me anywhere!"

"Get up," he said. "Will you please?" He started walking toward the car, without turning around even once.

CHAPTER SEVEN

As Aaron drove the silver station wagon through the cool night, he shifted his eyes back to the clock. It was 3:17 A.M. He vowed if they were home within two minutes, he'd drink a glass of brandy when they entered the house. He'd begin ignoring Jack until Jack asked why. Until then, he swore he wouldn't think about Pria's hand touching his, or how Suzanne drank too much and wouldn't ever let him take care of her.

All the car windows were open; the wind provided an excuse for not talking. As he focused on the road's yellow stripe, the car felt shifty under his seat, as if it could drive away without him. A musky smell invaded the car, a trace of Pria's living room rug, of rain-sodden gazebo wood. During yesterday's rain, he and Suzanne drove north in this car, and he'd thought about woods, about the pond and house, about keeping her in one place away from campus, from people with names he could never remember.

"What's on your mind?" Jack said. It seemed like the first time that Jack had ever solicited a conversation. The wind was cold, but Aaron didn't want the quiet of a closed-in car.

"Nothing," Aaron said. The car followed the yellow line and he heard Suzanne laughing, saying, "Oh, my God." They were headed down a hill at top speed, Aaron having pressed the gas by mistake. Suzanne screamed and Aaron tried to pretend that he'd done it on purpose; he tried to cover the fact that he was shaking.

"Holy shit," Jack said. "You should not be driving this car."

"I'm fine," he said, gripping the wheel so hard it hurt. "What are you saying? That you want to drive? Why the hell aren't you driving?" He was starting to sweat.

"Because we'd all end up dead," Jack said, and Suzanne laughed again. It wasn't much farther to go; they were pulling into the dirt road and the yellow line was gone. He started speeding up, a little faster and then a lot, daring one of them to try to stop him. They passed the trees; small rocks popped and crunched under the tires.

"Aaron!" Suzanne yelled, and it was as if she'd undone his belt with her teeth, it felt that good. She was scared. The pines and dirt

133

and compost sheds flashed by, drawing them right back to where they'd started, to where the house waited patiently in the dark.

"Take it easy," Jack said, and as Aaron pulled into the driveway, the wind became a breeze. Suzanne stretched her right hand out the window. Her fingers trailed the leaves on a low-hanging tree. Aaron stopped the car, and as they emerged and stepped up to the porch, the car began to roll down the slope of driveway.

"Shit!" Aaron hissed, as Jack ran and immediately put his weight in front of the car, stopping it from going farther. Aaron ran to join him as Suzanne walked toward the car, shaking her head, running her hand over her face.

"You left it in neutral," she said to Aaron as she began to bite her nails.

"That's what it looks like, doesn't it."

"I'm just saying."

Aaron put the car in park and didn't respond. They climbed the porch steps, and the silence felt like another person breathing.

"Jack, do you have a house key?"

"Course not." He flicked a burning cigarette into the bushes. "I lost mine months ago. They never lock the doors."

"Well, we're locked out now."

"Brilliant," Suzanne said. "Let's go swimming."

Aaron attempted to put his hand on her neck, feel the warm skin with the strands of damp hair, but she squirmed away and stepped off the porch, bent down to pick up gravel.

"I'll go around to Lila's room and try to go through her window," Aaron said. He waited for Suzanne to offer to go with him, which she didn't. "Do you want to come with me?" he heard himself mutter, and at least she nodded.

Jack lit another cigarette, dropped the used match to the ground. He looked wasted. "I'm going to the pond. You should come," he said to neither of them while looking off in the direction of the highway, as if wondering how they got home. They walked around to the back of the house; a few fireflies hovered by the hydrangea bushes, but no one pointed them out. Jack kept on walking down toward the water. "See ya," he said as he was walking. As he left, Aaron realized Suzanne hadn't touched him since early on at the party, when she kissed him roughly in a hallway, biting his lower lip.

"C'mere," he said to her, putting his hand on the small of her back. She was right there but she wasn't touching, and she wasn't talking either. "C'mon, I'll go in, and then I'll open the front door."

"Then why don't I just wait around front?"

"Just come with me, okay? I don't want you waiting alone long. Look, if she wakes up —"

"I know. You'll have to talk to her and explain."

They walked up to Lila's open window, where their quiet was necessary instead of awkward. He raised the window as far as it would go, hoping she wouldn't wake up. It was tough to get all of himself through the small space, and he could already hear the scream she'd more than likely emit upon waking. Lila didn't have an easy time with anything vaguely out of place in the night. When he was home over Christmas, she slept with the light on, watching her room until she couldn't keep her eyes open any longer.

He landed at her bedside with impressive quiet, and looked through the window for Suzanne's legs but was met with the dull reflection of himself. Aaron watched his sister sleeping, how her round face shone in the darkness. She was wearing her white nightgown, and the blankets barely covered her, as if she had thrown them off in the midst of an overheated fit. Aaron pretended that she was his, his own daughter, scared in the middle of the night. He searched for his features but couldn't find them. She was so light, all water and air, and he was wood and earth. Lila breathed loudly and the whole night with Jack seemed far away. He moved his foot slowly, the toes first, felt the waxy wood, and he was almost at the door, across the small space of the room, when he heard:

"Jack?"

"No, Lyle, it's me. It's Aaron. Go back to sleep."

"What are you doing?" And the dark room was filled with pale spots of light, as if someone had just taken his photograph. "Where's Jack?"

Aaron was ashamed of himself, as he felt a powerful urge to slap her. "Jack is out. He's out with his friends. I'm sorry I woke you, Lyle. Suzanne and I got locked out. So I thought, What would Lila do in this situation? And I knew you'd use the window. Go back to sleep, okay?" He wanted a quick exit before Suzanne became impatient, before his parents woke up and this got any more complicated than it needed to be. He heard a tap at the window, and Lila gasped. His sweating hadn't subsided.

Don't worry, Lyle, it's just Suzanne — he thought he'd said this, but as he went to the window to give Suzanne the *I'll be right there* sign, Lila started to make a moaning noise, and he was so afraid she'd wake his parents that he retreated from the window before he got there and sat beside Lila in bed.

"Shhh, Lyle, I swear it's okay. You're just tired from waking up in the middle of the night. In the morning you won't even remember this."

"Why are you lying to me?" she said, and he shook his head.

"No, no, Lyle — what are you talking about? I'm just saying we got locked out. Suzanne is waiting for me outside. You want to see?" He went over to the window and opened it, but she was gone. She probably got restless, had to go around and wait on the front porch, had to sit on the porch swing, pouting. And instead of getting truly frustrated with her, he warmed at the idea of Suzanne all alone, sitting in yellow light. He decided it wasn't so terrible to make her wait a little longer. "Lila, I'm gonna go, okay? I'm gonna get a good night's sleep so we can run around all day tomorrow. Okay?"

"I can't sleep. I had a dream that Jack was coming . . . that *he* was gonna come through the window. Can you stay until I'm sleeping?"

He could not say no. He couldn't tell her, *Sorry, honey, I have to go get Suzanne; I have to tell her what it is every day to keep her, that I'll do it anyway, that there's nothing I wouldn't do. I have to say these things so she understands that I am patient, that I'm good, that I'm the best she'll ever hope for.* Aaron lay down next to Lila, worrying about the smell of smoke and alcohol that must have been awfully strong, and he asked her what it was that scared her so much.

"Everything at night. Sometimes Mom wakes me up."

"Mom wakes you up in the middle of the night, like this?"

She didn't say anything, and Aaron tried to fight the small lump in his throat in the face of her terrifying innocence. Lila somehow always made him feel powerless. Whether it was this, her fear, or times when she couldn't stop laughing — the purity of her emotions left him weak.

"Does Jack wake you up also?"

"Shh," she said, "you're talking too loud."

"Sorry," he said. "Does he?"

"If he's staying here, sometimes. Uh-huh, sometimes." Her voice softened into a whisper. "And sometimes I just have a *feeling* that someone is coming, and then I can't go to sleep."

The car, the drink, the wanting Suzanne, the driving, were beginning to fade into his sister's small voice. They lay still. Lila's foot touched his calf. He thought of Suzanne and wished his sister were already asleep.

Twice he got up and went to the door, then realized, with shallow breath, that he hadn't left the bed. "I remember when you were born. . . ." he said, because he knew Lila liked that, because he imagined the storm that came that March, blocking the roads and making snowdrifts as tall as he was. Eleven years old, too young to do much but play outside until the midwife Tessa Pape arrived to bring their sister into the world. He thought about all the snow and how it didn't seem to melt and how Jack had a cold and had to stay away from the baby.

Lila loved all the details and he tried to tell them well. He went again for the doorknob and when realizing it wouldn't open, that it was merely a fistful of comforter, he looked at Lila and she was asleep. The clock said 4:34 A.M.

He had slept. He had slept at least a half hour and it was so little that kept him from cursing out loud, from waking his sister and starting this again.

Aaron left the bed, and before he let himself listen to Lila's sleeping moans, he got out of her room and down the small hallway to the locked front door — in front of which he expected Suzanne to be either passed out on the swing or in a nail-bitten frenzy. But when he stepped out onto the porch, the swing was empty. Suzanne wasn't there. The night seemed blacker, the porch light brighter, and he realized that she probably went to the pond. Because he didn't want to believe that yet, he checked the car, the cluster of pines where he sat earlier today, the blond-wood deck. The crickets were quiet, as was the breeze, and he knew the pond was where his brother and Suzanne were probably smoking another joint. He hoped they were talking about him; then he quickly changed his mind because if they were talking about him, it might be ridicule; it might be how wrong he did everything. The idea of Jack near her, near the scent of her, the neck, chest, and breasts of her — the idea — he couldn't get past it, though he probably should have. He should have imagined more. He should've imagined she'd do it, and Jack would too — the beginning of a kiss, the knees hitting stones, toes in the mud, the breathing. He could imagine her doing it, all of it. She would lick Jack's ear. She would climb on top. She would touch herself and touch him too, as she'd stay there, as she'd move over him. And he'd be under, he'd be grabbing her breasts, he'd be looking at her, moving — louder than he ever was in conversation. He'd have plenty to say. He'd be loud; they'd be rough. They would.

On the grass, he stood almost still, waiting for his decision, although what was there really to decide? He had to go down there, to the pond; he had to see. What he needed to decide was how to act, and out of a gaping lack of alternatives, what he decided was: calmly. If they were doing anything, if Jack's disgusting hands were in any way near her, if she was even looking at him in a way he recognized — he'd be level, he'd be straight. He'd be hurt and wronged and they'd be dumb and humiliated. Her nail-bitten fingers would rise to Aaron's face and he wouldn't let her touch. He'd grab her wrists very tightly.

What he couldn't believe was that he was thinking this way. He'd crossed over into treacherously humiliating thoughts. When did things get like this? When, between the day and night, did he feel an overwhelming urge to have Suzanne come to him, her head bowed, sorry for leaving him? Because in the last couple of hours, she had left. And this part he knew he was not exaggerating. Suzanne hadn't been with him in the same kind of way — the way that brought his heart into his thighs, when his mouth was full with the back of his ribs and everything moved better. None of that had been a part of him today, and now — in the dark, on the lawn — it seemed as if everyone knew it: Jeb, his

mother, Lila, Jack, everyone had been waiting
for this instant in which he realized that he'd
been left.

He was afraid to move, afraid that if he
moved this sense would grow stronger. So
when he heard a car pull into the driveway —
a car, at nearly five in the morning — his skin
felt as if it had briefly melted, and his heart almost stopped. He waited. He should've gone
around to the driveway to see who it was, but
he felt incapable. He waited for whomever to
come to him, to find him in the damp grass.
He was sick of looking.

And when she walked up to him, Pria
looked ready for anything. Her eyes were
heavier than an hour ago when they all muttered thanks and drove off from her party.
Jack had invited her to come swimming, but
Aaron certainly didn't think she'd show up.
He didn't say anything as she came toward
him. He couldn't think of anything to say. He
watched her move from the pines to where he
stood on the grass, out in the open. Her
breasts, which he'd avoided looking at earlier,
were barely contained beneath the thin cotton
dress. It was a pale pink dress, embroidered
with white. It almost glowed in the dark. She
ran her hand through her long black hair. Pria
stopped moving only inches away from him.
He didn't know what to say. "Hey," he said.

Pria laughed, shook her head. It was clear that was the wrong greeting. He was grateful to see her in the dark, as he felt more alone than he possibly ever had. He also wanted to yell at her to go away, to at least step back a few inches. He could hear her breathing and a small sound that was somewhere between a laugh and a sigh. Her eyes were yellow. At her place they'd looked green, but now they were remarkably yellow. "I thought you'd all be down at the pond," she said.

"We got locked out. I . . . they're down there, I think. I fell asleep. Now I'm going. I'm going swimming."

"Is that what you think they're doing?"

"Yes, that is what I think," he said.

She sat in the grass at his feet, and it was as if he were now bound to this spot — one foot on the incline of the hill, the other next to Pria, who leaned back, her weight resting on her hands. "Why don't you sit down," she said, looking out in the pond's direction, and he knew he should've been rocketing through the familiar wooded path, the branches scraping his legs, the ground pliant and soft underfoot. He knew he should go get Suzanne, find out for himself why he felt so small, but Pria lifted one hand and placed it on his shoe, and just this touch brought him down to the grass. To think, he assured himself, he just needed a minute to think.

She reached into the small purse at her side and pulled out two little pills. "They're like No-Doz," she said.

He gave her a skeptical look. "What do you mean, 'they're like No-Doz'?" he asked, and then laughed bitterly as he decided to accept, as he decided not to care. His palm outstretched, his glance elsewhere, he waited for the small landing of the tablets, and when they arrived he swallowed one at a time without looking at her, and then he let himself look, ready to listen. He needed help.

"Why did you come?" Aaron asked her.

"Jack invited me, didn't he?"

"Yeah, but, I don't know, aren't you tired? It's five in the morning."

"Am I unwanted here?" she asked, with the slightest trace of a smile.

"Well, no, but —"

"Why aren't you down at the pond, Aaron?" The way she said his name, it was as if she were swallowing syllables, as if his very name were the secret they weren't mentioning. She was so voluptuous that her legs could've sunk into the soil and started flowering — petals rising and drowsing, big exhausting scents. He was hard and didn't want her to know it, but he could sense her looking at it, at him.

"I told you, we got locked out."

"What do you think they're really doing down there." She said it as a statement, and he hated her for the certainty in her voice, the way she seemed to know everything, one clear step at a time. Pria shook her head and didn't smile. "What do you want to know? I talked to her. She told me."

His heartbeat was so fast he couldn't differentiate it from the new steady buzzing in his head. "What," he barely got out. "Just what."

"Do you find me attractive?"

"What?"

"I thought we were flirting tonight. Don't you think we were flirting?"

"No."

"You weren't flirting with me?" She didn't seem angry, only sincere, and he couldn't decide what to say.

"No. Um, I don't think you understand."

"I came here because I think you can be treated better." She said it all smoothly, without shifting her yellow eyes. She touched the fine dark hairs on her arms. "And even if you love her, even if you do, do you think that really means something? I mean, where is she? I'm just saying . . ." And then she mumbled something, something he didn't imagine was an optimistic turn.

"What?" he asked, as it was the only word

that seemed to belong to him. That vague question, that tactic of avoidance, it felt like his only kin. He asked again.

Pria moved toward him, and she smelled like peppermint and cigarettes. She gently took his face in her hands, and her nails grazed the stubble of his beard. She kissed his neck and as he began to pull away, she kissed him full on the mouth, her lips sucking his lower lip, her tongue searching its way inside. He didn't try to stop her now. He knew he shouldn't try. He didn't take her hands away. The pressure in his chest began to give way, and his penis was hard, and as she sat herself on top of him — her breasts right there, her tangled hair skimming his face — he couldn't breathe. He turned his face to the earth, hiding his panic from Pria, who probably thought he was simply embarrassingly turned on.

Her skirt was up; it touched his arms and felt like gauze bandages unraveling. It was Suzanne he wanted, and he thought of what could have happened if only he hadn't fallen asleep. Pria moved her hips dolorously, and he wondered what he could have stopped if he hadn't listened to this woman above him, who was muttering, whom he tried not to hear, as she said, "I want to taste you. . . ."

And as he turned Pria over, as he rolled on top of her and heard her gasp, he knew it didn't make any kind of difference what he did or did not do. And as he clutched her luxurious ass, as she ripped open his pants with her hands, he knew that this was maybe the only thing that Suzanne really wanted — to have him fucking a girl he didn't want to fuck, so that she could have his brother in peace.

He looked at Pria and she reached for his dick, tried to put it in her, and he winced as she swallowed him up. It felt like another person was moving up and down, taking her shoulders in his grasp. He leaned down so she couldn't look up at him, leaned down and drove forward fast and faster, and her hands covered his ears, and he couldn't hear anything but siphoned breath, which he knew to be only the slight motions of her hands on his ears. If he could've ended this without having to watch Pria walk away to her car, hooded eyes nearly closed, he would have. But because he didn't want to see this aftermath, and because he was, of course, aroused, he kept driving into her — hard, then harder, until he couldn't believe he hadn't come. And he didn't come. He thought of Suzanne and her thin arms moving through water — off balance, delicate, or spread out in the damp sand. He thought of Suzanne's shoulders, freckled and sloped, and as he did, he pried Pria's hands from his ears. The sounds emerged — of the breeze, the crickets, and the distant vehicles. These sounds were louder than they should've been. He stopped moving, and for a brief, embarrassing moment, her hips thrust toward him. He pulled out and it hurt — this desire, this misplaced longing. "Why did you come here?" he asked and felt his voice cracking. Her legs tightly closed together; the curve of one hip turned on its side. He pulled Pria's dress down, and smoothed the fabric gently. When Aaron tried to say something, something apologetic, he got only as far as raising his eyebrows, taking a hollow breath. His eyes were unblinking and his hands pulled at grass, and his dick was still comically pointing straight into the dark. What he did say was: "Tell me," which was vicious, leaving far too much to interpretation. "Tell me what she said," Aaron muttered.

"Aaron," Pria said, spitting the word in his face, but she didn't get up from the ground. She lay under the smoothed-out dress, beneath the mess of where his hands had just touched.

CHAPTER EIGHT

Suzanne couldn't hear anything through Lila's window and she was grateful for this small thing. If she heard Aaron talking to his sister, Suzanne would have just stayed there, full of sentiment, rooted in this patchy grass where she and Aaron started up last night before going for a swim. Suzanne knew she had the uncanny ability to be full of feeling in one moment and — in a different light, or at a slightly different hour — totally devoid of emotion. She realized that most people who didn't know her all that well would probably call this quality being focused. But she knew that it was less about being focused and more about being, actually, kind of cold. But she was a sucker for Aaron's kindness and a sucker for the nightlife of children. If she heard the little girl, she would no doubt feel bound to stay and wait. Yet, since there were no sounds of Aaron and Lila, she felt free. It was that puzzlingly simple. Aaron and Lila were inside on Lila's bed, and Suzanne

wasn't about to crouch down and look.

The sky was charcoal blue, starry and lush; clouds moved quickly. She could feel the motion through her body as she fixed her gaze upward, and dizziness engulfed her. Circles in her head felt larger than anything, larger than the desire to run, which was threatening to carry her down to the pond and straight underwater. The stars were colliding with the sky, the sky with the moon, and the moon with her spine. The moon was climbing up her back. *Energy never dies,* she thought, *it just passes on. The universe feels so personal,* is what she wanted to say, but the words stayed deep within, mixed up with the revolutions of her stomach and the quick images of a neck, a hole in a T-shirt, a finger barely tapping on a window.

When she ran out of abstract desire, she let herself think of Jack. She could picture him well right now because she knew he was not thinking of her. He must have just been lost in the pond and the sky right then, wound up in the density of trees. Jack might not have been surprised if she arrived at the pond alone, but Suzanne could bet that he wouldn't be waiting. She could imagine him floating, drifting on the dark water — his pale skin and the oval shape of his whole shaved head.

Now she closed her eyes, and lowered her

face from the sky. *I'm standing still,* she thought, *as still as I possibly can. But even so, there's activity, there's motion, there's no way to stop it.* A small voice said something about tomorrow, about the morning with embarrassed postures in bright revealing light, but even as she heard this voice, even as she could feel it, she had already started to run.

The grass slid under her sneakers and the hair on her arms stood straight up. Her hair flew in different directions and she didn't bother to move it away from her eyes. *This is why I have come here,* she thought, *to feel this kind of running, this kind of force behind a decision that is wrong and still to decide it.* As she entered the wooded path, she remembered how Aaron moved in front of her last night, how his broad back stood straight, how he pulled back branches so they wouldn't scratch her, and how he didn't talk until he hit the water. She wondered how long he'd stay in Lila's room, and what he would do when he realized where Suzanne had gone. She thought of this as if it had already happened to someone she knew a long time ago, someone whom she remembered with considerable tenderness. *He was a great guy,* she could picture herself saying; *he really was way too good for me.*

Midway through the path, where the trees thickened, she stopped to pull back the branches and was pricked by thorns. She couldn't hear any disturbance in the distant water, any splashes or plunges or rocks skipping. The night was so still, and for an instant Suzanne was scared. Not of Aaron and Jack or herself around them, but of the dark, the unnameable, the woods and sky, the energy that existed without her. As she approached the pond, the trees thinned out and the soil became rockier. A mosquito bit her right ankle, and she balanced on that foot, scratched with her left. She could hear a faint buzz of insects, and she waited a moment, scratching her ankle, before she went any farther. She tried to remember last night, kissing Aaron on the damp grass, pulling at his shirt, but she couldn't remember how he tasted, how his hands felt on her body. She could picture Lila in the window, the feel of the thin curtain, but she couldn't remember the rush of kisses, and this very same path to the pond. Sometimes it was difficult to conjure her own memories. Suzanne's memories were fragmented, not worth all the emotion everyone else always seemed to be feeling. When she got emotional, it seemed to be over small things — forgetting to meet someone for lunch, being underdressed at a party. Or seeing strangers fight on the subway, a little boy in the park crying over staying or going.

People always went on and on about the senses of recollection — the feel of the floor, the particular music, the taste of something sweet. She could remember floorplans of houses, how to find lost things, but not the feel of people's skin, their bedsheets, their clothes. And not Aaron's breath, even now.

Suzanne grabbed hold of a branch and stayed balanced on the one leg. She listened for Jack in the pond beyond the trees, and for Aaron's possible approach after finishing with the task of opening the front door. She continued listening, starting for the water again, dosed with possibility.

When he had touched her pair of gray underwear that afternoon, she thought her face would betray how the rest of her was shaking. With Jack, she thought she would stop asking for so much. Jack might teach her to demand.

And then again he might teach her nothing. She knew this wasn't about any kind of reason. This was about being alive in New England well before sunrise and running away from your boyfriend, and how running away seemed like quelling a fire, and how it most of all felt like beginning. This was not about imagining love, or trying and failing because you needed it too much. There was no place to be now but out in Jack's direction where everything rose at the lift of an eyebrow, at the slow long pace of arms stretching skyward — waking up a third, a fourth time in a lazy day. To keep on going was the only way to go, until what might happen just simply did, and there was nothing left to suppose.

It was then that Suzanne came to the end of the trees and watched Jack at a distance — she, rooted in the mucky sand, he in the black water, floating faceup on what looked to be a log. She liked to think she could've been sure it was him even if she hadn't known he'd headed this way. She liked to think she could've identified the angle of his neck, the position of his feet, how his chest sat on his narrow hips and his hips on his long legs. But now she was just too far away, and she would've never been sure if his clothes — Levi's, gray T-shirt, Nikes — weren't clumped in a sandy pile at her feet. Jack could've been anyone, any tall, thin white male, probably lonely or full of hope to be out on a lake alone at this hour. This was what her life looked like now — alone on a shore she didn't know two days ago, alone between a house and a body of water. She had always wanted a house, a real house with old things and history behind its walls, while water she'd been afraid of for years. And it was the water she chose now, swimming instead of calling to him. Swimming alone and silently until the figure became whoever it became, whoever Jack felt like being right then.

She wondered what she should take off her body and what she should leave on. Wearing any more than a bra and underwear would only look amateurish and prudish. But it was strange getting undressed, and as she removed her worn white jeans with the pale blue patch on the thigh, she was thankful that her underwear were the good ones, with the flattering shape, not too skimpy around the rear. It was a decent bra too, one that she pocketed from a rack of a Chelsea street fair, right before exams. She let her shirt fall where it fell, and as she stepped into the weeds, she began to shake. As she eased into the pond, it was as if she were pouring herself through a sieve. Something released through the imperceptible parts of herself — smaller than her pores, smaller than the pale hairs on her inner thigh. There was shivering, then greediness for motion, and as she began swimming, the water was smooth and everything smelled clean.

Suzanne kicked, reached and sliced the water with her arms, and as she gathered speed — breathing to the side only when she really needed to — the water became her own. It surrounded and engulfed her, guided her strokes in the right direction. It was no longer

Aaron's pond, no longer attached to a house in the woods, but a simple body of water — one of many, as her own body was one of many, as was Aaron's, as was Jack's. Bodies moving through water, moving through bodies — the water was warming, and as she came up for air, she began to tread water. Suzanne looked toward the shore. She had come farther than she'd thought, but was still a good distance from Jack, who had sat up on his log, maybe deciding whether to wave.

She could've gone back to shore. She could've just turned right around and swum back before Aaron even showed up. But Aaron might not have shown up. Aaron might have gone straight to sleep, angry and set in the assumption that she'd be back and they'd have a fight that would end affectionately. Aaron maintained that she liked any kind of drama, that she was indiscriminate about it. Maybe he thought she was playing a game. And that's what this could be, no more than a game, nothing more than giving him a little scare. She could turn around right now.

Nothing needs to happen, she thought as she began to breaststroke onward. Maybe all she was doing was drinking and swimming — nothing kids hadn't been doing for years. Grandparents, people long dead, they swam after drinking moonshine, brandy; they kissed and that was nothing but summer fun. *And maybe,* she thought — as her heart started to pound so hard that it was difficult to swim — *maybe as soon as we start talking again, it will feel like Jack and I are friends, even old friends, between whom the flirtation is already out of the way.* Five breaststrokes without a breath — six, then another pause. As she came up for air, she couldn't see Jack, and briefly panicked, until she realized she'd gone too far to the left, and everything had slightly shifted. In that split second of Jack being missing, and of being the only body around, she missed his presence so badly, so much, that when Suzanne set to swimming again, she breathed right after each stroke, keeping her eyes right on him, watching as he grew nearer and nearer, his features taking shape. And then he lay back down on the log, actually a few logs attached together, and the question of whether he was naked or not was answered as a full, resounding yes.

She kept herself down low, water up to her eyes and at the same time wanting nothing more than for Jack to dive down. She felt that as long as she remained underwater anything could happen, but once she was exposed in the air, listening to the sounds of the night inching by, she'd begin to think of Jack as Aaron's brother and of herself as someone she knew too well, someone with a fleshy middle who was freckled where she should've been white. Jack wasn't acknowledging her. Maybe he was just so drunk, so stoned, that she was no more than a ripple in the surface of the pond, a fish at best, something facile and light. Suzanne waited, quietly treading, blowing small bubbles in the water. She could see only one side of him, his ear and neck, shoulder and rib cage, his curve of ass and length of leg and foot. It was almost frightening how still he was lying. He must've been either utterly relaxed or else rigid as hell. It was difficult to see what his body really looked like at this limited vantage — his thinness could've been doughy soft or else all angles — edgy and naturally strong. His thigh had swirls of dark hair, maybe not all that dark when dry. She couldn't see the full view of his body and she was glad for that. This way it was almost like glimpsing a silhouette.

"Howdy," he said, remaining completely still, and she gasped.

"Christ," Suzanne said, still unable to breathe right, and she choked on water that tasted like the science room in fifth grade — stones through a tumbler, cheap orange ices, a hint of whatever wasn't meant for consumption, eaten on a dare.

"Jesus," Jack said.

"Well, you scared me. I'm sorry, but you did." She fought to breathe normally, and before she thought about it too thoroughly, hung her hands on the logs for balance. Jack didn't sit up, but he bent his knees, and Suzanne didn't look below his shoulders. She looked up at the stars and waited. Neither of them said anything, and Suzanne could hear her breathing, the heavy, ugly breath escaping her body. It was cold now that she'd stopped swimming. Jack's eyes were closed. "Are you asleep?" she asked as she allowed herself to see the concave chest, the uneven slope of his rib. His arm reached out, almost skimming the water. She could've touched his hand.

"No, I'm not asleep," Jack said. "Are you crazy?"

"What do you mean?"

"Where's your boyfriend?"

"You mean your brother?"

"I mean, where's Aaron?"

Suzanne didn't answer and she let go of the log, water swallowing her hands again. She floated on her back, ears in the water. Stars overhead made this all a little easier, presenting a safe distraction. She didn't want to stop floating or grab onto the raft again. She didn't want to choose. She wanted to be chosen, plucked from obscure waters, as if she were drowning and unaware, as if only Jack could

160

see she was sinking, and his vision alone — of Suzanne falling through the murky waters — would be all the catalyst they'd need.

When she stopped floating, she had drifted a few feet away from the raft. She could circle him like a planet, a shark, a tired girl still drunk on vodka, buzzing with weed. Or she could pull herself onto the buoyant wood. She could be scrutinized as she pulled herself up. She could just do this, now. But as she tried to hoist herself up, Jack did nothing to help her. He didn't even seem to open his eyes. He only moved over, allowing her the space she needed to flail and eventually sit herself down. He started whistling a corny tune, over and over again. It sounded like a military rag, a cheery camp song. His whistle was clear as a bell, pitch perfect and obnoxious, as it cut through the air between and around them, the air that now felt not only cool but cold.

"It's freezing," Suzanne said, not looking at Jack.

"You get used to it if you lie still for a while. You think you're cold, but I'm colder. Biologically. Women have more fat to protect them."

Jack was back to whistling, but this time a slower bluesy tune. She could dive and swim away, but she recognized the melody, one of

161

her mother's favorites, one that used to echo in the narrow apartment hallway: *It's only a paper moon, floating over a cardboard sea, but it wouldn't be make-believe, if you believed in me. . . .*

"How do you know that song?" Suzanne asked him, holding her arms around her knees, stomach in, neck straight, eyes watching the water.

Jack kept whistling.

"How do you know it?" she repeated, and when she looked at him, he kept on whistling and gave her a definitive shrug. It was time to dive, to let this go, but she couldn't help looking now, couldn't help looking at all of him. And his body seemed mangled somehow. Besides the broad bony shoulders, which went straight across, none of him was even. His rib sloped on the one side with a corresponding scar, his nipples were tiny, and his lack of chest hair made him look younger, far more vulnerable than she'd expected. His legs were twisted in such a way that she couldn't really see between them. He looked almost female, with his neck cocked to one side, his prominent collarbone jutting out. Or maybe feline, with those long strides and confident strokes, and a way of moving through open spaces that suggested other people, other voices, without doing more than shrugging, staring closely for little more than a moment. Then again, he was an unknown creature — part fish, part snake — whistling, naked, and yes, unfurling, legs now splayed in front of him. Suzanne should have jumped off the raft, as she was no cat, snake, or fish. She was just a girl — cold, arguably chubby, afraid, but curious enough to look at his body — and she was, against what was left of her better judgment, watching Jack in the barely there moonlight, and wanting.

CHAPTER NINE

Pria rose from the ground, stumbled just the slightest bit, and purposefully brushed off her behind. Aaron saw her ignoring his question, holding back what she knew. He shouldn't have needed Pria's or anyone else's version of Suzanne. He shouldn't have, but he did. He wanted to hear who Suzanne was when he wasn't around. He was always curious about it — he even followed her briefly, when she went to the art studio, when she went shopping — but now he needed to know. Maybe it was the pills he swallowed, or maybe the unfinished sex, but he felt an unprecedented impatience, the sense that everything was moving too slowly for him, that he belonged somewhere else. The shiver of pines and the sky up above felt threatening, as if the stars would all fall and the trees would loose their needles.

"I just feel strange," Aaron said. "Like I can't see correctly, or something."

"You can't see right. That's true. Jesus

Christ, is that true."

"Look," Aaron said, still half-expecting Suzanne to come walking out of the woods, "I'm sorry about this. I am. This has gotten messy, and —"

"Messy?"

"I just want to go backward for a second. Can you tell me what she told you? I really . . . I need to know."

"What difference will it make?" Pria said, and she turned back toward him. He stood up and felt a bit better, with his feet planted on the ground.

"You tell me," he said, and for some reason, he smiled. You want something, you have to work for it — this was something he knew, as well as he knew math: as every number has a personality, each part of his body did too. A smile, a shoulder, a hand: parts of him added up, spoke a certain language of persuasion.

"You're really confused," Pria said, looking at him slightly differently.

"Maybe," Aaron said. "But I know I want to hear what my girlfriend told you." They both sat down again without discussing it, and no part of Aaron could believe that they were, just moments ago, grabbing body parts and holding on. He couldn't believe they'd been kissing.

"Well," she said, taking a cigarette from the little purse, placing it neatly between her lips, "she said you were sweet."

"But —"

"You don't seem like such a sweet person to me."

Aaron watched Pria smoke, how her cheeks hollowed as she took a drag, drew the smoke down and deep, then let it out in an almost violent beam. I am sweet, is what he wanted to say, but he wasn't sweet anymore. He was rotten inside where he had, last night, last week, been ripe.

"She said she felt guilty, how much she wanted your brother." Pria didn't look Aaron in the eye, and Aaron coughed though he didn't need to. He looked at Pria until she looked at him. Her eyes were still yellow but not as wild. Her lips were pale without the pink sheen of gloss that had long since been kissed off. "She also said she had power over you, which made me want to throw up. Maybe she wants to see how far she can take this power of hers."

"Are you telling me the truth?" he said, not at all lightly.

"She said they'd already kissed," Pria said. "She and Jack. Sometime during the day. She said that she was already sneaking around."

"What else?" He felt strong, not sick. The

166

muscles in his legs contracted.

"Suzanne said," Pria started, maybe deciding what would hurt the most, maybe deciding whether to go on, "maybe she should leave tomorrow because she's been bored with you. I told her she was crazy. I told her to stay."

Just Suzanne's name in Pria's mouth made Aaron want to take a shower. He didn't believe her, but those things had been said; they'd made their way out into the air. Even if they weren't true, they affected his blood, his headache, his stiff neck, his stomach — like when he had nightmares, how waking was only somewhat comforting, because the dream had still occurred. And here, Pria was real. She had said these things, and even if they weren't true, he was left to wonder, even more deeply than moments ago, just what it was Suzanne had been thinking, and what she was doing right now.

"I'm sorry we did that," Aaron told her, and he was; he was sorry.

"You've made that painfully obvious," she said, stubbing the cigarette out in the grass, making no move to pick it up. And it pissed him off, her leaving the butt in the grass, like she had come here to do indiscriminate damage. "Why did you, then?" she said, and Aaron couldn't take his eyes away from the ground.

"Come on," he said, and his foot started tapping one two three four, one two three. "Give me a break," he said, and his voice divided between smooth and hard. Something was pulsing too fast for his foot to keep up, something deep and coursing, something falling. "I know you're lying to me about Suzanne," he said, finally looking Pria's way. "I know you're fucking with me, like you probably did with my brother, when you were all tied up with him."

"Jack and I are friends. We've always been friends."

"Whatever *that* means. Tell me you're lying about Suzanne." She looked at him but didn't say a thing. He was careful not to raise his voice too loudly, and the effect was a hollow sound. "Tell me."

"I'm going home," she said, and as she got up a second time, he got up too, and he grabbed her arm tightly, then held both her shoulders. "Okay," she said calmly. "You are not who I thought you were. I'm sorry I came here. Now get your hands off me."

"What is that supposed to mean?" he asked. "Just who did you think I was?" He didn't take his hands away, and she glanced at them — hairy and clutching her almond skin. "Who? You don't know anything about me. You didn't know anything and you came here. I didn't ask you to come."

"Let go of my arms now." And he did. Instead of running for her car, as he'd anticipated, she lit another cigarette. "I did know about you. Some things. I knew that you and Suzanne had been together less than a year, that you never had a girlfriend before her, not really, but that you used to fool around with your best friend Dana in high school. You're way too scared to try acid; a couple of years ago you took pictures of your little sister all the time, and some people thought it was weird. You were never a very good guitar player but you have a good singing voice. You have never smoked a cigarette —"

"Jack told you all this?"

Pria nodded.

"Why?"

"Because I asked, mostly."

"What do you mean, mostly?"

"Sometimes in conversation, you'd come up. You're his brother."

"Right," he said, but he was shocked that Jack mentioned him in any way whatsoever. "I don't want to know about what you know. I want to hear that you lied to me about Suzanne." He knew he sounded like a child, that he was forcing her to make things okay. *Take it back*, he used to say to Jack. *You'd better take that back.* Pria wouldn't; he was sure of that, sure that she would leave as coolly as she arrived.

"Fine," he heard her say. "I lied."

"You did?"

"That's right. I lied about all of it. We never even talked about you."

"What?"

"You didn't come up."

"Really?" *Shut up*, he told himself. *Just let it go.*

"You're a selfish guy," she said, her voice almost shaking. "You're worse than Jack." And she walked off, the little purse swinging at her side, looking flimsy, looking cheap. He almost called out to her, but the only thing that came to mind was a yell — somewhere between *fuck you* and *help me* and a shadow of apology — and he couldn't yell now, not on this lawn at this hour. His head pounded the rhythm of his foot — one two three four, one two three. He would make his way through the trees to the bank of the water, where he'd see Suzanne and what there was to see. He'd leave this spot on the lawn after Pria had driven away. If she drove away he'd feel better about moving, as if this part of this night had fully ended, had been taken away with her on the highway. When she was almost at her car, almost gone, she called out to him: "Don't go down there," not a yell, but loud enough for him to be sure of what she'd said. Pria stepped into her car and drove out the driveway, taillights glowing like two red eyes and two white ones.

And he pictured Suzanne and Jack in the pond, knee-deep and silent. Then not in the pond, but in the woods; in and out of both pond and woods, maybe not together at all. And if Suzanne was waiting, if she was upset with Aaron for making her wait so long and was simply waiting at the pond's edge, he would be the one who had done something. He *was* the one who had done something. He cheated on Suzanne. Pria disgusted him now more than he could stand. And that she knew about him through Jack — Jack pimped Pria to him was how it felt, and that everyone knew something more, though he himself couldn't figure out what. And Jack. Jack stopped speaking to him and he couldn't say when it started. Jack seemed as real as the people Suzanne introduced at school, whose names seemed completely irrelevant.

The kitchen, this morning, smelled like burnt fat. The room was contaminated with sunlight, with Jack breathing into Suzanne's space — into where her fingertips met the air, where her hair touched the middle of her back, and her voice ranged from very high to very low, lingering a beat longer on *L*s and

171

*W*s. He'd felt as if he needed to get her out of there, as if a gas jet were slowly leaking, but he hadn't listened to those thoughts because they'd felt irrational. But he'd been right. Something had been leaking and the day had gone by and it continued to leak. It had followed them everywhere. And by the time night came around, he couldn't say when the gas leak became a bomb, a specific fear that had accumulated around Suzanne, and they couldn't get away from it because the bomb *was* Suzanne.

She had said: what's the point of having a relationship if there isn't passion, if we can't show vulnerability? She seemed to know what she was talking about. She always seemed to know, and so he'd told her. Some things, anyway. She knew about the pictures of Lila for Senior Photography that some teachers had found disturbing, and how his mother told him those teachers were ignorant, that they were lovely shots and that most people were afraid of beauty. She knew about Jack and how he used to never shut up, and how one year he got quiet, and how one night last year he cut himself with a beer bottle, threw a rock at Aaron's head and didn't miss. She didn't laugh at that story, or the fact that he and Jack had only recently started talking again after the rock incident, and that Aaron wanted them to be talking, to go back and change things if possible. She knew how his father scared him with silence, how his mother seemed to love everything a little too much, and how he felt detached a good deal of the time. She knew these things.

Aaron inevitably began walking toward the woods, the path, the pond. It was inconceivable that his parents and sister were sleeping in the house that loomed behind him. The place looked empty.

A flash of Jack placing his hand on Suzanne's lower back, guiding her through a doorway. He couldn't remember if this happened or if he was imagining that it did. Her shirt lifted slightly in the back, and his brother's fingers grazed her skin. He touched her and Aaron looked on. Did this happen?

Did he let it?

Aaron wanted a crash, a new release, a way out besides moving forward. The slate gray sky had lightened considerably, or maybe his eyes were finally adjusted to the dark. He had no idea what time the sun would rise, when the circles under his eyes would fix themselves as one more night gone by.

He could smell the pond. It felt like only a minute had passed since last night, when he led Suzanne toward the water, heard her halting footsteps behind him. The stillness had made words such a challenge.

Aaron found a way to postpone the pond for just a few more steps. He remembered a clearing to the right of the path where it was possible to see the pond, and he snaked himself through some tricky branches to get there. Being up higher seemed to promise whatever sight he was to see would be somehow more bearable.

The scent of the pond was mossy, thick with chilly weeds; it came just before the pond itself, and what lay far out, down on the surface. Floating there, Aaron confirmed, was Suzanne. Suzanne alone, facedown on the raft. He waited to see Jack, but there was no Jack in sight. He turned from the pond and began to make his way through the woods, back onto the path. Aaron's heart did a small dance as he set out to meet her. He should have known she would have found that raft in the bushes and pushed it right out on the water. He should have known Suzanne would be there where she was, smack-dab in the center of things.

CHAPTER TEN

Suzanne watched Jack jump into the water, with barely any splash. She could picture him ten years younger, never staying where he was supposed to stay, getting wet when he needed to be dry, dirty all the time. Was she supposed to follow him? Was she supposed to jump too? He disappeared into the darkness with no more than a faint ripple on the surface. And he stayed under. Suzanne was, for all purposes, alone on the lake, and it was hard to discern how much of her buzz was still drunk and how much was simply a desire to have Jack surface and stop circling her. She wanted to pounce, to, for once, stop talking altogether.

But she waited. She waited for Jack to break the surface, and finally he did. She heard his heavy breathing, saw his shaved head, how his submerged body treaded water. She lay on the raft, on her stomach, and her neck stuck out, so they were almost head-to-head. "You were down there a long time," she said, and didn't know why she'd said it.

"You should try it. See how long you can stay under."

"No, thanks," she said. The color of the sky was changing; she could swear it was. Granite and soupy, the sky no longer fully belonged to the night. "You should come up here."

"No," he said, putting his hands on the raft and pushing himself up, "I shouldn't."

She touched his shoulder lightly, as if she were tracing a shadow projected on a wall. His skin was slick and slightly rough as she felt farther back, along the shoulder blade. He stayed half in the water as her fingers teased his skin, calling him out altogether. She touched his neck, which was smooth, thin-skinned, the hollow between the collarbones — a place to put her fingertip, a place for her tongue. But not yet. Her hands kept moving, drawn by the crisp air, the endless water. It was difficult to imagine daytime, to imagine being dry. His nipples were taut and in both sets of her fingers, the few fine hairs dried off in the cold. And then a line — her palm took a direct course from his neck to where he made himself visible, to where he modestly came out of the water. He had an inny. A barely muscled stomach that could fit between the shallow bowl of her hips, that could bear down without bruising.

Her breath buckled, her hand shook, and once he let out a sound — a noise so high and barely male — there was nothing she could do but pull him, pull until he was with her on the raft, wholly out of the water, wholly hers. And kissing wasn't what it was, not really. It was gnawing, sucking, biting, pressing, mashing. It was clawing. She thought she heard herself moan but she wasn't sure, it didn't sound like her, it didn't sound like it could have ever been her, but it wasn't Jack because Jack was still making that eerie wail, that small constant keening, as if he were barely alive.

"Do you want me to take off your bra?" His voice was hard, too loud; it shocked the base of her spine.

"Do you want to?" she managed, in between flights of breath.

"I'm asking you what you want."

"I want you to. I want —" And his tongue in her ear, nothing soft about it, and the swift unfastening of her bra, which she was sure had ripped, made her feel as if she were swimming again, as if she needed to push herself to another place, because something was chasing her and threatening to bite and transform her into nothing. He was grabbing her breasts, raising them toward her neck, as far as they could go. He was burying his face between her breasts like he wanted to burrow a hole. And then he bit them, one at a time, slowly. He held her hips between his hands, keeping her in place.

She heard his breathing, the uneven shift of the raft on the water, the occasional splash and ripple. The sounds blended together and created a path of music, a lulling agreement between her limbs and hands, between the patterns of her lips and tongue. She looked down at his head, bobbing and nestling, the smooth skin of his forehead. She wanted to touch it, but when she lifted her hands to do so, he grabbed them and held them still. Her wrists in Jack's hands felt smaller than anything she could imagine possessing or being. His fingers pressed her skin in separate fixed spots, and he continued from her chest up to her shoulder. She felt the air more acutely on the places where his tongue had left a trail of wet and where the heat of his face had been. "When did you know this would happen?" she managed.

"Shh," he said — an order.

"Okay," she said, "I won't."

And the shore looked far, so far away, that no one standing on it could possibly see what she was doing, how she was feeling. Aaron, if he stood on the shore, would be an obscure figure, a person who, by the time he'd caught up with her, would hear only a short and obvious good-bye, peppered with the words "too young." *I'm too young,* is how she'd begin. *Bye-bye,* she thought, as she let Jack lay her back on the raft, her spine making contact with the knobs of sodden wood.

He lay down on top of her, but so his face was at her navel. She couldn't see his body, just the outline of his back. As his lips brushed her stomach, she tried to hollow out her body, think scooped-out and emptied. "Tell me you like this," Jack said, as he kneaded her thigh with one of his hands, which she began to wish he'd lay to rest, or at least slow it down.

"I like this," she whispered, something she'd never said. The words seemed so bald. "I like it," she tried again, and the sound of her own voice sent her spinning, gripping his shoulders and trying to bring him to her, so she could feel her body under his, so his pressure could cover her skin. But Jack didn't move, only held her down and began to kiss her inner thigh. He removed her underpants, and she squirmed now, as an ache was beginning to replace desire, a shrillness between her legs as if she suddenly needed to pee.

"Where are you going?" Jack whispered. "Don't you like this?"

"I wish —"

"What?" he said, no longer a purr.

She tried to sit up but he wouldn't let her,

kept kissing and stroking until she wanted to scream out, not so much with yearning as with greed, with an urge to be buried, filled until she couldn't feel a thing.

"You want to sit up?" he asked, not un-thoughtfully.

She nodded, and his hands loosened their grip on her hips. She tried to touch him, and when she did, when she touched his uneven ribs, he kept looking at her until she knew she should stop. They were face-to-face, upright again. His pupils were huge in the center of his hazel eyes. "When did you know this would happen?"

"I don't know," he told her, and he started kissing her again, and she tried to touch him lower, and he moved her hand away. "Push your tits together."

"What?"

"You don't want to?"

She rarely touched her own breasts, besides getting them in and out of bras. Aaron claimed to love them, as did other guys she'd been with, but she couldn't tell how Jack felt about them, and so she did as he asked her to do. They felt surprisingly satisfying between her palms, comforting to the touch. Jack was watching her, nodding, murmuring approval, but he seemed agitated as opposed to appre-ciative.

"More," he said, "closer." And Suzanne noticed he was touching himself too, jerking himself off. She was repulsed, but she didn't take her hands away from her breasts because between this revulsion and her original throes of urgency, she felt daunted. These shouldn't be bad things, she convinced herself — this distancing, his wish to watch her, a dose of voyeuristic shame. She squeezed her tits, and let them go. She tried to tease, watched him wince, and caught his narrowed eyes.

"You like this?" she managed. "This is what you like?" And again she tried to move in, kiss his long neck.

He said, "Okay, yeah. Uh . . . uh." And she drew him down and onto her, and he made his wincing straining sound, like a disappointed child. She was suddenly sorry for him, as he jabbed at her and held on to his dick as if he didn't trust her with it, as he tried to find his way inside her. There was finally nothing doing. "Goddamn it!" he grunted, and pounded the dock. He smoothed the line of flesh at her waist, not so much a caress as a reminder to himself of where he was, and why he was there.

"It's okay," she said, and Lord help her, she believed it. She believed because she had to, because at this point, the risk had been taken, and it was going to be, it had to be, worth it. If this wasn't the way she'd imagined, she thought, there must be a reason for it. It was perfectly natural that this would be the case because, after all, they were both over-whelmed, right? Both heavy with an unfamil-iar pull toward each other, helpless, and —

"Jack," she said, and she loved his name, loved its jaunty feel on her lips, how the sound escaped her throat. "It's fine."

He didn't respond as she felt a flapping back and forth against her thighs, a digging of his bony pelvis into hers. He was still breath-ing heavily, still in motion, as if there had been no change. She cupped her hands around his shoulders, and tried to soften his jabbing motion. She tried to draw him near.

"Come on," Jack urged, "come on."

"It's okay."

"Stop saying that," he said, and shook off her touch. She tried to roll on top of him but he wouldn't budge. "You think I'm always like this?" he asked her, still on top of her, the wood at her back beginning to scrape.

"No, I . . . it doesn't matter. I just think —"

"What?" he muttered. "What do you think?" He sat beside her now, leaving her body exposed as a useless limb.

"I think we like each other, I mean —" And she sounded unconvincing, though she knew she was telling the truth. "I mean, I like you,

it's not just this" — she gestured ambiguously
— "so I think *this* is just . . . well, obviously . . .
complicated."

Jack brought a finger to his lips, began
gnawing on his nail. His body seemed to go
slack altogether. "Let's just forget about this,
if you don't mind." Jack wasn't looking anywhere near her; he'd adapted a focus fixed between the far-off rocks, as if there was
something essential to see out there, a bril-
liancy about to flash, that he'd regret not con-
sidering.

"Do you want to forget about it?" she asked
him, taking caution to keep her voice on the
strong side.

"That's what I said, didn't I?"

"But," she said, and forced herself to look
at him and take a full breath, "this is right."
She was pushing now — no stopping — *this*
she knew how to do. She leaned over to kiss
him, and at first it worked. He turned his head
almost all the way toward her, and that amazing sickening feeling jump-started. She was
doubly conscious of the shore, the trees, and
just how far she had traveled tonight. Suzanne was ready to explain anything to anyone. She was delirious with selfishness.

Jack abruptly grabbed her shoulders. "You
want it?" he whispered, gruff in her ear. His
breath was hot and it made the rest of her

cold, in need of more and more.

"Just — *yes*," she said.

"Are you sure?"

She could barely talk now; she was all talked out. "I am," she managed. "I don't care about —" He took his hands away, kissed her hard. She tasted him in a way she knew she could never forget.

And then he stopped. He pulled away, and when she reached for him, he hit her arm away, hard enough that it stung. She had to think fast and brace herself so as to not fall back and hit her head. Her heart raced so profoundly she thought she'd pass out, and seconds later she wished she had, because Jack stood up slowly as if he were suddenly in another time zone. He rose and grew remote until he might as well have launched into the faded stars. He looked down at her, and then — something Suzanne knew she'd also never forget — he shook his head and expelled an almost inaudible: *"You . . ."* He didn't finish the sentence because he plunged into the lake, leaving her naked on the raft. As she watched his long arms freestyle away, she put her own arms around her body, not so much an attempt to cover herself up, but a chance to feel what he had felt so briefly, and what he had turned away.

Suzanne reached for her underpants, sitting wet and bunched at her toes, a splotch of powder blue. She pulled them on — freezing, full of raft dirt, and *hers* — and she imagined a line being drawn with her body as it slid into the underwear. Before. After. She was on both sides of that line, thinking: *From here on out you'll be changed.* Things would be different but she didn't know how, and she wondered if she couldn't just walk away. She'd be punished, she knew. It could happen soon.

Suzanne saw Jack come up briefly and dive under again. Jack went farther and farther, toward his jeans and gray T-shirt, to where she and Aaron had discarded clothes last night. Suzanne knew she had to get off this raft eventually, as she knew that the sun would rise. It would be a clear, sunny day, she thought, the kind she had wanted, and now anything else seemed preferable. She lowered herself facedown across the raft, stretched her hands into the freezing water, and pointlessly splashed her face.

When she opened her eyes and looked out at the shore again, she tried to tell herself she had known that this was coming. And as she saw Aaron — so unquestionably Aaron — standing on the shore with his hands behind his head, she knew she should have stayed by Lila's window, that whatever freedom she had felt had mainly been fear. It was the fear she had wanted. And it was fear that she got, for Suzanne was afraid of everything now, from the fragmented shards of clouds overhead to what she supposed Jack would tell Aaron. She tried to remember what making this decision had felt like, when she had chosen Jack and believed. She tried to recall exactly when she'd made the choice, when, though she knew she was doing the wrong thing, she just hadn't thought it mattered. Jack was out of view now but there were no splashes or kicks, so she knew he was still under, with the water in his ears and eyes so thoroughly erasing her. It would be almost warm, the water, if she stayed under for as long as she could. She held on to the side, and she saw Jack emerge on the shore. Aaron and Jack stood together on the shoreline. As she let go of the raft and began to swim, she thought about how they were brothers, how they would stay, and she would go. The water stayed cold, and for a moment she lay on her back and looked up at the sky. It was silvery and timeless. She would pack up her things and take a bus. She wouldn't talk to a soul.

As she swam on, she made herself look and the figures were more in focus. Jack, thank God, had on pants. Aaron threw a stone toward the forest, or she thought it was a stone: his arm drew back and he let something fly, and although she couldn't see it, she could imagine the perfect arc of his throw, the way it was sure to make contact with wherever he had aimed. And she also knew that he would care, he'd check, he'd get it right. He'd throw, if he had to, over and over again.

CHAPTER ELEVEN

The sky shone pale through the darkness in an indecisive dawn. It was to be the sky of his imagination, the one he'd see when he closed his eyes for the rest of his long life. The sky looked this way at 5:32 on the third Sunday of May in 1987 when Aaron saw his brother Jack swimming toward him, when Suzanne remained on the raft. Because Aaron didn't want to stand there waiting for Jack to emerge on shore, and because he didn't know what else to do, he picked up five rocks, and with unprecedented precision, hit the rotting maple tree, one throw after another.

He'd let it happen. It was happening now. Jack swimming toward Aaron's turned back, Jack watching him throw stones at a tree. Each moment was because of the preceding one. There was no time-out now, no stopping his own rage from climbing his spine and meeting with the arc of his throw. The blood rushed to his temples as he bent over to collect more stones. His back cracked as he hurled the stones toward the tree trunk. He did it again and again, and he thought of the night last year, when Jack threw the rock at his head. Jack had picked up the rock — a considerable one, far larger than the stones Aaron now threw at the tree — and had hurled it at Aaron. Jack had released a growl along with the rock, as their fellow workers from the Caraway Café stood slack-jawed. It was the girl who came to him first, Aaron couldn't remember her name. *Wasn't it always the girls who were less afraid in the end?* his mother had needed to point out, days later, upon hearing the story.

Now it was Aaron who lobbed the stones one after the other, not caring anymore whether or not they hit, and he thought of how casually Jack had thrown the rock, and how Aaron could've sworn he'd smiled, if only a little, when the rock made contact with Aaron's head. He wanted to tell Suzanne that story again, but this time more convincingly. This time he would say, *Stay the hell away from my brother, he is dangerous, he is full of venom, no matter how it seems.* Aaron had to now convince himself that this was true, that no matter how he wished otherwise, it was simply the case that Jack hated him, even now, especially now, as Jack drew closer, making audible crawl strokes in the pond.

Aaron turned around and released his remaining stones toward the water, skipped the stones far away from where Jack approached. Three skips to three stones. He had always been good at that. His brother emerged from the lake, ankles submerged, and water fell from his rangy body in fast silver flashes. It was plain that Jack — smiling and, yes, naked — had plenty to say.

"Hello." Jack said it, just like that. Aaron heard him say hello, the last syllable higher than the first. And Aaron thought: *He is nothing like me, nothing at all, except now — how he glances at his ribs, how he stumbles almost imperceptibly on a mass of shale. Now he* is *me. He is my mother and my father. He is the blood in my veins and there is no escaping how, as he comes out of the pond, he is coming from Suzanne.* Jack walked forward, though Aaron tried to will him backward, back to the moment when he first left the water, before either of them would have to speak. And even as Jack kept coming with a bitter misunderstood smile, Aaron imagined him rising from the cold water, bursting up and busting out; he imagined the air meeting Jack's moves, the roar of silence propelling him.

"Put your pants on," Aaron said, the words stuck low in his throat.

"What?"

"Your pants," he managed, "just put them on."

Jack walked among the weeds and leaned over to pick up his jeans. As he put them on, Aaron wanted to push him over, step on his lopsided body, and bear down with all his weight. He wanted to see Jack squirm in the weeds, suck up leech-laced mud. The silence was sickly, weighted with every bug in the forest, the underground motion of leaves growing, branches stretching, the spinning and breaking of spiderwebs, the unrelenting blooming.

Aaron didn't look at the raft on the water, didn't want to let Jack see him look. Suzanne would be here soon; she had to swim out eventually. "Why didn't you come down earlier?" Jack tossed off. Jack's eyes were too big for his head, and he had a sore on his neck, some kind of inflammation. His shoulders were wide and the veiny rest of him slouched, as if from their comparative weight. Aaron wanted to kick in his back, to straighten him out and force him to talk without insinuation, without one shred of disrespect.

"I got sidetracked by Lila. She woke up."

"You should've just come down with Suzanne."

"Yeah, well." Aaron could feel his teeth set in his mouth, the exact placement of his

191

tongue. "I didn't know she was coming down here. I thought she was waiting for me."

"I've got to tell you," Jack said almost gently, "she seems like she gets impatient pretty easily."

"Oh, really," Aaron heard himself spit out, "d'ya think?"

"She seems like an impatient kind of person. More than that," Jack said.

"What, then?"

"I don't want to insult you or anything, I really don't, but," he said, "but," Jack stated, "I don't think she's good enough for you."

As Jack leaned down and picked up his shirt and a pack of Marlboros, Aaron said, "How do you mean?" And while keeping his distance, he began tapping the side of his leg one two three four, one two three. Jack pulled the shirt over his head and stuck a cigarette between his lips. He lit it and inhaled. Aaron let himself look out at the raft and it was empty. Suzanne was swimming to shore.

"You should just pay attention."

"Just what are you saying to me? What the fuck are you saying?" Aaron dug his fingers into his sides, glimpsed Suzanne getting closer.

"Do I have to say it?" Jack asked, sucking on his cigarette. "Is it just so inconceivable? The possibility of a girl being curious about me? It would just never occur to you?"

"Shut up, Jack."

"You're too stupid about people. You're stupid about me. I've lied to you so many times and I know you've believed me." Jack's voice was fierce. If Aaron didn't know better, he would think Jack's voice was full of love. Jack said, "You need to look out for yourself. You need —"

"I said shut up. Stop talking now. Stop!" Aaron felt as if he would take Jack's neck between his hands and watch it go limp. Jack was lying; he had to be. Aaron's head hurt with mistrust. And Suzanne was getting closer to shore. "Tell me what happened," Aaron said quietly.

"What?"

"Just — tell me what . . . tell me why did you do this?"

"Do what?"

"You want to tell me? I know you want to, and I'm telling you to go ahead. What happened?"

For the first time all evening, Jack, his brother — he looked panicked. "I really think you should be with someone better than her. Someone who's good. You know what I mean? *Good?*" He was anxiously looking out to where Suzanne was getting closer — white flashes of arms stroking through the water.

"She came on to me," Jack said, as if he were embarrassed.

"How."

"Why do you even want to know? I tried to get out of it. I told her to get a grip."

"If you don't tell me what happened —" Aaron's sides were pinched where his fingers dug into his skin. He could feel Suzanne watching him, waiting for him to do something. He could picture her wet face, up close to his own. She would tell him to calm down, that there was nothing to get so worked up about. She'd say, *Let's get out of here. Let's drink tea with honey; let's watch late-night TV.* Aaron kicked at a mound of dirt and stones, and some bits of ground flew in Jack's direction.

"Take it easy," Jack said.

"What happened?" He could hear Suzanne's sloppy crawlstroke. He looked — he couldn't help it — he wanted to see her face, but she was underwater, ears submerged.

Jack flicked his cigarette away and said, "She was all over me. I tried to tell her to go and find you, but she wanted to —"

"You sick fuck, you —"

"I didn't think you'd believe me. I know you don't —"

Aaron saw Suzanne's clothes sitting in a careless pile — the muddied white jeans and

194

the thin striped shirt, two blue canvas sneakers. Her feet were so small.

"Why?" Aaron said, but Jack didn't answer. "Have you done this before?"

"Done what?" Jack looked nervous, as they stood at an impasse, facing each other like dogs — one mad, one sly, both furious at heart.

He could hear Suzanne, splashing closer to shore. "You had sex with my girlfriend?" Aaron said, and he knew he was about to cry. He thought of Lila sleeping peacefully in her room, her small fingers clutching the worn yellow blanket. He thought of how she screamed when she was afraid. His throat constricted. He walked past Jack toward the comforting slabs of rock. He sat on one of those slabs and watched Suzanne switch direction and swim toward where he sat. Her features were twisted and blurred. Jack approached with his hands behind his back. He stood next to Aaron, so they were side by side.

"You asshole!" Suzanne yelled at Jack, or Aaron hoped she was yelling at Jack, as she stretched her arms in faster strokes, approaching the slippery rocks. When Suzanne reached the rocks and grabbed hold of one, she looked up at the two brothers and didn't come out of the water, which was obviously, in part, due to her lack of attire. "What did he tell you?" she asked Aaron, and he couldn't stop himself from wanting to pull her out of the cold water. Suzanne looked at Jack. "What did you say?"

"Suzanne —" Jack said.

I'll kill him, was what Aaron thought, as he heard Jack say her name. Aaron thought he'd kill him, and he thought he should, and he knew that no matter who said what he would never know, never as long as he lived, what happened between them. Suzanne said, "Aaron?"

And when he didn't look at her, when he couldn't look down at her, down there in the water, when he didn't look because he knew he'd fall apart, Aaron heard Suzanne say, "He's making it up." The scent of Pria's neck momentarily surrounded him, and he was so sick with anger that his hand twitched at his side, and it took only Jack's expression — the way he looked at Suzanne like she was nothing — to set his arm in motion.

When Aaron hit his brother the first time, he felt like he was cleaning out a filthy place. He hadn't swung a second time yet, and didn't realize that he was, in fact, becoming filthy himself and sinking into a darkness that light would not grace for an interminable time. The first thing he felt after he short-armed the punch was an exquisite pain in his pinky knuckle, where he'd clipped Jack's cheek with the outside of his hand. He didn't hear Jack's reaction, if, in fact, there was one. But he did hear Suzanne yelling. She came out of the water, and he heard the water. He never knew that water could be so loud. The water fell from her bare breasts, from a pair of blue panties he'd always appreciated. Her breasts were obvious, her arms gangly as they stretched around herself in a pathetic sort of modesty. She yelled, "Stop, please stop it," but she couldn't have meant it. She yelled, "Aaron," as the pain in his pinky throbbed, as Aaron noticed that Jack, though tenderly holding his jaw, hadn't fallen down. As Suzanne moved behind Aaron, and tried to talk to him over his shoulder, he was amazed and impressed that Jack's gangly body had withstood his punch.

"Stop," Jack said. "Please."

"Come on," Aaron spit out, breathing hard. "Just give it a try. At least fight back if you're telling the truth."

Jack swallowed, wiping his nose with the back of his hand. "You're stronger," he said quietly. "You know it," he breathed.

The three of them stood on the granite slabs, frozen, for a moment, in the shock of Aaron's anger. "Come on," he repeated.

And then Suzanne's voice wouldn't let up,

and Aaron could barely tune her out, but tune her out he did, enough to quickly react when Jack swung his right hand wildly back at him. Jack wasn't quick enough now, now that he had gone too far, and had overshot just how far he could push his big brother before his big brother pushed right back. Aaron could tell that Jack was shocked to have overstepped his bounds. But Jack *had* overstepped them, and Aaron was finished with being patient and understanding of everyone's flaws but his own. *I have every right to do this,* Aaron thought, as he grabbed Jack's shoulder with his left hand.

Aaron let loose a blow that sprang from somewhere in his guts; his whole body moved in agreement from his feet through his legs and hips. He moved the air aside — that was how it felt — and he let the light of the morning into his eyes as he remembered to aim farther than where he wanted to go. He remembered to move closer, to use two knuckles, to keep his wrist straight and to use the whole hand. His thoughts assumed the kind of clarity that he'd never have again — the untainted action and powerful flash of a young man unaccustomed to consequences.

Aaron felt the slick scrape of his brother's teeth, but it was not this particular sting that snapped him out of his seamless thrust. It was the sound of seriousness that broke him out of his trance, the sound he had wished for. He heard Suzanne, lovely Suzanne, saying, "Oh, my God," with her voice at least an octave lower, a voice that sounded as though every part of her absolutely believed in what she was saying.

His hand hurt, and he was puzzled by the intensity of his own pain. He hadn't remembered turning toward Suzanne, but he was face-to-face with her flushed round cheeks and splotchy chest, her arms still crossed over her breasts and her hands still gripping her rib cage. She didn't say anything, and the sudden silence propelled him to turn back toward his brother.

Jack was down. His brother's foot was caught between two slabs of rock. Jack looked like a rag doll, flung down sideways, headed toward the water. There was blood on the rocks, a dark stain beginning near his head. Aaron knew right away that Jack had fallen sideways as he had taken the punch and slipped on the wet granite. "Open your eyes," Aaron told his brother.

The sun was a thin glimmer, greeted by the pond and the trees. Suzanne was close enough to touch, and Aaron wanted her back so badly, wanted to kneel under her sloping breasts, to grab hold of her skinny legs and hide inside her softness, the softness in which he would always continue to believe. He wanted Jack to get up and go far, far away. "Jack," he said, "come on." But Jack didn't stir.

The sky would be blue today, a mean, bitter blue. The air would be too perfect not to mention. "Get up now," Aaron said as he kicked Jack's wrist gently. Suzanne, still undressed, leaned down and looked at Jack's bloody face. After one half-attempt, she touched his long, girlish neck. She put her fingers on Jack's pulse. She said, "Jack?" as if she somehow knew him better.

"Why didn't you wait for me?" Aaron wanted to ask her, as the pond grew ablaze with light.

"What?" he heard Suzanne say, and he bent down beside her.

"Did he say something?" Aaron asked, and then Suzanne told him no, no, he didn't say a thing.

CHAPTER TWELVE

Lila woke up at 5:30 A.M., sweating and out of breath. She couldn't remember what she'd been dreaming, and the more she tried to remember, the more panicked she became. She was sure her brother Aaron had been sleeping beside her when she went to sleep. It was a vague recollection, and maybe that could have been her dream, but Lila felt certain he had been there. She could even smell him on her pillow and stuffed lion — a smoky smell, somewhat sweet and heavy. Lila sat up in bed and looked out the window. The world was still dark. It seemed that Aaron had sneaked out of her room. She wondered if he really went to sleep, as she knew she was supposed to think, or if there was some kind of party down at the pond, even though no one was supposed to go down there after eleven P.M. Jack went down there all the time by himself; he said he liked to watch the sunrise. He said to his parents, "I'm appreciating *nature* — who can argue with that?"

Although it was close to morning now, Lila was seized with the fear of being the only one awake in the house, and too far away from whatever fun was happening at the pond. She knew her brothers were breaking the rules, and that her parents would want to know, but she also knew Jack and Aaron and Suzanne would be disappointed and angry if Lila woke her parents and told. Lila knew this fear would pass if she could fall asleep again, that if she closed her eyes long enough it would be morning for real, but when she closed her eyes she felt, as she often did before going to sleep, that something was going to happen. Mostly she was afraid that the house would catch on fire, that a loose wire or smoking ember was spreading flames in silence. Her heart beat faster until she had to sit up and turn on the light. Lila decided she would go find the older kids, maybe spy on them, before letting them know she wasn't as dumb as they probably thought, that she knew things went on all through the night, even when she was sleeping. Jack had taken her night swimming once, and he acted sleepy and kept singing "On Top of Old Smokey" and wouldn't get out of the water, even when the sky started to rumble with rain. It was scary down there by the pond, there was no doubt of that, but Lila thought they'd all be so surprised and impressed if she made it down there alone, that it had to be worth a try.

Lila grabbed her flashlight from the night table, then decided against it. She could do this without a bright pink light, and besides, it was nearly morning. Before going outside, she went in the kitchen and took a big plastic bag of chocolate–peanut butter cookies from the cabinet below the silverware drawer. Bringing food never hurt, Lila reminded herself, when she went somewhere she wasn't supposed to be.

As she stepped outside through the kitchen door, Lila realized that she ought to be wearing a bathing suit. They would probably all be swimming and they'd want her to come in the pond too. So she went back to her room and stepped into her red one-piece with the three gold stars on the chest, and pulled on her gray hooded sweatshirt that Jack had given her, which went down to her knees.

Outside, the grass was slick. Lila wasn't wearing shoes, even though she should have been, and she was surprised how cold the ground felt as she quickly ran to where the path to the pond began. Before entering the woods, she hesitated briefly, listening to the night sounds. Everything buzzed if she listened closely, and the dark ceased being black and looked more like green, everything green.

The ground was damp loam laced with soft bark, and as she made her way onto the path, the temperature dropped very slightly. The buzzing wouldn't stop, and it was difficult not to think of all the bugs that she couldn't see, how everything was alive. She wanted to go back to the house but the house seemed as frightening as the path, unless she woke her parents, which she couldn't do because her parents would worry that she was having nightmares.

The boys came down here all the time in the dark. It was difficult to understand how they did it, how this path seemed, to them, like no big deal. There was a force down there at the pond, something secret and revealed only during the night. Maybe it was in the water, and it had to be something worth this thorny run of trees, the pebbles and rocks that stuck out underfoot. The moon wasn't even visible, the sky was beginning to lighten, and Lila tried to picture the raft, the one she would be allowed to swim out to, if she passed her Minnow test this summer. Jack talked about building a slide on the raft and Lila agreed. She agreed, for the most part, with everything Jack said. Unlike Aaron, who talked to Lila about their parents, or about her friends at school, Jack didn't discuss people much, but rather ideas for clubhouses and slides and plans to get unusual pets like snakes, tarantulas, porcupines. To Lila, it was Jack who seemed different, who was always lying about what time he came in when he stayed at home — the way Lila liked it, when she was his trusted secret-keeper, his Lyle Bug, his squirmy sister sister.

Lila heard splashing going on down at the pond. The sound was unclear enough that she thought she might have been imagining it. She noticed the air seemed warmer and the trees smelled more like summer, even flowery, and she was sweating on her upper lip and everywhere, as if she'd just woken up all over again. It felt almost hot out, as if the elements were converging somewhere, as if the world were listening to her anxious thoughts. Maybe a huge thunderstorm or a forest fire was brewing. She made herself keep very still. Lila made promises to the trees. She promised the pines, the soil, and the grass that she would take special care of them forever if they got her down to the pond unharmed. She took back any thoughts about killing bugs. She would help everything live, if they helped her.

By the time Lila heard the yelling, she had realized that she was truly scared and that maybe everyone was right about her, that she was a frightened kind of kid, the kind of girl who is always scared and never gets over her fears. The yelling was almost not surprising; it articulated her worries. The yelling was male and indecipherable, an unabashed cry that came from the direction of the pond, and Lila ran there faster than she thought she knew how, so quickly that her feet hurt but didn't hurt, and her arms were scratched raw by skinny branches. Lila's body bristled with fear, but her arms and legs felt like they belonged to someone else, someone who was much slower, much calmer than she felt right then. She held on to the bag of cookies (and Lila would look back, as little as one day later, and wonder why) very tightly in her hand.

The pond grew closer, the air dampened and smelled like sludge, and she heard Aaron's voice: "He's fine, he has to be."

And then Suzanne, in a voice Lila could barely make out: "I swear, Aaron. Oh, my God."

Lila stood at the end of the path, unnoticed, where the sand and soil merged, where some clothes had been cast away. Just a few yards in front of her, Aaron and Suzanne weren't swimming but standing on the rocks down by the shore, where her mother liked to lie and dry off on a sunny day. Suzanne was naked now, her breasts dangling, her long hair matted and wet.

Jack was lying between Aaron and Suzanne. Lila couldn't see his face.

Aaron sat on top of Jack, but carefully, as if he were afraid of crushing him. Aaron leaned over and put his lips on Jack's and started breathing into Jack's mouth. Lila saw this happen on television, but she couldn't remember which show. Aaron didn't seem to be doing it right. Suzanne was shaking her head.

"We have to get help. Let's go," Suzanne said quickly, her skinny arms loose, swinging back and forth.

"And leave him here?" Aaron asked, in a voice Lila almost didn't recognize.

"Let's go!" Suzanne yelled so loud that Lila shrieked; she couldn't help it. Then Suzanne was running toward her, away from Jack, who lay immobile on the rocks, with Aaron hovering above him.

Lila hurriedly picked up the clothes in the sand, and held them out for Suzanne, who was running, her eyes wild and her matted hair in her face. "Suzanne?" Lila managed, and her voice sounded terrible — like whining, but louder.

"Holy shit," Suzanne said, tugging at her hair, as she saw Lila standing in the tall, tangled grass.

"Here," Lila said, and handed Suzanne her

clothes, "What happened to —"

"Lila!" Suzanne said loudly, and Lila knew she was angry as she took the clothes and called: "C'mon, Aaron, get her out of here!" Suzanne was talking about her as if she weren't there. *"Aaron!"* Suzanne repeated. *"Now."*

And Aaron ran toward them. And when Lila knew Aaron had seen her standing in her sweatshirt, holding a bag of cookies, she was humiliated and sprinted toward the uneven rocks where Jack was. Lila barely dodged Aaron's grasp. *"Lila!"* Aaron called loudly, but he might as well have been miles away, as Lila didn't even turn her head. "What the fuck is she doing here?" Aaron said; his voice was shaking and pitched higher than Lila had ever heard. Then Aaron let loose an unintelligible yell, the very one she'd heard from the path, and began to sob. He yelled and cried and strained his throat, and ran into the woods.

"Lila, come with me," Suzanne said, but she was looking after Aaron, watching him through the trees. Suzanne began backing away, telling Lila to come, while trying to keep sight of Aaron. When she'd either lost sight of Aaron or seen him in a state so terrifying it was hopeless, Suzanne turned back to Lila, who was at the base of the rocks, and going to Jack, no matter what. "Come on," Su-

208

zanne yelled at the little girl. "Do you hear me? Come here right now." But Lila didn't so much as acknowledge Suzanne's voice. Suzanne was no more present than the trees and the soil and the grass, who had led her down to the pond unharmed, but had punished her for asking too much. She was being punished and she knew instantly that this was the thing she had been afraid of, this moment, which must have been coming all along. "Lila, please," Suzanne begged. And then, "I'm not leaving you down here all by yourself."

Lila, if she could've seen anything besides Jack, would have seen how Suzanne yanked on her clothes and brought her sleeve to her mouth. Lila would have seen Suzanne suck on the end of her sleeve, and Lila would not have known that Suzanne hadn't done such a thing in fifteen years, that Suzanne herself didn't even remember this habit. Lila would have seen how Suzanne's pale skin was overcome with blotchy red, and how Suzanne was, finally, too stunned to move.

Lila dropped the bag of cookies in the sand and climbed the wet rocks to where her brother Jack lay still, in what seemed a very uncomfortable position, his right shoulder higher than the rest of him, pushed up by the tip of a rock. He looked like a fallen scarecrow, only he wasn't wearing a shirt. There

209

was nothing but fear in her when she saw his face, the bloody smear from his long nose to his chin, the grainy wet sand covering his thin face, and the way his shaved head cocked to the side, offering a view of the gash. There was a cut at the base of his skull which poured blood — trickling downward, on and in between the gray rocks crawling with bright green moss. He was dead. She knew it. This was what dead was — this absence of everything but fear, this quiet, airless terror. Lila knelt down beside him, not feeling the chill of the morning air, nothing of the scratches from the branches on the path. Only the heaviness that rose from between her lungs was present, the heaviness that passed through the dark of her throat and extended from her fingers as she put her hands on her brother's face. The skin there was soft and warmer than hers. Sparse hair grew from his chin down his neck; he barely needed to shave. On his left cheek, where the hairs were even fewer, a purplish welt was rising and swelling below the bone. Lila remembered, as she touched the swollen spot with her fingertips, that now they couldn't go to the bird sanctuary on Wednesday, as they'd planned. Her hand stayed still, in front of his mouth, in order to feel the absence of his breath, but Jack was breathing, he was fine after all, and as she moved her fingers to his neck, just to touch it, Lila leaned in close and kissed his dirty forehead, his soiled cheeks, and his soft bloody lips. "Is it morning?" she wanted to ask him, but Lila knew that it had to be, for without her having noticed, the sky had torn itself into strips of pale light.

Aaron was gone now and Suzanne was right there behind her. Suzanne was quietly waiting. The rest of the morning hadn't happened yet. Her parents were not running down here themselves and pushing Suzanne aside, or Aaron and her father carrying Jack to the house. There was no ambulance tearing up the driveway, no gruff paramedics shoving Lila away, no curses from her mother, no tears from her father, no speeding to the Portsmouth hospital on the near-empty Sunday expressway. Right now there was nothing but shimmering light, and Lila laid her head on her brother's soft stomach, careful not to give him too much of her weight. It was as if they were together, following through on Jack's plan to stay up for the sunrise. Lila closed her eyes and imagined Jack pointing. She imagined him telling her, *Look, look up, but don't look for too long. Check that out,* he'd say. He'd say, *Man, is that something, or what.*

But he didn't say a thing.

PART TWO

LILA

The truth must dazzle gradually.
— *Emily Dickinson*

CHAPTER THIRTEEN

What Lila never talked about with her parents: Aaron who was gone now for ten years and Jack who had been dead for the same amount of time. Her summers had been spent fighting the urge to yell "Don't fall!" when anyone went down to the pond with a towel. "Don't drown drunk!" she once called out last year to her father, when she would have done anything to get him to talk, to talk about anything at all. Lila got out, got away from the silent house in the woods by coming here, to New York City — supposedly to attend NYU — which was certainly second, if even that, to simply getting away. But really, it wasn't even simply to get away that she was after. She knew it all along, that it was here, New York, where she wanted to be, where her brother Aaron went to Columbia and majored in chemistry before dropping out, where Aaron met Suzanne.

He should have found her. That was what Lila thought about her brother Aaron, and why she hadn't really ever considered looking until recently. He disappeared after Jack's accident when she was eight years old, and he should have been the one to find her. However, when she looked (one night last year after a party, when her parents weren't home) and could not find his Social Security number anywhere in the house, and after she could not find one trace of Aaron in any of her parents' drawers or conceivable hiding places — Lila, from that night on, became intent on procuring this information. In Manhattan, away from the house, among the random grid of strangers, she was becoming increasingly ready.

What she wanted from her mother and father now: Aaron's Social Security number, and what she never said when her mother asked, "Do you need anything?" was: "Yes, I need Aaron's Social Security number." She never said, "That is what I need." What she also wanted was any information about Aaron's girlfriend at the time of the accident: Suzanne Wolfe, who was there that weekend. Suzanne who was from Manhattan although who was wholly without a trace in any directory, maybe never even left, and whom Lila imagined as an ally, an older beautiful friend. Lila had already checked all the obvious places, spent most of her productive hours of the past month on the phone with Columbia Student Records, with New York Information, each borough, each suburb. Nothing. Whenever she spoke to her mother, they talked about none of this. They discussed Lila's suitemates, their different cultures, different homes, places her mother always wanted to go. And to her father Jeb, she spoke of transportation in the city, the best and safest way to get from here to there.

And something was happening with the phone calls. Besides humorless and false reports once a week, Lila was calling her parents up to three times a day, calling and, when her mother answered, hanging up the phone. It started out of loneliness. One night at three A.M., she woke, terrified of the shadows on the wall, the sirens in the street, and she did, that first time, call her mother out of desperation, out of needing a familiar voice. But when Vivian answered, Lila was struck with the immeasurable distance between them. She hung up, and slept a long, fitful sleep.

She tried her parents one Sunday, after hanging up only once, for the weekly attempt at communication, and her mother answered immediately. Lila couldn't remember a time when Jeb ever picked up. "Hello?" her mother said, impatient with whomever she expected might hang up again. All the crazies after the accident offering strange sympathies, the townie publicity — her mother was still used to the mystery of the telephone.

"It's me," Lila said, and she heard Vivian take a short, full breath.

"You didn't just call, did you?" Lila could discern how her mother sat by the tone of Vivian's voice: her mother was sitting on the couch, with her narrow feet poking out of the burgundy afghan.

"You mean call and hang up?"

"Or get disconnected — something — you know, with the phone?"

"No," Lila said, distractedly, even shaking her head slowly for effect, "huh-uh."

"A prankster, or whoever, has selected our little abode."

"A *prankster?*"

"Or whoever."

Lila couldn't help smiling. "I'm sure it's just some kind of wrong number or something. Anyway, I'm sorry I haven't called for a while."

"I had a dream you got married," her mother said plainly. "You're not married, right?"

"No, Mom, I'm not. Where's Jeb tonight?"

"Well, thank heavens about that. Hmm? Oh, your father's gone out. How did you know he wasn't here?"

"I just can tell. Have you thought about what I said about the letter?"

"Hmm?" her mother said, and gave a small cough.

"Look," Lila said, her right fingers digging into her left palm, "I want that letter badly enough to have asked, which, as you know, says a lot. I just want the letter. What are you going to do with it? You don't look at it. I know you don't."

"It takes more than you think to turn a sow's ear into a silk purse," she said. Lila didn't even bother to say, *What?* "That letter will only frustrate and upset you," her mother continued. "You've already read it; I know you have. It's not even interesting. I don't see why you need to have me send it to you."

Lila wanted it, she just did, and it was too exhausting to argue, although arguing would have been preferable to the underhanded jabs, which they both took freely, while pretending that everything was essentially fine. Fine, that is, besides the loss of a now-sanctified Jack, and the successive disappearance of Aaron, who threw his family and his life away. Her parents seemed to pity Aaron for taking Jack's accident so hard, but they also couldn't help letting slip that they were angry at him for disappearing — too angry and hurt, apparently, to even want to discuss him or persons related. So, regarding Suzanne's letter, Lila couldn't imagine that her mother would ever budge. But three weeks later, she received a package in the mail. A multivitamin ten-pack, three pairs of black tights, a vanilla-scented candle, and wrapped in violet tissue, an envelope postmarked December 1987, addressed to Mr. and Mrs. Jeb Wheeler, and inside the envelope, the letter from Suzanne. It was on yellow-lined legal-pad paper, and her handwriting was neat and small:

November 11, 1987
Dear Mr. and Mrs. Wheeler,

I'd expect you didn't bet on hearing from me, after you told me I was the last person who should have been included in Jack's funeral, but I thought I'd try again in giving you my condolences. I figured it couldn't hurt. I also wanted to let you know that I am going back to Columbia next term and that I haven't heard from Aaron and I wondered if you had. I know he loves you very much, and it can't be long before he comes back from wherever it was he went.

The weekend that I spent with your family changed my life, and I want you to know that not a day goes by that I don't think about all that you have lost. Maybe one day something good might come from this. I have a hard time imagining what. I am sorrier than you know. Please forgive me for bothering you, but I send my condolences and my regards to Lila and to you.

Sincerely,
Suzanne E. Wolfe

Lila always wondered what the "E." stood for. After she found the letter two years ago in her mother's bureau drawer, she would return to the letter whenever she could — hold it, smell it (embarrassingly enough), and wonder — when Vivian was too far gone on Halcyon to notice or to care — why the middle initial? Ellen, Elena, Eleanor, Ella, Elizabeth. It was postmarked from Ossining, New York, where Suzanne might have been staying with her mother, or maybe with a friend, at a center for young depressed people, at an ashram. Lila had mined the given address for all it was worth, but there were no traces of Suzanne by then. Lila's parents wouldn't say one way or another what they knew about Aaron's girl. Lila's mother seemed to think she was the worst thing that ever happened to their lives, this stranger, this Suzanne, considered her a bad influence, which hardly made sense, for even Lila remembered Jack's sneaking around, his permanent badass grin and sense of secrecy. It was unlikely that Aaron's girlfriend could have been much worse, could have led her brothers down any surprising paths. Jack had been drunk. Jack had been dumb. Jack had dared himself onto the rocks and fallen. Who really knew who Suzanne was, anyhow? Besides the times over the years — when Lila woke her mother up, and fragments of Suzanne peppered her mother's dream accounts — Vivian claimed she knew as much as she needed to, and that such a girl would have probably gone on to cause a lot of people damage. Lila didn't believe this version. She thought her parents were afraid of acknowledging their guilt over not looking for Aaron hard enough, for letting their son, her big brother, slip off into obscurity without much of a challenge. As far as Lila could tell, her parents had just let him go.

Vivian seemed to dream of Suzanne, or at least *say* she dreamed of Suzanne, when she stopped taking the drugs, and tried to move on with a new sonless life. Her parents never had company anymore. Guests — all guests, they both said — were exhausting. Lila thought her mother dreamed of Suzanne because it was Suzanne who could help them find Aaron, and that her mother was too afraid of the time they had already lost. That, or (and this was a peripheral thought, one that Lila had recently begun to allow) her parents knew something about where Aaron was, and they simply weren't telling her. It was possible that Aaron was confiding in their parents and they were all hiding it from her. Lila was on the outside, no matter how she assessed the situation, and she was banking on Suzanne, her estranged ally, to lead her on in.

Suzanne's letter didn't help her with any information, of course. It was short enough that Lila could have copied the words down any number of times. But the feel of the paper in her hands, the knowledge that Suzanne had stared at this paper feeling guilt, sadness, anger, feeling anything at all — about her family, her brothers, about *her*, it was as thrilling as it was comforting. She wanted to call her mother and hear her say hello, but she fought off the urge, and went to dance class instead, the only class she'd attended in the last two weeks.

That evening, a cool Wednesday in November, Lila sat on a bench in dirty Washington Square. She liked to come there after dance class ended, let herself cool off and watch people. That particular evening she was watching some kids play bongo drums, and she hadn't noticed the young man approach, his too-big gray coat trailing the pavement.

"You're the fattest girl in your dance class, but you're clearly the best," was what he said as the sky drained of color. After this opening line, she ignored him, and he didn't say anything more. Her sweat began to dry and her muscles ached. Then she stood up and saw, behind her, the hem of his coat, the mussed-up mousy brown hair. Lila's first thought was that he looked like a shrunken version of her brother Jack, but she was always thinking that. Shrunken Jack, bearded Jack, Asian Jack, goddamn fatter Jack. Jack was all over the place. His particular slouch and delicate neck were surprisingly commonplace in Greenwich Village. Aaron could be sighted as well — at least his aquiline nose, broad back, or dark hair — though not many people looked like Aaron: he was harder to project. New York was full of boys and more boys who could have been her brothers. To her dismay, Lila looked like neither of them, and not much like her parents either. Theirs was a family whose children all looked like obscure relations.

"*What?*" Lila said, after the guy didn't go away.

"Fuck, fuck, fuck, it's fucking beautiful

224

here. I love this fucking country." He turned and he was wearing a thin white T-shirt. A T-shirt and a long coat, faded black pants.

"You're British," she said.

"That's right." He took a silver flask from his coat pocket. "Would you like a nip?"

"No." She gave him a look that said, *Are you nuts or what?* "No, thanks." The bongo players shook their heads, shook all over, gave her something to look at. Lila stood up, prepared to get moving.

"I'm Ben," he said, looking a bit up at her. He was a very short guy.

"So you think I'm fat?" When she spoke now, she sounded loud, unfamiliar. She had spent her first months of college having polite interactions, which led to nothing but drunken not-so-polite interactions. Everyone she'd met had seemed in a great hurry to be friends or enemies. Ben was older than her, but not by much. She could tell from his skin, which was smooth and almost translucent, hints of wrinkles around his eyes and mouth. He was laughing softly, kicking a stone back and forth between his feet, coming up with an answer.

An ambulance drove by, sirens sounding off; the bongo players didn't seem to notice. She saw the flashing blue and red lights, so commonplace in the city — in the middle of the night, the morning — the lights and sirens, and still, each time, she dug her right nails into her left hand. "You're a shrimp," she said, and started laughing with him. Who was he anyway? He had money. She could tell from his shoes, from his T-shirt, even if he was faking the accent. Something about the coat, even though it was old. She could always guess people's lives. "When did you see me dance?" she asked, and already she was lying. She'd seen him for weeks, looking in the studio window, as the class began to warm up, before the windows steamed. He shrugged and started jumping up and down, on and off the bench, like he was on some kind of exercise course. She couldn't help but laugh harder. By the time he stopped, he was out of breath, and his nose had run like crazy. He didn't have a trace of a beard. The drum kids packed up. Two cops walked in the distance. The streetlights came on, and he squinted. His eyes were bluer than hers.

They started walking down West Fourth together, as it was nighttime now, and they were each supposedly going to wherever it was they came from. Lila knew she was basically following him, for she wasn't going anywhere in particular. In the short time she had lived in New York, she rarely spent any time in her dorm room. Usually she spent her money slowly, sitting at all-night coffee shops, diners, going to the movies.

"I'm in acting school," he said as they hit Sixth Avenue.

"Why aren't you in London?"

"I despise British acting."

"You *despise* it?"

"It's a load of bullocks."

"Oh, right," she said, pulling on a pair of gloves.

"It is," he said, "it's completely phony."

At a busy corner, they both stopped but she couldn't decide who'd stopped first. She figured he was about to leave. "So you're into honesty, huh?" she blurted out, "like telling me I'm fat?"

"That's right," he said, "like telling you you're the best."

"I'm eighteen," she said, though she wasn't sure why she'd said it. She wasn't fat, she told herself. She was top-heavy.

"I'm twenty-three," he said, and looked up at the Waverly Restaurant sign. "I came here to meet Robert De Niro."

"At the Waverly?"

"No," he said without a smile, "not at the diner, just here, New York, America, sure, why not the Waverly Restaurant? Why not?"

Lila thought about how she'd been in college four weeks and how she'd attended classes for two of those weeks, not counting Modern Dance 301. She said, "If Robert De Niro came walking down the street right now —"

"You came walking," he said, "you did."

"Are you talking to me?"

"That's right, that's good. You talking to me?"

"Are you?" she said, looking him more or less in the eye. "For real."

Ben started walking uptown, and she went along, both of them dodging crowds, who were coming home from a day of work, of school — coming home or running away.

"The film," he said, "*Taxi Driver.* 'Are you talking to me?' "

"Right," she said, her face blushing. "I know."

They both stopped at the crosswalk, even though the sign said WALK. "So what's your name?" he said.

She didn't hesitate. She didn't lie. "Lila," she said.

He nodded, took out a pack of cigarettes, offered them to her. She took one, though she rarely smoked, but when she did smoke, it was packs at a time. Ben lit his own cigarette first, making a tent with his hands, blocking out the wind. By now it was really cold. Her feet hurt. "C'mere," he said, and she stuck out her neck as he lit her cigarette with his. People rushed in waves around them, most with dirty looks for the two jerks standing still in the middle of the sidewalk. "I live right there." He pointed to a doorway across the street, and she nodded. "What'll it be then, Lila?" he asked as they smoked. "D'you want to come to my little flat and keep talking or should we say 'bye?"

She said, "Um."

"It's okay," he said. "Think about it while we finish the cigarette. Let's not talk for a minute, if that's okay with you."

They leaned against a gutted-out store-front. Water dripped from an awning next door. What, she wondered, was this? "What are we doing?" she asked.

"Don't you think silence is so much more revealing than conversation?" he asked her, deeply serious, and waited half a minute before laughing. "I don't live right there," he said with a smile. "I just thought I'd see if you'd come with me. I had a feeling you wouldn't."

It wasn't as if her heart stopped beating or anything, but that moment — with the water dripping onto the cracked sidewalk, and the sky easing itself into night — it declared itself in Lila, deep inside, like a spectacular view, or a shooting star. Then he said he'd better get on the A train, it was a long way back to Queens. Somehow, the fact that he lived in Queens, a place she'd never been and never had thought to go, was incredibly disappointing. She was certain as she walked away that she should have stayed under the awning, in that moment, just a little longer. She had a feeling that if she had kept them there, then things just might have been different.

After saying a light "Nice talking to you," she left him there and walked away. She'd never remember what she did afterward, that night, and she'd certainly never remember with whom she spoke at Student Affairs when she quit college without even a phone call to her mother and Jeb. She moved into an SRO on Seventeenth Street. She got a job teaching English as a Second Language from a woman named Louise who hired out young women for private lessons. Businessmen mostly, a few bored wives. Lila kept dancing but at a different studio, in exchange for sweeping up at the end of each day, doing the towel wash, cleaning the mirrors. She bought herself expensive chicken-and-mashed-potato dinners whenever she succeeded in *not* calling home and hanging up more than once a day. She allowed herself one daily hit of her mother's voice — the panic of the second hello, her obvious struggle not to yell. Lila wasn't sure what she wanted Vivian to say, but she thought it was more the tone of voice she craved, the unleashing of her mother's tightly wound secret: her anger. On the best days, her mother yelled, "Who is this?" or better yet, "Just who the hell are you? Speak up!" The yell, the shrillness — it delivered, no matter how briefly, a thrill. And however pathetic Lila knew this sense of power was, it was still knowledge. It was the knowledge that it was only her, just Lila, on the other end of the telephone. Worrying and unsettling her mother gave Lila a sense of comfort.

During more honest moments, she'd admit that calling this "comfort" was no more than a shot at feeling blameless, and to hide from what was coming clear, now that she was more or less on her own. The fact was: Lila hated her parents. Not that she didn't love them, but she also hated them. She hated how they managed to get through each day, and how they remembered to do all the activities of living, one chore after another. It was as if nothing had ever gone awry in their comfortable ramshackle home. But the home was not comfortable, it hadn't been for ages, and *awry* was putting it mildly. Everything had exploded. And it was as if after an earthquake, her parents simply convinced themselves and their remaining daughter to live amid the rubble, never attempting — not even sort of — to rebuild the foundation, or at the very least, to hire a good contractor. Jeb didn't believe in therapy, so that was out of the question, and Vivian convinced herself that exercise — yoga for the first six years, Pilates for the past five —brought her all the self-reflection she could handle. At some point in the last few years, Lila realized that what she'd originally taken as her parents' snobbery was no more than earnest dread of the common questions people tended to ask — all those incessant questions that pertained to their life as a family.

So the phone calls. They were frequent. Lila convinced herself that she couldn't afford those expensive chicken-and-mashed-potato dinners anyway, so she might as well go ahead and call. It wasn't as if she were sending them hate mail. It wasn't as if she were hooked on drugs, or dangerous sex; she wasn't causing damage. Not much, anyhow, so she called. She called and hung up between lessons, while waiting for the crosstown bus to take her from Mrs. Nogucci's West Side apartment to Mr. Tasake's Midtown office. She called before dance class, she called after dance class, she called upon waking and she called — and this was the constant — right before going to sleep.

After she met Ben, the Englishr   fo
park, she tried to stop the calls (ι   sh
fully), and tried to think of hin   riჳ
Thinking of Ben felt like watching   hi
movie — not sad or sexy or part of a   sp
— but a series of specific odd iı   sh
which she was somehow privy. Sh   nϲ
these flashes of him — jumping up ɑ   pʰ
to the bongo drums, dramatically s   hϲ
cigarette, wiping his pointy nose or
gray sleeve — but she knew Ben's   w
nothing to do with hers. He was a g   E
sort of person, an actor who spoke   fϲ
strangers. He probably made frien   tϲ
day. When she walked through the ρ
day instead of walking a quicker rϲ
told herself it was because she liked th   g
or the chess players, or the dirty,   tₓ
fountain. She tried to tell herself sh
waiting for Ben to show back up in
and that, really, she had a life worth in   e
ing.   ℕ

As she started walking through the
least two times every day, she deve.
routine. Five minutes of chess watchi   r
minutes of doing nothing but look   ι
Aaron in the crowds (is he suit-w   i
grungy shirted? pierced through the   ϲ
one revolution around the fountain, aɾ   ]
briefly, almost like not doing it at ɑ   ℎ

233

nd the bench where she was sitting when
e met Ben, and if it was unoccupied, she sat
ht down. It wasn't like she was waiting for
m, not really; she only liked to mark the
ace, and claim it, somehow, as good. When
e came out the other end of the park, having
t met Ben again, she usually submitted to a
one call, to the satisfying sound of panic in
r mother's voice.

Mrs. Maruyama, a sweet-faced young wife
no served her Mallomar cookies during
nglish lessons, asked: "How to say — until
ur hours, my husband come home — how
say what I'm doing?"

"I'm working?" Lila suggested.

"No, I finish. Here I am." Mrs. Maruyama
stured, a small, delicate, and slightly frus-
ated sweep of the tidy space.

"I'm waiting," Lila said, nodding.

"Ah! I wait." Mrs. Maruyama nodded, her
es bright. Lila reached for another
allomar, and began conjugation.

Lila never really did stop waiting for Ben to
eappear, and even on the coldest days she
sually found a reason to check out the activ-
y in Washington Square, but she did move
ut of the SRO and into the apartment of a
apanese girl named Kisa who'd briefly been
er student before telling Lila she needed to

be in a class with other people. The apartment, dark and decorated, was on West Street, overlooking the highway, but also the river. A Robert Mapplethorpe poster of a male nude statue in the bathroom, framed photographs of Kisa's friends out clubbing in Tokyo, and brightly colored fifties furniture. Kisa wanted to open a hotel and restaurant, "fifties style," in Kyoto. Besides a newsstand, Lila had never seen so many magazines in one place, and was quickly becoming addicted to advice columns. She read them aloud to Kisa, in the pretense of helping her with idioms.

In an underdeveloped explanation for quitting school, Lila had eventually told her mother and Jeb she was "taking some time." Her mother said, "That's fine, we always thought you would, you should figure out what you really want to learn." Her father said, "Your college money doesn't need to be for college." They'd offered no words to dissuade her, which was infuriating. The college money now came to her through a personal banker named Linda Meeks. Linda's office was in the Seagram Building, and the elevator rode high and fast, popping Lila's ears.

"I'm interested in young women coming toward money from a position of power," said Linda Meeks, her jet-black hair cut so bluntly it looked dangerous. "I'll treat you with respect; I won't ask you when you plan on using this money for education. I just want you to talk to me unapologetically. Call me up! Ask for your maximum amount! Ask for more! But no cowering, no claiming to be bad with numbers. Get into the habit of demanding," Linda Meeks said, and winked. Her lapel pin was made from some kind of welded industrial tubing. Lila took her personal informational folder, said thank-you, and gave Linda Meeks her best conspiratorial smile. Lila, no fool, was thrilled to have access to the money, but vowed to use it only in the case of emergencies. She silently thanked her grandfather, Jeb's father, who had died long before she was born.

When Ben found her again, she had just turned nineteen very quietly. Spring was on the distant horizon, and she was dialing her mother from the pay phone near the park, trying to screw up the courage for a full-on confrontation. She wanted to begin an official search, and she'd had no idea how difficult it would be to simply obtain Aaron's Social Security number. Just those nine digits would be a serious start. There were incredible ways to find a person now, probably even more ways than she knew. Being in a city was beginning to make her feel as if her brother could actually be found. He could be anywhere. Lila called her mother and hung up before the phone even rang. Then she dialed again, let it ring, and when her mother picked up and said a particularly cheery hello, she saw Ben walking toward her, and she gratefully placed the phone in its receiver.

"There you are," Lila said, as Ben approached and, strangely enough, shook her hand enthusiastically.

"Good God," he said, "I've been looking for you, and here you are. How are you then?"

"How long have you been looking?" she said, not believing he'd been looking, not ready for anyone who would lie to her so soon. His thick hair wasn't as unkempt; she'd liked it better before.

"Just a few days, recently," he said. "Meeting like we did was rather strange. I thought if we saw each other again, something would be ruined."

"Like what? Nothing happened." She made a supreme effort to stand up straight, to not crack her knuckles or her wrists.

"But that's not true," he said. "I've made some good decisions since then. I think you probably have too."

"You've been okay, then?" Lila asked, attempting to appear smaller while standing up straight. She tried to glow.

"Oh, yeah, fantastic. You?"

"Peachy," Lila said, and Ben was smiling at her as if he knew she'd been waiting for him. Then he looked down at the pavement, which was slightly damp from the afternoon's freezing rain, and Lila could swear she saw a look pass across his face that said, *You know, don't you, that I'm not really worth the wait.*

"Can I buy you coffee?" he asked, and she said he didn't have to buy her coffee, that she would buy her own coffee, and he said no, he wanted to buy the coffee for her, and when she agreed, they turned in to the Washington Square Diner. They slid into a booth, across from one another, piled coats and scarves in comfortable humps, and Lila smiled, afraid she would start hysterically laughing, as she tended to do in inappropriate situations, afraid the hot chocolate they ordered would stream out her nose and send her into a red-faced, bleary fit. But the hot chocolate arrived with towering whipped cream, and she didn't laugh as she watched him remove the cream from the cup, carefully shaving the sides in a circle.

"What," he said.

"Nothing, I'm just watching the way you do that," she said, suddenly feeling how little sleep she'd gotten recently, like a pang of sadness on a sunny day. He nodded, and she ate some whipped cream before stirring.

"This is really good," he said seriously, and his thin brow furrowed as he took another sip.

"Why did you tell me I was fat?" Lila asked, attempting not to sound humiliated.

He didn't look flustered at all. "I don't know," he said, and she was prepared for another insult, at least something besides "I don't know."

"You don't know?"

"Well," he said, "I wanted to talk to you. I watched you dance a few times through the window with all those skinny little girls. Amazing coincidence, I thought, that you were alone on a bench while I happened to be walking through the park. I wanted to talk to you because you stood out. You looked confident. I didn't — you know — want you to think I was being too friendly."

"You solved that problem," she said, thinking how deceiving looks could be.

"I want to stand out," he said. "You're really only eighteen?"

"Actually, I'm nineteen now. I look older, I know. So you're an actor?"

"I'm learning," he said. "Happy birthday."

"Thanks," she said, and finished her hot chocolate.

"I'm, ah, about the fat comment —"

"Don't apologize," she said, avoiding his

eyes. "I'm very nearly over it," she said, and smiled.

They sat for hours, ordering water, ordering French fries, rice pudding, coffee. They talked about him, how his parents lived in the Bahamas, where he never went. They talked about his penchant for mimicry, and how he tended to insult people without meaning to. When she asked, he did an imitation of her, and she pretended not to be insulted. He portrayed her as a sloucher, an eyeball roller, a tapper of fingers, a biter of nails. He didn't ask any personal questions, and she was grateful, was tempted to ask if he did it on purpose, if he could tell she would lie about her family, lie about why she chose New York for college to begin with.

"Are you expecting someone?" he asked.

"Huh?"

"You keep looking around."

"Do I?"

Ben gave a small laugh, which said, *You know you do, of course you do.*

"Sorry," Lila said. "I'm not expecting a soul." She made an effort to look him straight on, while she cursed herself for how she couldn't keep her eye on the present or the future, and how she always looked a little bit longer than she knew she should, at the strangers around her, anywhere.

Night spread in a wintery light as they left the diner and walked. "What kind of decisions were you talking about?" Lila asked him, as again they were walking aimlessly.

"Hmm?" he responded, and she wondered if he maybe wasn't going to try to kiss her at some point on this walk.

"When you told me you'd made good decisions, what were they?" She tried to imagine kissing him and couldn't. She never could imagine that sort of thing.

He stopped walking and ran a hand over his head. He pulled out a pack of cigarettes. "I moved," he said. "I actually live right there." He pointed across the street, not far from where he had pointed the first time they met. His smile acknowledged his previous fake-out, his initial brazen tease. "Smoke?"

"Oh," she said, "there?" and became acutely aware of the crowds around them, the cracks in the pavement, the pockets on his olive green corduroy pants. She nodded yes, and took a cigarette from him without saying more. She told herself she wasn't nervous, and that even though she didn't know this guy at all, going to his place would be perfectly normal. She told herself quickly, *You're not shaking, see? This is what you want.*

They smoked, and exchanged phone numbers, saying they should see a movie sometime. Ben asked if she liked old movies, if she liked sci-fi flicks. And she said yes to every-thing, everything he said, but didn't think, even with her best agreeable side, that they'd ever see each other again. He hadn't asked her to come up to his new place after all.

But at some point within the following week, she got used to the fact that whatever day or evening they spent together wouldn't be the last, that in fact, they would see each other constantly. But even though each mo-ment was clearly fun, nothing even close to a kiss ever transpired between them, which was, Lila maintained to herself, exactly what she was comfortable with. She had wanted only a friend. Ben said Lila was talented, that she could do anything she wanted, and Lila said she just happened to want things that weren't really possible, and when Ben said, like what? Lila didn't answer, and then when he didn't look away, when he expected an answer, she laughed too loud and said, oh, you know, to touch my tongue to my nose, to witness an alien spaceship, all kinds of things.
She saw him act in a play about two brothers living in Manhattan with money and women to spare. It was a comedy, with Ben copping an American accent that fell between Georgia and Boston. It was a pratfalling silly

242

story, but she cried — the brothers, the lightness of it, the brothers — and she told Ben she
was crying because he was good. And he *was*
good. He had an invisible ring around him,
something fragile and quick and one step
ahead of the game. She told him she wasn't in
the mood for the cast party.

"It'll be fun," he promised.

"I'm sure it will," she said.

He looked so happy. He leaned in and a little bit up to where she was biting her nail. He
grabbed her by the shoulders and didn't let
go. "Okay," he said. "Okay. Listen. I'm getting married."

She didn't do a thing. He let go of her
shoulders and kept on smiling.

"You're what?"

"Isn't that amazing?" He laughed as if he
were joking, but then he said that his fiancée's
name was Caroline, that she was coming over
from London soon, and that he'd known her
forever. They'd been talking on the phone
and it just kind of happened. Didn't she think
it was good to be with people who'd known
you forever? Didn't she think that was ideal?
He spun her around and let her go, and she
made a mad dash out of the dressing room
door.

Then Lila headed back to the apartment
she shared with Kisa, telling herself the whole

way that she never really knew anybody anyway, that she'd wanted things light and distant, and that's what she had gotten. Lila passed the gay hustlers and the porno video store, ignored the abyss of the highway traffic, and walked up three flights of stairs to find the apartment empty, as it usually was. Lila called her parents. She called her mother and Jeb and hung up the phone.

What was coming clear to her was this: Lila wanted to tell Ben about all of it. *It goes a little something like this,* she would say. She would start with those seven words. She'd tell her story. She'd even do a little mock tap-dance routine after she was through, so he wouldn't feel pressure to respond. *Ta da,* she'd say, *ta da.* And he'd probably say nothing. Maybe nothing at first, and then, surely something aside from, *Lovely, pass me that lighter,* or *Do you fancy an ice cream?*

He really didn't listen all that well, she'd known that right when she met him, but listening skills seemed not at all important, not in comparison with the way his eyes watered when he heard Frank Sinatra sing "A Very Good Year," and even, bless his soul, "New York, New York." In fact, she wasn't even sure she needed him to listen, so much as she really needed to tell him. About the Suzanne letter that she always kept with her, about the restless nights she spent calling Information in every state, and how she became disoriented in time, and that she often couldn't remember what she did a day or two ago, but, before sleeping, could recall the exact arrangement of her room when she was seven, eight years old, even though her mother had redone the house when she was ten. That she couldn't drink orange pekoe tea because it smelled like Suzanne's hair. And, what she was most afraid of saying: *Sometimes I wonder if I didn't make all this up — these memories I swear by.*

She wanted to tell Ben that one May weekend ten years ago, she went from being the youngest child to the only child, that Jack died from a head trauma, from falling on the rocks, from having way too much to drink, and Aaron disappeared after blaming himself, which made her parents angry and desperate and cold, and she somehow thought there was more to be done besides waiting to forget the details that still lingered in her memory. Since she left home for New York, the particulars of the family she no longer had were not diminishing but magnifying, and she didn't know if she wanted this flood of past to stop or go on and grow stronger.

Lila wanted to tell Ben all of this. Ben, who didn't know anything besides the fact that she came from New Hampshire and that she had a brother with whom she wasn't close. The way he looked at her sometimes — worried might have been the only way to describe it — she had a feeling he might understand.

"Do you like milk and honey?" said Ben, the second Sunday afternoon in April, soon after his play had closed.

"Am I in paradise?" Lila was lounging on his wicker chair, under his open window. His new apartment was a sunlit, hardwood-floor wonder, which belonged to his Aunt Flora. Lila had been there only briefly at night, when Ben forgot his wallet.

"Absolutely not, but it's rent-free." He went to the stove and poured milk in a saucepan. He poured carefully, no splashing around. It was quiet, quieter than she ever remembered being with Ben, or with anyone lately. A fly buzzed up and down the window, getting ready to die. The sun struck the walls yellow, light holding everything up, maintaining this kind of silence. All his surfaces were bare, his bookshelves overflowing. She smelled cinnamon, and something waxy, faint stale cigarettes. "Are you in a queer mood?" he asked, pouring two glasses of warm milk. The milk made a sizzling sound when it left the hot metal.

"Yes," Lila said, and watched him twirl honey in the glasses, felt an extra breath in her chest, another set of arms at her side. "I want to ask you," she began, and she smiled and stopped speaking.

"What's that?" he said, looking up from the milk. He looked like a little mole in a little hole. She felt like a bear.

"Nothing, really," she said, and looked around the room, up at the vaulted ceiling, where the paint had begun to splinter. "Why don't you ever talk about Caroline?"

Ben handed her a steaming glass of milk and said, "Why don't I know anything about you?" And sat down on the couch, put his feet on the table between them.

"What do you mean? What do you want to know?"

"Well, I thought I wanted to know what you wanted to tell me, but I've known you over a month now, we see each other all the time, and I know that you're a good dancer, and that as far as I can tell, you have no other close friends, you've never mentioned your family, or a boyfriend, even an ex-boyfriend. I can't picture what you do when I don't see you. Why did you drop out of school?"

"I didn't like it," she managed, although her throat seemed shut down, air hard to come by. She looked out the window, and a cloud moved quickly east. "What else?" she asked, and looked directly at him. "So you think I've never had a boyfriend? You think that's strange?"

"Have you?" he said, smiling, even though he must have heard how her voice shook, even though it must have been obvious that her hands were sweating and that the light in the room made her feel like she would stumble if she tried to walk away.

"No," she said, "no one like that."

He looked at her with quiet surprise, as if she'd taken off her clothes. "Okay," he said.

"Okay, what?" She wanted to leave, to even go home to her parents, and grab onto something familiar — her pillow with the ripped-up stuffing, a pale speckled frog from the edge of the pond.

He took a sip of his drink and put it down, leaned forward with his elbows on his knees. "I must tell you something then." He cleared his throat and blurted, "I don't have a fiancée. I made all that up so that you wouldn't feel pressure around me. You seemed like you felt a lot of pressure. It just kind of happened, and I thought I could pull it off as a joke, but it —"

"Not funny," Lila said.

"Exactly. Not funny, and the joke didn't happen, and I just kept to the story because, I suppose, it was easier."

"...stand that," she said, and thought ...es she had told during her one ...lege — that she had a brother ...tor in Hawaii, that her parents ...ced, that she had a sister named ...ine. Those were just the ones that made ₅ome sense. Some days she'd made up anything at all. "So there's no Caroline?"

"Well," he said, lighting a cigarette sort of sadly, "there is, but she is, by no means, my love."

Lila shifted her weight in the wicker chair. She examined the small scratches on her fingers, the dark silver polish on her short nails. There was something breathing in the space between them, more like an invisible other person than their untapped potential. What she felt inside wasn't potential; it was fear. It was small where it should have felt big, hulking where she wanted whisks of air, and there was speed where elegance should have been, in polished easy breaths. She knocked over the milk, straight into her lap, and the warmth felt almost good.

And Ben didn't do anything but laugh, pick up his own glass, sit farther back, and look right at her. He said, "What do you want to do?"

But he also didn't let her answer. "C'mere," he said. "C'mere."

Lila got up — the milk, grown cold, se
down her jeans, on her thighs — and m
her way to the couch, and Ben patted t
place beside him, and she sat. "What is it?" he
said, and that was when she thought she'd
cry. "What?" he asked, as if he maybe didn't
really want to know.

"Ben," she said, just to say his name; that
was how badly off she was. "Ben."

"That's right," he said, and handed her a
napkin, as if it were the only thing to do.

They sat together on the couch. He wore a
gray sweater with two holes in the cuff. She
wanted to tell him she had brothers whom she
could hear across most silences, that she was
sick of remembering more than anyone else
seemed to.

"Can I touch you?" he asked, and she was
somewhere outside with the crowds, with the
clouds, falling and getting up again, bruising
her knees. She was grabbing onto her pillow,
her frogs, tearing at pieces of lavender tissue,
reading one word at time: *I'm sorrier than you
know. Be someone,* she thought; *please.* And as
she nodded *yes, yes, you can touch,* she
watched his soft brown hair, and when he put
down the glass of milk he was holding, he
came closer, smelling of salt and honey. She
was within his small arms, he did his best to
enclose her, and that was when she knew she

250

had to remember more, in order to feel something besides keeling over, which was how she felt right then. Lila took off her sweater, and showed him her big huge breasts, which no one had really seen.

"Ben," she said, "why don't you show me how?"

And if he had, if he had shown her, instead of respectfully telling her to put her sweater back on — and if he had not given her a deep kiss when she did put her sweater back on, the kind of kiss she had never received and had always desperately wanted — she might not have insisted on leaving right then, out of sheer incredulity. Because his lips, his hands, they couldn't be happening, a kiss could not possibly feel this good. If Ben hadn't held her knotty curls between his fingers and looked her exactly in the eye, Lila might not have left in such a rush and literally tripped on the last step of Ben's brownstone. And if she hadn't tripped, she might not have walked home with such attentiveness. And because she chose to walk up Bedford Street slowly, and because she was walking on the right and not the left side of the street, it happened that Lila saw a table of four through a small restaurant's window, and on seeing one of the two women, Lila's teeth began to ache. Only briefly did she wonder why the long-haired woman looked familiar. She realized: this moment — one of the top three she'd imagined for years — it was happening right now, and exactly this way. How could Lila have had any idea that she was to find her — not in a foreign country, not in a hotel bar, not at an airport or at jury duty — but here? In the most obvious city, at a Middle Eastern restaurant on a Sunday late afternoon? Lila watched how she sipped a glass of red wine — lips parted on the rim — and how she touched her lips briefly after swallowing. The tall man beside her refilled her empty glass. Lila watched her run a hand through her still-long, still-straight hair, look at the dark man seated across from her, lean her head against the window as he spoke, and then with all the others — these strangers at her table — Suzanne began to laugh.

CHAPTER FOURTEEN

Lila stood outside the restaurant, behind a convenient tree. As her face pressed against the bark, she was careful not to press too hard, not to make bark imprints on her face, as she looked through the ordinary glass window at Suzanne. The air was slightly wet, the sky blank but brilliant, maintaining that weather knew a thing or two about subtlety, and what was required for someone who was heading toward mystery. A blond couple hurried by and opened the skinny restaurant door, letting escape a salvo: scallions, rose water, burnt pita bread. A craving began unraveling inside Lila, a raging hunger, and for a moment she wanted nothing but to scoop pieces of seasoned lamb into fresh pita bread and down a dark, rich beer. She could be stunned into silence, she could forget her name and who was president, and still, she imagined, she could come up with an answer to "What would you like to eat?"

Suzanne was sitting next to a tall man in a

gray jacket. The man had a high forehead and dark, thoughtful eyes. He was less handsome than Aaron, but more wiry, like Jack, in a way that suggested intelligence, not danger. No matter how smart Lila knew Aaron to have been there was something, in hindsight, about his countenance that called his intelligence into question. Even though he really only liked the solitude and steadiness of running, he'd looked like a team player, a guy who could model bathrobes and make you want to buy one. The man with Suzanne, on the other hand, looked like a scholar or maybe a cardsharp, someone with at least one foreign language under his belt. Lila saw him place his hand on the back of Suzanne's neck, giving it a brief squeeze. They were both listening to the couple across from them — a petite Asian woman with peroxide-tipped hair, and a man with remarkably thick eyebrows. Suzanne seemed to lean away from the tall dark-eyed man, and the way she rested her head on the windowpane, Suzanne looked as if she belonged, unquestionably, leaning against that particular window, but Lila guessed that Suzanne most likely looked that way wherever she happened to be. Some people, Lila knew, (and she counted herself among them) would never, not on their best day in life, acquire such a look.

Suzanne still loved Lila's brother Aaron, had been waiting ten years for him to appear. Suzanne was never serious about Aaron, never thought of him anymore at all. Suzanne and Aaron kissed passionately outside Lila's bedroom window. Suzanne and Aaron fought outside Lila's bedroom window. Suzanne was beautiful. Suzanne was plain. Suzanne was eating a green olive behind a restaurant's window. A woman with long henna-red hair who looked remarkably like Suzanne was eating a green olive. It wasn't Suzanne. It was.

Lila could've just knocked on the window right in front of her. She could've knocked and startled the woman leaning her lazy head against the glass. Lila could have gone inside. But Suzanne's party was getting ready to leave — they had that worn-out look about them — and while the food was certainly not gone, it looked, nonetheless, discarded. Dressing-soaked lettuce sat next to dabs of hummus-type salads. White ceramic plates held up the delicate bones of fish, the leftover phyllo dough and its mysterious colorful filling. Lila would stand there and watch until they left. She would stand there through the night if she had to. "I know you," Lila could say to Suzanne with a smile, as the elegant group departed, and Suzanne would say, "You must be confused," and she would answer, looking deep inside Suzanne's green eyes; she would say, "You're right, I am. I am very confused." And Suzanne would know her right away. She'd just know.

Suzanne's dark-eyed man was smoking now, and Lila saw Suzanne take the cigarette from his long fingers, and without looking at him, take a slow drag. The spilled warm milk from Ben's apartment had dried onto her thighs but left the fabric of her pants and underwear damp and cold. As Suzanne exhaled, Lila wondered how long it had been since she left Ben standing in his red wool socks on that beautiful hardwood floor. It couldn't have been even a half hour ago, but really, it seemed like ages. The exact taste of Ben's lower lip suddenly came to her — a honeyed, sleepy taste that reminded her of her own body, its hidden childishness. Lila realized she was now biting her own lip, absently running her tongue along it, as she kept her gaze fixed on Suzanne, and the bluish cloud of smoke that settled in the air around her.

Ben had kissed her, and that wasn't the half of it. She had embarrassed herself, and still, he'd kissed her. She had felt as if she couldn't breathe, and it wasn't in a good way. It was too much. Everything felt ridiculously heavy, way too much at once. As Lila pictured Ben's hands — how they were too thin and too small, how they barely covered hers — she saw Suzanne say something to her friends that was evidently smart and serious because everyone nodded, and their expressions went somber. Soon afterward, they gathered their things, the dark-eyed man held Suzanne's coat for her, and she gracefully put her arms through the narrow camel wool sleeves. Seeing the group's departure, Lila felt colder, as if she were newly experiencing the chilly air. As she shivered, she also began to sweat, and her heart zipped around her chest and throat, furiously pounding. "You know me!" Lila wanted to shout, but she didn't, she couldn't, and with her teeth buzzing, she bent down, pointlessly pretending to tie a laceless shoe, as Suzanne and the others walked right past her.

It was unnecessary, Lila knew, to hide, for she looked so different, she really had no need to worry about being recognized. For one thing, she was big now, and everything larger than what people would have predicted if they'd met Lila as a delicate-looking child. Her once honey blond hair had turned brown, and she'd opted to go dye-free, or at least not blond. Every so often she'd get creative and dye red streaks or on the rare occasion blue, but now her shoulder-length hair was brown, saved from being mousy only by the spiral curls. She looked up and saw, a block north, Suzanne and the dark-eyed man say good-bye to the other couple who were holding hands. Suzanne and Mr. Dark Eyes were walking west.

Lila ran to catch up, and followed them onto Grove Street, where sparsely leafed trees made skeletal patterns on the charcoal blue sky. The sun was setting, and soon it would be cold. Suzanne and her *boyfriend?* weren't touching, and from what Lila could see, they weren't talking either. The man had a loping walk, as if he'd bumped his head in one too many doorways, and even through his long black coat, it was clear he had an impressive back. Maybe he, like Aaron, was a fan of individual competition, and was a swimmer, a good one, excellent at butterfly. Lila watched the two of them move and she tried not to step on the cracks in the sidewalk, tried to keep perfectly alert, ready to strain her hearing and understand their conversation, should they begin to have one. She felt like an old-lady detective, another sexless crime solver who talked to smelly cats about her cases. The man put his hand on Suzanne's neck again, beneath her glossy hair, and Lila refused to think of her brothers, to let either of their faces push their way into her mind. She refused to think of the house — sinking farther and farther into the soil — of her parents alone in it, turning lights on and off. And she refused to think of Ben, of his watery blue eyes squinting — watching her run away.

The relative bustle of Hudson Street felt like a small victory, and there, Suzanne and her tall man stopped at a flower stall, after Lila heard him (in what seemed to her, a falsely cheerful tone) suggest they get some flowers. Lila couldn't help but get as close as she possibly could, and there, within the cool scent of lilac and lily and rose, Suzanne's right hand grazed an orchid, fingered the shape of the white-and-purple petal. Suzanne's fingers were bare, no polish or jewelry, but then, as Suzanne's left hand tucked a loose strand of hair behind her ear, Lila noticed a very thin gold band with a spectacular yellow diamond. Married. To this man, Lila assumed, at least she would assume so for now, as the pair gave off no illicit glow.

"How much for the lilies?" Suzanne asked just then, and the tone of her voice — both eager and doubting — transported Lila precisely to the first of two dinners Suzanne shared with her family, when Aaron's girlfriend asked questions. Lila couldn't picture the meal, didn't recall the conversation or who sat where, but Suzanne's voice she remembered exactly.

"Ten dollar," the flower vendor said. "Ten dollar."

"Let's get the orchid," Suzanne's husband said softly, but Suzanne shook her head.

"Too much work," she said. And he shrugged, pushed his expensive-looking glasses up further on his nose. "You sure?" he wanted to know. He had a sober face and a heartbreaking smile.

"Richard," she said, "it's okay." And she smiled back, a slightly strained smile, and pointed to a large bucket of lilies.

"Excuse me," Lila heard herself say, way too loudly. Suzanne didn't look, and the vendor did, and Lila ignored the vendor. "Excuse me," Lila repeated. "Hello?"

Suzanne E. Wolfe finally turned her attention on Lila Wheeler, whose mouth went immediately dry. Suzanne gave Lila a look that said, *I have no idea who you are.* Suzanne took her wallet from her black leather shoulder bag, and handed the vendor a twenty as she looked Lila's way. "I'm sorry?" Suzanne asked, as if Lila were a senile neighbor, known for roaming sidewalks. The sight of Suzanne's face straight on was more than she could handle. All Lila could picture was how this same woman who was buying lilies as if they were a carton of milk — this woman being offered orchids — one miserable May morning, ten years ago, had pond-wet hair and smelled like mud, and stood beside her brother Aaron, who was crying, and Suzanne had said *Oh, my God,* over and over again.

"I thought I knew you," was all Lila could manage.

"Hmm," she said, curling the same strand of hair behind her ear, the diamond glinting in the streetlight. The vendor handed over the wrapped-up lilies and a few bills. "Thanks," Suzanne told him, as she put away her change, and took the flowers in her arms like a newborn. "Um," she muttered, returning her minimal attention to Lila, "sorry, I'm afraid I don't know who you are. Richard?" she asked him, as if it were highly unlikely that Lila was worth the effort of being this polite. Richard shook his head, shrugged his lovely shoulders, and grinned. "Do you know Freida?" Suzanne asked, with a brittle smile.

"Who?" Lila asked, and almost laughed. She wanted to tell Suzanne to stop smiling already, to say, *Listen, I'm no one you need to smile for.*

Suzanne moved closer to Richard, who was lighting up a cigarette. Something flashed across Suzanne's face — recognition would have been too strong a word, but recognition was what Lila sensed, and she took a deep breath spiked with Richard's smoke. "I don't think we've met," Suzanne said plainly, and gave her shoulder bag a small adjustment as she reached for Richard's long arm. "I must have a familiar face," she said as the two of them backed away. "People tell me that sometimes."

And they were off. They took a few steps away from her and Lila's head felt far above her body as she heard herself yell, "Suzanne!"

Suzanne and Richard turned around, Suzanne looking more annoyed than perplexed.

"Listen," Lila said, and every cell in her body felt as if it had decided to speed up, as if the air around her, that she was so conscious of breathing in and out, were a limited, extravagant gift. "Listen," she repeated, although it was clear they were both listening now, "you do know me."

Suzanne looked as if she were about to laugh or pull out a gun — in accordance with her expression, either would have seemed appropriate. "I'm really sorry," she said, "but we don't recognize you."

"*You* know me," Lila heard herself say to Suzanne, as she stared straight into her eyes. There was a lifting somewhere; she could feel force rising through her hands at her sides, shooting up her arms to the back of her neck. "We know each other," she said in a more neutral tone.

A silence existed for a second, no more, before Richard exhaled a little laugh and gave Suzanne a look that said, *She's nuts, then, right?*

"Suzanne," Lila said, "I'm Lila. Aaron Wheeler's sister."

The night was dark, but the sky overhead was still adjusting to the sun's absence; burning blue and dusky pink, all about to go black. Cars whizzed by; building lights turned on. Lila waited for a response. "Oh, my God," Suzanne said, as if the situation were, if only for just one moment, really beyond her control. "You look so different," she said, and Lila felt stunningly ugly. "Well, of course you do. You grew up; you must be in college by now."

Lila nodded, Richard looked confused, and nothing was cleared up when Suzanne politely said: "Lila Wheeler, Richard Hannon — my husband."

"Nice to meet you," Lila said, as she shook his outstretched hand. "Um," Lila said, directed toward Suzanne, "I'd really like to —"

"We'll have you over," Suzanne gushed, "of course we have to get together."

Richard Hannon, Lila noticed, seemed to take this meeting in stride. He had the look of a man who was accustomed to going nowhere on this earth without running into someone that his pretty wife knew.

"Look," Suzanne said, with a look that was so conspiratorial it was almost sexual, "we're actually racing to get home to receive a phone call." She smiled as if rushing anywhere, or waiting for phone calls, were all part of something funny. "Why don't you take my card," Suzanne said, reaching into her black shoulder bag and unzipping a little case. "Take it," she offered, and Lila did. There were smiles all around. "Give us a call." Suzanne's smile left her face as smoothly as it came. "It's good to see you," she said, with more than a hint of meaning, and Lila nodded. Suzanne was excitedly friendly, but unquestionably removed. Lila doubted they had been in any kind of rush: they had just been buying flowers, and even now, Suzanne's eyes sparkled with all the time in the world. "What a coincidence," she marveled, and Richard smiled his crinkly smile, and gave a little wave.

"Which way are you going?" Richard said, his voice deep and soft.

"East." Lila pointed, and she took a few steps in that direction. "Have a good night," she managed, and she crossed the street, going east, forced herself not to turn around, at least until she reached the other side. The card was white with simple black script, but she was so afraid of dropping it that as she crossed the street, she stuffed it deep in her pocket with her keys and lip balm, before she could give it proper attention. She needed to make sure they'd stopped watching. Once on the other side of Hudson, she could see they were continuing to walk downtown.

If Lila could meet people without feeling a lifetime away — if she hadn't needed to leave Ben's apartment that day — then maybe she wouldn't have kept following Suzanne and her husband down Hudson Street, even after she had their number. Maybe, if there were ways to believe the lies she had grown accustomed to telling, it would not have been necessary to be certain not only of Suzanne's phone number, but more important, where she lived. There was just no way that Lila could keep up with lying to people, but there was equally no way she could conceive of meeting a new person and telling the truth when the subject turned to family. It wasn't as if she worried what people would think of the truth; it was that if she said it out loud and began getting condolences and opinions, it would be impossible to think of anything else. Lila knew she would talk about it too fast, too much — there was an accident when I was eight, she could say, and my brothers disappeared. She'd be more alone after her story than when she began. Lila knew this was what meeting people really meant. But if she could talk to Suzanne she'd feel different, of this Lila was sure, for they shared the same story.

So Lila waited a few moments and ran after them. She walked back across the street and followed Suzanne and her dark-eyed husband down Hudson, telling herself that Suzanne might ignore her phone calls out of fear, and their reunion was far too important to both of their lives to let one person's fear get in the way. Lila told herself she wasn't angry that Suzanne had clearly moved on, that Suzanne had a whole life now, one that Lila was sure had little or nothing to do with Aaron and Jack. Lila understood that; it was what she wanted for herself. But they were always there — Aaron and Jack — they tapped out drumbeats from room to room wherever she made some kind of effort — if she sat on Ben's floor, trying her hardest to be a person who knew about sitting and smoking and talking about anything at all. Aaron and Jack were always there, and here was Suzanne, walking quickly away, knowing who Lila was and hoping — at least Lila hoped she was hoping — that Aaron's sister, Jack's sister, could be counted on to follow through and find her again.

Night was closing in on the city, the twilight being replaced with true darkness, and Lila followed Suzanne and Richard as they walked quickly, barely looking at each other. The lilies bobbed in Suzanne's arms, and her hair made a gentle rise and fall. Time seemed to be limited to this rush down Hudson, a rhythmic passage to which Lila had a hard time imagining a conclusion. It was difficult to believe that these two people were going home, that their home could be on any of these upcoming streets, and as the walk progressed, as it went on and on, it seemed strange that they hadn't taken a cab. The blocks got longer, the streets quieter, and they were farther downtown than Lila had ever been. Suzanne and Richard seemed no longer rushed, but rhythmic, as if they had hurried to achieve this state — inhaling lilies, gliding under scaffolding. Without warning, Suzanne made a left, and her husband followed, then turning right and walking one block to Greenwich Street. They slowed down, and both of them seemed tired now, as if arriving were a disappointment.

Lila hid herself in a neighboring doorway, and watched Suzanne hold on to the flowers and wait for Richard to take a set of keys from his pocket. "I'm tired," Richard said, and Suzanne nodded, muttering an agreement that Lila couldn't make out, as her husband turned the key in the lock. Richard gestured for Suzanne to go first, and as Lila marveled at this small gesture of politeness, Suzanne disappeared behind the muted green glass door. Lila wondered if Suzanne appreciated being ushered through her own doorway, being touched, so briefly, on the small of her back. Did Suzanne make a habit of counting her blessings or had she always expected a life of plain and simple good fortune? Before going through the door himself, Richard looked both left and right, almost as if he'd heard his name being called, but was too exhausted to care. He closed the door behind them. They were home.

Lila approached the doorway, but she couldn't see inside. She imagined Suzanne and Richard riding the elevator, looking at the lilies or each other, and maybe, because Suzanne was so shocked at seeing Lila, and because it was usually she who pressed the elevator buttons, no button had been pressed at all, and Suzanne and Richard would arrive on a strange floor, disoriented, having missed their stop entirely.

Lila was certain that whether or not she had stayed in Ben's apartment when he had kissed her was a key choice in a larger picture that was beginning to come clear. This meeting wasn't accidental; it certainly was not. This kind of thing happened all the time when she was younger. Everything was connected by Lila's rules of timing, and somehow, then, things had made sense. She would decide not to go to sleep, for instance, and on those nights when Lila stayed awake (in her favorite cotton nightgown, leaning on the windowsill) either of her brothers — as if they knew that she was waiting — would come into her room. *If you want something,* her brother Jack had said, *it will happen, or even if you don't know what you want, you'll find out soon enough. Like it or not,* Jack said. *Like it or not, ready or not;* he'd said that all the time.

There was nothing that happened before the age of nine that Lila didn't think she had, in some way, caused. Lila didn't — she knew this — *cause* Jack to get wasted and fall on the pond's granite outer edge, resulting in a cerebral hemorrhage. And she didn't cause Aaron, the handsome one, the smart one, to drop out of college, to blame himself for Jack's death and run away forever. She had done enough remembering of that night not to think she was in any way responsible. Lila had been a little kid — this she knew — but still, there were times when she wondered. She could have just woken her parents and told them to worry. She could have, if she were a different kind of kid, not cared what Suzanne would have thought of Aaron's bratty kid sister, the pain-in-the-ass tattler. Lila could have told on the boys, and kept them safe in the house. Lila and her parents could have gotten in the way, because, really, that weekend, what else were they good for? It had to have been up to them. Adults and children were responsible, in the name of love, to stop those in the prime of youth from killing themselves in the deceptive name of fun. But at the time, their mission of fun seemed more important than her parents, much larger than any serious danger.

But now Lila was alone on Greenwich Street, where she had never been, looking up at a row of expensive shades and good yellow light. Above the darkened rooms were light rooms, and then light ones again — light with curtains and shades, and inside there were conversations she wanted. Lila waited for action in one of the lit windows, but there was barely a shadow, and she waited for a light to come on in one of the darkened rooms. It looked like, in Suzanne's building, one apartment took up an entire floor. The list of these huge apartments by the intercom was ice gray on black, six numbers with no names.

It was so quiet here, way downtown, as if everyone were inside and having a better time. Without Suzanne in front of her, Lila was getting cold, and she wanted to call her parents and hear the anger, the panic in her mother's voice. She saw a pay phone not far away, and told herself she would check her messages, just go and check her answering machine. But when she reached the phone, she dialed her parents' number, heard the ringing, and stayed on the line. The phone rang until it was clear her parents weren't home, or weren't picking up, and still she held on to the receiver. Lila pictured the phone on the butcher-block kitchen counter, surrounded by colored pencils, the phone on the tree stump table by the couch, the hollow vibration of ringing within the unfinished wood walls, the endless ringing absorbed into the framed black-and-white photographs of Lila as a baby, of the Mojave desert, of Vivian among winter birches. Their answering machine had broken two years ago, and they'd put off getting another one, until Lila realized it was the last thing they desired. As much as they said they wanted Aaron to come back, whenever Lila asked, it was all too obvious they had given up hoping, or were so shocked and angry at his disappearance that they couldn't bear the machine's blinking light — five messages, two messages — the continuing signal of false hope.

As Lila left the pay phone, she walked farther downtown and saw the streets with the new knowledge that this was where Suzanne lived. A gourmet market with an old-fashioned sign was closed — a chain-link gate hung over the entrance. Perhaps Suzanne got her watercress there, her ricotta cheese, her truffle oil. Or Suzanne didn't cook, and she ate only Italian chocolates, three-berry muffins, and milky coffee. Lila imagined Suzanne was a good but infrequent cook, and that she would eventually make Lila dinner and tell stories about Aaron — tearful stories, true ones. There was nothing to do now except call her. Call her and come back to this apartment building, to come back and wait. But for now, she couldn't give up getting one last glimpse.

There would be a better view of Suzanne's apartment building on the other side of the street, so Lila crossed, looked up again, not knowing exactly what she was doing besides putting off going home, and avoiding thoughts about the rest of this day with Ben. She looked up — at the lights and at the parchment blinds, at the brief silhouettes of strangers in and out of view — and she was filled with such a wave of exhaustion she knew it was time to go. Only right when she was about to leave, exactly right then, the open fifth-floor window filled with ocher light, the shade raised slowly, and there she was. Suzanne was looking down at the street, one hand holding the string of the blind, as if she hadn't quite decided to keep it raised. Lila couldn't see her eyes, there was too great a distance, but they were easy to imagine. The green iris, the large black pupil, the arched eyebrows, unraised. Suzanne took her hand from the shade's string and lifted the window as far as it would go. Lila tried not to blink. Then Suzanne turned — having had the breeze, having had the view — and disappeared from sight. The light stayed on, promising another appearance, and Lila waited as long as she could stand, without any luck.

CHAPTER FIFTEEN

Lila spent Monday at the Museum of Television and Radio, watching interviews with Lana Turner and comedy specials starring Bob Hope. All the women were curvy and smiley and the men were openly lascivious and very polite. These shows transported her as far as it was possible to go. She had found the museum by doing an assignment for her sociology class during those long-ago weeks of school. She was supposed to have analyzed a favorite television show from childhood with the aim of placing her childhood in the context of society, but ended up watching old interviews and the childhood shows of another generation.

Lila never said so, but she maintained a certain pride that she hadn't watched TV much as a kid. Her house had a TV but it functioned only with a VCR, and even though she watched as much as she possibly could anywhere else, she never questioned that her home was without channels and news, without talk shows and game shows and sitcoms and cartoons. TV

was the time spent uncomfortably longing in the homes of well-meaning friends. TV from the late eighties was altogether too real. She preferred the television shows from eras when she wasn't alive, when even her parents were mere children. Those programs made her feel dour and dark in comparison with all the cheery young women, and her darkness inspired her to finally get up and out into the city before the day was wholly gone. Lila went to Bloomingdale's and bought lipstick after an Estée Lauder lady gave her a makeover, and she walked through Midtown in a mildly uplifted state, wandering in and out of shoe stores and watching people escaping their office buildings one after the other. It was spring, an almost unseasonably warm day. The sun glowed behind a white and yellow sky; the metallic buildings loomed strongly, undaunted by heat and pollution. Lila walked and walked and headed downtown, but passed each subway stop that she thought she'd walk into. She found herself walking, and walking all the way home, to Kisa's apartment, where Suzanne's card was placed in the drawer of Lila's bedside table. The card said:

Suzanne Hannon Fine Art
Specializing in Sales and Appraisal of
Twentieth-Century Paintings

and it listed the address as that very same Greenwich Street locale, a phone number that Lila immediately committed to memory and wrote down on ten separate sheets of paper.

Once in her apartment, she sat at the small table by the window, and thought about how Suzanne took Richard's name and how she was now an art dealer of some kind. On the message machine, Ben had mumbled about being sorry, then about how she was being overly dramatic, then how he was sorry again, though he wasn't sure what for, then that they should go see a movie or eat a meal, just that, no big deal, that she should just pick up the phone and call him, if only because he wanted her to.

Lila picked up the telephone and called her parents. The room was darkened by drawn shades; the shadows of the furniture made Lila want to lie down, although it was still sunny outside, a perfectly pleasant day. "Hello, Mom," she heard herself say, surprised that she hadn't hung up.

"Well, hello, darling. How are you?"

"I'm okay."

"What's doing?"

"I bumped into Suzanne on the street." It came out of her mouth the exact moment she thought of saying it, and the result was disconcerting. She felt dizzy with fear and vague uncertainty, as if her mother were a stern boss or a doctor with life-threatening news.

"Suzanne who?" her mother said, and Lila could hear, faintly, the sound of a knife on a chopping board — a lemon, no question. "Do I know her?"

"Suzanne," Lila repeated, refusing to explain.

Her mother's silence was like the inside of an ancient cave — a place so pleasantly terrifying that in no circumstance would a careless move be made. Lila could sense how her mother still held on to the knife, though she doubted that Vivian realized she was holding on. Then she heard her mother swallow, presumably iced tea swimming with lemon, though Lila wouldn't have been surprised if her mother were taking a neat sip of anything alcoholic within reach. "And?"

"That's it," Lila said, backing out of the conversation even as she wanted to go full steam ahead. "I'm just saying; I'm just, you know, telling you."

"I don't want you having anything to do with that girl."

"Mom, I'm just saying I saw her. She's not, like, a girl anymore either. She's, you know, married and —"

"I don't want to know," Vivian said, almost

shyly, as if Lila had offered an extravagant gift.

"Great," Lila said, "fine."

"You are living independently in a dangerous city. Your father and I don't make any demands of you, and I would think I'd have some say, just the smallest dose of influence, over you. Is that too much too ask?" Her voice was ugly and hard, with an unmistakable undercurrent of begging. "Just stay away from her," Lila's mother said, without a trace of lightness. "It would make me very uncomfortable to think of you spending any time with her. You know what I think of her. You know how hard this is for me to talk about."

"I know."

"So."

"So I have to go now."

"Please don't," her mother said, in the tone she used to tell people, *We lost our youngest son.* Lila wanted to hang up just then, and she was so used to the option that she began to grow panicked at the idea of having to say anything more. "I don't know why I told you," she said.

"I do. You think she's important somehow. I understand that. Sweetheart," her mother said deliberately, "she was here at our home on the worst day of your life." Her mother's voice took on a feral quality, untamed and determined. "She was a manipulative kind of young woman. I didn't like her — accident or no — and I'd strongly prefer you didn't spend time with her."

Lila didn't say anything, and as the silence returned it was no longer her mother's silence but her own — stale and ineffectual. "Fine," Lila said, without any effort to be convincing. "Say hi to Jeb for me."

"Well," Vivian said with an odd enthusiasm, as if making up for her true self, the one with vehement requests, "he'll be awfully sorry he missed you."

With the phone hung up once more, the room, even with the brightly colored pillows on the couch and photographs of Kisa and her friends in the Tokyo nightclubs, took on a look of dead people or certainly old people, with just enough air to stay awake. Lila opened the windows facing the West Side Highway, and watched the trucks and the hazy river. She reached for the phone again to return Ben's phone calls.

"Hullo." Ben answered on the third ring.

"It's Lila," she muttered, and then cleared her throat. "It's me."

"There you are," he said. "Listen, let's see each other, all right?"

"All right. Okay," she said. "I'm sorry I disappeared," she made herself say.

"Forget it," he said. "Listen, I've been thinking." He sounded a shade deeper, thoughtful, nervous though blunt, basically exactly how Ben sounded, only now he had seen her breasts and they had kissed each other. Her Tangerine Breeze lip-balmed lips had connected with his chapped delicate ones, and he had touched his tongue — which seemed considerably less delicate than the rest of him — to hers. "Right," he continued, "I think we should meet far away from either of our apartments. Neutral territory and all that."

"Sounds like a plan."

His friend Anthony told him about a place out in Brooklyn, a thirty-year-old café devoted to Frank Sinatra, whom Ben worshiped as a close third after De Niro and Pacino. Neither Ben nor Lila had ever been to Brooklyn, and Anthony already gave Ben the directions, so didn't that just sound ideal? A subway ride in itself sounded good at this point. The fact that Ben called at all, that he was making plans, getting directions, choosing locations, was positively overwhelming. "Um," Lila told Ben, "that sounds fine."

"They're open late," Ben said.

"Oh, you want to go now."

"Well, tonight, yes, I'd thought so, it's such a lovely day, but, if you don't want to . . ."

Lila peered out the dirty window, noticed how the sun was barely visible behind the silvery haze, but that the sky still burned with light. Evening would arrive soon, but it was still too difficult to picture. It was difficult to picture the whole thing — that the sun would descend, that trains would take her to Brooklyn, that Ben would meet her there, someplace she'd never seen. "That's fine," she said loudly. She almost shouted, "Just tell me where to go."

The apartment, after the phone was safe in its cradle, was back to seeming dead. "I ran into Suzanne E. Wolfe, Suzanne *Hannon* last night," she could tell Ben, as a way to begin their conversation. "Do tell," Ben might say casually, taking a drag on a cigarette, "who is Suzanne?" Then she'd tell her story. Lila imagined Frank Sinatra's sympathetic voice in the background, hanging in the smoky stale air, and how, when she began to tell, that air would become electric, and the big-band horns and the trumpets would give way to the whisper of a snare, just in time for Lila, in time for her to explain how things just might be different now, how Suzanne might tell her things, things no one but Suzanne could know. *This is what happened,* Lila could say, just like that.

She quickly showered, looking at herself in

the mirror as little as possible, throwing on her favorite blue jeans, a loose red T-shirt, a tight black cardigan, and low black boots that reminded her of places she'd never been and wanted to go — Western places, Southern places, stupid and dreamy places. She put on mascara and red lip gloss, then took both off, washed her face again, and grabbed her keys, heading out to meet him.

Carroll Gardens was green. A wash of deep blue and sooty gray swirled around the evening sky. The heavens were punctured by streetlights and headlights, but all was serene nonetheless. Small shops lined Smith Street: barber, tailor, deli, junk shop, bagels. A large concrete schoolyard loomed empty, and a few scattered people were going home. This place felt like it contained homes; there might be old people here, grandparents, people who ate cake with coffee and took their coffee with cream. The street was mostly quiet, and there were dogwood trees in almost supernatural states of bloom, pink and white against the deepening sky of evening. Who lived here? she wondered; who looked at these trees in the morning, and did they have a better life because of it? Lila quickened her pace and wondered — as Lila had wondered before, but could do so more immediately now — if

Suzanne or even Suzanne and Aaron had walked these very streets for any reason at all. She thought of one of her favorite movies, *Two for the Road,* and how Audrey Hepburn and Albert Finney pass their younger selves on the highway and don't even know it. These streets felt that way to Lila, that she was passing an invisible familiar person, someone who was telling her that this was one day out of many days, and that she should get to the café, because Ben, never mind who he was or would be, simply had asked her to be there.

Lila was ten minutes late, but when she saw Ben from a block away, he was leaning on a storefront, looking straight ahead, not even looking at his watch. He was running his hand through his hair slowly, as if he were thinking something, and Lila realized that she wanted to know what that something was, and that she wanted to know all about him.

"Fantastic," Ben said, when he looked up and saw her.

"Hi." She was sucking in her stomach from the very depths of her soul.

He looked at her with those watery blue eyes and said, "Fantastic to see you."

"You too," she said, looking away. "I'm late."

"No matter," he said. "You look radiant."

"I do not look radiant," she said, with as little commentary as possible. Lila thought her voice sounded remarkably even, while inside, she was someone else, insecure to the point of tears, thrown completely off-kilter by the one word: *radiant.*

Ben shook his head as he threw his cigarette to the ground, then nodded to the café. "Shall we go on up?"

The café was on the second floor, up a narrow stairway, and the room itself was covered from floor to ceiling with photos and mementos of Frank Sinatra. And although it was smoky, the room was not dimly lit as she'd imagined, but bright and garish, with television blasting Frank footage and a group of older gentlemen watching reverently. "You'd think," Lila whispered, "if this place has been around for thirty years, they'd have seen this a few times before."

"Maybe it's an evening ritual."

The café served a basic coffee and tea selection, "Homemade pizza — best in NY," and besides that, basic gas station products — Twinkies, Ring Dings, mini apple and cherry pies, some chips. Ben stepped up to the counter and plied the man away from the television long enough to order coffees and an assortment of Hostess goods. Lila watched him from the table in the corner.

Ben dumped the plastic-wrapped goodies on the table and put down two coffees, sat and lit up a cigarette.

"Weird place," Lila said.

"What do you mean?"

"You know what I mean," Lila said, and made sure to smile. "Didn't you picture it a little more, you know —"

"I didn't picture it at all, actually. I think this place is all right, really, and incidentally, that chair you're sitting in — that was Frank's."

Lila looked at the chair. It was a bright green fake velvet disaster, but she noticed all the rest of the chairs in the joint were the basic church-basement variety, and for a moment she felt special, for a second, kind of pretty, sitting in Frank's chair.

"So I did a bit of research for our little field trip," he said foppishly, while tearing open a packet of Twinkies. "I have to say, I thought most of Brooklyn was more —"

"Tough?"

"Well, okay, yes, that's right, I did. Laugh at me now, go on."

"I'm not laughing."

His eyes blinked rapidly as his slightly crooked teeth were bared in a smile. Lila thought about how she'd soberly removed her shirt, how she'd *propositioned* him, and here they were, talking uninformedly about not much at all. She thought about Suzanne, and how much she wanted to do none of this with her. *Did you love my brother?* Lila might start with that. No "how are you," no compliments about her home, her shoes, just: *Did my brother love you? Did my brother love me?* and *Where is Aaron? Just tell me that.* How to create conversation with Ben should hardly be as difficult, she thought. *He's just a guy I met in the park; he's someone I will have met and gone out with, the way that people do.*

But then Ben put out his cigarette, and laid his small pale hand on hers, which had been fiddling with a Twinkie wrapper, folding it into the thinnest of folds. The men in the corner weren't laughing anymore but quiet and slouched and listening to Frank and Juliet Prowse sing about how they were wrong for each other. Ben had his hand on hers and it wasn't sweaty but dry and soft, with two blue rivulets, fork-shaped, strong. She found herself turning his hand over, so that the palm faced up, and she held his palm like that, looking over the lines as if she knew what they meant.

"I think you have beautiful shoulders," Ben said, as she was swallowing. He cleared his throat. "Nice tits, of course, but that you must know already. Right, I'm blushing now."

And he was. His face was pink and his ears were red, and his mouth twisted up like a knotted balloon. "I don't know," she managed to say. "I mean I didn't know. Thanks. I think I'm nervous," Lila said in a smaller voice than she'd intended. "You were right about me feeling pressure." Juliet Prowse was dancing on TV in a lush white knee-length dress; the fabric rippled and billowed, and Frank grabbed her waist. The men by the television whistled, and Lila felt that invisible familiar self for a moment whispering, *You have beautiful shoulders, so shut up and get on with it,* and she smiled at Ben, as he whistled just like the men from Brooklyn, watching the green glow of the past.

Ben did his Sinatra impression for the men by the television. The manager of the café told Ben how he wanted to go to England for his honeymoon twenty years ago but his wife didn't like the rain, and that same manager made Ben say a few lines of Shakespeare because the manager loved the theater, the good stuff, not the junk. And then the café closed up, sending Ben and Lila onto Court Street, both buzzing with sugar and caffeine, and not least of all, each other. They walked. They walked because they were used to walking with each other, and because somehow, if they stepped onto the subway and went away from these quiet unfamiliar streets, the tenuous sense of shared experience would fade, and the hours that had passed richly and carefully would somehow compress into the routine of transportation.

"Did your high school have cheerleaders?" Ben asked, as they passed more closed stores, pasta and meat shops, a pharmacy.

"No, I went to a small Quaker school. There were five other girls and seven boys in my graduating class. I don't think I'm really the cheerleading type anyway."

"I suppose not. I grew up watching all those movies in the eighties about high school in America. It looked like one big party."

"Not mine." Lila tried to think of something pleasant to tell Ben about her schooling. "I spent a lot of time in the woods," she offered. "We made fires. When it was warm we swam in a pond."

She could count the times in high school that she swam in the pond. If she tried, she could probably count how many times she ever really swam there at all, after the age of eight. Lila loved to swim — in the Atlantic Ocean, lakes in Massachusetts, swimming holes only miles away from home, but almost never in the pond by her house. She was convinced it was somehow toxic on the bottom, that even besides the bad memories there were way too many fish for such a small body of water. This never seemed irrational to her, and no one questioned her very much. Lila cultivated wearing hats by the pond, when she had to be there. She said she liked keeping her skin very pale and never exposed much more than a downy forearm, her ankles. She was proud of her ankles. Never showing much more than this, she reasoned, was a good tactic for drawing attention to the positive. When she did swim, it was always a surprise. *In high school, I was popular,* she could say to Ben, and it would be truth. Lila was surrounded by people when she wanted to be. Her morbidness was appealing, and this was something she had figured out by junior year. There were always a few people willing to listen, to hear Lila talk about her family and somehow relate it to their own. But she knew that everyone talked about her, as if she didn't care. "She doesn't care," was something she knew was said about her by friends, teachers. Talking freely had that effect. She'd created that person, the girl who sat in the shade and said things like, *Careful on those rocks, my brother died there.* Sardonic, her mother pointed out, sardonic and bitter. And her mother, in this case, was right; Lila had to give her that, for Lila she hated that person, the pale-skinned brat in the woods, because she cared too much, and about every wrong thing. Now Lila cracked her knuckles and cleared her throat too loudly.

"What about you?" she said to Ben. "No cheerleaders?"

"None whatsoever. No girls at all."

"Boarding school?"

"That's right," he said. "But I've told you that before, haven't I? I was sent off when I was eight. We got to come home for weekends, and all week long you'd just dream about your mummy's face and smell. And then you'd come home and she'd have a nice tea waiting for you, and then you'd snap your fingers and you were being sent back in time for tea at school, which, to give the school credit, was really lovely. I suppose it was to make Sunday nights less depressing, which was altogether impossible. And you'd be so sick about leaving your mummy that you wouldn't eat any of the lovely tea, and the dinner was never very good, and you'd go to sleep hungry, dreaming of your mummy, who was most likely taking a healthy dose of sleeping pills, and dreaming of the Riviera, or the time she met George Peppard, or anyone besides your father."

They'd stopped walking at some point, and were looking at a bakery storefront, at cheap cakes and day-old bread, just for something to look at. "Very Dickensian," Ben said.

Lila nodded, but privately she was distressed by the idea of a sniffling little Ben, after lights-out in some stone dormitory, surrounded by other little sniffling boys under navy blue blankets with empty stomachs.

He smiled at her, not a sad smile either. "Things got quite a bit better later on," he admitted, not being one, she knew, to dwell on anything so embarrassing as childhood. They walked on quietly, turning onto a residential street where proud rose gardens and bougainvillea vines glowed beneath the streetlight, the half-moon. Lila hummed "Witchcraft" so as not to seem too sullen. The brownstone windows weren't all draped with curtains, and there were views of other people's living rooms, paintings, computers. A man sat, reading, in a tall chair in a first-floor apartment. He was young and almost bald.

"I like it here," Ben said, and Lila could sense him watching her, but she couldn't quite look his way. She thought of him admiring her breasts and shoulders and how he wasn't insulting, even though she realized she was waiting for him to be. Lila felt hopeful in a way that was as tenuous as Suzanne Hannon's business card and the places it could lead. Everything felt as fragile as the tender insides of these strangers' homes, and how all of this could be revealed as dull, the young bald man not content, but depressed, and the gardens nothing but ordinary.

"I do too," she said, "this is nice."

Ben stopped and she couldn't just keep walking and she knew that he would kiss her and that she would let it happen, and even as she felt it happen, how his soft skin smelled honeyed, but also like seeds and smoke and new paper, and how her ears rang and her legs pressed together, Lila knew this would be over soon, and that it would be unlikely she'd recall the feeling and believe in its ease. She would remember the bald man, and the tall amber chair, and maybe the way the sky was truly dark, but not the small burn at the base of her spine, the near painless release from herself.

At Ben's apartment, there were two huge amps, an upright bass, a guitar, and a suitcase that all belonged to "a musician friend" who'd been called out of town unexpectedly. Lila was immediately reminded of how little they knew one another, but within an hour she was fairly relaxed, curled into the chair under the window, and laughing about the cast of characters that were Ben's "good mates." There was Milo the obsessed Jimi

Hendrix fan, whose father was England's poet laureate a few years back, and whose mother was Hungarian royalty; Lucas, a recovering coke fiend, who'd spent his two years out of university earning scads of money "making computers sexy," and Lucas's sister Claire, a lesbian pianist who was the most intelligent of them all. Milo spent a fair portion of his time embarrassing his parents in ways that Ben was relaying to Lila, making her laugh harder than she could remember laughing in a long while. "Poor Milo," Ben said.

"Poor Milo," Lila mimicked him perfectly.

"Poor Milo's parents," Ben said, and poured himself more whiskey. Lila still nursed hers, and as the night progressed, she grew slowly accustomed to the bitter, hollow pull of it, down her throat, through her blood. She liked whiskey right then, in an unfamiliar way — a way that didn't cause worry. Lila had gone through a puritanical phase when her friends began to drink, revolted by the part alcohol and drugs certainly played in Jack's death. He fell. Just a fall on those jagged rocks. The easing away from control did not seem, to Lila, worth the happy blur. Then, a year or two later, she loved to drink, and had some fun letting something inside fall away smoothly, but this feeling always worried her, and the worry came forward in heavy hits —

lying in the backs of speeding pickups, on her bed, postparty, when she was finally alone. But right there with Ben, nearing midnight on a Monday, she felt fluid, and interested in Milo and his parents, and Ben; in anything Ben had to say.

"My dad and mum weren't concerned enough to be embarrassed by me, had I thought to try," Ben said lightly, "which was probably a good thing actually. Probably saved me a few years of quality piss-off time."

Lila wanted to know whether asking further about his parents would be pushing it too far. She didn't want to insult him by taking him too seriously. "I think I'm doing that," she said, and realized she wasn't sure it was true, as soon as the words escaped her.

"What? Pissing off?" he asked, and before she could answer: "Well, thanks," he said not a little bitterly. "Cheers."

"No, no," she said, then, "*No.* Not with you. I mean," she said, making sure he was listening. "I think, maybe, I'm trying to piss away my time and my money so that they'll notice."

"Your parents?" Ben asked, and she nodded, shrugged.

"I'm not sure. I think —" she said, and then felt as if she were about to laugh again, remembering Ben's elastic face, his ridiculous imitations. "I think, maybe, I'm just doing what I really want to do." Lila wasn't pissing away time, she knew that, but it was hard to believe, when she realized that she could care less about school, about which facts she knew and which ones she didn't, and about learning what kind of life would one day be appealing, and laying the groundwork for getting there. Ben had gone to RADA, and now, in New York, he took acting class, to keep on the ball, all the time. He had an agent and he auditioned, and rehearsed and performed. He had shelves of plays that he knew by heart. He knew *King Lear* and *All's Well that Ends Well* and *Hamlet* the way she knew her memories of being five, six, seven years old. It would be one thing if she were directionless. That would be flaky and even romantic. But directionless she was not. She wanted to find her brother. She wanted to hear him tell her about one night out of both of their lives. This was her direction, and she didn't have another. And yet Aaron wasn't in on her plans, and neither was Suzanne. She knew their lives didn't converge anymore but she was sick of heading in this direction alone.

"Why don't you tell me," Ben said, and she poured herself more whiskey.

"About?" she said, her heart sick with

speed. She wanted to. She wanted to pour forth every detail of what happened to them all, and the great urban miracle of finding Suzanne.

"Dunno," he said, and she had an urge to touch his face again, to do so with a measure of confidence. He was all light and easy now, now that she agreed to come into his place, now that the evening was going on and on. "How did your parents meet?" he asked, and Lila forgot about her reserve for a moment.

This was her favorite story.

"My mother was staying with her brother Aaron, who lived in Portsmouth, because she was saving money to go live in Spain."

"How bohemian," Ben said, and she flinched inside. *Yes, it was bohemian,* she wanted to say. *My mother thought she'd be a woman set loose in the world, a girl on a ship bound for freedom.*

Lila explained how her mother was living with Aaron, and earning some money as a substitute teacher, and never going anywhere because she wanted to leave as soon as possible. And how, because her mother was also driving Aaron crazy, he sent her out one autumn night to a place called Cal's, where one of his friends tended bar, and at that bar, Lila told Ben, was Lila's father Jeb, who'd come down from the woods for a burger and a beer.

Jeb told her mother about the house he'd just built, which was one of five houses around a pond, which glowed green from the reflection of the pine forest. Her father told her mother — a small-waisted, wild-haired, freckled girl — about his friends Michael and Louisa who lived in the house nearest to his, and how on clear nights they all ate dinner outside, and other people from the houses brought their dinners too. Communal living, but not without the joys of solitude. It beat the city, he told her, and he took a big bite of his burger.

"Was he a good-looking hippie?" Ben asked. "Women can't resist those. I'm picturing Peter Fonda."

"He was no Peter Fonda," Lila said, and laughed. Her own life disappeared, for the moment, into the telling of this story, into the perfection the world seemed without her. "But I suppose he was pretty intriguing. He had — has — a glass eye, which kept him out of Vietnam, and he was as pale and Waspy-woodsy, as my mother was dark-eyed and Jewish. So" — Lila looked around her, the wood floor and cool light, the glint of the bottle and glasses — "so did she want to see it? is what he asked, after she was through with her beer." Lila tried to keep this a romantic story — two young people, how they fell in love. "And they drove in his light blue truck to the houses and the pond." Lila pictured the house, the pond, how they were impossibly the very same places. " 'I love it,' my mother immediately said, after Jeb showed her each room. And she never left."

"What is your mum's name?"

"Vivian," Lila said, and she thought, as she said it, what a beautiful name it was, and how what was familiar to the ears could be so foreign to the tongue.

"She never went to Spain?"

"Not until my brothers were born, and by then, I guess she spent most of her time curbing them while they ran around on a churros-and-chocolate sugar high."

Ben shifted in his chair. "I didn't know you had more than one brother."

Lila tried to smile. She didn't know what to say, and the more she tried to think of how to put it, the more the silence expanded. The air smelled different, like cloves, vanilla, musky perfume. It smelled good and nothing like her. And some cast party pictures on the mantel loomed unfriendly. *You were not here when these pictures were taken,* Lila thought. *You were probably alone, calling your parents, listening to your mother's voice, without a single decent response.*

She kissed him then, surprised as she did

so, surprised how it seemed the only thing to do. They kissed as cars passed outside Ben's window, as the world became slightly larger, as time did not stand still. "I should go now," Lila finally said. "I really should go home." But she didn't go home, and things went slowly, very slow, and they did no more than kiss until something felt different, softer somehow. The sun was beginning to rise.

She wanted to tell him how the streets of Brooklyn felt sacred now, that Frank Sinatra never sounded like much until she listened to him sing while watching Ben's face, that he was a good kisser, a great kisser, the only great kisser she'd known. Lila wanted to ask: *Remember the bald man? Remember how hard I laughed?* But she only smiled and said good-bye.

The apartment was empty and refreshingly clean. It was seven o'clock in the morning. The card was in the drawer, but she didn't even look at it. She held one of the copies she'd made, despite already knowing the number by heart, and though Kisa wouldn't be home for hours, Lila closed her bedroom door. She sat on her futon, her feet tucked beneath her, and waited until it was eight.

Then Lila watched the numbers as she dialed the cordless phone.

She answered immediately, as if she'd been expecting the call.

"Suzanne Hannon?" Lila asked.

"Who is *this?*" the voice replied. *Smart girl,* Lila thought, *for there are pranksters out there, there certainly are, just dying to know all our names.* And Lila told Suzanne that it was Aaron's sister on the line, the one from the flower stand, and Suzanne said yes, hello, it's been such a very long time.

CHAPTER SIXTEEN

As Lila stepped off the elevator, into the stark white hallway, she counted the time that Suzanne had actually been involved with her family. Aaron brought her home on a Friday evening, and she left, care of Bonanza bus, little more than twenty-four hours later. "You don't know her," Lila said softly, before knocking on Suzanne E. Wolfe Hannon's door. She realized the door was open, and from inside the apartment a cross-breeze was blowing the scent of clean worn cotton with a hint of something sweet. Before knocking, she inched the door open far enough to take a peek, and Lila stepped inside without thinking, transfixed by a small black-and-white photograph of a still body of water at the base of a moon-shot mountain.

"Oh, you're here," Lila heard from awfully far away. Lila looked up and saw Suzanne in a doorway across a huge, spare space. She had really meant to knock. "Come in," Suzanne said, "take off your shoes, if you don't mind."

Lila took off her black boots, which looked filthy in the sparkling loft, and set them side by side. "Sorry," Suzanne surprised her by saying, "but the floors have to be cleaned an obscene amount of times in order to stay in decent shape, so we try to be shoeless."

"It's nice," Lila said, and it did feel pleasant — a sense of comfort and ease, however false, was there nonetheless. She thought of Ben sliding on his floor in red socks, and the Brooklyn night, almost a week ago, he was wearing one green and one blue. She knew, or at least she thought she knew, that Ben would find Suzanne attractive. She wondered how he'd describe her. "Thanks," Lila said, not sure what she meant to address. *Thanks for having me here? Thanks for making me take my shoes off?* "Beautiful apartment," she said, as Suzanne came toward her, barefooted, with perfectly red toenails. Suzanne and Lila didn't touch — no handshake, nothing.

The far wall was lined with paintings. The colors were deep and bright, as if lit by a hot setting sun. The paintings looked like landscapes, just by the shapes and composition, although, she realized, they could have been inspired by just about anything. One looked a bit like a woman's back. Lila could tell the paintings were good. She wanted to keep looking, and Suzanne noticed.

"He's my new artist," Suzanne said, turning her attention to the wall, and smiling a gentler smile. "My only living artist," she said. "Mostly, I sell dead artists' work, but he's good, don't you think? I want to do what I can with him, before he gets swept up by a big gallery."

"They remind me of home," Lila said.

"Sit down," Suzanne said brightly, and Lila did, on a bloated pale sofa slung with blue chenille. Lila touched the blanket and sat patiently, as Suzanne orbited around her, stopping in the open kitchen to bring out two plates: thin chocolate-chip cookies, fruit. And what would she like to drink? Coffee? Me too, Suzanne said, I've had enough of herbal teas. And within minutes there was hot mocha java, to which they both added milk, and Lila noticed Suzanne's even smile, as if they were really two women having a casual coffee date, engaged in the business of sharing secrets small enough to smile through.

"How long have you been married?" Lila asked.

"Three years," Suzanne said, and crossed her legs. She was wearing tailored black pants and an antiquey-looking shirt, which probably cost a fortune; it was short-sleeved and button-down, the faintest shade of blue. "Lila, you look so different! It's amazing," she said. "You look great. It's strange, but really good to see you. How did you even remember me?"

"I just did," Lila said, making sure not to smile. "I remember you vividly."

Suzanne plucked a few grapes from their stems and sat back on the couch. "Well, I've changed a great deal," she said. "It's hard to remember how everything seemed when I was at Columbia. God," she said, breezily, "I was almost your age when I met you."

"You were a year older."

"I mean, basically. Basically I was where you are now. Are you in college?"

Lila thought, *You were nowhere near where I am now. You were a girlfriend, a student, unused to consequences. You were flirtatious, I remember.* Lila shook her head. She told Suzanne, in brief, the trajectory of her New York experience.

"You live on the West Side Highway?" Suzanne asked skeptically.

"It's all right," Lila said, feeling, for a moment, that Suzanne was only a kindly aunt, one who had her welfare in mind.

"You know," Suzanne said, "I could probably talk to someone I know and get you a better place. I know a lot of people who are always coming and going. Maybe I could get you somewhere where you didn't even need to pay rent. You could house-sit."

"I'm fine where I am," Lila said evenly, "but thanks."

"If you need anything, though — if you get sick of teaching or something — I could maybe even get you a job. You probably have plenty of people to turn to, but —"

"I don't," Lila was quick to let her know.

"Well, then," Suzanne looked a little less comfortable. "If you need anything . . ."

As Suzanne trailed off, maintaining her considerate services, Lila noticed that the lilies Richard and she bought weren't in a vase, and she thought maybe they were in the bedroom, but then she realized they were probably long gone, that these purple wildflowers were their replacement. "Do you buy flowers every week?"

"Oh, I don't know." Suzanne shifted in her chair. Again the smile. "I love flowers. I mean who doesn't, I know, but I do. Richard" — she hesitated a moment, as if rethinking what she intended to say — "he's away a lot, this year in particular, so he sends them, which is nice."

"Very." Though Lila knew it must indeed be nice to receive flowers from one's husband, it somehow didn't seem so just then, with the air smelling like orange rinds and strong coffee but somehow divorced from the people who might have touched the oranges or stirred the coffee. The sofas were pale caramel and the softest, cleanest suede, and the low dark-wood table had not a speck of dust. The coasters were bright green and looked heavier than they were; Lila suspected they were from some Scandinavian country, where a very wealthy woman made nothing but coasters and possibly small round bowls. "Where was that photograph taken?" Lila asked, nodding to the matted black-and-white mountain and water, knowing that while she was genuinely interested in where it was, she was also trying to make Suzanne focus on the placid water, the moonlit silence, the fact of why, indeed, Lila was here. Lila knew she could observe Suzanne's style and listen to her talk about flowers and art and coffee and Richard for hours, but Lila also knew that she was listening to Suzanne through a ten-year-old filter, and the Suzanne that Lila wanted, and for whom she was waiting, was someone who didn't know these conversation topics were possible.

"Oh, do you like it? I took that photograph. It's in Vermont."

"When were you there?"

Suzanne plucked some more grapes. "Oh, I don't remember. Sometime in college."

Suzanne had perfect skin. She wore

apricot-colored lip gloss. "Sometime in college?" Lila repeated, trying not to rise in volume. "It's all more or less the same in your memory?"

Suzanne returned Lila's stultifying look. "Of course not. Of course. I just mean, you know —" Lila was aware that Suzanne had been thrown off-kilter very easily. It only took being firm, a good strong stare. Suzanne continued, trying to backtrack: "I mean, it's just funny. One person can remember everything about a place, nothing about who was there, and some people are the opposite, or they can only remember smells. I'm just the worst. You'd think I *would* remember about that photograph. I know I labored over developing it."

"I remember everything."

Suzanne didn't, to her credit, say anything. At least not for a moment or two. There was the faintest sound of a horn blaring. The glass on the windows must have been the thickest possible option. Lila felt as if they were very high in the sky, floating in this moment of Suzanne's pretty face in deliberation, and the anticipation of just how much of her elegant babble would be revealed as distinctly artificial — no more than an attempt to see how far this meeting could go without ever mentioning the past. "I remember you," Suzanne said, and Lila set her cup down.

"What was I like?" she asked, her face opening.

"Sweet. Sort of. You were smart. I hadn't spent any real time with little kids at that point, so I wasn't sure which things about you were average and which were not, but I've known a few more kids now, and I think you were definitely the sharpest." Suzanne looked at Lila, who merely returned the look, so Suzanne continued, looking away, toward her living artist's colors or maybe the white of the wall. "You watched me," she said. "I wasn't used to that."

"Kids make me nervous," Lila said suddenly.

"Exactly."

"We played rose garden," Lila said, "the torture game."

Suzanne nodded. "On the lawn."

And just as Lila felt a detached kind of calm, the closest to composure she was going to come right then, the phone rang in the other room and her heart punched hard. "I need to get that," Suzanne said, and muttered an apology as she exited toward the phone. Lila could hear Suzanne, for the door didn't close all the way, and as Suzanne spoke in clipped tones to whoever was on the other line, Lila wondered if Suzanne didn't leave the door ajar in order to show off a little, to say, *Look, I have a life, a real business that is not some errant pursuit.*

Suzanne raised her voice, clearly unhappy. "We went over this again and again." She said, her voice lower and sober. "I said Friday, which is tomorrow . . . Do you want to try to sell someone a fifty-thousand-dollar painting by fax? No . . . I said . . . don't —"

And Suzanne hung up the phone. Lila knew she should say, *This is clearly a bad time,* and leave, politely. But there was no way, after ten years of wanting this moment, that she was going to let it go, and take the chance that it might not come again. She stayed planted on the couch, and began to eat a chocolate-chip cookie. She sipped her coffee and smiled at Suzanne, who emerged from the office with her hair scrambled atop her head in a tortoise barrette. "Framers," she said, and smiled sharply. "What can you do?"

"Does this happen often?"

"Often enough." Suzanne took the last of the grapes, picked them violently off their stems. "How are your parents?" she asked, as if it were impolite that she hadn't asked already.

"Great," Lila said, with inexplicable loyalty that seemed to rise up from nowhere. "They're both doing well."

"They hated me," she said.

Lila shrugged. "They needed to blame someone," she said, and Suzanne nodded, and in an instant, Lila dropped the delicate teal coffee cup — the coffee splashing on the pale couch, the cup smashing on the specially cleaned floor. "Oh, no," Lila said, and went to pick up the beautiful pieces of china. They had an iridescent sheen to them, and she felt genuinely sorry.

"Don't touch," Suzanne said, and then, "don't worry about it. It's fine."

But it wasn't fine; that was plain. "Please don't tell me these are some family heir-loom," Lila said.

"Not *my* family," Suzanne said with a laugh. "Don't worry," she said again, in the worried voice. And she swept the mess quickly in silence, sprinkled powder on the couch, and Lila moved into a low-slung chair. Suzanne's face was flushed.

"Um," Lila said.

"What," Suzanne urged, as if she were ready for a question or two.

"Where's Aaron?" Lila asked, and to keep the pressure off, she added, "do you think?"

"What do you mean?"

"What do I mean? I mean, it's been ten years, and we don't know where he is."

"Are you serious?" Suzanne asked, "He

hasn't contacted you?"

"No," Lila said, her throat constricting, "has he —"

"Not *me*," Suzanne said, as if she barely knew him. "Lila, it was a long time ago."

"I know exactly how long ago it was."

"I'm not saying you don't. I can't imagine what you must have gone through." Suzanne looked away, looked around, almost as if they were being watched. "I don't know what to say. I haven't heard from your brother since I left your house that morning," she said, lowering her voice. "I knew that he went to Europe because I got a postcard."

"We got postcards for a few months. The last one was from Israel."

"Well, I only got one. From Logan Airport, 1987. It seemed like he just wanted to move on. I would have thought that —"

"Did you love Aaron?" Lila interrupted, not caring how stupid she might sound, not caring what difference it made if Suzanne did or did not.

"Lila, I'm married."

"I know, but —"

"It just doesn't feel right to be talking about your brother this way. I suppose I did love him. But it was so long ago, and I'm a different person than I was then."

"I'm not. I feel exactly the same."

"Lila, what do you want?" Suzanne suddenly said, her voice brimming with impatience.

Lila realized that she wasn't exactly sure. Besides help finding Aaron, she knew there was something she wanted from Suzanne, beyond just to be in the presence of someone who knew her life without the necessity of explanation. "I don't know," she said, and as she said it, she knew that what she wanted more than anything was to hear about what happened from someone besides her parents. "They sat me down, that day at the hospital, after they knew it was official. They told me there'd been an accident, that Jack had fallen. Then later, when I asked more questions, they told me about how drunk he was. That he had gotten out of control and into trouble. They said Aaron tried to help him, but Jack didn't want help. And my mother wouldn't mention you much. She thought you were trouble, you're right, which never made any sense to me. They told me Aaron couldn't handle not being able to rescue Jack. But I can't picture it, the way it happened."

"Why do you want to picture how your brother died?" Suzanne was gentle, and for the first time, Lila could tell she remembered it all, every horrible moment.

"I want to understand how it could have happened."

"It just did, okay? Terrible things happen all the time. And this terrible thing happened to your brother, and I'm sure it is hard to live with, but *you* are fine. You are a whole other person."

"Like you? Like you're fine, and untouched, so it doesn't really matter?"

"I'm not saying it doesn't matter. I'm saying you're not going to get it all back."

Lila looked at the paintings and the tall clean windows. Suzanne lived here. Suzanne bought and sold art, and talked about color and light and made love to her husband and ate meals in good restaurants around town. She probably traveled frequently, and talked on the phone consistently with a few friends. Suzanne didn't fall on the rocks, and neither did anyone Suzanne knew even relatively well. A college boyfriend's brother died, and the boyfriend broke up with her and took off to Europe. What was Suzanne supposed to say? She might have never even discussed the weekend she spent with Lila's family. When Suzanne remembered that night, Lila realized, it might be, simply, a negative memory, not personally tragic enough to be a secret. "I want to know what happened," Lila insisted. "We had dinner, and then I was forced to go to bed. I was having the best time; I didn't want to go to sleep. And then . . ." Lila felt herself fading into the distance of her memory and made sure to cut herself off. "I wonder about it, you know?"

Suzanne muttered something.

"What?"

"We were going to that stupid party." Suzanne laughed nervously. "It seems so far away. I can't believe any of this ever happened." Suzanne seemed irritated, and Lila couldn't tell if she was irritated with the party and what happened afterward, or with having to tell Lila anything at all. "We, you know, just went to some party at Jack's friend's house." Suzanne spoke as if she couldn't believe her own words, her own life. She seemed shocked to remember it at all.

"Who?"

"I don't think you would have met her, the woman who gave the party. She wasn't exactly the kind of girl you'd bring home to Mom."

"Not like you?" Lila said, not meaning it as sarcastically as it came out.

"No," Suzanne said, "not like me. Not like you, either."

"What, was Jack *involved* with the girl or something?"

Suzanne looked frustrated, took out her

barrette, and her hair fell to her shoulders, exactly how it had been. "It was a party, Lila, that's all. I barely remember what anyone looked like. I was just saying . . . look . . . the party was a whole separate thing. It could have been any number of parties."

"But the woman who gave the party? What was she, super trashy or something?"

"You know what? Yes. She was. She was nobody you'd know and nobody I would have known either. She was just some woman with a weird name who was into your brothers. It was kind of sad, actually."

Lila smiled at Suzanne in a form of collusion. She took a breath and emitted an odd laugh. The laugh lied, the smile lied; they said, *Don't worry, you're right; I'm letting this all go.* "Weird name?" She smiled again and acted as if they were in the halls of any high school, indulging in their very worst selves. "What was it?"

The glint in Suzanne's eye looked like glass and glitter. "Something foreign — who knows, maybe she made it up — Pria, I think it was. Something like that. I don't remember," she said.

This was a coincidence too good to be unimportant. Her favorite jewelry store in Portsmouth was called Pria. She was, in fact, wearing a beaded bracelet from that very store, one that she rarely removed. Lila was careful not to seem too interested. "Did she make jewelry?"

Suzanne laughed a darker laugh. "Lila, she was a stripper. Okay? She was no artsy-craftsy type, believe me. I wouldn't be surprised if she'd ODed on any number of substances." Suzanne let out a sound between a sigh and a laugh, and looked at Lila with a plaintive smile. "Aaagh!" she said. "It was so long ago. Meeting your family . . . I don't know. . . . What about you? Do you meet your boy-friends' families? Richard's parents would only meet someone if he thought he might be engaged soon. They didn't want to put in the effort. That made me like them even before we were introduced."

"Did Richard know who I was?" Lila asked.

Suzanne nodded. Her neck was covered with pink splotches.

"You're lying, aren't you?" Lila said, "You're lying."

"Excuse me?"

"You've never even told him about Aaron or anything, have you?"

"Listen," Suzanne said, the same voice that she used with the framers on the phone, "I've invited you here, I've been more than willing to talk. I honestly was happy to see you. But this is obviously something you need to deal

with, and you are making me very uncomfortable in the process." She let down her hard
voice, and the slightly flustered teenager that
Lila remembered emerged with unwilling
emotion. "I don't know you and you don't
know me. I dated your brother for eight
months when I was nineteen. Lila, really. I
don't know what you want me to do."

"I just want to be in the presence of someone who knows."

"Who knows what?"

"My life," Lila admitted.

"But I don't know your life," Suzanne said.

"Yes, you do," Lila said quietly, more quietly than she had ever planned on speaking in
this empty beautiful space. "You do."

"I could tell you stories of how wonderful
Aaron was. But Aaron, don't forget, broke up
with me, and no matter how devastated he
was from Jack's death, it didn't feel good to be
dumped." Suzanne drew a sharp breath, and
winced a little. "But he *was* wonderful. I'm
sorry," she said, and smiled the brittle smile,
which lasted only a moment before fading
into a look of genuine confusion, when she
said, "I think maybe you should go."

"You have no idea how badly you will make
me feel if you don't talk with me again."
There it was — straight guilt. The only card
she could think to play.

"You want to know what happened."

"Yes."

"And then you'll be . . . okay."

"I just want to hear you tell it."

The sun was setting, and the sky was gray, full of loose, thin clouds. The grapes were all gone and what was left of the cookies were broken up into halves and quarters. Suzanne made more coffee. "Do you have a boyfriend?" she asked Lila, and without thinking, Lila said no.

"What is it?" Suzanne asked. "Is there someone you like?"

"Yeah, there is," Lila said. "I'm too sensitive," she confessed.

Suzanne nodded, as if she knew all about it. "You said that to Aaron, that day, on the lawn. You told him he was too sensitive."

"I don't remember that."

"It was funny," Suzanne said, and she poured more coffee, gave Lila another cup.

"Well, I am," Lila said. "Was he?"

"No," Suzanne said, and her voice grew almost stern. "Everything he did, he wanted to do the right thing. He got nervous."

"And that night?"

"How much do you remember about Jack?"

"I remember a lot. He was the one whose approval I wanted. To get Jack's attention

318

seemed to take more work; maybe that's why I wanted it again and again." Lila paused, tried to read Suzanne's blank face. "He made me feel so good," Lila said, feeling good just saying it, "he did."

"You were so little," Suzanne said abruptly. "Jack — and I don't want to color your memories — but Jack was the one who insisted on going down to the lake. He was really drunk and really stoned, and Aaron and I just wanted to be alone, you know, together, and Jack told us he was going swimming, and Aaron insisted on going after him. I mean, I didn't know how Jack was, I just wanted to go inside and be with Aaron, but Aaron told me that he felt responsible. And so we went after him, which is what Jack wanted, and he. . . ." Suzanne paused, as if she might stop talking, but before Lila could urge her, Suzanne pressed her fingertips to her eyes and continued. "We went swimming. All of us. But Jack needed an audience. That's what it seemed like. He kept saying, 'Dare me to go out farther!' and Aaron begged him to come off the rocks, but he didn't, and he did stupid moves, jumping up and down, pretending to fall." Suzanne spoke with almost no expression. "And Aaron and Jack started yelling back and forth. Then Aaron came after him, to get him onto the shore, and Jack jumped away."

Suzanne looked at Lila desperately, or desperately was how Lila would come to think of it, when she'd look back on this moment as the one that somehow shifted things and revealed Suzanne as completely separate, no help at all. Lila didn't know why, but she was sure Suzanne was lying; she possessed the kind of determined assurance that was not up for discussion. "That's when he fell, Lila," Suzanne said, and she covered her face with her ring-finger hand. The diamond picked up light.

"Thank you," Lila knew to say.

"Okay?" Suzanne said. "Okay?"

Lila nodded, placed the cup in its saucer. She looked out the tall glass windows.

"Looks like rain," Suzanne said, clearly relieved.

Suzanne's story matched her mother's story and her father's story. Almost word for word. This was the first thing about Suzanne that really made sense, not because Lila was any closer to knowing more about Aaron and Jack, but because she was finally certain of something: both her parents and Suzanne knew something she didn't. It was not her imagination: she was indisputably alone in this life, but she steeled herself against sadness; she was sick of the very word. Lila listened to Suzanne and recognized the tone of voice, the absence of contemplation. Never did her parents or Suzanne question, out loud, what might have happened if one little thing went differently, if anyone could have done something, anything else. There was stubbornness to this story that defied the horror of the situation. As certain as she was that rain would not come until nightfall, and the air would be static as she walked uptown, Lila knew right then that as much as her parents loved her, and as kindly as Suzanne was meeting her gaze — Lila knew that these were lies. Whatever happened that night to her brothers, clearly this was not it.

Lila had been right about the static air. While walking home, all around her it had felt as if something were about to happen. In her apartment building corridor, the scent of fried vegetables filled the cramped space, adding to the humidity. Kisa was locking the door to go out for the evening. "Take an umbrella," Lila told her roommate, and Kisa told her to eat the tempura that was lying out in the kitchen. "You look tired," Kisa said, and left.

In the kitchen, Lila picked up a zucchini disk and doused it in soy. She shoved it in her mouth and looked at the phone. The carrot tempura was her favorite; it was soft and sweet. The cauliflower wasn't bad either. Lila nibbled and picked up the phone then put it down, thinking of Ben and how much he somehow mattered, how she didn't want to screw up. She went on this way, eating and thinking, till there was no more sunlight, and a measly few onion strips were left. Lila took the phone into her bedroom. It finally began to rain.

It had been two days since she'd last called her parents and hung up. By now, it was embarrassing they hadn't thought to get caller ID, although she figured they probably viewed such a device as a fundamental act against privacy. They were big on privacy. Big on the right to do nothing but hole up in the woods and talk with the same people about the same few years when they all never worried about privacy, when the world made it easier to share. Lately, Jeb didn't attend even these gatherings, was known to use the word *hippie* disparagingly. He stuck to his welding studio, where he spent hours fashioning wine racks and candelabras, doorknobs and chairs out of hot molten metal. He gave his products to schools and to halfway houses, neighbors who came by quietly. He had never made anything for Lila, and lying on her futon, with the rain beating against her windowpane, she wished she had even a little candlestick, something of his time.

The phone rang twice and, surprisingly, her father answered.

"It's me," Lila said.

"Why, hello, me. What's shakin'?"

"Why are you answering the phone?"

"Felt like it," he said. "Everything okay in the Big Apple?"

"Steady," Lila said. "Up there?"

"Oh, fine, fine." She guessed he was in the kitchen, either fixing a meat-based dinner, which her mother wouldn't touch, or else rolling himself a joint. Silence floated over the telephone. Outside, on the West Side Highway, trucks drove by, pelted by rain. The television bled sound from the apartment next door.

"Raining there?" Lila asked, realizing as she always did when she spoke to her father that her speech fell into his pattern. That was how it was with him. People went his way, in his time. Lila wondered if he was always this way, long ago as a child. Did he always take the lead in distinctive silences, in scattered bits of affection? Animals followed him home from the closest general store. Women, Lila noticed, behaved in basically the same way.

"No rain here," he said. "Your mother's gone to exercise class. What's going on?"

"Not so much."

Jeb sighed, emitting a grave rumble, and said, "Kiddo," mildly. Lila thought of Suzanne's smooth face, and how its expression had undoubtedly changed when Lila mentioned the party.

Again, the silence. She literally timed it; watching the clock, she dug her nails into her hand. *Peter Fonda,* she thought, and almost laughed. *Yeah, right.*

"Your mother told me you're teaching a lot. That's good. You're getting the money okay?"

Lila muttered a yes, embarrassed, as she'd been taught to be, by the subject of cash.

"You take care then," Jeb said loudly, having had enough of the phone.

"I might not be around on Sunday," Lila blurted out, finally arriving at the point of her phone call, "so I might not call."

"Going on a trip?"

"Maybe," she said, "Long Island." And she thought *Pria, Pria, Pria,* until it sounded like utter nonsense.

"It's lonely up here without you, bug."

"Well, it's lonely here too," she muttered.

Her father told her to have a good trip, and they both shyly hung up the phone.

The rain was relentless, and she was glad for the rain — it sealed her inside her purpose and everything seemed clearer. Ben, she remembered, had access to a car. Lila dialed his number and he surprised her by picking up right away. "Do you want to come away with me this weekend?" she blurted out.

There was barely even a pause. "Brooklyn wasn't far away enough, was that it?"

"That's right" — she smiled — "I thought we'd go north."

"Then north it is. I want to."

"Do you think you could get hold of a car?"

And to her relief he said that shouldn't be a problem, but where exactly were they going?

She wanted to go to New Hampshire, to get away, she said.

"Do I get to meet Mum and Dad?" he asked. "Might you then sleep in my bed, if they like me?"

"We're not going home," she said.

And when it was all set, she felt excited and sure that Suzanne was not her friend, not her ally at all. There had to be allies somewhere — real ones, not created from her daydreams. She had to find another ally, and Portsmouth didn't seem like a bad place to begin.

Lila looked down at her wrist as she hung up the phone. The bracelet on her wrist was cool and glass and she had always loved the way it reminded her of stones. She remembered the day she'd bought it as being rainy and dank and how the store called Pria had smelled sweet and dry. She couldn't deny how she had returned, over the past three years, in search of the simple pleasure that — however subtle — she'd found there in the jewelry store, on just another rainy day.

CHAPTER SEVENTEEN

Ben had insisted on driving. By the time he and Lila approached the border tollbooth, there had already been three near-accidents, each one causing Ben to mumble something about blind spots and Japanese-made cars. The day was unremarkable — late-April pale — windy with patches of sun. The speed of the car, and Ben seated at her side in his too-short Levi's and requisite moth-eaten cashmere, made Lila more sure of herself than just hours ago, when they had crossed the Whitestone Bridge, fleeing the city. Ben stuck out his narrow hand, upturned, and she dropped in the quarters.

"Not like that," he said, and didn't close his hand. It was one car away from their turn. Ben smiled, and said, "Come again. Go on, give the coins a good smack. I need a solid contact — quarters to palm — or else it's bad luck."

"Bad luck?" Lila said, taking back the quarters. "I don't need that."

"Then on you go, give a firm quarter slap."

"It's our turn!"

"So get it right!" he said, mock serious, stiffening his palm for effect.

And Lila smacked the quarters down without any jangling around, Ben paid up, and they were now in New Hampshire, speeding down 1A and listening to Elvis Costello. Ben lit a cigarette, mouthing the lyrics; he still didn't know the details of their destination. " 'He thought he was the king of America,' " he sang out, knocking on the dashboard, tapping the wheel. The familiar green signs and green trees along the highway made Lila feel this could have been almost any time in her life, years before, or even years to come, this travel north through beginnings of spring, this waiting to arrive. It was absurd, she knew, to have asked Ben along without having told him the purpose of the trip, and it was almost unfair to keep this much from him. But each second she thought about explaining, it seemed impossible. She feared the whole story would seem too complicated, or not complicated enough, or the meaning would be lost in the clumsy delivery. Lila looked at Ben. He didn't seem as if he were waiting for her to explain anything. It was possible that he simply took her at face value, that this trip *was* purely in the name of fun, and all she was after was a salty change of scenery.

"Do we eat fishy things in Portsmouth? Chowder, clammy clams?"

"Anything you please," Lila said, giddy with his presence. She felt like leaning over and kissing where his hair brushed the tip of his small rounded ear. "I don't know," she stammered and then recovered. "I like to get grilled cheese and tomato at an old tin diner by the water. But fishy things sound good too. At your speed, we'll definitely be there in time for lunch."

Lila didn't mention that she'd have some searching to do, that, no matter how much fun he was, she would still have to go her own way for a while, to wade through the currents of strangers. As much as Ben felt good beside her — and he did, he felt better and better to her — he was also too much of an unknown to consider bringing along. Lila had wanted to explain to him, and even planned on telling him everything during this car trip, before they crossed the New Hampshire state line, but the opportunity, she realized, was not going to present itself without drastically changing the mood. And she loved the mood. She loved being on the highway, in transit, just two people going to the same one place. She couldn't, at the moment, imagine needing more than this — the basic back and forth of two people listening to music and discussing lunch. To disrupt such a pleasure didn't seem worth any interruption.

"Are we going near your home, at least?"

"Sort of," Lila mumbled. "I used to come into Portsmouth on the weekends. I learned how to drive when I was really young. I'd take the car whenever I could."

"Your parents never found out?"

"They probably did, and just didn't feel like doing anything about it. But I have my license now, not to worry. I drive far better than you do, believe me," she said, "though I have to say, I enjoy watching you drive."

"Why, thanks," he said, and nothing more. The tape stopped.

"I also came to Portsmouth and stayed with my brother Jack," Lila found herself saying. The car seemed to speed up. "He lived here for a short time, when I was a little kid." A simultaneous relief and discomfiture worked a spell where the music had been.

"And where is Jack now?" Ben asked easily enough, but Lila thought, for a moment, she could detect a certain carefulness in his tone.

There was nothing else she could think to say: "He died," she said, "when I was eight."

"Oh," Ben said, "I didn't know."

"Well," Lila said — as much to Ben as to the trees, the sky, the stretch of highway gray.

"I'm sorry," he said stiffly, looking as far toward her as he could, while keeping his hands on the wheel. Lila smiled, not for any reason other than the fact that she had avoided lying. Ben didn't ask how Jack died, but in a way, this was better for now.

After eating a terrific amount of fish 'n' chips, and checking into one room at the Blue Spruce Motel, Lila and Ben sat on separate beds, making nervous fun of the art on the walls. Lila couldn't help but notice that it was nearly two-thirty, and she had to get out of the room and on to the jewelry store. When she'd pictured the weekend, it seemed entirely feasible that she could slip away alone, possibly unnoticed.

The morning after Ben agreed to come away, Lila had called the store called Pria and asked the man on the phone if she could speak with Pria herself, who turned out to be just across the street getting a tea. Did she want to leave a message? Lila said no, she'd come by on Saturday, and would Pria be working? And Lila was assured that Pria would be there until five. It was just that simple.

Pria would be able to tell Lila something, if only what kind of an impression Aaron and Jack had made at one party, years ago. Lila knew, biased as she was, that her brothers were memorable, especially as a pair. It didn't occur to her that Pria might not remember, whatever kind of person she happened to be.

Lila realized that in her projected version of today, she and Ben were ghostlike, far more separate entities than it felt like they were right then. In fact, it seemed impossible, now, that she could make anything close to a graceful exit. If she were Lana Turner on a Bob Hope comedy special she could don a mysterious smile, twinkle her eyes, and invoke pleasant anticipation. But Ben wasn't prone to admiration for coyness, which was one of the things she liked best about him.

She really had thought she could find Pria on a kind of parallel track, with Ben along but not knowing. She shouldn't *need* to tell him, was what Lila had truly believed, in order for them to have a good time. But watching how relaxed Ben was, lying on his own queen-sized bed, drinking a Coke from the vending machine without any idea of how important this day could be for her, was creating such a mounting sense of anxiety, it was embarrassing to admit it to herself and somehow more impossible to share.

The clock said 3:42. She had to get out.

"Would you mind," Lila asked, as naturally as possible, "maybe splitting up for a while, and meeting later, around dinnertime?"

"You know, we *can* get separate rooms if you want," he said, laughing. "I mean, it seems like a real waste, but if it's making you *this* bonkers —"

"No," Lila said, "I'm not bonkers; this" — she gestured around the thin-walled space — "is all fine, terrific," she said, giving her most uninhibited smile. She even kicked off her shoes and sat in lotus position. "I just have some errand kind of stuff I want to do. Boring stuff."

"I thought that's the point of a weekend getaway," Ben said, sitting up. "Doing stupid errand-type things with the person you've committed to spending two days with."

"I know, but —"

"But what?" He hung his feet off the side of the bed and leaned forward, elbows on his knees. "You thought the drive was about as much time as you could spare?"

"No, I . . ."

Ben was pissed. His eyes weren't watery, but icy clear, and their gaze was demanding.

"I didn't tell you. . . . I forgot, but I —" It was a quarter to four. Even if she wanted to tell him everything now, she just couldn't spare the time. "I promised my mother I'd meet her at a store. I got pressured into it," she said, trying not to seem nervous, which was like trying not to breathe.

"Am I so embarrassing?"

"What?"

"As a friend? Your mother would be that disapproving?" Ben got up and rifled through his bag, procuring a different sweater. "I would have liked to meet her," he said, pulling the sweater on roughly. He started in with his shoes.

"Ben."

"What? You can't talk about it? There's some great big reason you have to lie to me right now, not even a couple hours into being here?"

"This is not what you think."

"I have no *idea* what I think. I would just like to know where you're going right now. This looks bad, you know?"

Lila nodded.

"Can you tell me?" He said it kindly. He did. But it was nearly four o'clock. She had to get to the store, wait for a quiet moment, explain who she was and what she wanted, and arrange a time to talk in private. There were all kinds of things that could go wrong, and she needed to leave time for Pria's tea breaks, the possibility that people leave work early, and sometimes never even show up.

"You don't believe I'm meeting my mother?"

"No, I'm afraid I don't."

"Well," Lila said, putting on her shoes and standing, so that both of them were off the beds and ready to leave, "I have to go, or else I'll be really late. Are you going to meet me later?"

"Where and when do you have in mind?"

She thought about Pria, and tried to leave room for the possibility of a long, informative conversation. "How about eight at O'Shea's. It's by the water."

"O'Shea's at eight."

"Will you be there?" Lila asked, walking out into the carpeted hallway, as Ben stood in the doorway.

"I'm not sure."

"You're not sure?"

"For fuck's sake, Lila, you can't be bothered to tell the truth, and you want me to promise to show up? It doesn't work that way."

"I know."

"So are you going to tell me?"

"Ben," she said, her voice sounding fragile and fake, "I have to go. I'll —"

"No, that's fine, that's all right. Go," he spit out. "It'll be nice to walk alone by the pier. I'll have a proper time of it, brooding, et cetera. Go on," Ben said. "Go."

He was disappointed. It was *almost* impossible to hear. "Ben," Lila said, "I —"

"What's that?" he asked. Lila couldn't speak. "Nothing? That's what I thought."

Portsmouth seemed larger than the way it had looked in her mind for the past nine months. She knew this town; she'd come for dinner at the Stock Pot with her family in its various stages, gone shopping with friends down on State Street, drank too much coffee at the Elvis Room. It was the closest thing to a metropolis that was near enough to their woods, and she'd always been grateful for its village delights. The streets never matched what she wanted in a town, though — quaintness never meant enough. But now, after spending a stretch of time in New York, managing to come back as little as possible — home only once for Christmas Eve and day — this town took on an appealing beauty for which she felt unprepared.

Lila thought about how odd it was that she had been to the jewelry store a number of times. A woman with short black hair consistently worked the counters, and Lila remembered being curious about her, because she usually said nothing. Even if Lila made a purchase, the woman remained silent as she rang up the purchase and carefully put it in a bag. Then she'd smile as she handed over the goods, as if she were letting you, briefly, into a better world. The store seemed less like a store than someone's home. This kind of laid-back sales approach seemed to work, for each time Lila came to Portsmouth, she always returned to the store. Judging from the decorative additions to the place, and the subtle price increases, she wasn't the only one. The last time she had been there was August, immediately before her stint in college. Lila had wanted to buy a few dozen tiny bottle-green beads, with which she'd meant to string together a choker, but the store had been too crowded, and the summer heat made nothing seem worth the wait.

Lila picked up her pace and passed one of the many salty-looking men in this town — men down on their luck for lack of naval-yard jobs. This man slouched on a bench in a roadside planter and made a strange kind of picture with his weathered skin and threadbare layers amid the newly planted crocus bulbs and tulip buds. He sat still as the cars passed him by. And there were two girls with green nail polish and too much hairspray, no more than fourteen years old. Lila passed these and many other people and thought about how Suzanne's comments about Pria were distinctly bitter. Suzanne had been such a great disappointment, and now the memories of

Suzanne, which Lila had somehow treasured, looked deflated in her mind's eye — not much brighter than the blur of other friendly older girls who'd attracted her brothers' attentions. Had Suzanne been important to Aaron? It was now tough to say. If Suzanne had no idea where Aaron was either, maybe all that intensity Lila thought she'd witnessed hadn't been so intense at all. Or maybe it was only the accident that cast Suzanne as romantic and exceptional, and really, she was just one more girl to pass through the house.

She wondered — as she rounded the corner, a block from Pria — about love: who had it and when, who has it and why, and if it counted when the one you loved did not or could not quite love you back. Her love for her brothers was surely unrequited, for she'd been searching for years in one way or another, for as long as she could remember. With every passing moment Aaron and Jack became more real, and she was left only wanting them closer with every year gone by. Lila knew she poured her purest self toward an empty space, and there was never much of her left over for whoever might be curious. Lila wondered, as she saw the store in the distance, if Ben would be at the bar later, and if it were even possible for her to love a person who actually showed up. It didn't seem that such a love — one who answered when you questioned — could compare to this fast silence that lived within her and told her where to go.

The store had a painted purple door, with a small black-and-white sign, as if it were a club. When Lila arrived, she spotted the dark-haired woman immediately, opening a glass case of necklaces for a group of what looked like college kids — maybe UNH — who were milling around. There were three girls and two guys and it was amazing that they were probably how old Jack was when he died. They even wore the same kind of clothes that Jack used to wear, clothes he wore in a certain picture that Lila kept inside her head, as the exact way he was. In the photograph lives Jack, perched in a tree, wearing baggy brown cords, a red, yellow, blue, and green thread-bare flannel over at least three more layers of thinner shirts. She loved how Jack dressed — as if he forgot that he could actually buy new clothes every now and then, instead of wearing what he found in the storage room or Jeb's studio — but on these kids, the kind of kids she grew up with, Jack's clothes were reduced to a style, a hippie-dippy style that was grating and made her pleased she'd showered this morning, that she was wearing black, nothing exceptionally baggy, and berry-colored lipstick. She felt proud not to be caught in another era's trends and then, of course, she was ashamed for caring at all.

But here was this group of people essentially her own age, who had agreed — at least implicitly — to wander into this store together. Lila realized she couldn't imagine how such a thing could transpire, how people became friends. She tried to think of a time when she did this kind of lazy wandering in and out of stores with other people, and although Lila knew she did it in high school not so long ago, the very nature of spending time with a group seemed foreign. They looked so comfortable together, these kids in the store, and without any apparent couples, their bodies seemed to know when to be close and when to be distant. A tall guy with wheat-colored hair rested his hands on a short girl's shoulders, and they both pointed out a bracelet to a freckled redhead who swung a plastic bag at his side. The yellow bag, the girl's blue shoes, scribble written on the tall guy's hand, these details were as vibrant as the sets of beads and rows of silver, and she felt like a Peeping Tom, searching for nothing besides what constituted a genuine sense of ease.

"Those earrings I bought last week brought me great luck," the short girl told the dark-haired woman who must have been Pria.

"I'm glad," she responded, and nodded, giving that same cryptic smile. Then she held a necklace up to her already adorned neck. "It's new," she told the group, who listened very carefully.

Any one of these people, Lila thought, would probably be showing Ben a good time now, or at least would be showing him some places to go. Any one of these people wouldn't be absurdly possessive of their past. Everyone did have sad stories, it was true, so why did she need to keep hers secret?

After the group left, the store recovered its familiar lull, and a gray cat appeared and slinked in circles between Lila's legs. The woman who was Pria sank into a pale pink velvet sofa, where an identical cat was fast asleep. She looked at Lila, smiled graciously, and then began to bead a nearly completed necklace. For a moment, dark-haired Pria looked surprisingly matronly. Her scoop-necked white shirt revealed a wrinkled chest, and a cluster of nut-brown sunspots. Besides the rows of oddly shaped beads at her neck, and the thin silver hoop nose pierce, she could have been anyone's suburban mom, smiling a daily greeting. Lila tried to keep her eyes on a row of earrings, so she wouldn't stare too obviously. The store was empty, besides Lila and the woman who just had to be Pria. This was just the way she had planned it, and she didn't want to blurt anything too suddenly. Lila knew Pria would never make conversation. This was the kind of place where you could browse for as long as you were inclined, where the management would close the place down before asking if you needed help.

She looked ethnic, but unidentifiably so, and could have been anywhere from a very weathered thirty-five to a very youthful fifty. She had circles under her eyes like Lila's mother, the kind that said, *This person will always look tired, but simultaneously attractive; they will never have to try to draw you into their gaze.*

"This pair," Lila began, "may I see them?"

Pria rose from the couch and both cats followed her. "Those are my favorite," she said, as she took the earrings from the case, sounding not at all, somehow, as if she were trying to make a sale. As Lila fingered the silver and blue glass beads, Pria said, "Try them on, go ahead." And Pria and Lila both looked at Lila's reflection in the mirror. Pria was nearly Lila's height, and she smelled like baby oil and newly blown-out candles. "They go with your eyes."

"Beautiful," Lila said, the only word she could think to say, and she told Pria she'd take them.

"Do you know," Pria said, after the exchange was made, "I'm afraid I need to close by four today. I'm sorry, I know the sign says five."

"That's okay," Lila said, fingering the earrings. "I've been here plenty of times."

"You live in town?"

"No, I . . . I grew up in the area. My brother used to live here, and I visited," she said, unsure of whether she should introduce herself first, or simply mention Jack's name. "I think you knew him, actually. Are you Pria?" Lila asked, as Pria nodded and kept her expression pleasant, unresistant.

"Pria Dajani," she said, holding out her hand.

Lila reached for the thin long fingers; Pria's hand felt warm and was as smooth as it looked. "I'm Lila Wheeler," she said, releasing her hand.

Pria's expression changed at that point, but she remained silent and kept nodding, as if she should have known.

"You knew Jack?" Lila asked, feeling the bottom begin to fall out of this day, the part that she'd kept held high. "And Aaron?"

"I knew there was a sister."

"That's me," Lila said, feeling proud and sad. "I just found out that it was your party, you know, the night of Jack's accident, and I was wondering . . ." Lila was talking too fast and she made herself breathe. She noticed, as the setting sun shone through the window, that Pria's eyes looked very light green, so light they were almost yellow.

"You want to talk about it."

"Please," Lila said, and Pria went in the back room to grab her things. Lila held on to the earrings, as she watched Pria lock up; then they both walked out into the April evening, brisk with fading light.

"I didn't have to close early for any good reason," Pria admitted.

"So you have some time."

"Well, you deserve a little time, don't you think?" And then Pria laughed a laugh free of bitter stitches, as if Lila were the guest, weary with travel, whom she had been expecting.

Up four flights of stairs in a yellow-painted house, Pria lived in the turret — an L-shaped studio with very high ceilings and wide-planed hardwood floors. The place was small, but clean and bright, with a sense of perpetual breeze. There were light blue walls in the front part, where Pria's bed stretched under three tall windows, and bright white walls in the back part, where the kitchen hosted small photographs tacked up, one pin for each, of a wide array of subjects from people in cities, to blades of grass, a black-and-white set of eyes and a forehead. Lila sat at the kitchen table, leaning into the dark oak, and watched Pria make tea with lemon rind and cinnamon sugar; steaming water poured from a copper pot.

"This morning," Pria intoned, in the slightly underwater timbre of her voice, "these lights up above blinked on and off, and seconds later this teapot spontaneously cracked, without my even touching it." Pria added mint leaves to the tea as she continued, "I knew something was coming today. I had a feeling."

Lila nodded, unsure of what to say. As Pria brought tea to the table, Lila's mind worked on at least two planes at once, commenting to Ben in one corner of her mind: the woman was a total flake. But in the other corner there was less volume maybe but definitely a voice: *This is all you have going, and it's going better than Suzanne went, so drink your tea. Open your mind.*

Pria sat down, bowed her head, and closed her eyes briefly. Lila realized she was praying. A moment later she opened her eyes and took a sip of tea. "I've gone through a lot since the time I knew Jack —" she began, then stopped herself. "How much, exactly, do you know about me?"

"Nothing," Lila said, and she couldn't imagine what there was to know.

"I've had a lot of crossroads, you know? I try to be honest about my past, because it fades quicker that way. I was stripping for cash and spending it quickly and unwisely. I had a lot more of it than I do now, but I live now, you know what I'm saying? That wasn't living." She reached for a tin on the counter, and took out a cigarette, and offered them to Lila. "My one remaining vice," she said, and smiled. "I like them with strong peppermints. You can really feel your breath."

"No, thanks."

"This place isn't much, but I have my store, and that's something I'm really into because it's mine." Lila wondered if she should interrupt and reroute Pria's disclosure, but decided against it. There was a silence, the sounds of her own sipping and swallowing. The tea was disgusting. "So," Pria said, which was close enough to the question of *Why are we sitting here?*

"I knew they'd been at a party that night, but I never bothered to ask about it, and —"

"Why?"

"I don't know," Lila said, surprised by the question. "I guess I didn't connect the party to Jack's accident."

"And now?" Pria asked.

"Now I want to know everything about that night. I want to know how it ever could have happened. Everything seems so precarious, I can never picture it. I . . ." Lila had an urge to stop herself; she let the urge pass. "I can't stop thinking about both of my brothers. It's as if it's occurred all over again, or I just recently found out. I feel like I don't know what happened to my family. The more anyone tells me the story of what happened that night, the more I can't believe it." Lila felt her face grow hot, as the full force of her neediness surged. "And I want to find my brother. I don't know if you know this, but Aaron went away after Jack died, and he stayed away. We don't know where he is."

"He disappeared?"

Lila nodded, and Pria seemed surprised. "He was smart," Pria said.

"To run off?"

"Oh, no." Pria laughed. "I meant he was intelligent. I remember. I've wondered what became of him. I've wondered what became of you, too, even though I never met you. Maybe it wasn't true, but I heard you witnessed it."

Lila was prepared to ask questions, not answer them. This was not the time to share her vivid picture of Jack on the rocks, his head smeared with blood, and drool down his chin.

"After," she eventually responded, "I got there after. I didn't witness the big event." She heard the hostile side of herself she knew and hated, the attitude that she'd been trying, these past eight months, to unlearn.

"That must have been difficult for you, growing up."

"It was okay," she snapped, then nicely, "It was fine." She imagined the phone calls home she'd made in the past months, how the image of the telephone ringing between wood walls that no longer contained her was definitely thrilling. She wondered if that was how Aaron felt — exhilaration from being gone.

"Did you *date* Jack?"

Pria shook her head. "Jack was a restless kid. He was still living at home, and was usually in no condition to go back there. I was restless too, but I was older, and a woman, so I ended up taking care of him, or that's how it seemed at the time. I used to tell people we were 'friends with a sparkle,' which seems so ridiculous now. We were really just screwing around, I guess." Lila felt embarrassed, and oddly annoyed, but Pria didn't seem to notice. "But Jack had a way of making me feel like I was doing a good deed, letting him into my bed." Pria took smoke deep into her lungs, holding it there for a few seconds. "But, really, we were friends. I guess he mentioned his brother pretty early on. First I knew just factual things, like his name, and that he went to a good school, and all that. Jack talked about you too. He was crazy about you."

Lila smiled, in spite of herself. She felt faint with relief.

"Jack liked to call Aaron 'the Ken Doll with Brains.' He thought Aaron was really arrogant; he was jealous of his big brother, no question of that."

This was surprising. Lila knew Aaron was the handsome one, the one who studied and succeeded, but Jack made decisions, or that was how it had seemed. He always seemed happier than Aaron, and more in control. She had thought Jack did exactly what Jack wanted to do.

"He really pissed Jack off," Pria continued, "but Jack pissed me off a good deal of the time, so I guess I began thinking of Aaron as a hero. I had a crush, although I'd never met him, and the more Jack answered my questions about him, the more I liked what I heard. After Jack and I stopped messing around, he'd tease me with promises that I'd get to meet Aaron. So one night I have a party, and Jack shows up with the famous brother, who has a girlfriend."

"Suzanne," Lila said, as neutrally as possible.

"Suzanne," Pria repeated, no more than confirmation.

"What was the party like?"

"Terrible," Pria said, and laughed. "They were all terrible. I was lonely and always inviting people over, and then I'd spend the whole night praying that they'd leave. It was not a good chapter. The house was basically toxic. I'm sorry, I know this is not about me."

"It's your life too. Your party."

"I just liked him," Pria said, lowering her eyes, the wrinkles in her forehead becoming pronounced. "She was lucky, I thought. I wondered what made her so special."

"Who? Suzanne?"

"Aaron was mad about her, probably unhealthily so," Pria said gravely, and Lila felt another wave of relief — the restoration of Aaron and Suzanne's unique intensity. *So I was right,* she thought, *they were in love.*

"I talked to her," Lila blurted. "I looked for her with no luck, and then I bumped into her on the street in New York."

Pria nodded. "Mmm," she said, "you called her to you."

Lila knew she should let that one go. "You believe that? That I called her to me? What about the fact that she lives basically in my neighborhood?"

"Fine. What about the fact that you always

come back to my store, and I notice you each time, and never know why?"

"You noticed me?"

"What about the fact that my lights short-circuited for the first time in years and this antique pot cracked, all today? I'm just saying things are maybe more connected than we can ever know. I'm saying it pays to stay awake."

"I'm awake," Lila said.

Pria smiled and put out her cigarette. Lila found herself smiling too, releasing breath she was unaware she was holding. She made a wish just then, a wish that Ben would be at O'Shea's. She, in fact, prayed. Because after all, Lila did descend on Pria today, the day of the flashing lights and crumbling appliances, bringing questions concerning a night of death. How could Lila say, after all, what or who was or was not a harbinger of her progress? Maybe she did call Suzanne to her, maybe signs were flashing everywhere, ones she maybe couldn't see but could learn to feel. Then again, she thought, reaching for the tin of mints, maybe not.

"You talked with Suzanne?" Pria asked, more subdued.

"We spoke just days ago. She said she didn't remember the party."

"Did you believe her?"

"No," Lila said, and something dissolved inside her, remembering the clean loft and Suzanne's glossy hair. Through Pria's window, the sky deepened; wind chimes sounded through the open window. Lila felt she was nowhere, yet moving forward. Pria may have been from a slightly different planet, but Lila realized that she trusted her, that it was right to come. "Tell me," she said. "Please tell me what you know."

"Would you like more tea?"

Lila shook her head. She wondered, at this very moment, what Ben was doing. "Please tell me."

Pria poured herself more tea, and looked at Lila as if to assess something she'd previously overlooked. Then she began. "Aaron was nervous. Jack hadn't mentioned that. He . . . for one thing, Suzanne was . . . after Jack. And from what I understand, Jack didn't object. I think they messed around behind Aaron's back."

"Jack? How do you know?" Lila said, feeling sick to her stomach — the small amount of tea she'd drunk sloshed around inside her.

"Apart from its being obvious, she told me. Jack was all she could think about. She spilled it all to me, after she threw up in my bathroom. She toyed with Aaron so viciously that night. As for Jack, he needed attention. Of

352

course he enjoyed it. He flirted shamelessly with everyone, men and women alike." Pria laughed again, crow's-feet framing her golden eyes. Jack and Suzanne loomed large and wild, while Aaron's aquiline nose, his hazel eyes, broad shoulders, and deep voice shrank into a boy's despair, a boy with a broken heart. "This was, what, ten years ago?" Pria continued. "But I remember it better than you'd think, and not only because Jack died. The night was memorable on its own. Aaron was so nervous, and the way she looked at Jack — it killed Aaron, you could tell. Everything was loose, too loose, though I would have never said that then. I have to confess this has haunted me a bit. I felt guilty for a long while."

"Why?"

"Good question. Guilt is nothing but energy circling in on itself, a total waste of time."

"Yeah, but why did you feel guilty?"

"Because I told Aaron how tricky his girlfriend was. Because I wanted him for myself, and tried my best to get him. And Jack, poor guy, was a show-off by nature, and when he was under attack he was at his worst. He'd do anything. That's what I think must have happened when Aaron confronted them." Lila pictured the jagged rocks, Jack's lanky body jumping higher and higher, missing his footing, with Suzanne standing by, egging him on and on. "You poor kid," Pria said, "you need some answers, I can feel it. You need some closure."

"I do," Lila finally said. "I do. I keep thinking there's some question I'm forgetting to ask. I don't know what else to say."

"Be with yourself for a while. Be in silence if you like. I'm going to do some things in the front room. Please feel free to spend some time here, whatever you need."

Pria left Lila sitting alone at the kitchen table, where she played with a pepper mill, and told herself to stop, to be still, to think of what she would say to Suzanne, of what she would say to Ben. She could swear she heard Pria singing or chanting, but when she listened more carefully the sound faded out into the radio playing NPR in low, serious tones. As Lila poured salt in perfect tiny piles, and watched the shaker's glass make soft indentations, she remembered Jack at a diner, calling to a waitress in a loud, funny voice, his eyes never stopping long enough to look at anything, how he rarely ate, but loved ordering exotic desserts, how he lifted her higher than she ever anticipated. She could still remember the feeling of being lifted high, how the difference between her brothers' lifting styles was that Aaron placed her on his shoulders, on his back, while Jack swung her around, and kept her dangled by the ankles, always until she screamed.

Maybe she'd tell Ben everything and leave it at that. Maybe Aaron really wouldn't want to see her at all; maybe too much time had passed, and she was forcing something that was never meant to be. Pria's story was an ugly story; the characters were common. Lila knew she should leave soon, at least to find Ben, who was out there somewhere, hopefully in town, and she looked out the window as if to find him where the sky was night-dark and hazy and the chimes barely stirred.

Pria sent her off with a charm: a bunch of dried sage tied by three strands of Pria's hair, an unpolished rose quartz, plus four beads — blue for peace, silver for time, green for the natural world, and a bronze lion for strength — enclosed in a purple cloth. For luck? Lila had asked, and Pria told her to smell it, and answered that it was for all good things, that a little beauty never hurt, when facing the unknown. The charm smelled like Aaron, or at least how she imagined Aaron to smell, and Lila tucked the charm in the bag from Pria's store, and put on the earrings she'd bought just hours ago, which looked better than she remembered. "Stay in the present," Pria also said, to which Lila said, "Huh?" but understood that memories couldn't replace anything, no matter how strong, and they couldn't make changes for you. Suzanne must have memories, Lila thought, as she descended the narrow stairwell, and Suzanne must ignore those memories every day, and think to herself how easily she got away with deceit, how she was near to death and was left unscarred. Suzanne had stayed in the present, that was for sure, and her place in the world must have been secured by immediately learning to forget. Lila had no doubt that Suzanne was good at letting go.

The house glowed in the darkness as Lila walked away. It was one house in the world, and she thought of her own rented bedroom, her parents in their house by the pond, Suzanne in the airy loft. She believed with all of her being that it was impossible to give too much significance to each one of these places. Each doorway was distinct and hallowed. For there was a holy aspect to all homes — a unique and singular power.

But when she closed her eyes and imagined Aaron, he was always at large in the world. Lila craved knowing where he called home, and she needed to know at least that: the one house, tent, boat, apartment, or motel, in the one particular place. And beyond knowing where Aaron lived, Lila needed to go further and attain some kind of closure, wherein the houses and lofts and rented rooms would be — first and foremost — places where people lived their lives, where the present was important and ever-changing and separate from the past.

As she looked into the closed shops — old-lady displays alongside surfer-chick style — she saw two teenage boys walking together, and something kicked at her throat and pricked her skin. Jack was jealous and disloyal, where she'd imagined him to be free and easy, and Suzanne was fickle at best. Maybe Aaron never even knew exactly what went on behind his back, and was so racked with guilt over Jack's accident that he not only couldn't face Suzanne but doubted everything that went on that weekend, questioned each moment to such an extent that he couldn't stand it anymore. *Maybe*, Lila thought, as she watched the boys turn onto a side street, *he was like me, unable to get beyond the same story, the same suspicious feeling, and maybe disassociation was the only way he could do it.* Because Pria was right: Aaron *was* some kind of hero, or at least that was how he tried to behave. To be betrayed by Suzanne, and to have also failed to save Jack, whom Lila knew he loved, must have shattered his sense of reality.

She sensed these events slipping away from her, as they changed shape in her mind. And as they changed, Ben no longer seemed as much of a stranger, for he was more familiar than this new version of the past. She needed to tell him everything, before she doubted what even happened and didn't happen that night.

O'Shea's had a good crowd. A game of pool had already started, and Ben was one of the players. He was a stylish player, which didn't surprise her, and the balls shot around the table in hard, fast lines. When he looked up and noticed Lila, she was already at the bar, and she offered him a smile he didn't return. People were watching him and she knew that made him happy. She felt what she would later identify as the first real pang of intimacy toward him, because she knew right away how he was feeling, without ever doubting. Even as his face was hardened, she knew the crowd was stirring him up, and helping him along. Lila drank a Coke, ordered a beer without being carded, went to the bathroom and fussed with her hair, put on lipstick and powder, came back and drank the beer, and then another, and watched Ben play pool until she nearly got up and yelled for him to please stop, to come have a whiskey, baby. He would have maybe enjoyed such a spectacle, had he been disposed to liking her right then, but Lila knew she had driven him to ignore her. At first she kept calm, or calm enough, at his utter lack of response to her presence, but as she failed, time after time, to catch his eye, Lila began to realize that no matter how honestly she chose to behave now, it would simply be too late. He smiled, and her heart sped up, until she realized he was smiling at two girls at a table. Of course he had made friends here already. Of course he was well taken care of with or without her, and he was probably ignoring her, not because he was hurt, but because he genuinely was sick of her, and had nothing more to say. So she sat and sipped beer, and fingered Pria's charm, devised systems of how to wish upon each bead, the bunch of sage, the quartz that felt cool to the touch. She wished for at least one more chance with Ben, and she wished for it over and over again, until she was familiar with each object in the purple cloth.

Ben's opponent was tall and stout, with a belt buckle in the shape of a dog bone, and he took his sweet time angling a shot, looking as if he might fall onto the table at the slightest turn. Color rose to Ben's pale face, no doubt in frustration, and he took off his sweater to reveal a V-necked T-shirt that made him look about fifteen years old. To her confusion, the longer he made her wait, and the funnier-looking he became, the more strongly Lila found herself tapping her foot on the bar, fighting with herself not to rush up to him for real, to tell him she was no longer nervous about the same things. She would change, she wanted to explain, and right then, she knew she'd mean it.

As Ben finally received the money he won, he stuffed it into his pocket without counting, and Lila did approach him, apparently not cautiously enough, for he stepped back and bit his lip before digging into his other pocket and handing over a key. "For the motel," he explained.

"Oh, come on," Lila said, and although she was smiling, leaning into one hip, she felt a sob spiraling up her throat.

"Look," he said, lazily running a hand through his hair, "I don't know what you expect; I really don't." The bar was filling up, and she thought she recognized two people who were arguing. The lights were orange and the air was cool, as if it were snowing outside.

"Please," she said, and she swallowed before speaking deliberately. "Please just come outside with me. Just come onto the docks with me for a minute."

"I don't think so, Lila," he said. "I don't know what you thought was going to happen here, but this wasn't what I had in mind. I don't appreciate being anyone's sidekick." And he pulled his sweater back over his head, picked up his bag, which was set down in the corner. He waved to a young woman who crossed to the ladies' room, who smiled at him as she went through the door.

"I see you've spent a lot of time here."

"Well, I wasn't going to buy souvenirs for four hours, was I?"

"Please," she said, and she reached for his hand, which must have shocked him as much as it shocked her, because he flinched and agreed to come outside, to take a walk by the water.

The blacktop path that ran along the water was functional, and although there were public gardens not far away, the patch of waterfront where Ben and Lila walked was empty of adornment. The water rippled when it caught a bit of wind, sloshing around the docks and the buoys. "You're good at pool," she told him, as he threw the motel key up in the air and caught it, for the third time.

"I'm quite competitive."

There was an impersonal silence, nothing peaceful about it.

"Come on!" Ben finally yelled.

"What?"

"What? You're asking *me* what?" Ben stopped walking, and stood solidly planted before her. He took a breath. "Look, what is it you want?"

She looked at Ben, his hair tossing in the wind, whipping around his head, and she remembered meeting him in the park that very first day. They had just walked away from each other. They had simply said good-bye and disappeared into crowds. And what an absence appeared when he was gone. Who would have known that she had enough room inside her to miss yet another person?

Now Lila wanted to tell him something better than the truth, something that would excuse her from all bad behavior. Her second chance had come, and now it was almost gone.

Everyone had sad stories, it was true, so why did she have to keep hers secret?

Lila kissed him with the kind of desperation she had never quite allowed herself, and the wind stung her skin nearly raw and blew her hair into wicked knots, and when Ben responded tentatively, putting his hands on her waist — that touch, even through her bulky sweater, was enough to set her loose, crying in dry heaves at first, her eyes wide open, staring at the black water below. "It's all right," he said unconvincingly, and they both sat down on a wooden bench to find out if it was.

She told him her story — from the moment she met Suzanne ten years ago, to Pria's psychic bent — and just as nothing came out how she had planned or imagined, she realized that Ben had his thumbnail between his teeth, and he was listening, actively listening, making sure to hear every word. When she was finished, and she had even showed him Pria's charm, he drew her down, so that her head was in his lap, and he started working out the knots in her hair. "Suzanne," Ben finally said, as if to clarify, breaking a spell of bleary quiet. Then he said her brothers' names, and the boys she knew them to be at the fatal ages of nineteen and twenty declared themselves in the briny wind before dissolving into Ben's voice, and the word *Aaron* and the word *Jack* were, for a moment, barely more than words.

Ben asked her if she'd like to go back to the motel, and she told him yes, in a minute, let's just watch this one boat pass. And Lila sat up, as they watched the boat — a cabin cruiser — fade out of sight. Ben's palm cupped the nape of her neck, and she held his other hand, but as she stared out to sea, eyeing the cruiser, she couldn't help but wonder about who was inside, if they were coming or going, if, perhaps, they were running away.

CHAPTER EIGHTEEN

It wasn't how she'd imagined. Lila hadn't known what to imagine before she did it, and now that it was done, and done two times, she still didn't have a precise feeling of *that* was what *it* was. The Blue Spruce Motel called to mind pale skin, which fit with what part and how, but the parts Lila recalled most vividly were the parts she'd already known. What she thought of, on the almost astral drive back to Manhattan, wasn't so much the act of sex (which wasn't nearly as painful as she'd expected; in fact, it barely hurt at all), but the surrounding elements of her own hair in her eyes, Ben's breath in her face, and her toes' light touch to his thin, shaking legs as he laid himself down beside her.

She'd felt heavy. Not fat, as she'd feared, but massive somehow, pinned to the bed by a force that was as assuring as it was confusing. A power had arisen on its own, separate from whatever power existed between her and Ben. This separate force shot up from beneath the mildewy carpeted floor and settled deep within her. Lila felt herself grow and expand far beyond the confines of her body. Her fingers reached farther than she knew them to reach; there had seemed to be more air. As Ben touched the knots of her spine, she'd felt diaphanous, and briefly laughed. She never closed her eyes. For that timeless couple of minutes or so, she had forgotten about Suzanne.

On the drive back to Manhattan, everything looked brighter, and her place in the world felt more sharply defined as separate from the trees and the highway and the thousands of other cars. She was in *this* particular car, and she was next to Ben, who sat his wiry body behind the wheel, giving off his particular sense of ease. While she had urges to touch him again, she also felt separate, moored to the car seat, but able to slip away, perhaps more easily than she would have imagined or considered possible. Lila had thought that if they went through with it, she would feel absorbed by him, and perhaps absolved from her range of discomforts, which, as it happened, was not the case at all. Though Ben kept squeezing her shoulder, running his hand over her messy hair, she was still on her own, still her addled self, looking out the same borrowed car window, and thinking about Suzanne E. Wolfe, Suzanne Hannon, wife, art dealer, fan of orchids and lilies.

When they returned that Sunday night, Lila hadn't intended on staying at Ben's apartment, but they were both hungry and Ben had a full fridge and felt like cooking. After linguini and pesto, an enormous pot of broccoli, and a bottle of red wine, they started kissing on the couch, and by the time they acknowledged it was happening again, they were skidding, naked, from the living room into the bedroom. Lila felt as if this were the most real part of her — the part that was naked and giggling — but as soon as she acknowledged how good she felt, she crashed into self-consciousness, making sure the lights got turned off, thinking about each moment as if she were being watched. Lila tried to remove Suzanne from her mind and focus on Ben alone, but as she did so, she questioned Ben's desire, even as he kissed her fingers, her neck, even as he held her shoulders — her strong, capable shoulders — gently, as if they were the first he'd ever held. She questioned him in her mind, even as he worked his way over her body with the kind of rapt attention she was sure she'd never known.

Streetlights poured through the windows, though the shades were drawn. A breeze filled the room as they lay facing each other, and above the bed, papers tacked to the wall lifted their sides like half-etherized moths, as Ben made his way inside her. She felt a flickering there, a piercingly good feeling, and it was all she could do not to squirm and pull her own hair, to stop herself from making sounds, which she knew would embarrass her beyond distraction. Ben rocked himself against her, as she stayed more still than she knew she should, while she wavered between pure thought and pure feeling. Good and bad didn't seem to apply to the world inside her body; it was too unfamiliar there to know yet what to call these sensations. She had never masturbated; she had never wanted to. What was happening inside was no more or less than shocking but she did not want it to stop.

Ben seemed to be terrified of stopping; he went back and forth in a kind of panic, until finally Lila grabbed his back and pulled herself beneath him, and he cried out in a lower voice than she'd ever heard him utter. For a long time, he lay collapsed on top of her, which was just where she wanted him to be. Ben was light enough that he didn't crush her but heavy enough for her to feel covered, and covered was what she wanted now. He worked his way down and kissed her breasts, then met her eyes in the darkened room. "Just call me Speedy," he said, in a voice that betrayed the lightness of his joke. As she smiled, he wove his fingers inside her ropy curls.

"Speedy," she said, "Speedy, oh, Speedy," and then: "As if I'd know what is too short a time! That seemed good," she said, apparently unconvincingly.

"Lila," he said in a small voice; her name never sounded so tragic. He rolled off of her and lay flat on his back, his hands beneath his head.

She had made him feel bad. *No,* she thought, *you shouldn't feel bad; it's me who's feeling the displacement, the self-consciousness — you? You're just fine; you have smooth sleek skin, and confidence. You have grace.* "Ben," she said, just to say his name, the way she did sometimes, "Ben." And Lila reached out and touched the lone blue vein below his shoulder on his chest. She knew where it was, after seeing it briefly in daylight. She traced it, and felt his small arm muscles, his slight but solid chest. Lila kissed his ear, without thinking. "You make me feel . . ." But she couldn't complete the sentence, for she wasn't sure of the word.

"I'm just not certain," Ben said carefully, "that I make you feel anything."

"But you do," she insisted, but as she said so, she unwittingly thought of when she could go find Suzanne and lacerate her. In spite of the importance of this moment, Lila couldn't help wanting to go right then. How had she even progressed this far with Ben? Lila couldn't possibly belong here, but she wanted to, and she knew that what she wanted was to convince Ben to love her, in order to leave. She wanted both.

"You can't be feeling bad or distant or whatever you are feeling, and not have me feel it too," he said simply.

"I can't?"

"I'm afraid not." She tried to kiss him, but he kept on talking. "Are you thinking about that woman?"

"Hmm?"

"Your brother's girlfriend. Are you thinking about her?"

"No," Lila said, and got a piercing flash of Suzanne's pondside nakedness, her long wet hair. "I'm not," Lila insisted, and persisted in a kiss, focusing all her energy into Ben's mouth.

"Lila," Ben said, dead set on meeting her eyes. "What are you doing?"

"What do you mean?" *If I get to Suzanne's before eight A.M.,* Lila thought, while stroking Ben's hair, *I'll be sure to catch her.* "I'm being affectionate."

"Well, I am too. I'm affectionately asking you to stop."

369

Lila took her hand from Ben's soft hair. She looked at him, and felt a dull ache in her back. It seemed impossible to sustain a feeling for longer than a moment; she seemed doomed to have a minimal attention span, sexually or otherwise. The only thing that stayed fixed was Suzanne and her brothers and the question of *why* they dominated, still, instead of receding into more current life concerns. In her head she realized she was always planning. At that moment, looking into Ben's blue eyes, she was planning how she'd wait for Richard to leave the apartment, and how, if he didn't leave by nine-thirty or so, she'd assume he was away on business, and she would press Suzanne's buzzer until Suzanne answered. The wall of paintings flashed through her mind.

"I'm sorry," she said.

"For what?"

"For the way I've been behaving. I must not be much good."

"You're splendid," Ben assured her. "You are splendidly good fun in bed."

"Just not now," Lila said.

"Just not now." He said, "The thing is, I'd just very much like to know where you are."

She answered quietly: "I'm outside Suzanne Wolfe's apartment building. I'm standing on the pavement and everything is quiet. I'm waiting."

"For what?"

Lila closed her eyes and felt how truly dead Jack was. As much as she tried to find him, there was no access to that place, the place beyond the blood bubble that hung from nose to mouth, beyond the quality of air that hung suspended, surrounding just the two of them, Jack and Lila, on the wet hard rocks, before he was taken away. "I saw him dead," she said. "Or almost dead. I hung on to him there, at the pond. And Suzanne — she was there too."

Ben touched her shoulder, but she couldn't quite feel his hand.

"Suzanne just stood there, watching my brother's body, and watching me. She not only saw how it happened," Lila said, "but she saw my last moment with Jack. What right does she have to such a personal — the most personal — view of my life? What right does she have to my memories?"

"To *your* memories? But —"

"I just need to get inside. I need to see her."

"You need to blame her."

"I think she deserves some blame, don't you?"

Ben waited a moment too long to respond.

"So you think I'm being crazy?" she asked,

drawing the covers farther up, so they nearly touched her collarbone. "You think these things happen, and she was young and stupid, and that was that?"

"I don't know what I think," he said, raising his voice. "I don't know enough."

"You do. I told you everything."

"But —"

"What was unclear?" she asked, and reached for her T-shirt, which was draped on the bedside table, and she pulled it over her head, which calmed her, if only slightly.

"Nothing, I —"

"What don't you understand? My brother Aaron was in love with Suzanne. In *love*, crazy about her, willing to do anything for her, and what happens when he brings her home? She charms us all, and then makes a play for my brother Jack."

"You talk as if this just happened yesterday, as if you were there with them in bed or something."

"It did — I was. It feels as if I was there this morning. That's just the way it is with me." As she said this, it occurred to her that Jack also saw Suzanne's naked breasts by the pond, and how he was no doubt conned into thinking he was special, how he was dazzled because she was dazzling. Lila, now lying in Ben's bedroom, having tasted her first real dash of lust, could imagine Jack and Aaron more clearly tonight than she perhaps ever had before. Both of her brothers felt very much alive.

If she left now, her familiar questions would be sharpened and defined, and when she saw Suzanne, she would be ready. This heightened state of awareness would only make her more impervious to lies. Lila knew or hoped this with the same measure of confidence that hinted at a time in her future when answers could never possibly mean this much.

"I guess I don't need to ask where you're going," Ben finally replied, and he sat back on his bed, not rising to say good-bye.

Although it was late, and these tree-lined Sunday streets were basically deserted, Lila felt less afraid than excited. It was not warm enough to stay outside for hours without getting a chill, but it was perfect walking temperature — a slice of each season hung on the air. The trees — the ones under which she had followed Suzanne and Richard that first Sunday — were greening; their skeletal patterns on the dark dusky sky were scattered with leaves under lamplight. Even as she moved ahead, as the night burned away, she could hear Ben's questioning voice less and less clearly. To forget his skin was more difficult.

For years she was always waiting. And now, she thought, as she watched the World Trade Center against the paling night sky, now she didn't wait anymore. Instead, she planned.

It was 3:45 A.M. and Lila was on Greenwich Street between Harrison and Jay. The lights in Suzanne's window were, of course, dark, as were all the apartment windows. Lila assumed Suzanne slept well and deeply. A person such as Suzanne could live successfully in this world and in the world of sleep with equal ease, not particularly attentive to dreams. Lila noticed that as she imagined Suzanne, and Suzanne's sleep habits, she was walking up and then down Greenwich, back and forth, like a nervous suitor before a make-or-break date. If she had been a shade closer to rationality, a degree closer to the self she knew, Lila would have stopped herself long before this vainglorious middle-of-the-night entrance. She would have been cautious, or at least somewhat considerate, had she been thinking, more or less, like herself. But instead, she watched her feet pace the sidewalk, which stretched in front of her, clear of garbage, like a shale-bottomed shallow river. Her feet instinctively skipped the cracks, which issued possibilities of curses, and her skin itched beneath her pants from the air's mercurial chill. There was a second — as an off-duty cab issued a rush of unidentifiable music — that seemed to eke itself out into timelessness, and then, as the cab was gone, the timelessness abruptly halted and Lila, barely halting her own rhythmic pacing, pressed the fifth-floor buzzer. She buzzed it twice, hard.

If Suzanne Hannon had been, as Lila suspected, a deep, satisfied sleeper, she perhaps would have ignored the buzz of the buzzer and willfully believed the noise to have been a part of her innocuous dream. But Suzanne was, in fact, a very light sleeper, and within seconds of hearing the buzzer, she was at the intercom, terrified that someone she knew was in trouble. And someone *was* in trouble; the someone was herself.

"Hello?" Suzanne's voice wafted through the intercom, an obviously fine-quality model, for there was none of the usual transmitting crackle and fuzz. Suzanne's voice was very clear for someone who'd ostensibly been asleep. Lila had thought she'd make up some lie, some reason for needing to come upstairs. Lila had planned on saying she'd been mugged, and she had nowhere else to go. Once upstairs, as Suzanne would be assuaging any guilt she might have still held deep in her enviable medium-size breast, as Suzanne would be in the middle of being polite and asking what Lila needed, Lila would tell her then that she hadn't been mugged at all. But as Lila stood, before dawn, on the desolate, expensively zoned sidewalk, and heard Suzanne's hello, she was once again sick of lies and exhausted by the certainty that she would certainly have to tell more lies, bigger ones, if her brother was to be found.

Hello? Suzanne said again, still a whisper, but more annoyed. Lila wondered, almost idly, if Richard were at home.

"It's Lila," she said, daring Suzanne to dramatically respond, to balk and try to send her away. Suzanne must have pressed the talk button; it gave a tiny *pffht;* it promised a response.

Suzanne said nothing over the intercom. A heavy room tone emitted shock and indignation through the sleek black lines of the machine. Suzanne's piqued silence wafted out onto Greenwich Street in an antiseptic chill; the temperature literally dropped. Lila didn't consider the possibility that Suzanne wouldn't let her upstairs. If she had been closer, again, to that careful analytical self, all kinds of considerations would have plagued her in that bridge of a moment, where nothing existed besides a dreadful spell of electronically transmitted silence. Finally Suzanne said, "What is it," still whispering, angrily, with not nearly enough concern to be considered an actual question.

"I need to come up," Lila said neutrally, amazed for a moment at her own brazenness. She had known herself to sit through entire classes in high school and the few sorry weeks of college, too embarrassed to go to the bathroom, not wanting to insult the teacher, to cause any heavy weather.

"It's barely four in the morning," Suzanne's voice quietly stated, as if to ascertain to what extent Lila's persistence was not madness, and was not, in fact, dangerous. Then: "It's okay," Suzanne said loudly, a voice clearly not meant for Lila, before Suzanne cut off the intercom.

Richard, Lila thought. *Thank goodness for Richard.* Lila waited for Suzanne to listen in again, but the intercom stayed quiet. Lila saw no choice but to press the buzzer again.

"*What*," Suzanne whispered fiercely.

"Oh, I'm sorry," Lila replied, with exaggerated politeness that seemed to rain down on her from a mysterious luminary of courage. "How rude of me." Lila, too, was whispering now, which she knew was almost unnecessary, given how much space lay between Suzanne and Richard's front door where the intercom was, and their bedroom. "I'll wait here until it's light out. Until your husband is on his way to work. I'll just stay right where I am. Then I'll reintroduce myself. I don't know why, but you seem to be nervous about the two of us talking."

Lila had passed through her doubts and anxieties, and even, briefly, the well-fought-for memories of her two absent brothers. She didn't notice the stain on her sweater, the hangnail stinging her left index finger, or the slouching passerby staring, relentlessly, at her bosom. She didn't think of all that was already wrong with her life. She thought of nothing, at that moment, besides her rising, glittering aggression toward Suzanne. If Lila had stopped, even only to notice her own labored breathing, she might have even apologized and retreated. But for some reason — was it the newly acquired knowledge of desirability and desire? Was it as simple and predictable as that? — Lila didn't stop to notice anything on that dark April morning besides the thin ebony lines of the intercom, and the locked green glass door before her. "Suzanne," she repeated, she dared. Lila knew Suzanne was listening.

No answer.

"Suzanne!" Lila could hear her voice rising, not only in volume but in pitch and — did she actually think this? — velocity. The syllables tripped off her tongue appealingly, as if she were shedding unwanted skin. Suzanne simply could not, would not, leave her hanging; the possibility simply never existed.

"Please," Suzanne whispered, and then her voice dropped even further. "Just go. We can talk another time. I promise."

"Let me up," Lila said, in a voice she didn't recognize, a voice that issued power from places inside her — places about which she had only read. "I'm not going to stop buzzing this buzzer if you don't let me up." Lila imagined doing so, and was so charged, she almost wanted Suzanne to deny her.

Suzanne said something unintelligible, so soft and scared was her whisper.

"I couldn't understand what you said," Lila said casually, buoyed by the surrounding air, which had begun its unveiling toward dawn. "Just let me up. I have some things to tell you."

The buzzer buzzed, and the door opened before Lila completed her sentence, and as thrilled as she was, that irked her. Lila hadn't finished speaking, and the way things were going, she wanted Suzanne Wolfe Hannon to hear every single word.

But as the elevator rose, Lila could feel her fury shrinking as the emerging thought of Pria's charm grew. The sweet bunch of beads and crystal and sage in cloth seemed so benign, even comical, because Lila knew it was no potion or spell or calling that led her to rise — at 3:55 A.M. — in a sleek gunmetal gray elevator. No, the only way she'd gotten here was through sheer dint of will. She alone was truly responsible, and the magnitude of her need, the need that brought her to threaten a thirty-year-old woman in her home in the middle of the night, was alarming. But there was no going forward before going backward, not for Lila Wheeler anyway.

With her eyes closed, Lila could almost start to see the New Hampshire sky, to feel the slimy wet of the pondside granite underneath her fingers. As the elevator door opened, she walked, almost trancelike, into that dove gray corridor, which, when Lila opened her eyes, smelled slightly of artificial sweetener and the absence of fresh air. So much had happened since she was last here, yet she still had no idea where to find Aaron. It seemed highly likely that there was more information that Suzanne hadn't troubled herself to disclose. There had to be more. A mysterious someone, a missing link, must exist who knew more than Lila, more, for that matter, than Suzanne Wolfe Hannon, regarding Aaron's whereabouts. Maybe Suzanne could lead the way. This time, Lila thought,

Suzanne would have to say something impressive in order for Lila to leave. No spilled coffee or business phone calls would intimidate her now. The previous visit had been filled with lies. Suzanne had wasted Lila's time. Thinking of Ben, she turned the corner; thinking of Ben, she saw Suzanne leaning against the wall of the apartment building corridor. Lila knew, as she thought of Ben, that she didn't have time to waste.

"Jesus Christ," Suzanne said, her lovely eyebrows furiously set, her hair loose and unbrushed and burnished amber. She wore gray drawstring cotton pants (probably Calvin Klein) and a white T-shirt (probably Richard's — Brooks Brothers, or Barney's, or even Banana Rebublic). The skin beneath her eyes was limpid, almost lavender, in the glow of the hallway light. "What are you doing here?" Her voice was no whisper, but low and resonant.

"Is Richard asleep?" Lila noticed that Suzanne wore green Chinese slippers. Her ankles were dusted with freckles.

"What do you want?"

"You want to talk right here? Your apartment is so big," Lila said, inching her way beyond Suzanne to where the doorway was, the door that was not quite shut.

"Don't," Suzanne warned, "don't go in."

She swallowed; she ran her hands through her knotless hair. "Please."

Suzanne was afraid. Lila could sense it, like she could sense the shifting of weather, the insidious tone in an underhanded compliment. Suzanne looked younger, smaller; she didn't wear her wedding band or the striking diamond ring. It was almost difficult to believe that behind that large blond-wood door lay a husband, a home, an accumulation of treasures. "You don't wear your rings to bed?" Lila asked, after a confusing stretch of silence.

"Please, Lila," Suzanne said, as if she didn't even consider the question, "I know you are . . . searching . . . and I understand how hard —"

"You don't understand," Lila said, without raising her voice even a little bit.

"I just don't think this is how we should talk," Suzanne replied, not without evident condescension. "I mean, in the corridor at four in the morning."

"So I should call you?" Lila asked.

"That would be better."

"And you'll get back to me?"

"That's right."

"And you'll tell me more lies, more excuses for yourself?"

"What are you talking about?"

Lila had no response.

Suzanne moved in closer to Lila and said, "If my husband wakes up —" Suzanne whipped around toward the door, as if she'd heard it opening, as if posing the hypothetical had caused Richard to stir. "He's a deep sleeper, but if he wakes up, I want you to tell him that you're drunk, or, I don't know, lost or something. That you had nowhere else to go. Promise me you'll do that."

"Why are you so worried?" Lila asked, and meant it. Suzanne seemed so afraid of this memory. Was it Richard's judgment or her own that Suzanne feared?

What was surprising then, given her fear, was that Suzanne hadn't put her foot down. If while she was on the neutral street, Lila couldn't imagine Suzanne saying no — now, standing in such close proximity to people sleeping behind their personal walls, it seemed particularly outrageous what Lila was requesting and it was even more outrageous that Suzanne was *granting* the request, and treating it as if it were a command. Control, Lila realized, was an altogether foreign feeling. For an instant, and with great shock, Lila felt as if her mother were watching, and she wished, to her own surprise, that her mother were actually here with her at this moment to witness this strange fulfillment. Lila knew, or thought she knew, that Vivian would be impressed. "She was a cheeky girl," her mother had said of Suzanne. "She was a little manipulator." It didn't even bother Lila, as she followed Suzanne the art dealer, the wife, the recipient of lilies and roses, that her mother had been right.

The loft was filled with a cool blue light and an eerie sense of serenity. Where was all their *stuff?* Suzanne probably threw away everything that wasn't currently pertinent. She probably unloaded clothes every season, making way for the new and improved. Suzanne poured two glasses of water and handed one to Lila, who actually thought, *Okay, I saw her pour the glasses from the same Brita water pitcher; therefore, mine cannot be laced.* To her credit, Lila did realize then that she had grown, if more tenacious, also considerably more crazed. So Lila, in between fantasies of Suzanne's spontaneous murder plots, leaned on the butcher-block island in the kitchen, and Suzanne did the same. Aside from the subject matter, they could have been friends casually late-night snacking. They could have been sisters. "I went and found —"

"Shh," Suzanne hissed. "Come on, keep your voice down."

"I went to see Pria Dajani," Lila whispered. And Suzanne — cheeky manipulator that she was, and Lila could now see how slick she really was — Suzanne said, "Who?"

"Pria. Dajani. You had such nice memories of her, remember? The stripper who gave the party the night my brother died." Lila raised her voice at the sound of that sentence.

"Oh, my God," Suzanne whispered, "you are sick."

"You told her, if you remember, that you were 'after' Jack, that you wanted him."

"What?"

"What?" Lila mimicked. Suzanne obviously intended to keep lying. "You remember. I know you do."

"Keep your voice down," Suzanne commanded. "Say what it is that you need to say, but keep it down." The tone, Lila thought, was unbearably condescending. Suzanne's unflappable denial made Lila want to shake Aaron's girlfriend until her narrow shoulders bruised, which probably wouldn't take much, Lila thought, for she'd wager that Suzanne had, very literally, thin skin. The thought of Suzanne bruising led her to think of Jack broken — lying dead or *almost* dead, which was even worse, for Lila sped through the common thought circle: What was his last glimpse of the world? Which words did he recall? Did he, even slightly, perceive that Lila was there with him, that she had made it down to that wretched pond through the darkness, all alone?

"You," Lila spit out, not heeding Suzanne's request. "*You* say what you need to say. Tell me what happened that night, and tell me why, and admit what you had to do with it."

"Lila," Suzanne said, she purred, and her name in Suzanne's mouth set something further askew, for the way she said Lila's name — seductively, definitely alluring — made Lila realize Suzanne wasn't about to admit a thing. Then, as if a wave came up beneath her arm, quite suddenly, Lila tossed her glass of water in Suzanne's direction, and not only did the water fly forward, as Lila certainly intended, but the glass left her hand also, and shattered on the teal ceramic tile. Both the water and the glass only grazed Suzanne, but the shock of Lila's display shot through Suzanne's attempted cool, and she was angry now, as only a woman whose secrets were coming back to haunt her could be. She grabbed Lila's arm and whispered, "You are a twisted, fucked-up kid, no different from your brother."

"I'm not a liar," Lila said.

"Congratulations."

"If you don't tell me something true, I'm not leaving. I'll tell him," Lila said, not sure she even meant it. "I'll tell your husband everything Pria told me. I can tell there's plenty he doesn't know about you. This is probably only one of many mistakes you have made. Am I right?"

Suzanne bent down behind the counter to sweep the glass away, and Lila instinctively bent down too. The shattered glass, on the teal ceramic tile, sparkled with what little light was available. Lila fought herself not to help Suzanne clean up the exquisite mess. She fought back the need to apologize. Lila reached out and touched a piece of sharp glass. She pressed her finger down hard until it drew the faintest prick of blood — giving her a place to focus, aside from Suzanne sweeping in this hellish limbo, and besides the sound of the bedroom door opening and the small space between the counter and the floor, through which Lila could see Richard, in a pair of boxers, walking toward the kitchen with the off-kilter steps of the newly awake, with the bewildered face of a good husband.

Suzanne stood slowly. Lila stayed down.

"What's going on?"

"I broke a glass, baby. I couldn't sleep, so I was getting some water. It's all cleaned up, though. Go back to bed, okay? I'm just going to do a little reading out here."

Lila realized the part Suzanne meant for

her to play, and so, after a moment's deliberation, she stayed quiet, thinking she'd surely get farther if she followed Suzanne's lead. Lila focused on the small pain of the prick of the sharp clean glass, and tried to will herself to shrink into oblivion until Suzanne successfully reassured him. As it happened, Suzanne must have known her husband pretty well, for Richard ambled back to bed without discussion, scratching his bare shoulder, convinced that his wife's late-night wanderings were no cause for alarm.

Suzanne and Lila were both silent for at least half a minute after Richard closed the bedroom door behind him. Suzanne put the broom back into the closet. Lila stood up. "Come with me," Suzanne said, and led Lila to the door.

"But —"

"I'm getting a jacket," Suzanne said, as if she were saying "I hate you." "I'm coming with you out this door, we'll take a walk, and only one of us will come back."

In the elevator Lila began telling Suzanne all that Pria had said. Before they exited the building, under the lobby light, Lila noticed how Suzanne's neck was spotted with color — bright red hives wide as quarters were spreading down her chest. The chill of the air was reviving, and Lila was reunited with her pacing self, her enraged anticipation kicked back into her bones. Suzanne was making excuses. Suzanne was failing miserably at convincing Lila of anything besides the fact that she was hiding something or many things. They walked briskly down Greenwich, their voices growing louder with each passing block. "I, okay, yes, okay? I flirted with your brother Jack. We flirted at that woman's party. Is that what you want to hear?" Lila was impressed by Suzanne's indignation; her yell was controlled and furious. It was almost convincing.

"Why are you afraid of my talking to your husband?" Lila shot back. "If it was no big deal, then what are you doing here with me right now?"

"I want you to leave me alone. I don't want you banging down my door anymore. So if this will do it, then fine. I don't want you bothering my husband. He doesn't need the headache. That's why. He's under a lot of strain."

"So am I." Lila was yelling now; she'd stopped her walking and was yelling. Her voice echoed in her ears like a honking horn. "I am under strain too. I know what happened," Lila said in a release of withheld breath. "I know."

Suzanne looked hardened by the glare of

the streetlight, under the bland haze of this patch of night. Suzanne, Lila realized, was listening.

"You knew he was jealous of Aaron, because Aaron told you all about him. You seduced him, you made him feel special, and you egged him onto those rocks. Aaron tried to stop Jack, and you made Aaron feel stupid and cautious. If you hadn't been there that night, no one would have died, and —"

"That's not —"

"No!" Lila screamed, hysterical now, tasting the salt of the tears that had sprung without her knowledge. "*No.* Just listen. Just be quiet and let it come out. It happened because of you. I have a right to know. Because you thought it was exciting to play around with two guys, to see how far you could push Jack, how" — Lila stammered, her brain giving thoughts too fast for the words — "how . . . far you could take your . . . your *power* . . . my brother Jack *died,* and your *boyfriend,* my brother who I know, I just know is out there, disappeared. And I don't blame him, because now, I blame you. I —"

"You want to know what happened?" Suzanne asked furiously. She was planted on the cement between two clean lines. She moved only to scratch her hives, which covered her neck and, apparently, her chest, for she opened the jacket and scratched on top of the bright white T-shirt. "You think it was because of me?" She looked not far from tears herself, if only in frustration at the perilous itches that were taking control of her body.

The sky, Lila noticed, was considerably lighter. That was the moment she panicked. It was before what came next. It was the sky that started the dread inside her. The thought of morning's inevitability made her weak with fear. It was as if she could sense each moment passing and dying before the moment even arrived. This view of the pearly sky, this view of passing time, made Lila want to hold back each moment from turning on its own.

"You want to know?" Suzanne repeated, "because I won't tell you unless you ask again. Ask me again," she said, half with terror, half with a grin. "Say: Tell me what happened."

Lila could feel the morning now. She could even feel, against her sharpest wall of will, the mornings of her days to come. She could actually envision — as Suzanne waited for her to speak — being awake at this hour each day in the future, for the rest of her life. "Tell me what happened," Lila said.

"You think it was me? You think if it wasn't for me, that Jack would be alive?" Suzanne didn't even pause. Lila would look back and remember that. She couldn't wait to say it. "It was Aaron, Lila." And then Lila understood. "Aaron killed Jack," Suzanne had to say, to make it absolutely clear. And then, as if her own naked language shocked her, she hurried to embellish. "It wasn't really an accident. Aaron punched him — pummeled him really — and Jack slipped on the rocks."

Lila barely breathed. She believed Suzanne, in a way that felt as if she'd always known. Lila had to have always suspected, somewhere, on some level, that this was the awful truth. "My parents?" she managed.

"They know," Suzanne said. "Of course they know. Aaron blurted it out immediately, before the ambulance even arrived."

"He found you and Jack together."

Suzanne nodded, looking worried. "It *wasn't* quite an accident, but you wouldn't — you can't, Lila — call it murder. We were young and drunk and selfish. All of us," she said.

Lila heard the word *murder* in her head. It called out to her like a roar.

Both of them, as they began walking toward Suzanne's apartment, had lost their steam. Suzanne looked tired, and Lila couldn't imagine what had become of her own expression. She could barely picture her features, consumed as she was with all she had lost for what seemed like a second time, and all her parents' stories that had been revealed, through meeting Suzanne, to be lies. Lila realized she had devoured nothing *but* lies, year after year, and though she remained angry with her parents, she couldn't help but feel that she had believed what she wanted to believe, because the truth now seemed so glaring. The truth, to her embarrassment, felt worse than the lies.

The two women walked in silence. Lila didn't know what she would do after Suzanne returned to her life five floors above the pavement, but she imagined that she would just keep walking. That was as far as she could see. Lila thought she would walk until she collapsed, and, in fact, perhaps she would have, had Suzanne been truly missing a sense of compassion, which she wasn't, which was, of course, what made the situation so difficult. Suzanne was not all bad. As Suzanne turned, almost bashfully, toward Lila, in front of the green glass door, Lila could barely feel her legs and her feet. She could barely feel her body at all. It was five o'clock in the morning.

"I know where he is," Suzanne said to Lila. Keys dangled from Suzanne's key ring. The sky split into pieces. The breeze came to a stop.

Lila couldn't say anything. She could not say a thing.

"Aaron." Suzanne took a breath, and she looked pallid from the chin up, florid from the neck down. She gave a neat cough. "Aaron has written me letters. Many letters. They keep coming to my mother's apartment. They keep coming with no return address. I have never tried to contact him. I have never opened the letters. My mother tells me when they arrive, and I ask her where the postmark is from, which she tells me, and then I tell my mother to get rid of the letter. It has gone on for years, and I've never told anyone about it."

"He writes to you?" Lila heard herself say, barely audibly.

Suzanne nodded. She scratched her neck with her pinky fingernail, in one downward stroke. "I don't know what to say."

"Why don't you read them?"

"Because I'm sure it's hate mail. I don't want to read them."

"Where is he?" And before Suzanne could answer, she asked it again.

Suzanne looked Lila squarely in the eye, which she had never once done throughout the course of their exchange. "If I tell you, will you promise not to contact me again?"

Suzanne was still afraid, and Lila realized

that her fears weren't simple ones. This went beyond the possibility that Lila would tell her husband nasty stories about her troubled youth. Lila pictured Suzanne's perfect loft — the delicate shimmering china, the paintings and the chenille blankets, the slant of light through the window — and Lila recalled Richard's concern, and the way Suzanne called him baby. Lila would never understand this kind of love, the delicate balance of security and deception, but looking at Suzanne in the dwindling darkness, at Suzanne's thin ankles in Chinese slippers, with her hives and nervous hands pushing aside stray auburn hairs, Lila realized Suzanne had never revisited the past for longer than a flashing instant.

"I won't contact you," Lila told her. "I promise."

"He's in Michigan," Suzanne said. "He's been there for approximately five years. He's in Ann Arbor, Michigan."

"Michigan," Lila said, testing out the word. "Ever been there?"

Lila shook her head. She thought of football, a girl she met on a ski lift once, who'd been on winter break from U of M. She thought of lakes on a map. She thought of snow.

"Good luck," Suzanne said, as she turned the key in the lock. "And I am sorry. I am."

"You're not like I remember," Lila said.

"You either," Suzanne replied. "But —"

"It doesn't matter anymore," Lila said. Suzanne stepped inside the building, closing the door behind her.

PART THREE

LILA AND AARON

All actual life is encounter.
— *Martin Buber*

CHAPTER NINETEEN

Ann Arbor was named for the love of a woman. There were at least three variations on how 640 acres of Michigan land came to be called Ann Arbor, and two of these tales depicted men blessed with wives named Ann. The third story was an unrelated legend about a woman named Ann d'Arbeur who, long before the men and their wives, led explorers through the Huron Valley wilderness.

Lila knew all of this because a peculiar professor had offered her university trivia, along with altogether too much information, during the long bus ride here. Lila pictured the latter Ann — wild hair streaming behind her — as she called out confident directions, as she bravely led the way.

Rising from her spot under a barely blooming tree, Lila stretched. She had fallen asleep on top of her duffel bag, in what, she assumed, was the college quad. She had napped for only an hour — it was still morning — but she felt refreshed, and finally convinced that she had made it out of Manhattan intact. Greyhound had taken her through a long sleepless night from Port Authority, a night she spent picturing each of her brothers' faces and willing those faces to make expressions, to not stare straight ahead, to not become photographs, stuck in time. Aaron had a habit of cracking his back. She tried to imagine how he twisted his face when he did it. There was always a small relief. And did Jack's eyes always crinkle at the edges or was it only in a few pictures above her mother's desk of a singular day when the sun was too bright?

An ordinary bus had brought her here, to Ann Arbor, chilly and green. She was in Michigan, and no one knew, not her parents, not Ben. She was missing. The sun pushed itself against the haze, struggling for exposure, as Lila picked up her bag and held on to her lime green drawstring purse, the contents of which were: Pria Dajani's charm, two hundred dollars and a ladybug purse full of change, two credit cards, one ATM card, Linda "the money lady" Meeks's card, three photographs of Aaron (one after he'd run the New York Marathon the year before Jack died, one close-up of him laughing, one candid profile of him reading), a berry-colored lipstick, and a blank book full of notes to herself, including Ben's address and telephone number, Pria's and Suzanne's surprisingly similar-looking business cards, a plastic pink locket with a picture of Jack (age sixteen) that she'd had since she was five, a mini bottle of silver nail polish that she always meant to take out of her bag but never did. She held on to it all and made her way into the concrete square. She walked past the benches, toward the center, where the library spilled tired students onto its steps. The small bright fields surrounding the quad were the only real indication that it was May — that, and the passing few folks wearing shorts, as if their optimistic wardrobe would bring on the warm weather. A guy with a pompadour chained his bike to a rail. An enormous black dog lay panting.

As it was a colorless day, there weren't many people lounging about, but a steady stream made their way with Lila across the quad by foot and by bicycle. None of them was Aaron. She observed the way people walked, the bearded and the bald, and there was no one at whom she looked twice, no one even close. The bell tower had rung its bells before she'd drifted off, and now, she realized, there seemed to be an absence of something, and that was what it was. No bells, just wind, and the inconsequential voices of strangers' hellos to one another, their casual good-byes.

In the middle of the square there was a

metal *M* cast into the concrete, about as big as her bedroom window in New York. The *M* looked old and important, a relic of those time-traveling stories she had loved as a child, where everyone always just barely made it back to the present. The *M* was the darkest of metal with a trace of oxidized green. People walked over it, around it, and no one stopped to look down. Ann Arborites were probably used to its strange and curious beauty. She inched toward it, thinking about how it was the center of a well-planned square, and how someone created this finishing touch. The *M* drew her in. She not only felt like touching it, but she felt like she had to touch it in order to go on with her day. The more she tried to ignore the *M,* the more she felt like something terrible would happen if she didn't go ahead and make contact. Lila reached, reflexively, for Pria's charm, as if one superstition could conquer another, but as Lila had suspected, that charm had little or no power over her own extremity. She imagined the circles under Pria's eyes, how they were the color of heather, of mushrooms. Lila extended her foot. The tip of her black boot grazed the metal, and then she stepped down with both feet, so she was standing right on it, on the window of the center of this town. She looked around, and she wasn't in anyone's way. She closed her eyes. A moment passed, two. The sound of women laughing, on their way out of the library. Car horns on State Street. The loud flapping of pigeon wings. She dared herself to keep her eyes closed for a few more seconds. It was a test of will, she told herself; she was lucky to have sight at all. Again she reached for the charm, and this time focused and squeezed it hard.

"You a freshman?" she heard a casual voice ask. On opening her eyes she saw a guy in a sweater, a green sweater with gray flecks. His jeans were too long. He wasn't Aaron.

"What?" Lila said, although she'd heard him perfectly. She had almost forgotten that she was visible to others, so consumed had she been with the act of watching.

"I just thought you were breaking the spell, now that exams are over."

"I don't go to school here," Lila said, and immediately wished she had lied. "What's the spell?"

"Oh, sorry. It's one of those campus things, you know; it's bad luck for freshmen to step on the *M* before they take exams. Now exams are all over, pretty much, right?"

"I was just standing here," Lila said. "I don't know why." Although she did know. She wanted to make a wish. She thought she would wish from the center — that, with

403

Pria's charm as her aid, her wishes would em-
anate to Aaron, whoever he was now, unlisted
in any Michigan directory.

"Are you meeting someone?"

Lila nodded, annoyed that he was talking to
her. Her loneliness was probably apparent,
and he was another nice guy who felt sorry for
her. She tried to feel blessed, and let the guy
off the hook. "I'm meeting my brother. He
teaches here."

The guy took out a red bandanna from his
pocket and blew his nose, then put it back in
his pocket, which was one of the most disgusting things Lila could think of at that moment. The guy folded it carefully with his
hands, which were nice hands, large and artis-
tic, she could tell by the way they moved.
"What does he teach?"

"He teaches Organic Chemistry," Lila said
with authority. "He's getting his Ph.D."

The guy raised his eyebrows, nodding.
There was an extremely lengthy silence, during which Lila assumed a tacit agreement of
no more chitchat between them.

"I had a first kiss with my girlfriend here,"
the guy finally said, and he looked off toward
the east, as if the woman might appear any
second. "We were friends. Then we came
back after Thanksgiving vacation and realized
we'd missed each other a lot. We called each

other the night we got back to school, and we met here, on the *M*. When we kissed, it began to snow." He shook his head as if he couldn't believe his own luck. "Isn't that amazing?"

Lila took another glance at the guy. Why was he telling her this? He was good-looking. He might have been earthier than she liked, but he was definitely kind of beautiful. Ben would describe him as exotic, because he had slightly slanted eyes, which were very dark, so dark they looked black. Lila missed Ben, suddenly; she missed how he extracted people's strongest characteristic and completely defined them by it. That was why he was such a good storyteller; his characters never blended together, and Ben rendered people far more interesting than they ever seemed to her. All Lila saw was a guy with a cold who had the same mellow desperation that tended to define a particular type of sexy man. Connecting to strangers was something this guy probably thought of as his own defining characteristic; not *chatting* with strangers, nothing so facile, no, it was a sense of sincerity this one probably defined himself with. Just when she was sure he was affecting nonchalance, he blew his nose again.

"That's beautiful," Lila said, and too much time had lagged; it came out sounding as if, not the story, but his nose blowing were the object of her admiration. But he didn't laugh and he didn't look at Lila, and she had a sudden intuition that his girlfriend was dead. Lila pushed the thought out of her mind. It was just like her to think that everyone was suffering. *Then again,* she thought, *it would make sense that the stranger he picked to talk to be me; if I lost someone, I'd want to talk to me, too.*

He nodded, no doubt pondering the girlfriend's beauty, exemplifying the kind of devotion Lila was certain she'd never provoke.

"How long have you been seeing each other?" Lila asked, trying to gauge how old he was, if he were older or younger than Aaron. She guessed he was younger, twenty-five or so, maybe finishing up school, slowly.

He looked at her, and for a second she saw his face in a completely different light. He had an angry look. "Oh, five years," he said, with a twisted grin.

Lila immediately said, "Sorry. I'm really sorry."

"For what?"

"It's none of my business." Lila realized, as the guy shifted weight from one foot to the other, and pushed his dark hair off his forehead, that if she had simply seen him walking by, she would have looked twice. She would have taken the extra moment to think, *He might be Aaron.* And standing here with this stranger, she realized how far off she would have been, and how, no doubt, she would have a million false hopes before her brother ever came her way. *If* he ever did. The guy looked up at the white sky.

"Is it always this unsunny?" Lila asked, steering the conversation in an easily escapable direction.

"Pretty much. It goes: fall, winter, summer. No spring really. It just gets hot, which is supposed to happen soon. I take it you're visiting?" he asked, glancing at her duffel bag.

"Visiting, yes."

"You're staying with your brother?"

"Oh, yeah, with my brother."

"Where does he live?" The guy shifted his gaze from the sky to her, and she found something about his eyes quite difficult to look at. His eyes were both masklike and gentle.

"I'm not really sure," Lila said, somehow not nervous about getting caught in a lie. "He just said to meet him. He was supposed to give me the information ahead of time, but that's the way he is. Kind of the absent-minded-professor type." Lila heard her voice fall in a comforting key, a tone that said how normal she was, how used to her brother she was, how she understood those closest to her, how she trusted. Her voice rambled on about the difference between being absentminded

407

and just being a total flake, a tangent about the difference between messy and dirty. Her voice was as light as air, while inside she could not escape a vision of Aaron pushing Jack into the position she remembered so well — his limbs rag-doll loose on the unforgiving rocks. And as Lila engaged in conversation — the guy's name was Keith, he was a Comparative Religion major — her heart began its familiar race, and uneven swells of tears tugged at her throat, jockeying for attention. As Keith explained that he'd traveled before starting college, that he worked on a farm in northern California, Lila spotted a broad back and thick dark hair in the distance.

A few yards away, there was someone bending down to tie his shoe, a someone that was possibly Aaron. As she watched him, the handsome stranger in the distance, she noticed how she felt something straightening her back, some sensation that felt a little like power. Where formerly lay confusion was emerging an urge to yell at the man tying his shoe. But when she imagined the new slant her ranting would take, she just didn't have the words. Hearing from him would be a start, hearing something that made sense. This had to have an end of some kind, didn't it? Didn't she get, at least, that? It made her furious that here she was again, making up cute stories about her absent brother, that she was in the midst of pretending to another stranger, another young man.

As Keith explained that this quad was called the Diag, because of its convenient diagonal path that connected the sides of town, Lila nodded and noticed that the possible Aaron bobbed his head rather pertly as he tied his laces in knots, and how, as he stood up, he was not nearly as tall as her brother, how he wasn't Aaron at all. But Aaron, at that moment, might very well have been tying his shoe somewhere else, somewhere close by, quite unaware that his sister, no longer an owl-like child, was watching a shorter man, an innocent man, and assigning him her brother's identity. Lila looked away from the would-be Aaron, and followed Keith to a bench.

"So what's your name?" Keith asked, with a confused look, which said: *This conversation has gone on too long for me not to know.*

She told him her name was Abigail. She said she had come from New York City, where she was born and raised. Even as she crossed her legs and scratched her knee, she felt herself changing, ever so slightly, into a woman who grew up taking taxis and express trains to get to her school and friends. She became a girl with a pedigree who was traveling, who was used to traveling, who got restless too long in one place. She could do this. Keith said: Nice name, and Lila smiled. He looked up at the sky again. It was as if the exchange of their names had given him license to sit, without apologies, in silence. There would be no sun today; the light was becoming less and less promising. In fact, the sky seemed to be darkening, and the air was becoming close. A storm was probably brewing, and Lila hadn't even thought about where she was going to stay. People walked by, dogs walked by, a guitar player and his drumming friend started something up in the farthest field.

When Keith looked at Lila again, he had tears running down his face. His dark eyes were darker, and his skin was flushed. At first she thought it was the wind, and that he had stared too long at the sun, no matter how dull its glow. She remembered how bright the sun rose the morning of Jack's death, in contrast with all that dark blood. When she realized that Keith was actually crying, she tried to form the words of concern, the "Are you okay?" the appropriate response, but a cloud came over her mouth, as if she were bound and gagged by her own intrusive memories. He was really crying — this stranger, this Keith — the first person she'd met in this college town. She obviously brought misery straight to her.

"Abigail," he said tentatively. Abigail? Had she really told him her name was *Abigail?* Could she do nothing right? Abigail she was now, and Abigail she'd continue to be. "Abigail?"

"Call me Abby," she said, like picking at a scab, making the situation even worse. "Listen, don't worry about me." There was someone who came out of the library. He was petting the big black dog in a depressed and loving manner, which made her look twice, even though he was bald and very thin.

"I can't seem to go anywhere these days without talking to strangers."

"It's easier," Lila said. The bald man with the dog — he had an even shadow of stubble the way Aaron's used to be. He kept on petting the dog, and would not turn around.

"A friend of mine says that strangers are meant for confessions, that they're the world's built-in system of input, and input is all any of us need to gain momentum sometimes."

Ssh, Lila thought, *just hush,* and she tried to will Keith to stop talking for a minute, to give her a second to do nothing but watch.

"Abby," Keith said.

"Uh-huh?" Lila muttered. The man stopped petting the dog and stood up, facing

Lila's direction. He couldn't have been Aaron; his eyes were too deep-set and his lips were too thin, but then again, this man was gaunt, and people's looks changed so drastically with weight loss. It was within the realm of possibility —

"I don't think *what* people's input is necessarily even matters," Keith insisted, breaking into her thoughts. "I think maybe that to stay on course, you know, moving forward, you have to spit out what's dragging you down. I think maybe if I say it enough times it'll lose its power."

"It?" Lila spit out, more impatiently than she'd intended.

Keith placed his hands on his thighs, like a kid who'd been told to stop fussing. "Maybe not, though. Most likely I should keep quiet."

This Keith, he was a nice guy; he was someone who needed something. "I wouldn't recommend it," she replied, as gently as she could. The bald guy walked toward her. He scratched his elbow through a well-worn jean jacket. He was intense-looking, he must have been around thirty, but who was she kidding? If it were Aaron, thin or fat, she'd know without scrutiny. Wouldn't she?

Lila could just picture Aaron walking behind her now, and how she wouldn't even notice because she was too wrapped up in projecting him onto unsuspecting men — her impatience causing her to miss out on the real thing. Lila turned around quickly, expecting her brother to be right there, and, of course, there was no one but a short boyish woman wearing sunglasses despite the sunless sky. Though Lila couldn't see her eyes, she was sure the girl was glaring at her.

"Where's your brother, do you think?" asked Keith.

"He's always late," Lila mumbled, a bit too eagerly.

There was an inevitable silence, a space to be filled with someone's story, the aforementioned confession to a stranger. "So," Keith said, not looking at the sky, nor at her, but straight ahead, in the distance.

"So," Lila said, disappointed to still be here, in her cowardice, in her false identity.

"When did you arrive here?"

"In Ann Arbor?"

He nodded.

"Last night, I mean this morning. I traveled all night."

"Do you need a place to stay?"

"Do I look like I need a place to stay?"

"You look tired. You look —"

"Well, I've been traveling on a bus all night. You'd probably look tired too." Keith's eyes fixed themselves on her, through the stillness of the air, through the persistence of Suzanne's voice in her head. *It was Aaron.* Lila felt the weight of Keith's strange gaze, and thought, *Jack will never know me.* She thought of how little she was when she had loved him with all of her energy and unself-conscious desire. For desire was what it had been and what it was; she had wanted both of her brothers with an urgency and greed that reigned in her jumbled memories as nothing short of hunger. She couldn't help but question her desire, and suspect that it was even more unnatural than she'd been suspecting all along. Lila feared she would never grow out of her wild need for attention from two particular boys who simply no longer existed. She was still saying, *Look at me,* with every step she took toward finding Aaron. *If Jack could see me,* Lila said to herself, as she gave Keith a weary grin, *just what exactly would he think?* And as this stranger, this Keith, kept looking at her, Lila felt a sadly inconsequential fear: *What if Jack had lived and didn't like me? What if we had grown apart?* There was something contemptible about growing older, about being the very age that Jack was when he died. With Jack's accident no longer an accident, and shrouded in the mystique of Aaron's explicit culpability, there was something almost inconsiderate, even shameful, about aging. "How old are you?" she asked Keith. Any minute, she knew, rain would be let loose from the clouds, and this conversation would be over.

"I turned thirty today."

"Happy birthday," Lila said meekly, for his birthday was clearly anything but happy. "Wow."

Keith laughed. "Yeah, wow." He didn't look thirty, she thought. Was this what thirty looked like? Was this what Aaron looked like? Whether goateed or ponytailed, conservatively dressed or, in fact, bald, she had to know — at the very least — the changes of his truly architectural face. Maybe even the shock of Aaron alive, no matter how changed, would loosen the hold of her constant images of Jack's shaven head hitting the rock.

As she swore she felt a drizzle, Lila noticed that the story of waiting for her brother was losing all aspect of believability. She was lying a lie so stupid, she almost resented Keith for going along with it. Plus she had to pee, and she dreaded finding a hotel. The prospect of being alone in a hotel room for the first time should have felt glamorous and independent, but in reality it was nothing short of depressing. She knew she wouldn't be able to stop thinking of all the other people who'd slept in the bed before her, with company and without. Such anonymous privacy would make her feel nothing if not expendable.

A crack of thunder finally broke through the sky, and within seconds, tiny fists of hail began to zing through the Diag, through the town; it was weather that ushered people along, that got decisions made. Keith looked at his watch. *A hailstorm,* Lila thought. *Of course.*

"What are you going to do?" Keith asked, wincing at the sky's display.

"What?"

"About your brother," Keith said, and Lila could tell he was at least mildly annoyed. People dashed into the library, into the various buildings that flanked the green.

"Don't worry, I'll call him." The words floated out of her mouth.

"You could come with me and use our phone."

As a sharp piece of hail nailed her forehead, she felt the odd sting, and noticed they were the only people, as far as she could see, who were staying in one place. She thought of the constant crowds of Manhattan and how she relied upon the masses. Crowds anywhere were somewhat comforting, if anxiety-provoking, full of the possibility of Aaron. She thought of how she could find a crowd at some café in town. But the thought of going into a café, and waiting for the hail to stop — over sugary coffee, overhearing other people's conversations — didn't do a thing for her.

"My friend's place," Keith repeated, as if to hurry her train of thought. "Where I've been staying." They stood up from the bench stiffly, wincing through the pellets of hail. "I have to go," Keith said. "Are you coming?" He asked her almost resentfully, as if he assumed she'd say no.

"My brother —"

"I'm sure he'll understand."

Lila ran with him to the tomblike arch facing East University, as if she had no choice. She was taken with Keith's puzzling eyes, his capable-looking hands and sense of loss. She had no designs on his attention. He only made her miss Ben, and he was way too old for her anyway. At best, he could help her navigate the town, find inroads toward a six-foot-two, thirty-year-old male, brown hair, hazel eyes, more likely than not, fairly strange. Besides, as hail fell in angry bursts, the idea of a house sounded increasingly appealing. She needed to talk to locals, she reminded herself, and it was a small town, wasn't it? This could be a perfect way to start.

A burgeoning crowd stood under the dark stone arch, waiting for the hail to stop, and Lila and Keith made their way through the sweet, heavy smell of the shelter seekers. Both of them ran with incredible momentum, as if stopping weren't ever going to happen, as if they didn't need to stop, as if, really, they each could dispense with their individual situations, at any given moment.

It was a hailstorm in May. Anything was possible.

His street was like a picture of a street, a dream of a street, where one asks repeatedly, *Where am I? Am I someplace I've been before? Am I on TV?* The houses were ramshackle Victorian; porches seemed to figure prominently for the denizens of Church Street. If there weren't people on the porches, watching the crazy hail, there were remnants of accumulated nights and days spent drinking and/or smoking, painting (easels stood proudly on two separate porches, stoic, waiting for their artists), gardening. There also stood a number of unfortunate cinder-block apartment buildings, probably born around the same time as Lila herself. Church Street sang of impermanence; it bragged about all the people it had known. The street had seen plenty of hail in its time, plenty of people on the verge, people needing comfort, needing change. As Lila ran behind Keith, she wondered what his whole story was. Did his girlfriend leave him because he was too possessive, too sure of his feelings? Was she a free sprit, a heartbreaker like Suzanne? Or maybe Keith did something so terrible that she could never, not ever, forgive him.

The hail was letting up, and Lila realized she was out of breath, so she slowed down to a walk. Her duffel bag weighed her down a little, and, anyway, it was good to look at the street more carefully, to try to get glimpses through windows, and see as much as she could. Keith had run farther ahead, and he now turned around. "Can I carry your bag?" he called to her, from half a block away.

"I'm okay," Lila called back to him, surprised at how much authority her voice could carry. He waited for her to catch up. "Thanks," she added with a smile.

He nodded and resumed walking, seeming to understand that she felt like walking alone. The hail had entirely stopped — it was as if there had never been a storm. The sky was white, it was blank, it went on forever. In the distance, Lila saw a white steeple shooting up against it. Could there be an actual church on this street — on an avenue of what looked like potential parties and easygoing days? She imagined the inevitable clashes of quiet and riot between the congregation and its restless neighbors, and as she walked progressively slower, the church looked that much more beautiful. Maybe she would tell Keith, *Nice to meet you, good luck, good-bye,* and enter the hushed and lavish silence of other people's faith. The church might be so opposite from the home of her atheist parents that it might offer something close to emptiness, a perfect hollow where she could listen closely to the confusion of all she now knew. She could tell a priest. Or what if there were no priests? Wasn't it only the Catholics who gave confession? She could tell a kindly minister. *Aaron killed Jack. Aaron pushed Jack onto slick rocks, and Jack bled inside. He bled until he died.*

Lila stopped between two cracks in the pavement, as if she were ordered to do so within an inch of her life. She felt doomed to fail, as if the failure were already happening. She was a coward for having lied to Keith, and for wanting to perpetuate her lie. What was she going to do, dial a phony brother's number, and leave a phony message? It was time to start describing Aaron to everyone she met. It was time to use her resources. What had she been thinking when she gave Keith a fake name? Maybe Aaron told the story of his life to everyone he met. It was not impossible that there were strangers who knew the story, who knew her name and her troubles and were ready to help. She shouldn't have been wasting a minute while Aaron still existed as the boy who lived in her mind as angry and misunderstood, laden with guilt. Until she knew him as alive and *here,* there was nothing to do but look, ask, get to it.

She saw Keith slow his pace and walk up the church steps. Maybe he stopped here daily on his way home, and imagining such a ritual made Lila like him all over again. She wondered what kind of congregation was housed inside, and if anyone were praying at that moment. Lila saw Keith search in his pockets. As she drew closer, she saw that dangling from his fingers was a set of keys.

"Hey!" Lila called out, in a fit of friendliness; "do you have special access or something?" But as soon as she said it, she realized that the church was merely the shell of a church, and that it had been converted, probably long ago, to housing. It was, essentially, no different from the previous houses-with-porches. "*This* is your friend's place?"

"Cool, isn't it?"

Lila felt oddly disappointed, as if she had been expecting to actually find God in one afternoon, all because she liked the drama of a steeple against the sky. This was just a house, another place where she didn't belong. "How many people live here?" she asked, just for something to say.

"Depends," Keith said, throwing the keys in the air, and watching his hand catch them; he turned the key in the lock. "Come inside," he said simply, as if coming or going were no decision at all, only different sides of a pretty coin.

The open space of the converted church smelled the way Lila remembered a ski lodge in North Conway. There was an underlying current of warmth in the atmosphere, as if a flannel shirt had just come out of the dryer, as if some giant with sweet breath had fallen asleep and let his mouth fall open. This was a house where meals were cooked, where savory steam from various pots had settled into the cushions and the blankets on the couches and rugs. The house smelled of dinners and brunches and faintly of lavender soap. The scent of the space was impressively complex, but the most salient feature behind the red church door was the amazing display of light. It wasn't, of course, a sunny day, but the steeple-shaped picture window filtered the *quality* of light inside, so that gray as the light was, it was still the light that one noticed so strikingly — mainly in front of the winding staircase, which divided the living room from the plum-colored kitchen.

Keith sat at the table by the window, and took off his gray-and-green sweater, revealing a surprisingly tailored Izod shirt — a faded hunter green. "It's warm in here," he said absently, while Lila looked around the downstairs. A painting hung above the couch — two tall women in similar robes, one gazing ahead while the other looked at the gazing one questioningly. "I did that," he pointed out, as if reading her mind.

Lila told him, truthfully, that she liked it. She asked him how long he'd lived here.

"Since the New Year. I think of it as a holding tank. I'd assumed I'd be gone by now."

"Why? This is a great place."

"It is a great place. A complicated place too."

"Why's that?"

"Money," Keith said. "Essentially, money. My friend David has got some, and he owns this place, and nobody has to pay rent."

"That's generous," she said, half paying attention, looking around the space and trying to guess if the type of person who'd live here would be the type of person who'd know Aaron. "I take it he's not a student."

"He kind of is. He just works at a bookstore and takes classes now and then. That's the weird part — how he got the capital. He had been a traveler, like I was, and a few years after I met him, he went on to the Soviet Union. Apparently he met an artist, a very old man, whose paintings David claims to have known were valuable in the Western art market. He wasn't a famous painter, of course, but he painted during a certain period, or whatever, and David convinced him to sell him fifteen of his paintings. All the money David had saved for two years of travel, he handed over to the old painter's nephew on a dock in the middle of the night, in exchange for sealed-up tubes. They could have been stuffed with fakes or even blank canvas, but they weren't. They *weren't*. And he smuggled them out from behind the Iron Curtain, and hit the London art market in a borrowed suit, and he sold those paintings for enough money to buy this church. No one knows how much money he has."

"Come on," Lila said, sort of annoyed.

"This is a fairly interesting place you have stumbled into." He smiled.

She fished for the question she couldn't quite deliver: *Do you know Aaron Wheeler?*

Keith made tea. This cup smelled and tasted deliciously of black licorice. They sipped as the light through the window waxed and waned, took form and took leave of form, simply flooding the entire space. Lila tried to fight against it, but she could feel the house working a palpable charm. She tried to picture the space full of people — chopping vegetables, arguing, playing loud music — it was impossible. The space exuded solitude, a familiar yet wholly unknown peace. For a moment she doubted Keith's entire explanation. "Where is everyone?"

Keith gave a shrug. Lila pictured Keith, momentarily, as the annoying guy who was staying on the couch, the guy who brought home young women and told them about David's groovy pad.

She finally just said it as if she were at a party, asking about a hometown acquaintance: "Do you know a guy named Aaron Wheeler?"

Keith — nice guy that he was — gave the question a moment of thought. Then he said no, so plainly and without doubt, that she felt surprisingly and deeply disappointed.

"I thought you did," she couldn't help responding, and she realized that she *had* thought Keith would know him; no matter how ridiculous it seemed, it was, realistically, the reason she'd probably followed him here.

"Does he go to U of M?"

"I'm not sure," Lila falsely mused, looking out the giant window, as a break in the clouds appeared. "I haven't seen him in years." The sun came out in a cloying instant, and filtered bright yellow through the glass, forcing Lila to shield her eyes. "Friend of the family," she explained, as her eyes began to water at the brightness. The dramatic light transformed the room: the prior warmth of the room turned stuffy, swirls of dust were illuminated, and the colors in Keith's painting looked garish. She could tell him everything right now. She could start over with the truth, and enlist his help. He would help her, she knew. "So what does she look like?" Lila asked. "Your girlfriend," just to be fair, she told herself, just to be polite. Keith looked through the sunlight, surprised.

Keith went on, telling about Mimi, how she sunburned easily, how her hair was the color of pennies, how everything in life felt slightly embarrassing without her personal slant. He said, frustratedly, that even his description of her felt dull and uninspired.

"Is she still alive?" Lila asked, and was instantly sorry, knowing, before Keith shook his head, just what the answer would be.

"Do you believe in ghosts?" he asked, with a weak smile.

"No. Not really, no. Maybe I'm just pissed off because I've never seen one. I had a brother . . ."

Keith looked at her and almost asked but she was thankful he did not. She should not have been doing this with her time. "Why did you ask if I needed a place to stay?"

"I took a chance. I thought you might have been lying, and maybe you were running away."

Keith looked not embarrassed, but curious, as if his own confessions had somehow earned him a place among the trusted.

"I'm not running," Lila said. And she looked out the window where the leafy branches of a tall tree were almost tapping the glass. Under the tree, a man was walking with a slender pale-haired woman with a long thin nose. The man turned to the window and saw Keith, to whom he gave a small wave. Then he casually gestured that he was coming inside, and they walked out of sight, to the door. Lila could swear she heard the branches moving, and the man's and woman's feet stepping on twigs and kicking pebbles out of their way.

Then she couldn't hear anything for a moment, not even Keith, beside her. For a split second, Lila was disappointed that her conversation with Keith was ending so soon. But as the sound of the front door came up loudly in her ears, she whittled herself down to a tiny breath. She reminded herself that, like it or not, she was now called Abby and that, no doubt, she was mistaken. She must be mistaken because really, how many times already had she thought she'd seen him before and been so disappointed? When she realized that the answer was never, not really ever, the door had opened.

She took a breath and the breath was loud, everything too loud. She wished for the hush after an accident, after *the* accident — a silence so rich, it would fill her up and absolve her of all wanting. But there were loud hellos and the clunky sound of bags landing on chairs; there was Keith blowing his nose. She wanted quiet as she fell and caught herself in between the noise and the years that led up to *this* year, to *this* day: that she was being introduced to him as a stranger, to this moment when he believed she was that stranger.

This is David, Keith said.

Hello, Aaron said.

CHAPTER TWENTY

It was not a moment in which time stood still. Time *could* stand still, and this Lila knew — it stood still when she last touched Jack and when Aaron went screaming through the trees, and time also stopped when she saw Suzanne on Bedford Street, leaning her head on a windowpane. But in this particular converted church, on this tempestuous Friday in May, Aaron's hand was as familiar to her as his name or his absence. He looked in her eyes and time rushed on.

He looked exactly the same. For all of her expansive imagining of Aaron bald, bearded, fat, and thin, her brother looked remarkably unchanged. In fact, to Lila's chagrin, he looked better. The faint lines in his face accentuated its sculptural structure, and his hazel eyes were greener than she recalled. "Are you visiting U of M?" he asked her.

He had no idea. Lila couldn't believe it, but Aaron clearly thought he was meeting her for the very first time. To her amazement, it felt like nothing out of the ordinary was happening — she had no tears, no fainting spell, nothing. In all of her daydreams and fantasies of this meeting, the specifics of the given scene would melt away and there would be no need for words. She never imagined other people would be around or that they would matter in any way. She certainly never banked on Aaron not recognizing her, or that an explanation would be necessary.

As far as Aaron knew, she was nobody, and yet he'd asked his common question with fierce intention, as if her answer really mattered. She could tell this was now his manner, his way, and if Aaron were, in fact, a stranger, Lila would have guessed he'd been through not the murder of his brother, but perhaps a bout with mental illness or years of AA — he had that visible will about his eyes and mouth, a determination to get clear. And maybe he *had* battled sanity and alcohol — maybe he'd been through all that and more. It had been, after all, almost exactly ten years.

"I'm traveling cross-country," Lila managed to tell her brother, adding a wicked glint in her eye. *Abby*, after all, would have a glint in her eye, when talking to a guy like this — a mysterious transcontinental art dealer, an indisputably handsome man. Abby would stand up straight.

Keith said, "Abby needs a place to stay the night," and looked at her, challenging her to disagree. Lila didn't say anything; she only returned Keith's conspiratorial smile.

The slim long-nosed woman, who'd made a beeline to the kitchen upon entering the house, suddenly piped up: "We could use a few extra hands this weekend."

"You picked a good time to come to Ann Arbor," Aaron said, not acknowleding if, in fact, she could spend the night. "It's Keith's birthday."

"Big celebration," Keith said dryly. "So she can stay, right?"

"Shouldn't be a problem," Aaron said. He looked out the window, like a peaceful despot, as if he were expecting someone —a visiting dignitary for this special weekend, a messenger of forgiveness.

"Thanks," Lila said, and added, "David," as if she were addressing a talk show host who'd given an initial compliment.

"I'm Sylvie," the woman in the kitchen called out, and then she came and shook Lila's hand. She was almost beautiful in a well-scrubbed way. Her clothes were nondescript but they fell on her thin frame nicely, and her blond hair hung stick-straight to her shoulders, the color of butter and wheat. "How many are we then?" she asked Aaron, who still looked out the window in silence, and Lila wondered if he was known for mysterious silences like their father was, if he was known for anything at all.

He told Sylvie "Nine," without looking away from the window, which didn't seem to faze her. She was a real blond with thin lips and turquoise eyes whose individuality probably lay in the rare combination of having a genuine knack for organization without being a bitch.

"I hope I'm not imposing," Lila said — a politeness so strongly rooted, she knew it would never subside. *You killed our brother,* she could imagine herself saying, *but are you sure you don't mind if I use your phone?*

"David," Sylvie said to his broad back. "She's asking you a question." Sylvie spoke gently but the effect was curt. He didn't respond to her, but he did turn and face Lila. She wanted to tell him *I hate you,* to be lifted on his shoulders; she wanted to see him weep.

"You're supposed to stay here," he said, with that same look of intention, and for a moment, she was certain that he'd not been staring out the window in basic contemplation, but rather in a state of shock after recognizing her and needing to be absolutely sure. *You're supposed to* rang in her mind, and she was sure he had to have been thinking of what to say or do. "This house is all about that," he said.

"All about . . . ?" Her mouth was dry, the nape of her neck sweating.

"You know, people who need a place," he said, "a place to stay."

"Well, great then," she said, keeping her voice light light light. Keeping it going. She was curious. Sickly so. She thought of her parents, how they would soon realize they had no idea where two out of three children were. "Great," she repeated. "What can I do to help?" She addressed Sylvie, feeling like an awkward social worker, new on the job.

"You can chop," she said. "We're having a dinner party."

The kitchen felt like a separate house. It overlooked the back lot's decrepit vine-covered wall and enveloped Lila with its purple paint and herb boxes and dark jars of oil lining the sill of the one small window. If the front room was about light, this back kitchen was about dark, and Lila had never been so suited to dark, to any kitchen, ever. All the darkness inside her, the unsettled questions, fiercely gave themselves over to Sylvie's domestic tasks. Sylvie gave Lila twelve yellow onions to chop, and she would chop to save her soul, chop with the precision and power of a concert pianist. Lila was intimidated by the onions, though she'd chopped thousands before, and afraid that the one correct way of doing this would, of course, elude her. It was as if she were handling a knife for the very first time. Her fingers meticulously worked the onion skin, and she chopped the bulb in quarters before getting down to business.

Sylvie was kneading a loaf of bread. Her long knobby fingers flattened the dough, pausing every so often to reach for a black olive in a small yellow bowl. "I love these," she said, each time she took one, as if the force of her craving was upsetting. "I could just eat these for dinner."

"Why the dinner party then?"

"Oh, we always have big dinners here. I guess you could say it's one of the stipulations."

"Stipulations?"

"The house," she said plainly, as if by way of explanation.

Lila nodded, but played dumb, and Sylvie said, "You know the deal here, right?"

"I don't know anything. Are you and David, y'know, together?" Lila laughed nervously, and Sylvie laughed also, which made Lila feel better.

"Ah, no," Sylvie said, "noooo."

Lila waited for more explanation but none came. "So . . ."

"It's David's house."

"And he likes a good meal?" Lila asked, as if her brother were some kind of Mafia don whom everyone was trying to please. Lila felt a spasm of tears about to flow, and she decided to just let them loose, let her face redden, and blame it on the onions.

"It's not like that," Sylvie said, washing her hands briefly, and starting to knead again, not noticing Lila's tears, or at least not commenting. "Everyone likes the setup. David — David and I — just think good food, actual meals, are important. Like a family."

Lila thought it all sounded suspiciously like a cult. Sylvie, she imagined, was probably a disgruntled, spiritually unfulfilled young housewife who'd left her family to run this communal household instead. Lila went to wipe her nose with the back of her hand, but Sylvie handed her a tissue. "Is this place like a co-op or something?" Lila asked.

Sylvie shook her head. "It's not that organized, believe me. Everyone here just met David at the right time. Jacob knew the couple that moved out last year, so he's the newest. But there's no time frame on how long anyone can stay. I was the first. I renovated everything. I put the place together."

"Was it always meant for others?"

"Oh, yes, of course. That was what David

always wanted — and me too, of course. He's very generous, you'll see."

There was something ridiculous about Aaron doling out places to live, trying to create some kind of cozy haven. He'd had so much time for people all along, so many good intentions, and yet none of that time or intent had ever been extended to her. Lila chopped and tore, diced and burned, and Sylvie put the bread in the oven. A silence descended and Lila's tears fell in plump drops, unremarked upon. A strange sensation was occurring: Lila was crying from somewhere deeper than where onions could reach, yet the tears weren't connected to feelings. She seemed to feel just fine — distant perhaps, but okay, and though she knew this wasn't possible, that she was bound to feel something soon, nothing was catching inside. Only a tingling sensation developed in her chest, when every so often, some more-or-less pleasant person popped his head in the kitchen and asked Sylvie what to do. Jacob, a stocky twenty-something, was sent out to buy booze. Keith, who by now felt like an old friend, hung around in the front room and straightened up, blasting dour music. Lila gave shy smiles to whomever she was meeting, smiles wired tight as a fiddle bow. "Onions," she said, and pointed to her bleary face. Each time a new person came around,

Lila's heart beat that much faster, for she was sure, before she looked up, that it would be Aaron, come to tell her that he knew.

But Aaron hadn't even asked about the meal. Lila wondered where he was as she stared at perfect slivers of onions — was he still staring out that vaulted window as Keith cleaned? Had he gone into his bedroom to practice meditation? To read? Masturbate? To write a letter to Suzanne? *Dear Suzanne,* Lila imagined him getting going, *you lying, crazy bitch.*

Lila wanted nothing more than to expose what happened that night as something that was still in the process of happening — yet here she was, lying to everyone within earshot, doing chores in her brother's house and cooking him dinner. She *wanted* to cook dinner. She wanted to see Aaron chewing and living his stolen lucky life.

She bore down on the knife with the force of her weight, as it sliced through another onion. She didn't come out and tell him from the start, *Aaron, it's me, Lila!* That moment had come and gone already, for it was the "me" part that stumped her. In the face of Aaron's unchanged physical self, it didn't feel valid to be the adult version of Lila Wheeler. Aaron would be disappointed that the Lila he knew, the real Lila (for this was how she thought of it), was not anywhere to be found. She imagined both of them standing around, pretending not to be disappointed and somehow embarrassed that Lila had grown up.

"So you're traveling by yourself?" Sylvie asked. She started chopping cloves of garlic, and gestured for Lila to do the same.

"Yep."

"Where're you coming from?"

"New York," Lila said, and wiped her face with a tissue. "Manhattan."

"So where are you from?"

Her breath was suddenly hard to find; it lay heavy in her chest. "There."

"This is your first stop then."

"That's right," Lila said, and cleared her throat, looking out toward the back lot. "Ann Arbor. Why not."

"You just inadvertently picked this town as a first stop?"

Sylvie chopped faster than Lila, and Lila tried to keep up, as well as alter the direction of the conversation. Her tears had stopped, but a panic was definitely beginning. She tried to suppress her heavy breathing, and instead, she cut her finger. "Fuck!" Lila cried, and the knife dropped onto the butcher-block counter with a thud. The blood rushed out, and Keith rushed into the kitchen, followed closely by her brother. "Sorry," Lila stammered, now clutching her bloody finger, "I'm fine." She smiled hard. As the blood seeped out, she did feel fine. In fact, she felt sort of relieved. The cut asserted a dull pain that snapped her into finer tune with her surroundings. The cut was good, she reassured herself, as voices urged her (her brother's the softest) to run her finger under cold water. Lila focused on how the water numbed not only her finger, but all of her, for a moment. Everything seemed to go anesthetic. What she had taken for Sylvie's suspiciousness now seemed to have been no more than good-natured curiosity. She was nobody; she was missing; she could say anything here, after all.

Lila pulled her finger from the running water, and before she could register how gently his hands were encircling her wrist, she heard Aaron's voice: "You okay?" deep and convincingly worried.

"She's fine," Sylvie said. "It's just a little cut."

Lila nodded, but pointedly ignored Sylvie's advice and gave her hand over to her brother's thrilling touch, to his skilled examination. The blood still trickled out, and Lila was grateful to her blood for its stubborn flow. Aaron took her hand, and she had an urge to paint his face with her blood, to touch it to his lips and say, *I know the truth about you.* His fingers were careful and so familiar as he wrapped her finger (left index, nail bitten down but not badly) in a paper towel on which was printed *Home is where the heart is* in blue. Her blood soon blotted out the words and she began to laugh. "Thank you," she told him, her laughter verging on hysterical. "Thanks a lot. I'm sorry about this," she said, and poked her bloody diapered finger in the air. "I must be more tired than I thought."

"Abby got in this morning," Keith explained. "She rode the bus all night."

"From?" Aaron asked, good-naturedly, reaching into a drawer and procuring a Band-Aid, and taking her finger again.

"New York," Sylvie said, before Lila could find the words. Sylvie then looked at Lila with the affection Lila imagined Sylvie reserved for, let's say, botulism, or perhaps bacon fat on the floor.

"Always wanted to go there," Aaron said. He carefully unraveled the bloody towel. He didn't ask Lila if she minded him presiding over her wound, if she would rather be doing it herself. "Someday," Aaron said. "I'll get there eventually."

"You've never been to New York?" Lila asked, as he wrapped her finger in a Band-Aid so gently she almost couldn't believe he didn't

440

kiss it when his work was complete. She felt a simultaneous urge to kiss him on the lips, so fully that she'd shock both of them, and to yell to the high ceilings what a fraud he was, what a complete and utter fake. Aaron let her hand go, as simply as he'd taken it. And while she felt dizzy with desire to make herself known, to be wrapped up in his guilty arms and thanked for her persistence, Lila was beginning to enjoy her anonymity. It would be like this: she'd take in as many lies as possible. She'd get good and informed.

Aaron shook his head.

"I can't believe that," Lila said. "I can't believe you've never been to New York."

"East Coast snob in the house," Keith said.

Aaron grabbed an apple from a hanging wire basket. He bit into it with gusto and smiled at her, making clear he hadn't taken offense. There was a piece of apple on his bottom lip, and no one told him it was there. This small thing was all it took to make her fully feel who he really was and what had led her here. She looked at Aaron and she could see Jack's mouth, though they never had looked much alike. Lila could smell the pond, how wet everything always was in the summer, how nothing ever quite dried. "I need to take a shower," she blurted out, as Aaron walked out of the kitchen. Sylvie looked startled and Keith did not, when Lila grabbed Keith's arm. "Would anyone mind if I took a shower?"

It was Sylvie who escorted her to the bathroom. "You can use my shampoo," she told Lila, and pointed out her basket of stuff on the corner of the tub. "Whatever's in there, feel free."

Lila nodded thanks, and looked at her bandaged finger, fought for the air to breathe. She needed to be alone. She needed it like shelter. *Please,* she thought, *just go.*

"And there's plenty of hot water, so don't worry. I despise bus trips, myself. So okay? Do you have what you need?"

"Thank you so much," Lila managed to say, through the dizziness and throbbing of her finger, and a wave of oncoming nausea. She sat on the lip of the tub and tried to pass off this sudden motion as exhaustion, plain and simple. "Whoa," she said.

Sylvie wasn't leaving.

"Thanks, I'm all set."

"Listen," Sylvie said, her hands clasped in front of her belt buckle, which was perfectly burnished silver. "I saw the way you looked at David just then."

"What?"

"Obviously you're not the first to try. I just

442

want to warn you, he's not exactly in the market for a girlfriend."

"What?" Lila said, and was too stunned to laugh. Too stunned and too annoyed. Her heavy breathing stopped. "I wasn't — I mean — I'm not . . . interested."

Sylvie gave her a look. "I'm just saying. You don't have to defend yourself or anything. He's a very attractive guy. I've just seen it happen before. It gets ugly."

"Yeah, well, I can imagine. Thanks for the warning. Who *are* you to him, anyway?"

"Who *am* I?"

"To David."

"Well," she said, as if she were extremely delicate, unused to such personal questions, "David's my best friend," she said, in a tone that made clear that he was anything and everything but.

Sylvie, Lila realized, had her own obsession to contend with.

"He's —" Lila tried to wrap up the conversation. *He's unavailable,* she had wanted to say.

"It's just that he's celibate," Sylvie said quickly, her voice riddled with confession, as if his celibacy had caused her own. Perhaps her cooking and cleaning and sense of order were only a product of sexually frustrated devotion. Everyone had a story.

"I don't want to be rude, but I just met the guy," Lila said. "I really just want to shower."

Sylvie nodded and closed the door, leaving Lila finally alone. The absurdity of Sylvie's perception gave her thoughts a little light. She had found him. There was no more searching to do.

The dinner consisted of what Lila's mother Vivian would call "peasant food" — linguini with garlic, onions, and olive oil, broccoli tossed with minced anchovies, and a light, unsalted bread. Lila found herself asking for more, unsettled, but not totally surprised that this entire meal was a staple of her mother's repertoire, usually served on rainy days. Aaron, it seemed, hadn't lost all connection to his past, and Lila bet Sylvie also knew how to make a good *penne arrabbiato,* as well as mushroom omelettes with just a little bit of plain American cheese.

Aaron ate like their father — upright in his chair but slouched at the neck — and Lila had trouble remembering if this was something Aaron had grown into or if he'd always resembled Jeb this way. "That was great," her brother told no one in particular, as if the meal had miraculously disappeared. "To Keith," Aaron said, raising his glass of apple juice. Everyone else, including Lila, drank cheap red wine. She could feel her teeth and tongue staining. Ben had told her that red wine was good for the heart.

"To you too," Keith responded softly, and sucked a last long strand of linguini with his pursed full lips.

When Aaron got up to clear dishes, Lila took up her own plate and followed Aaron into the kitchen. He scraped the food into the yellow trash can. His forearm was older, the veins defined; he stacked the dishes in the sink. "Hey there," he said to Lila. "You're so quiet."

"You're one to talk." It came out with no inhibitions. She smiled.

The dark kitchen was lit by one bare bulb, now that it was night. Lila could no longer see the lot out back, or the vine-covered concrete wall. She could hear her own breath and she could feel how her eyes kept blinking. "You got me there," he said. "I suppose you're right about that."

"I like your sweater," she said, in part to see what he'd say about the green Shetland with the paint stain, and in part because it was her habit, when a person made her nervous, to give compliments, genuine or not. "It looks comfortable," she continued, and the words themselves felt fragile, as if they weren't getting enough air.

"It was my father's," Aaron said. He was watching her as she set her plate down on the countertop.

"Really?" Lila asked, and a charge — something she was almost sure was mutual — began to flow between them. She felt drunk and pleasant and attractive, not what she would have predicted. "There's a stain," she told him, having no other words at her disposal, because there was too much to be said. She saw herself reach over and touch the yellow paint. It was easy enough to do. She reflexively wondered where Sylvie was, and if she was somehow watching them, for it was clear Sylvie had acquired a kind of impressive household stealth. Lila heard her own voice: "Where are you from?"

"Idaho," her brother said, completely straight-faced, completely cool.

"Idaho?" she spit the word back. People who turned statements into questions were narcissists — a tidbit from a book she'd read whose name she couldn't recall. She remembered this as she said it again: "Idaho."

"You?" Aaron asked, as he opened the freezer.

"New York," Lila said.

"Oh, right," Aaron said, as he took out a bakery box. "That's right."

"Is this for Keith?" Lila asked, basking in

this absurd familiarity, hanging around her big brother, unaware of the next step.

"That's right," Aaron said, "Keith's birthday. He's not in the best mood, and I don't suppose this will do the trick, but you do what you can."

"Sure," Lila said.

Aaron transferred the ice-cream cake from the box to a plate, his brief concentration interrupting his sentence. *What*, Lila thought, *tell me something*. But Aaron, apparently, wasn't one to rush his words. He meticulously slid the cake just so, arranging it perfectly centered. "These guys in the house — they're like brothers to me. They're my brothers."

Lila felt a choking sensation deep inside her throat. "Excuse me," she said. Lila started coughing and coughing and she knew she'd never stop. She knew she'd cough to her death if she didn't tell him the truth. Aaron handed her a glass of water. "You —" she said, but then shut herself up, because she was panicking and she knew it. She tried to focus on calming down. She tried to stop choking, and choked harder. She wanted to sip the water alone, and not be stared at by Aaron or anybody.

But Sylvie came in and made herself useful, her long arms like tree boughs lifting Lila's in the air. This was nothing if not comedy, she thought — first the bloody finger, now this, and didn't comedy come in threes? Sylvie was telling her to breathe, and she was breathing all right, she was breathing heavily, in and out, and she stood watching Aaron's face. His eyes were deep-set, even deeper than she'd remembered. For a flash, he had looked alarmed, or even — maybe — terrified. "I'm okay," she said. "I think I just need some air."

Outside, on the front steps, the air was clean and cool. "Happy Birthday" was being sung inside; she could faintly hear its highs and lows, and she could imagine, after only knowing him half a day, what Keith's response would be: he'd shake his head with a serious face; then, unexpectedly, he'd smile wide. Lila understood it was possible to know someone so quickly, to know exactly what expression an essential stranger would make in the face of kindness, and yet it could take a whole lifetime to understand your family — to put together memories with an unallied present and have faith that you are, in fact, related.

CHAPTER TWENTY-ONE

A lone saxophone wailed under a stone archway as if each note would be its last. An hour or so after Sylvie's familiar meal, Lila wandered up and down State Street, admiring the ancient movie marquee, watching more people pass in and out of bookstores and sidewalk conversations. Still hungry, she ate a mint-chocolate-chip frozen yogurt cone. She gave five dollars to a man with radio antennae attached to his head and a sign that read: *Help me get back to my planet.* A small sign for vintage clothing appealed to her, and she made her way up a narrow stairwell that smelled strongly of weed and geranium perfume. The floral smell was remarkably strong through the pot stench; it was winsome and feminine and reminded her of Pria. "Evenin' " a male voice welcomed her to the tiny room full of clothes.

Lila nodded at the guy, who was about her height and wiry, and playing with a pink plastic yo-yo. His skin was smooth like crème café.

"Everything's fifteen percent off," he told her, as if he were letting her in on a secret. He had thick hair black as licorice, sleepy dark eyes, a tattoo of an orange fish on his muscular forearm, and on his neck a cobalt blue circle enclosed a light brown mole.

Lila nodded again and noticed a tall unlabeled bottle of amber liquid sitting beside the antiquated register. She detected the varnished smell of whiskey through the musty air. "Well . . ." she began, but became distracted by the shape of his broad shoulders, the whole of his carelessly clothed body.

He was looking straight at her; his eyes were deep stains, threaded with copper. Lila had to look away. There was mostly junk everywhere. Purple polka dots and vinyl pants, vinyl pink panties. "Vinyl seems to be a theme."

"True," he said, and laughed. "Too true. What are you looking for?"

"A dress," she said matter-of-factly, and she suddenly really wanted one. She wanted knee-high boots and thigh-high stockings, a one-way ticket to Rome. She wanted a chain-mail bracelet, a true-blue T-shirt. She suddenly wanted *him*. "I want a dress." She looked at herself in the full-length mirror, surrounded by ridiculous costumes. Her face was unnaturally flushed. "Is this all you have?" The words felt heavy on her tongue, as if she were telling lies.

The guy shook his head, and took off his thin brown sweater, as if he were about to begin doing physical labor. She couldn't even bring herself to laugh at her reaction, which was pure unadulterated wonder. His muscles were long and lean, delicately close to the skin, and between the worn T-shirt with the word *ponytail* in lime green, and the very dark jeans, she could make out slivers of his hipbones. His hands made her think of her own ample hips. Those hands, smooth and brown, inspired strength and motion. "Let me show you something," he said, and even Lila could recognize what this guy's most salient feature was, his one defining characteristic. This guy was all about sex.

"Oh, yeah?" Lila replied, surprising herself. The guy raised his thick eyebrows and smiled.

She thought of kissing Ben. She could feel his lips, in a way more strongly now, than when they were actually on hers. He had been too much to take in all at once. But Ben had been coming back to her — in flashes, really, bit by bit — since she'd left his apartment less than two nights ago. If he were here now, Lila thought, as the guy went into the smallest walk-in closet she had ever seen, Ben would be trying on a pair of vinyl pants. He would be asking where the guy got all this stuff. Ben would find out about each tattoo, and consider, for a least an hour, maybe getting one himself.

"What can you fit in there?" she asked him, trying to see beyond his shoulders.

"Close your eyes," the guy said.

"Close my eyes?" There she went again, repeating. She shut up and closed her eyes. There was a rustling of fabrics, the sound of plastic bags, a lightening of her limbs. She felt dizzy as a mold-heavy scent rose and fell before the guy spoke up.

"All right," the guy said, "you can open up now. Check this out."

He was holding a hanger draped with an ivy-colored dress, so rich it had to be velvet, but when she touched the fabric it wasn't. It was light and soft as silk, with thin straps and a peacock feather on each side where the straps met the dress. Little beads, ink blue, adorned the low neckline.

He handed the dress to Lila in silence, and instead of going into the tiny closet to try it on, which appeared to be the only option in terms of a dressing room, Lila found herself unbuttoning her blouse, undressing right before him, her eyes lingering on the guy's brown neck, where the blue circle safely enclosed his beauty mark. Waves of chills shot through her skin and waves of heat too. There were no windows in the store. The ventilation whirred behind the sexy clothes — the wall of fishnets and beaded bags and leather gloves almost shook. Lila stood in her bra and underwear. Her fine hairs everywhere stood up at utter attention. The door to the store was open. Anyone at all could've walked up the stairs.

He said, "You shouldn't wear a bra with this." So Lila unhooked her white cotton bra and hung it over a clothes rack. Her nipples were so taut they almost hurt. Her breasts were now part of the ridiculous fashions; they belonged to the scent of whiskey and mold, to the marijuana- and geranium-heavy air. Her breasts were far away from Ben, from Aaron in his pious house, from anything familiar. They felt suspended, even, from her very self.

The guy — he nodded, he just nodded and swallowed, and with every bit of a smile, took the dress gently off the hanger, and handed it over to Lila.

It slid over her body like a second skin, a phrase that had always sounded creepy to Lila until now. How could she have known that her second skin was so sensual, female — as smooth and strange as mystery?

"Damn," he said. "Damn."

Lila laughed like a wholly different person, a woman accustomed to such exquisite retail therapy. He handed the liquor over to her with a questioning look.

"You bet," she said, and leaned on a clothes rack, accepting the tall bottle. The liquor singed her throat like a flame to fabric, made her good and raw and awake. She passed it back, and he took a swig, making as if to toast her.

"I'm Lowell," he said, as if his name really mattered.

"Well," she said, "cheers. I'm Lila." Abby seemed demure just then — nothing particularly special.

"That dress . . ." he murmured. He took a step closer.

"I never had a prom," she said. The heat of his body made her sleepy and tangential, incapable of making sense.

"You're kidding," he said. "I fucking loved the prom."

"Is that right?" Lila asked, and raised her hand to her neck, which was damp beneath her heavy hair. "Did you score?" she heard her voice ask. She briefly wondered what the hell she was doing.

He shook his head, looking grave.

"Then I guess you missed out on something too," she said, and Lila downed some more liquor, which really tasted like hell. She gave him a huge smile, reaching past him toward a pack of Camels. This store was a house of vices. "May I?" she asked.

"Don't know if you should," he told her.

Lila took one and smiled again. "I'm usually very healthy," she said. "Healthy as a horse." He lit it for her, and she inhaled deeply, closing her eyes. She felt his breath nearby, or maybe she imagined it, and she exhaled a thin stream of smoke. There was a loosening throughout her legs.

"Easy," Lowell said.

She opened her eyes, and saw him reach out and touch one of the peacock feathers. He was supremely graceful as he fingered the green dress that belonged to nobody's body but hers. Lila could see his hands tentatively feeling their way at her sides, but she couldn't quite feel them. She could hear his breath as he touched the skin above the neckline, and then she felt the air underneath the dress, how it snaked up her legs and slowed her down. "Okay," she heard herself say, but he didn't seem to hear her; maybe she hadn't said it. "Hang on," she said, as his lips were near her ear now, and she could smell his smoky whiskey breath. He kissed her neck sloppily at first, and then progressed to a kind of precision, stopping in between each kiss, to see what she would do. She pulled back from him silently and looked at his unfamiliar face. She just looked at him, without questions, without searching his eyes. Lila only wanted to see him; she didn't care if he saw her. This seemed to make him nervous.

He pointed amusedly to the cigarette she held, which she gripped in her hand like a pencil. It was burnt down to a fine ash, at least one inch long. She dropped it to the floor. "Sorry," she said.

Lowell didn't look too concerned. He reached out to touch the dress again, but this time she could feel his hands, how entirely strange they were. They palmed her chest and pressed on the beads and feathers. He leaned into her neck again, and she drew herself away.

"You're kind of crazy," he told her. He tried to kiss her mouth.

"Come on," she said, pulling away, as if they were actually friends.

"What happened to prom night?" he asked, not cruelly, but as if they were in this together.

She picked up her purse, shook her head, and then, not quite coldly, handed him one hundred dollars in cash. "I'll take the dress," she told him, and he eyed her strangely. "And I don't think I'll undress again."

The night was quiet now, as the church stood tall in the distance. The white steeple illuminated the surrounding sky. There was barely a sliver of moon. Lila thought of New Hampshire, of her parents sleeping under the chill of a navy blue heaven. The house, the path, the pond, were all frozen in time, fixed as a child's diorama. Green construction paper trees and tinfoil stars. Blue cellophane for water and sky.

She hadn't meant to expose her body to a stranger, to play games with herself like that, but she couldn't deny that she felt excited by the danger of doing so, by the sheer thrill of anonymity. She hadn't even intended wandering so far from Aaron's house, or to stay out for such a long time. But before she began to cower at Aaron's door, Lila reminded herself who she was. She could lay claim to this place. She could. She could tear it all apart.

Inside, the space had the haunted aura of people dreaming. Keith slept on the downstairs couch, flat on his back, snoring. His loss could be a ghost in the curtains, a sudden wind, or a surprising taste in his mouth.

Jack, in fact, could be watching.

The table was cleared of dishes but strewn with playing cards. Coffee cups and glasses still adorned each place. Someone's headband and small-faced silver watch were also left behind, as well as one lone Oreo cookie. Also on the table was a piece of paper, writing side faceup. *Abby,* the note read, *if you found your way back in, go on upstairs and crash on the upstairs couch. Why did you leave so abruptly? Hope you're O.K. . . . Keith.*

Lila promised herself she would thank him tomorrow. He would understand — or at least she hoped he'd understand — soon enough. She would thank him her whole life. And she would certainly thank Pria for her honesty, for her charm, for being the ally she was supposed to find. *Thank you,* Lila would tell her. *I know it was you. Even if you're not sure.*

She climbed her way up the stairwell that stood between the front room and the kitchen. She walked very carefully past the bathroom and out onto the loftlike landing. Her duffel bag sat on the large ragged couch. This much, in itself, seemed like a miracle. She sat down, took off her shoes, and was quickly sobering up, because right in front of her, a few feet ahead, was what had to be the steeple door. Up those stairs, her brother would be sleeping.

Lila told herself she shouldn't do it, that it was the worst thing she could do, but even before she could change out of her dress to rid herself of her boozy, smoky perfume, she was upright again, the carpet soothing the balls of her feet, as she padded toward the door. She

458

put her forehead on the dark wood that smelled like nothing, told her nothing, and issued not a clue. He was upstairs — not David in his sleep, but Aaron — just a stairwell away.

The door opened without fanfare. She was a fantasy now, she told herself. Her actions at this moment were merely some illusion he was having. Lila could feel herself crossing over into the permissive realm of dreams. She told herself, repeatedly, that she was completely over her preposterous fear of the dark, that the dark couldn't hurt her any more than the light could, any more than the blinding sun. She told herself this, but telling herself did not stop her heart from speeding or her hands from shaking. It did not stop the familiar images of blood and water, blood and Jack, the same useless horror shows. Her fear of the dark had been with her as long as she could remember, but Lila knew she had no choice but to conquer it now, because her fear of staying in the figurative and more powerful dark about her past was ever so much stronger. If Aaron lay in a strange dark room, well, then, into strange darkness she would go.

She ignored the creaking of the short, steep stairwell. When she reached the top, the room itself was fortunately lit by outside streetlights and a nice piece of moon. As her eyes adjusted, she saw that the room was like the cabin of a fine antique sailboat or a house in the trees. A mobile hung from the ceiling in long shapes of green, yellow, and blue. The window was open, pushed out into the night. The room smelled like breeze and like soap faded out by a good, clean sweat.

He was on his side, way to the left, as if a person were missing from his bed. The covers were pulled up to his waist. Aaron's mouth was only slightly open, and his breath was nearly silent, moving his broad chest up and down. Had he watched her like this when she was a child, and wondered just who she was? Lila couldn't help searching his nakedness for signs of herself. There were none, besides, maybe, the color of his skin, which was pale, but like hers, it was the kind of pale that tanned. Jack had it too. They all inherited it from Jeb, who — unlike their moon-white mother — had an even olive glow.

Aaron was hairy, even more so than she remembered. And Lila recalled, right then, that she used to call him King Kong. Neither Jeb nor Jack had had half as much hair as Aaron at twenty. Aaron's shoulders sloped slightly into knots of shoulder muscles; the one closest to Lila had the tea-colored birthmark she remembered. This letter-pressed petal, this miniature bas relief — it was the smallest yet most perfect proof that he was, indisputably, her brother. On his skin above his elbow was what looked like a faded cut — purplish and recently acquired. Of the rest, what could be said? He had a man's chest, rounder at the stomach, which hung down slightly, like a small sack of sugar. Outlines of muscle prevailed.

Lila watched with the curiosity of love, with the scrupulous eye of infatuation. She watched as a sister who could finally appreciate not only the difference in men's bodies, but that her brother was, ultimately, just a man.

Her brother, Aaron, he was beautiful.

The moment she leaned over, she was convinced — she must have been — that she, too, was dreaming, for the only thing that she wanted right then was simply to be closer. She sat on the mattress where the missing person was. At first she only sat. She was very aware of the cigarettes and alcohol, what a strong scent they created. Lila felt dirty and — for a moment — that she was corrupting him. He looked so maddeningly innocent. She fought the urge to smooth his hair away from his forehead. The sheets were dark blue with a neat white piping. Everything was so clean. The sheets felt new between her fingers, which were not, somehow, shaking. Then she lay down on her brother's bed. She just set herself down beside him. *If he wakes up,* she thought . . . *if he does . . . I'll disappear. I can do it. I will simply will it to happen.*

She'd felt afraid ever since that night when he had laid himself down beside her, but she was no longer afraid. Now she lay back, looking up at the ceiling, so similar to the wooden beams of their home, where their parents lay together just like this. Maybe desperate, maybe not, but still married after all these years. Lila finally understood why her parents remained together after every wrong thing that had happened. It had something to do with the silence here in her brother's very bed. It had something to do with the rage Lila felt toward him and the fantastic sorrow too. It had everything to do with relation. With wanting to touch and worrying over that touch, with guarding it and finally doing it.

It was the lightest of touches on Aaron's bare shoulder, these ten years later. It was only with her finger, and not for very long. She was pointing and making an invisible mark. She would follow it tomorrow. She would touch it again.

After he was told.

CHAPTER TWENTY-TWO

In a way, waking up in the church house, on the upstairs couch in her purple NYU T-shirt, was the strangest moment of the past few months. Lila heard quiet activity downstairs, and she assumed that the first up (probably Sylvie) was making a pot of coffee. She closed her eyes again, being not at all ready to do anything quite yet. The night was coming back to her in unnerving fragments, and she was disturbed by the images pressing upon her eyelids: the finger cut, a coughing fit, Jeb's old sweater. Lowell and his hands, the dress. The haunting presence of dreams.

Had she really lain down next to her brother, or was that part of a dream?

It was real, and she knew it. She could remember the wood beam ceiling. His long brown lashes. The expanse of space at his side that she had decided to fill.

Lila would let him have his hot shower and coffee. Then she would ask him to take a walk.

★ ★ ★

There were no clocks in the bathroom, or on the landing beside the couch. Although she didn't want to talk to anyone besides her brother, she wanted to find out the time, so, after dressing, she crept down the stairs. If it was really early, she'd hit the sidewalk and walk, taking in the energy of a Saturday morning, the free lift that happened when she stood in the midst of any kind of crowd.

But the table was cleared of its cards, watch, headband, and Oreo, and the clock said ten after one.

It was afternoon.

She had slept ten hours when she usually slept only five. "Hello?" Lila called out, but no one answered back. Where was the person who was making noise just minutes ago? Had she imagined that? She looked for another note, another kindness from Keith, but no notes were around, and no clues of her brother. It was possible, she supposed, that no one noticed she had come in, which was definitely preferable to everyone passing by her sleeping form, questioning, out loud, what she'd been up to last night. "Hello?" she called again, and still, no one. There was no coffee out, but there was a bowl of fruit, and she plucked some grapes, thought of Suzanne, and ran up the stairs to the steeple

464

door, where she knocked three times.

She opened the door without caution this time and in a more nervous state, somehow, now that Aaron wasn't around. This was thoughtless and she knew it, for anyone could return at any moment, and rifling through David's private sanctuary was not how she wanted to be found. Even disturbing Aaron's privacy was wrong — she knew — however entitled to it she actually happened to feel. She thought of Suzanne plucking green grapes from their stems, calling her husband *baby*. If Pria were an old friend, if that were possible in this lifetime, she would tell Lila to do whatever the hell she felt like doing. She would say, *Fuck privacy — you have a right to know for yourself what has happened to your family.*

The bed was made. Of course it was made. Of course the room was essentially spotless, and advertised its sense of correctness. Suzanne and Aaron both looked fantastic and kept their different spaces with the same flair for order.

The wood walls in the steeple were polished the color of weak coffee. A hand-tinted photograph of two shadows on a wall was matted and finely framed, and it hung above a metal desk. The photograph looked like it was taken in a desert place. The light was that clearly hot. And the bookshelves took up an entire wall. From what Lila could tell, they were all religious books. Martin Buber's *I and Thou*, and *The Tibetan Book of the Dead* were the only ones she recognized. One shelf was entirely in Hebrew.

Some kind of Balinese or Tibetan mask hung on the wall above her brother's pillow. Green and red and gold, with nostrils the size of silver dollars, it was the face of a monster, or that was how it looked to Lila, and she was amazed she hadn't noticed it last night. She couldn't imagine why anyone would hang such a thing above his bed. Then again, she could. This demon ruled over the bed — the domain of sex — which, in Aaron's case, was sex and death. It was more effective than a mirror, which could present the good angles and the possibility of innocence. This mask presented nothing but the monster, could remind Aaron of demons everywhere, in every country in the world and beyond. Inside himself.

She was speedy with greed, and her hands moved too quickly for the quiet nature of this room. Her fingers — still with a Band-Aid, bitten and unpolished — skimmed the cool desktop and opened all of the six small drawers. She listened to the faint skitter of a creature between the walls. She listened and *became* that creature — ears pricked up and ready for Aaron's return. But even as she listened, the outside of this room was beginning to fade away. The real possibility of being interrupted didn't weigh all that heavily, for the papers in her hands (graph paper with building sketches, a list of books, a series of names and telephone numbers — some with check marks, some without) were so mundane, so amazingly ordinary, that she didn't feel culpable of any wrongdoing. The content of his drawers was like a postcard addressed to somebody else: its utter predictability made it completely fair game. There was a drawer of rubber bands and tape and glue, blue Post-it notes and paper clips. One contained gas and electric bills addressed to Mr. David Silver.

Silver.

The expensive colors are Jewish. The plain colors are not. Who had said that? Nana? A friend at school?

Miss Vivian Beth Silver married Mr. Jebidiah Samuel Wheeler.

Her mother's maiden name. How unoriginal.

Lila knelt down on the red-patterned Moroccanesque rug, and searched under the bed. There was a box down there. Lila reached for it, amazed at the lack of dust. She imagined herself hitting her head on the bed frame, passing out with Aaron's life in her sneaky hands. Lila envisioned herself being found by all of his loyal fans in a huddle, who'd fight over which one would get to inform David that *Abby was snooping around.*

She dragged the box out from its hiding place. It was metal, red-painted, with a big fat lock. She looked for a key in every possible place — through the desk again, under his pillows, mattress, in his shoes. She searched between the books in a time-crunching frenzy. Finally, as she was getting nowhere and progressively frustrated, she decided to put the box back and look in other rooms, to see what Aaron's friends could tell her. What the woman of the house was about.

Sylvie's room was the only one downstairs, off of the living room, and Lila shouted for good measure to double-check that she was still alone. The door was painted white and the room was also white. A small copper mirror sat upright on a wooden bureau. The bookshelf was small and the books were surprisingly mostly fluff. Best-sellers and airport paperbacks. Some cookbooks and self-help titles. A few Jane Austen, a few Brontës. Her bedspread was white with light blue dots, the kind found in a Cape Cod guest room. The floor was hardwood, the area rug woven blue and white. The room's decor gave off no whiff of personal space. She could have stepped into a catalog room. However, unlike Aaron's, and to Lila's surprise, Sylvie's room was a mess. It was *after* the catalog photo shoot, in a warehouse studio in Jersey where no one ever bothered to clean up the set. Used and crumpled tissues lay like painter's rags to the right and left sides of the twin bed. A banana peel and a yogurt-crusted bowl and spoon sat on the nightstand. Newspapers littered the dresser top, as well as a dead plant, which scattered its leaves in crisp brown bits. Lila had the feeling that Sylvie didn't let anyone in here and that she had truly crossed a line.

Lila started with the drawers. Quickly. Nothing caught her eye. Then, once again, she was lying cheek-to-floor — this time braving dust bunnies — while searching under Sylvie's bed. At first she saw nothing strange about the box that lay there. But when she brought it out, along with an unmarked manila envelope, she was struck by how the box was the very same as the one under Aaron's bed. Metal, red-painted, with the same fat lock.

Lila put it back, in favor of searching the envelope, which wasn't even sealed. And sitting on the unswept floor, just like that — in her jeans and favorite blue sweater, Lila saw them pour straight into her lap. It was, needless to say, a surprise.

They were pictures of her.

Some of the black-and-whites that Aaron had taken for his high school project were enlarged to eight by ten inches and were curling slightly at the edges. She held the small pile in her shaking hands and nothing else was real.

Lila, age four, sits on a rock, next to a pale bullfrog. The pond glimmers in a silver strip behind them, and the sun is obviously shining. In a three-quarter profile her eyes are big and bulging and her little nose and mouth are scrunched up in a smile. She is missing two teeth, and the bright light washes over her curly hair, making it appear almost white. Her hands reach tentatively toward the frog and are extraordinarily tiny.

Lila, now in Sylvie's room, looked down at her own grown hands in a kind of misplaced shame. The child on the rock looks silly, joyful, and capable of becoming anybody, doing anything. She is bound to nothing but the very earth, and it's plain that she's surrounded by love. You can see in her eyes the trust she places in everyone, in everything. She is four years old and happy.

Another picture, and she's staring right into the camera; she's in the woods and the light is darker, saturated with oncoming evening. It must have been one of the last photographs of any given day, as she looks spent and sensual in a way that is particular to children. She is slouching against a tree, and something in her mouth suggests that there is something she means to say.

What was it? And did Aaron listen? Did he make her laugh a moment later, or did she ask if they could go home? To step into the photograph and find that fleeting second — this was something for which she yearned as strongly as food or sleep. To feel herself in her brother's gaze and hold on to the dying light — it would be beautiful there; it would be frightening. Colors would look different; everything would.

Here in Sylvie's room, in a stranger's room, was this trusting child's future. Here was where she let the tears come as that child stared back with light eyes and a dark mouth and a hint of a stubborn chin. Lila watched and became unaware of the act of watching. She became that child as the pictures kept coming: she was holding a stick, looking down at that stick with a pure, indelible focus. Here she was again at the water's edge, sticking out her tongue, holding up her hand to block the sun. In the distance a white plastic shovel looks lonely and discarded in the mud and gray sand.

She imagined that these were his favorites. On the back of each one were titles in black careful print: *Lila and the Frog. My Sister in the Woods. The Stick. Spring, 1984* . . . There was also one small faded color photograph that he must have taken from their mother's box below her desk. On what is clearly a winter's day, Vivian brushes Lila's hair in front of the old woodstove; both mother and daughter are in crimson turtlenecks and are seemingly unaware of being photographed.

Lila let the tears come and they kept coming in a great hurry, barely granting her time to breathe. She thought of Aaron, sick with guilty grief, searching their mother's things for a fragile photograph, before flying away from them all.

What were they doing in Sylvie's room?

She barely thought about that glitch as she pored over the photographs like secret text, as if these young Lilas were somehow very different from the ones in her parents' house. She looked for more pictures, ones of anything and anyone else, but there were no others.

They were all of her.

Aaron did not want to leave her, Lila realized. He did not want her to recede into the horror of that early summer morning. Her brother took the best of her; he took what he knew how to take. He did not want her to pass into dreams and threads of dreams, into every child he ever saw. Lila was this child, *here*, committed to paper, and therefore to memory. He'd tried to make sure of that.

Aaron had not wanted to lose her, she thought, wiping fat tears with her wet sleeve. He hadn't wanted to, but he did. And because of that loss, she was extraordinary. She was somewhere else, stopped in time, full of possibility. She was Abigail.

Holding the pictures, holding them tight, she imagined that Jack hadn't died. What if Aaron had fallen asleep in her bed, a deep sleep of mercy, and she had woken him up to make waffles? She imagined her family sitting down to waffles, and how she would've become impatient listening to everyone talk about people she didn't know. She would have stared at Suzanne's long hair. She would have reached out and touched it, braided a few shiny strands. What if her own sleep had been powerful enough to draw her brother in? Say the whole night had passed into morning, and Lila hadn't let him go. She might have asked him to sing her lullabies, or his version of lullabies, "Wild Horses," "Wild World," anything from Neil Young's *After the Gold Rush*.

Looking at the pictures, at her own young

face, it seemed that all the possibilities repeatedly lit up their lives like punishing fires, and that her family was no longer composed of individuals, but instead — almost like stillborn children — the cruel abundance of possibilities. Each time Lila looked at a picture, she was surrounded by the sense of a deep long breath, and was startled by the small tight curls at her child's forehead, the unabashed toothy grin, the direct gaze that seemed to ask, *What's next?*

Her little face looks nothing like the face it would become. In the pictures her features show no hints of the large, dramatic shapes her nose and mouth would acquire. Some children grow into their features; Lila had grown right out of hers. There is, of course, no indication that large breasts were lurking, or that her honey blond hair would darken. There is no darkness anywhere, in fact. She held the pictures and held on to herself, trying not to fall into the vortex of the past, into reliable and pathetic sadness. But the girl in the picture looks so light. She is perfect and unaware that in less than five years the world will change in a moment, without any warning at all.

Aaron developed these photographs. He'd stood in the darkroom at the high school for hours. He must have loved the intensity of the process, the concentration it required. She pictured the gradations from dark to light, and how perfectly he would have been suited to the chemically scented silence. He was like that, meticulous, but who knew how she would have thought of him by now, had he, on that fatal morning, simply fallen asleep beside her. His meticulousness might have grown into fussiness, someone rigid and difficult to please. She could have grown sneaky on him and hidden from his judgment, his stern and perfectionist ways. He might have bought her infuriatingly practical birthday gifts. If he had fallen asleep beside her, these pictures might have looked extremely different. They might have looked ordinary, sentimental. They might have looked discarded.

But they didn't.

The pictures didn't merely *look* like anything — they *were* something, a tangible proof and a tender piece of evidence that said he had not wanted to leave her.

Lila looked around the room, Sylvie's room, which was a blur of blue and white. She had to get going, get out of this room, but it was difficult to think straight. Her breathing was irregular and it was hard to do much. She wanted to lie down. She wanted sleep. But she watched herself return the pictures to their place under Sylvie's bed. She thought of

Aaron's religious books and photograph of two desert shadows. Then, still sitting on the floor, she closed her eyes and saw *Aaron* asleep, how his chest hair had looked soft and his eyelashes long. How he'd rolled so far to one side of the bed, as if he loathed to take up too much space.

That was something she understood. For a long time now, Lila had been trying to take up less space in the world. She wasn't fat or unthinkably tall. She had only wanted to go backward for so long, to be quiet and unnoticed.

In Sylvie's unknown but average room (it was no ship's quarters, no tree-house steeple) Lila stood up, and began to feel a strange rush of incongruous excitement. She felt expectant, even though what she was expecting was a dark conversation about her brother Jack's death. About the *why* of that loss.

At least that was what she thought she was expecting.

Lila didn't know it, but she was actually skipping that step, and, in fact, what she was anticipating was simply the business of living. In Sylvie's neutral room, she was having a glimpse of forward motion. She had a taste of it, for a moment. And then she didn't.

"What are you doing?" an alarmed voice cried at the door. It was a true-blond, thin-lipped, long-limbed voice. With the sharp tang of suspicion.

The room was in its place, she reassured herself. Pictures of herself were bizarrely returned to Sylvie's dusty floor. Aaron's room also — she'd left it in place: shadows, desk, mobile, mask.

Lila stopped herself from bolting, and from blurting out the truth. Her lonely truth that belonged to no one else. "I'm just looking," she said to Sylvie.

"Just *looking?*" Sylvie stood in the doorway, in overalls. Not cute. "What are you looking for?"

"Just looking," Lila said, as if Sylvie were a salesgirl.

"Don't you think you should ask someone if you can look around their room?"

"You're right," Lila said, "of course. I was just . . . I was so curious what it would look like. You have great style."

"You must have been pretty disappointed."

"No, of course not. I love that copper mirror."

Sylvie looked as if she was struggling to stay on track. "Just *ask* before you go in my room again, okay?"

Lila nodded solemnly, walked out of Sylvie's room, and closed the door behind her. She then followed Sylvie into the kitchen, and watched her take a broom from the closet and start sweeping the linoleum floor with an unreadable expression. This was what Aaron had ended up with: not Suzanne, not a similar careless sexiness, but someone to clean up anyone else's mess before her own, someone who wanted him coldly and purposefully, but with fundamental ferocity.

"Can I help you with anything?" Lila asked.

"How long are you planning on staying?"

"I'm not really sure."

"Look," Sylvie said, holding, but not leaning on, the broom, "David is a very nice guy, which is a rarity. But his kindness is also his downfall. This is technically his place, but I get very angry when girls like you use his kindness against him —"

"Girls like me?"

"Wait," Sylvie said. "You come here, it's a good deal, and you take advantage. I heard you sneaking around here last night, looking for God knows what. This is not a hotel, and David isn't up for grabs. Okay?"

"I never thought he was."

"Then what were you doing in his room last night?"

"What?"

"You went into his room."

"I did not."

There was rustling at the front door and

Keith and Jacob wandered in. She raised her voice at Lila: "I saw you!" Sylvie looked as if she were five, and Lila had taken away her toys. Panic glazed her arctic eyes so madly that Lila almost reassured her with the truth.

Keith came behind Sylvie and gently touched her shoulders. "C'mon, Syl," he said.

"She was searching our rooms," Sylvie cried. "All of them! She tried to sneak into David's room last night."

Keith looked at Lila apologetically. He didn't even question that Sylvie might have been telling the truth. He smoothed her narrow shoulders with the denim overall straps. He encouraged her to relax.

It occurred to Lila that maybe Sylvie didn't actually see her last night, and that this was her routine with any woman who stayed here. Maybe Sylvie was paranoid — accurate this time — but paranoid nonetheless.

Sylvie shook her head and looked away. "Nobody believes me."

Keith gave her shoulders more attention, but Jacob ignored everyone and reclined on the couch as if he were the only one in the room.

"Where *is* David, anyway?" Lila asked her, as if to say, *Truce, okay?*

Jacob surprisingly piped up: "He's running.

He goes every Saturday — insanely long runs — twelve miles or so. I usually pick him up at a schoolyard outside of town. Why don't you join me?"

"I will, thanks," Lila said, giving Sylvie a smile.

"I know what you're up to," Sylvie said uncompromisingly, and for a moment Lila didn't doubt that she did.

The sky through the large windows was an innocent blue, the kind that always put her slightly ill at ease. "What's the weather like?" Lila asked Keith.

"Warm and beautiful. You should really go check it out," he said purposefully, and she understood that she was being ushered out, as he nodded toward Sylvie, who, having just returned to the kitchen, was beginning to bang pots around. She was making a whole lot of noise.

"I'm gone," Lila said.

"We need to leave here in about an hour," Jacob reminded her with a smirk. "So just don't go and disappear again."

After slipping out the door, she followed the aborted curve of the street, where a deli stood incongruously amid the old houses. There was no one around. She bought a coffee and stood still on the sidewalk. Lila stood there, in her same old clothes and hair and fingers, with her same lime green purse with Pria's charm and the business cards and dirty dollars, and suddenly felt as if she were being watched, as if every moment counted in a way she'd never fully understood.

Those pictures had just poured out of their envelope as if they'd been waiting all along — if not to mock her, then to make her good and aware of just how fleeting time really was. *Every* moment counted, every passing day, and as she thought of how she'd left Ben's apartment without once looking back, Lila knew she had really only been keeping track of the past.

Without Ben knowing where she was, Lila realized she felt — perhaps surprisingly — *less free*. And though she had expected, with each step toward Ben, to feel more and more afraid, in fact, she was less so than ever. Before she could think it over for much longer, Lila dialed his number.

The breeze blew the weeds between the cracks in the sidewalk and her no-longer-honey-colored hair. Lila was far away from the child in those pictures; she took a breath and trusted that it was the right place to be. She wasn't missing and she wasn't dead. She was nineteen years old and very much alive with someone important to call. Lila strained at hope's edges and prayed to the telephone that Ben would not only be at home but that he'd also be awaiting her call.

He answered on the third ring. "I'm in Ann Arbor, Michigan," she told him, laughing at that one simple fact. Said out loud it really seemed absurd. She described the church, the movie marquee, her new dress, and how she wished he could have been there with her at night to see the streetlights and the trees with the wind passing through them. "You see," she said, "I found him."

"What, already?"

"Yes," she said carefully. "Ben, it happened right away. I met someone on the campus, and it was hailing." She realized there was no easy way to explain any of it. "I was taken to his house. Just like that. He came through the door and then he introduced himself as *David*."

"But —"

"David," she said, with more bite than she'd intended. "He *introduced himself*. He didn't recognize me. And obviously he's changed his name."

Ben said nothing. She could hear him light a cigarette. "And then?"

"And then we shook hands."

"How did he take it, *then?*"

"Well, I introduced myself as Abigail.

Abby," she said archly. "Right back at him."

"Are you telling me that you found your brother and lied to him? That he doesn't know who you are?"

Lila didn't say anything, surprised at how Ben seemed to have an awfully accusatory tone.

"Lila?"

"Ben — yes, that's right, that's exactly right. He lied to all these people who he lives with and to *me* first. He did it first. What was I supposed to do? So that's right, I've been lying. It's complicated."

"It *is* complicated," Ben said. "I'm sure you're doing what you need to be doing." He sounded as if he would say something more, but then he stopped himself abruptly. "You're so far away."

"You don't feel so far away to me," she said.

A silence slipped through the telephone, through the cracks in the uneven pavement. Across the street a large red house loomed as large and abandoned as history. Its contrast to the blue sky was like a portrait of people grown apart.

"Lila," he finally said, in a bad-news tone, "it is good to hear your voice, but I *don't* understand your situation. I don't understand why you would deceive your brother after all your obsessing and finally finding him. I don't, to be perfectly honest, understand you."

"But —"

"I want to. I want to know you better than anyone does. I want all of it. I was in, I really was. You're slightly mad, but I find you terribly interesting — and I am wild about your face and your big luscious body. Do you understand what I'm saying? I've been waiting by the phone like a little girl, all right?" He started laughing, but there was something spiky beneath the laughter.

"Ben?" she said, wanting more than anything for him to keep on talking.

"I'd like to sit somewhere with you," he picked up, "without the threat of you leaving if you don't like the expression on my face. I want to stop having to prove so much. But Lila, I want a lot of things. I want a job. D'you know what I mean? I can't just wait for you to throw me a bone every now and then. That's not on." He cleared his throat and he sounded older somehow — experienced in the ways of irrational women. "When you tell me that you have found your brother by way of — from what I can tell, *sheer magic* — and that you are still playing around —"

"This is not a game," she said clearly. *Fuck you*, she thought, *this is not*. "You're right; you don't understand."

"Stop it," he said, real hurt in his voice. "Just stop doing that. Stop telling me I'm either out or in. Just give me a little bit of a break."

"You want to take a break?" she asked, with the sensation of being dropped into a deep brown well.

"I want you to do what you need to do. Selfishly, *I* want you to talk to him."

"Selfishly?" She could see, from where she stood, the white steeple of the churchhouse. A bleached cross on a blue sky. In her wildest fantasies she could have never imagined that this was where Aaron would be.

"Because I don't think you can stop getting angry at me every time I say anything if you don't go get angry at him. Who knows?" Ben said. "Maybe you'll always be this way. Maybe it has nothing to do with how many lies you've been told, and how many you tell on your own. Maybe you're just angry with me because I piss you off. If that's the case, well — we'll see what that's all about." He took a breath.

"You don't piss me off."

"No?"

"Of course not." She found herself shaking her head, touching her fingertips to the telephone. "Do you think I've been taking all this out on you?"

"I do, in a way, yes. But I know I've also invited it. I'm intrigued with all of this and you know it, but only to a point."

Ben continued, "You do know you're like an addict, don't you? You're absolutely addicted to this search. And as long as that's the case, the only role I can conceivably play is the poor sap who keeps on about how distant you seem. I'm afraid that's too limited for me. I'm not one for endless mystery."

"Yeah, well, I'm not either. I'm the one who's been searching for my brother."

"And now you've found him," he said firmly. "So why don't you go and speak with him."

What could she possibly say to that?

"Lila?"

"Believe me," she said, "I intend to."

"Well, then," he said. "That is awfully good to hear."

Their voices were both muted and suspicious, but somehow more certain as well.

"So how is it there?" Lila asked — saying anything to keep talking.

"It's a shitty day outside. I went out for a coffee earlier, and everyone was in a foul mood."

"You should see it here," Lila said. "It's a good day here."

There was silence on the line but it wasn't

so bad. Lila closed her eyes and pictured the white-trimmed window in Ben's apartment where she imagined he was standing. All around her, on the sidewalk, there emerged an abundance of clean, new air.

Ben coughed, breaking the spell of quiet. "Where's your brother now?"

"He's running," she said, and she pictured that run. She understood in her bones why he ran, why he had always run. He ran to obliterate the voices of others and to clear a straight path toward what was undeniable. He ran to hear his particular truths and to find out, without the encouragement or discouragement from others, of just what exactly he was made. Aaron had always needed that kind of time. She knew, intuitively, that Ben would understand this.

"I have to say," he said, "I wish I knew the bastard."

"Aaron? I wish I did too."

Lila pictured Ben and Aaron meeting, and felt sad because that would never happen. Everything was so separate. They'd never shake hands and talk about music. They'd never take a drive to pick up the missing ingredient for the big festive dinner that they'd never share. They wouldn't disagree about some stupid thing and ask for her opinion. They would never meet.

"I'm completely afraid," Lila finally said.

"I know," Ben replied. "But until you do this, until you finish it up completely, you'll never really be with me."

And standing on the sidewalk, after telling Ben good-bye, she imagined the white cross going up in flames against that perfect sky. She saw all those pictures beneath Sylvie's bed burning away, and Aaron being left with nothing.

The breeze passed her by just then. She could see as well as feel it. The breeze carried something as it passed her by, and Lila saw what it was. It was the day opening up, putting every last card on the table. It explained to her — patient as seasons — that this was not what she wanted. *Look,* the day told her, *listen now: It doesn't need to be this way at all.*

CHAPTER TWENTY-THREE

Aaron ran in a pair of black running shorts and a faded blue T-shirt. He ran with a fierce expression, which looked as if someone had tightened every nerve in his magnificent body. Lila didn't care how far he'd just run — the look on his face was more than physical exertion. His jaw looked clenched and a line wrinkled deeply between his furrowed brows, but it was more than any one physical attribute that made something very clear: he was tortured. Here was something ephemeral and true, and she felt considerably relieved.

They were sitting in an unkempt schoolyard. Jacob and Lila sat in a makeshift amphitheater beneath huge pale sycamores that blew in the pollen-heavy breeze. Lila noticed Aaron see them and give a minuscule wave, but then he veered, purposefully, in the opposite direction. He slowed to a halt and stretched his hands skyward. Lila and Jacob watched, dumbly, as he stretched. "I hate running," Lila said.

"I hate it more," said Jacob. And Lila couldn't help liking him. He was stocky in stature but had a bouncing walk, probably due to lifting weights and doing nothing else in the way of exercise. He had colossal arms and skinny legs, and wore thick biker boots, which served to balance out these somehow endearing proportions. "But I like coming out here. By truck," he added with a grin. "I like sitting and waiting in this wide-open space. I know it's not *that* wide and open, but it does the trick."

Aaron looked up from a side lunge and smiled. She felt the smile inside her, way down in her cells' nuclei, in her timorous beating heart. She saw a flash of her father Jeb, his silent kind of love, the kind forever questioned and mistrusted because of its quiet ways.

Quiet was becoming increasingly hard to take.

"Hi," Lila shouted. "How far did you run?"

Jacob looked at her as if she were chanting obscenities.

"What?" she asked him softly. "What's so terrible?"

"He just needs some time, that's all. He's just run twelve miles. Give him a second to breathe."

As her brother eventually walked toward

her, all she wanted to say was: *Sit down. Let's all just stay here in the midst of all this green. There's a swing set and a slide, and monkey bars too. What more do we really need? Jacob, David (Keith, you can come too), let's take a little break from the world as we know it.*

But she just grinned at Aaron, feeling — despite her best efforts — shy.

"Good run?" Jacob asked him, gripping, briefly, Aaron's sweaty hand.

"It was fine," Aaron told him. "You had some company?" he said, looking at Lila. "A little tour of . . . what would you call this? Some trees? Trees and an old school?" He laughed. "Not exactly road-trip material. But I guess after leaving New York, you're not in the mood for a Saturday in town?"

"It's nice out here," Lila said, looking around: tall trees, blue sky. "It's fine."

He seemed very mellow. Too mellow. Granted, he'd just run about half a marathon, but there was something strangely toned down about his energy, as if nothing at all would surprise him.

"How 'bout food?" Aaron asked dreamily, as if food were something he'd heard about but never actually had. "On me."

Aaron's choice of a late-lunch spot was located where they designated as "downtown,"

north of State, on Liberty Street, at the vegetarian restaurant where Keith had briefly
waited tables. Everything inside was dark
wood and wall hangings and there was a little
gift shop in the front, selling various healthy
things. The car ride had been a surreal jour-
ney in which sitting in the backseat placed her
directly in back of Aaron, close enough to run
her fingers through his sweaty hair, or tickle
his neck as she had done on countless long-
gone car rides. Now, Jacob, Aaron, and Lila
sat in one of the many booths, ordering.

"Grilled cheese and tomato, please. And a
Coke," Lila said.

"Oh, we don't have any pop here," the
waitress, a pasty-faced woman, said with sullen disapproval.

"The carrot juice is really good," Aaron offered.

"Just water, thanks," Lila said.

Jacob ordered spinach lasagna.

Aaron cleared his throat and smiled at the
waitress. Then he said, "I'll have a big bowl of
brown rice" — he illustrated with his hands
— "a side of avocado, a side of tomato, a side
of cheddar cheese, and an order of stir-fried
carrots."

The waitress only smiled.

"Oh, and carrot juice. Large."

Lila sat next to Jacob. She was on the inside

of the booth, leaning onto the dark wood, trying to both watch and participate as this meal unfolded.

"You don't seem like you're from New York," Aaron told her.

"I don't?"

He shook his head. "No," he said plainly, and — if Lila wasn't imagining things — kindly, as if he were saying, *I know you.* Aaron was, Lila decided, someone of whom it could be said, *He looks ya in the eye just a little too long.*

"I thought you've never been there," Lila said. It was one thing for him to lie, but another for him to do it carelessly. "How can you tell who does and doesn't seem like a New Yorker?"

"That's true," Aaron said. "That's fair. So what were you doing there?"

"Working," Lila said, as cryptically as possible. It was difficult not to feel as if this were a contest — who'd crack first, who'd lie so outrageously that they'd have no choice but to come clean.

"Doing?" Jacob asked. She detected impatience in his tone.

"I was teaching people English. ESL. English as a Second Language."

"Have you seen *Stripes*?" Jacob asked.

"That's always the first question anyone asks me," Lila said.

"Well," Jacob said, "*Stripes* was an important film for ESL. Terribly important."

The food arrived, and Aaron smiled as if this were a fortunate surprise. It was difficult not to stare, as her brother embarked upon creating his meal from the variety of sides that he'd ordered. He chopped the avocado into tiny cubes and sprinkled them into the brown rice. Then he did the same with the cheese and tomato, added salt, pepper, and some kind of seed that was in a bottle on the table. But he didn't eat it right away. As Keith put away his lasagna, and Lila nibbled on her grilled cheese, Aaron ate his carrots slowly, one by one. Only when he was completely finished with the carrots did he douse the rice with soy sauce and begin eating from the bowl. To both her amazement and chagrin, his food looked incredibly delicious. The delicacy with which he approached his rice bowl made a grilled cheese sandwich seem like a limited choice of fare. "That looks good," Lila told him.

"Would you like a taste?"

She remembered bites from his fork, pieces of his cookies; she remembered how he'd always offered. He liked to make her chocolate pudding, the real kind, on the stove. Sometimes, on weekends, he made three peanut butter sandwiches and took them to his room.

If she came to say hi, he'd give her one of the sandwiches, as if it had been prepared especially for her. And Lila shook her head now, though she did want a taste; she wanted to dig right in. He was genuine in his offer, as he always had been. He ate as if he hadn't tasted anything so good in a very long while. He was starved for his life, desperate for it. "No, thank you," she told him. Then something occurred to her. Something almost unthinkable, but perhaps unavoidable.

She didn't have to tell him.

She could have this weekend, this checking up on Aaron, and then she could move on. She didn't *have* to disrupt Aaron's ethereally constructed life, and break down every boundary she always thought should be broken. Maybe Aaron's choice was the right one. Jack wasn't coming back, so why should Aaron? Maybe, after that long-ago night, Aaron didn't belong to a family anymore. It was clear that he commanded respect from at least all the people Lila had met here so far, and perhaps he shouldn't look back for an instant. Maybe it wouldn't do anyone any good. Discovery can be violent, she thought, and hadn't there been enough of that? She could set him finally free, and he would belong to the world at large, put in his place among strangers.

Something relaxed inside Lila, and no matter how temporary, she felt a strange acceptance of this alternate reality — the world where she was Abby and Aaron was David.

Lies could be useful if everyone agreed to believe. Maybe it was *not* the truth, but rather the acceptance of lies, that this experience would teach her to appreciate.

Jacob said, "There's a party later on, so we should get going soon."

"Where?" Aaron asked.

"Jim and Dahlia's."

Aaron shook his head. "I don't feel like it."

"A party?" Lila piped up enthusiastically.

"I'm not in the mood," he maintained.

"Come on," Jacob said, "we've got a guest here." He smiled, charmingly, and Lila was grateful.

"I want to go," she said, looking right at Aaron. Then she said, "Please come."

Jacob chose that moment to head to the bathroom, and Lila was unable to eat anything right then, as she was, for the moment, across from Aaron in a restaurant, in a dark-wood booth, as if they had always done this together, and she were only here for one of her many visits. She gripped her fork. He kept eating in silence. In her lap, she tore her napkin to shreds. Lila waited for him to say something, but he didn't, and *awkward* wasn't the word for what the silence felt like — it was more like a spell that Aaron was weaving with his choice not to speak.

"So," Lila said, unable to do it, to just sit.

"So?" he asked, without sarcasm or insinuation, but as a clear-eyed invitation for her to speak up.

"I don't know," she said. "Will you come to the party?"

He nodded and kept on eating, meeting her eyes in a perfectly friendly manner. The thing was, Aaron *looked* completely honest. And in a strange way, she believed he was. She was beginning to accept that he meant well. He had the curse of good intentions. "You wanted to ask me something?" he asked.

"What do you mean?"

"I mean, you seem as if you want to."

He knows, she thought. The thought was pure, without any doubt. *My God,* she thought, *he has to.*

"Do I?"

"Maybe not," Aaron said. "Maybe it's just your eyes. You have startling eyes," he said. "They're very beautiful."

She started nervously giggling. "Thank you," she said.

"Why does that make you nervous?"

"What?"

"If I say you have beautiful eyes. They are."

497

"It's just —" She didn't know what to say, and he wasn't about to help her. "Thanks," she told him.

He cleared his throat again. "You're searching for something here, aren't you?" he said. "I'm not saying you're not taking the Great American Road Trip, but maybe you came to our house for a reason."

Lila didn't respond. She thought of her parents and wondered what they were doing. She thought of asking Ben to call them and explain what she was up to. It would be a while before she could talk to them, but she no longer wished them storm and stress. She was beginning to pity them, and to pity not only Jack, but Suzanne and Aaron as well. Their specific houses in the world, those hallowed sacred spaces, were beginning to seem like prisons.

Aaron was sitting up straight, looking good. His seventies-style Adidas sweatsuit was red and white, and his skin was still flushed from his run. He had some beachy freckles on his Greek-statue nose, and the way his lip curled slightly upward gave him a look of persistent innocence.

Lies were just lies — from them there was nothing to be learned. Of course Lila knew this; she knew what she had to do, but the truth seemed too elusive, too perverse.

Beauty, she thought of telling him. *I've been searching for your beauty.*

She might be left with this and only this — his ruthless, precious face.

CHAPTER TWENTY-FOUR

Aaron, it's me.

Who are you?

It's me. You know.

Oh, my God. Oh —

I've come all this way for you. I searched. Look at me.

I'm looking.

No. Look at me. How could you not have known me?

She could not get the words out. She couldn't, but she would. Lila promised herself this, as she thanked her brother with a nod, and walked through another doorway.

In the country, on a lake, this house was everything that Aaron's church was not. The floorboards were warped beyond belief, and though the place was huge, and probably had stood for at least fifty years, it looked as if each minute might be its last. It took Lila about a minute to register that this was the party house. That was what this place was about.

The people who lived here were most likely uninterested in nesting and eager to supply fantasy and escape — that and probably a fair share of drugs. Lila watched as Aaron said hello to everyone with the same level of respect and concern. The guy in the corner whose pupils were the size of quarters? Aaron shook his hand and settled into a folding chair for a chat. The fat woman with the huge saggy boobs who wore a T-shirt that said *Everything in Life I Needed to Know I Learned from My Cat*? She got a big hug — an eyes-closed, the-world-is-gone, body-close hug. The couch smelled like dead skin and looked as if it had been dragged in from the street just minutes ago, but behind the couch was a decadent, truly beautiful Japanese screen, in fiery reds and oranges, touches of blues and emerald greens. Lila stared at the screen as a method for taking a break from people.

"Hi," a voice next to her said.

It was Keith, whom she was extremely happy to see. "Hey there," she said.

"How was your day?"

"Weird," she said.

He only nodded and looked at the screen with her. She felt like kissing his cheek, but instead they both wandered to the bar. This place actually had a panel wood bar stocked with kitschy inventory — there was a huge section of old-man liquor brands, bottles of olives and cocktail onions, small bags of Planters peanuts that Lila suspected were pillaged from a plane. Keith and Lila poured rum and Cokes into mason jars. They sat on vinyl-upholstered bar stools and glanced around the room.

She drained her drink quickly and poured herself another. She made a napkinful of cocktail onions and green olives, and nibbled as she watched the room like a circus. Keith sipped and laughed now and then, at things never all that funny: a line from a movie he'd recently seen, the way Lila drank her drink as if it were a cup of hot cocoa — two hands around the glass — and the face of one of the figures on the Japanese screen who apparently looked like one of his former teachers. Time passed quickly or slowly, Lila wasn't sure which, but after her second fortifying rum and Coke, she found herself laughing at whatever Keith said. If someone had told her a week ago that she'd be in this house, getting drunk quickly, watching her brother across a room of misfits, she would not have laughed. The idea of her brother had been so sacred, so untouchable, so ridiculously inhuman. But here he was, flesh and good bone structure, in the middle of living a life. A seemingly temporary life, but his own life, nonetheless. Here was Aaron — not in the midst of a jealous rage, but with his arms crossed at his chest, nodding at the fat woman's gestures, at the trippy guy in the corner, at the tall skinny guys with poofs of Elvis hair, at the terrier on the couch, and finally — Lila realized (and maybe it was only this the whole time) — he was nodding at her.

Keith's laughter sounded so obviously stoned, so desperate, like canned laughter on a sitcom. Lila watched Aaron crack his back loudly and smile apologetically at the crowd. She felt a stab of recognition.

Lila would ask him, *Do ten years of strangers believing and supporting you accumulate as true forgiveness? Does that count?*

"Does what?" Keith asked.

"What?" Lila said.

"You said, 'Does it.' Does what? I was asking. I just didn't know what you meant." Keith's eyes were so dark and impenetrable. They were like animal eyes — lovable, yes, but ultimately unknowable. *It was his eyes,* Lila imagined saying. *They would not let me go.* She let loose a hideous laugh.

Keith joined her and they let the poison laughter consume them. She saw the room through teary eyes and aching cheeks. Keith pointed at the onions and olives. "You're like a little mouse," he managed to get out, "hoarding your snacks and your secretive ways." His face was animated and mocking.

"I'm a spy," Lila said. "I'm a terrific spy."

They both stopped laughing and then started again. The clumps of people in the room, including her brother, stared in a kind of shy jealousy. *What could be so funny,* their faces said; *could they be laughing at me?* The Japanese screen looked like something from a Hollywood version of a brothel, and so Lila undressed everyone with her eyes. Their concerned faces and illusory nakedness fit together well. The fat woman's breasts dangled with nipples the size of teacups, the skinny guys' skinny dicks hung shyly, someone's smooth skin shone lunar in the dim light, and slim hips revealed prominent bones like almonds in white chocolate. Everyone but Aaron was naked in her mind, naked as Suzanne and Jack ten years ago. She poured herself more rum, no Coke this time.

"You should maybe slow down," Keith said softly, not laughing anymore.

"I should," Lila said, and drank. She dressed everyone back up, until it was only a room full of vaguely young people again, talking away their energy, drinking away their desire. Jacob ambled over to the bar. He refreshed his drink and ate peanuts. "Where's Sylvie?" Lila asked them.

"Not here," Jacob said with a wicked smile. "Look outside." He pointed to the surprisingly lovely bay window that rose up behind the bar. There was a perfect view of the lake. It sulked between the sky and the earth, just waiting there, between them. There wasn't much light, but the water reflected the color of night and the thick stand of trees that surrounded it. A yellow crescent moon gleamed through the darkness. It was the moon of a children's story, with the hint of stars lingering above and below, stars that would be seen clearly when viewed from the lawn just outside. It could also most likely be seen on the shore of her family's pond, where at least one of her parents was probably fooling around with a fairly new and handsome telescope. Lila pictured Jeb adjusting the lens for her mother. Her father knew more about every last thing, but her mother knew how to appreciate. She was a better audience for everything from people to the sky. Vivian knew how to marvel.

" 'It's only a paper moon, floating over a cardboard sea,' " Lila sang softly, truly absentmindedly, " 'but it wouldn't be make-believe if you believed in me . . .' "

"You have a pretty voice," Keith said, surprised.

" 'Without your love,' " Lila continued,

mugging like one of her old-movie heroines, " 'it's a honky-tonk parade.' " She sang louder and then stopped, laughing it off, not noticing Aaron had come up behind them, and that he had been listening.

He said, "I love that song."

She almost gasped when she realized what she'd sung. *Of course you do,* Lila wanted to say. *Our father whistled it nonstop, our father who didn't speak, and spoke less after you and Jack were no longer there.* "Me too," she said.

Aaron smiled a crooked smile. She could smell his clean smell, ripened by all that running. He was drinking chocolate milk. His hair was the port-dark color of their mother's with the heavy texture of Jeb's. His eyes were good and complicated.

The alcohol was helping but not dissolving the physical pain that was increasing every time she looked at him. As the day had gone and night had fully arrived, she could feel the darkness grabbing hold of her spurious self and tearing away at its guise. There were multitudes of possibilities, a decade to be explained, and she was waiting for the precise moment to take it all in — her brother's story that was her story also, that she was here to claim.

She turned back to the bar and poured more rum, no Coke. It tasted like summer and it was summer outside, and this had to happen and she needed a bridge, she needed something strong to get to him. She drank and fought the weakness inside her: the pale soft skin of Ben's wrist, her mother's exhausted eyes, her secret desire to sleep all the time. She fended off the habit of tears, which were accumulating like a choker. She protected her tears by burning them with rum, staining them before they were fully formed. Lila knew Aaron was watching and she let him watch, let him see what he was doing to her, what he'd been doing all along.

"What are you doing?" he asked her, not quite alarmed, but not cool anymore.

She spun around and the room spun too. Her eyes were wet and itchy. "What do you mean?"

"I don't know." He looked at her with a face revealing nothing, still handsome still young, everything intact.

"You don't know?" She was wound up now and her strength was returning. She imagined Jack, full of spite; right now she understood why. "You seem so in control," she found herself saying.

"I don't get drunk, if that's what you're talking about."

"Why?"

He shrugged. "I don't like to drink."

"You don't like to lose control?"

"No," he said plainly, "I don't."

"You've never lost control? Never?"

"I didn't say that. I —"

"You've never done something reckless? Something stupid? Do you think so rationally, so *carefully* about every single thing you do?"

"No," he said. "No, of course not." He looked at her quizzically, as if she'd just slapped him across the face and he was quite sure he hadn't deserved it.

Lila took a breath. She took another. Then she watched herself reach out and touch his wrist. His skin was smooth and hot. "I'm sorry," she said. "Let's go."

It came into focus slowly.

The lake extended far into the distance, a green darkness that smelled like blood. There seemed to be less air the closer they came to the lip of the lake, and the house seemed very far away. There were no rocks here, just smooth banks of sand that blended into the slope of unkempt grass. Sounds from the party reverberated like wind — the music and talking only a minuscule part of a much larger picture that not even Lila could see clearly. When she looked out at the still water she felt the fishy feeling of everything that was living and swarming and growing. She felt the sensation of things unseen.

Lila caught Aaron smiling, and she smiled too.

"I used to love to swim," she heard her brother say. She looked up immediately, expecting him to be watching her, but he was staring only at the water.

"Used to?" she asked, keeping up her end of this pageant, this play they would act out until her brother finally broke down.

He barely shrugged his shoulders and shook his head. He looked at her blankly. He gave her a little grin.

"Don't you like to swim anymore?" She couldn't stop. She could not.

"Not really."

"That's too bad," she said. Lila looked at her brother. Now that she was standing right here, right at a *lake,* in Aaron's direct line of vision, she wanted her zippy urban life back, a life she never really considered to be much. She wanted Ben — not *back* but forward — just a chance with him and him alone. The temperature here was perfect and she was affected by its perfection — it made her dizzy and weak with appreciation to be alive, to be equally guilty and angry.

Aaron was watching her. She could feel it. He watched how she leaned forward, how she was listening to everything a little too hard.

She had him now; he was looking. "Abby," Aaron said, as if to reiterate the rules of this night, to tell her just who she was.

Lila looked at her brother, without saying a word. She opened up her eyes and really looked, putting on no mask at all.

He met that look and doubled it. The sky melted a little. The stakes rose, as she felt her skin rise like drizzle in a heat storm. For an instant, Lila almost forgot who he was, who *she* was. There was an animal lurking, smelling blood; she could feel it coming.

"Listen," he said, and looked stunned somehow, as if she had again physically harmed him. Then Aaron reached out and gripped her arm, as if making sure she was there. "Are you listening?"

Lila managed to nod, under his grip, under his searching gaze.

He said something so quietly; she couldn't even hear him.

"What?" she asked. And what was she expecting? What could she?

Then, like a blind man, Aaron touched her face. He touched her forehead, and along her cheekbones. He put his finger to her lips. "I feel like I know you," he said, fear in his voice, and he threaded his hand through her heavy hair, resting on the base of her neck.

"What's that?" she muttered, her voice

gravelly. She looked out at the water. The world turned on its axis. She was queasy with motion, as they hurtled into the present moment, where she was, as it happened, not at all prepared to be.

He said nothing, and with his hands on both sides of her head, Aaron came closer, his lips against her forehead in a soft kiss.

Lila had no idea where she was running, only that she was running away. She passed through the mouth of the woods into the massive pines that surrounded the lake, the haggard rock-hard soil. She knew this smell, or its softer sister, its well-tended cousin back east at her parents' house. Once inside these woods, she could have been inside a cave. Lila could hear him calling her back, but it wasn't her he was calling; it was someone named Abby. She ignored his plea and pitched herself into the dark, which was impressive and murkily terrifying. She tried to remember all the different times she'd run through woods, all the many days and nights on different friends' properties. And although she could remember plenty, she thought of the only run that mattered: the one she knew with all of her senses, the same worst hustle of her life, when she carried cookies and wore a red bathing suit, when she thought she was being so brave. She ran, and then, unwillingly, her body came to a halt. Lila bent over and began heaving dry heaves until pounding began in her head and then, through her cursing, she let herself throw up.

When she stood, she continued to reel but felt considerably clearer. To move forward was what she wanted, but unlike the woods at home, these woods didn't have clear trails. They required navigation — avoiding sharp branches and circling the trees. It wasn't as if she wanted to get lost; she only knew she wanted to move, to hide away for a while.

There were birds landing on branches; they rustled new leaves and cried out, and there were bugs, of course, ones she couldn't see, but they were creeping along and creating a stir, spinning webs and inching out of wintry snug cocoons. Her skin felt itchy and she balanced on one stone and then another, until she found herself close to the lake. There was a clearing that tapered off into the water. There was no sand here, only dirt and muck, but it was the same gorgeous water, blackened emerald with glints of moon. Lila took off her shoes, and breathing hard and damp with sweat, sat on an uncomfortable rock. She looked out toward the direction from where she had come, but the trees blocked her view. She'd have to wade out a bit in order to see the house, and so she stood and took off her pants and plunged her feet into the chastising muck, one foot after the other. It was cold and sludgy and, for some reason, it made her want to pee. She rinsed her mouth out with lake water, and then she trudged on out, noticing the blowsy shape of the lake ripples, the lulling sound of nonexistence. There was so much life beneath the surface, she knew it, yet right now, while she waited, the lake water seemed to be no more than a great expanse of nothing.

"Don't be scared," he said.

She didn't turn around. What Lila did was focus on the muck between her toes, and the lake water drying on her bare legs, leaving a film of invisible dirt. She wore a pair of black underwear, a black T-shirt, and the blue beaded sweater on top. The air teased the fine hair on her thighs. She tried not to turn around, but she couldn't stop herself. She was drawn to the sound of her brother's voice, still pitifully new and magical even after these strange two days. He, Aaron, was still what she had looked for and found, her big fucking prize, her jackpot after years of deprivation.

He was watching her with interest, with calculated warmth and affection. Lila could imagine him thinking that if he treated her like everyone else — all those sad saps that he'd met and helped out so successfully, she would become just another charity case. She would gain perspective over her difficulties and leave him alone. His hands were in his pants pockets, keeping him in place. He was looking right at her. He seemed to be nodding.

"What are you nodding at?" she asked him.

"I know you're afraid. It's okay."

"Is it?" she asked. "Do you think so?"

"I don't really know," he said. And then he just stood there. "I *don't* know you," he said. "I don't know your mind, but I do think so. I think you'll be fine." He was cryptic as anyone she had ever met. He talked like some kind of sphinx. She waited for him to say anything more but he didn't say a word. The space between them thrummed with possibility. She remembered how he smelled like good clean sweat. He looked like he belonged here, in the dark, in the woods. She couldn't see him all that well; he was a figure in a forest. This seemed more honest, somehow.

"Why are you celibate?" she asked him. It felt strangely good to ask.

"Who told you that?" he asked, coming closer, filling in the gap with his legs and his shoulders, with his puzzlingly labored breath. He was looking at her, and what she felt was complicated. He didn't look as if he were about to answer. She didn't know if she wanted him to. What she knew was that everything she had ever felt was brimming all around her. Her misplaced longing was being placed, and her self-conscious attention to detail was at work: the way each breath was followed by the next; the seconds lost and minutes gone and time perpetually dying.

He seemed to be coming closer but at the same time receding. He seemed to come closer and then — then he was close. He put his arms around her and she felt herself dissolve. She could feel her sturdy body diminishing straightaway, yet she realized that though she was smaller than he was, she was not that much smaller after all. He didn't pull her to him, and she didn't settle in, so his arms did not enclose her as much as outline where she was, exactly, on this earth right now. There was still the smallest whiff of air between them. They were not exactly pressed together, and not quite set apart.

For a long time, there were no words.

She came closer. His arms reached further around and he breathed. He breathed loudly and slowly and she could feel him shaking. She was shaking. It might have been only her tremulous breaths that shuddered between their bodies. Her eyes opened and closed and she was not quite waiting anymore. She was in another place where thoughts did not and could not possibly apply, where longings were so powerful that death seemed very near. Death seemed appropriate now, only she couldn't imagine what form it would take. A tree could fall, lightning could strike, or Aaron, her brother, could fly into a rage. Anything was possible, anything at all. Lila knew nothing. For instance: denial. She had no idea about its power, how terrific a force it could be.

Aaron stepped away. "This is very strange," he said. He sounded younger and different. He sounded genuinely confused.

"Why don't you just say it."

"What do you want me to say?"

Lila knew that her deepest desire was to be named. She wanted, she *needed*, to hear him claim her. "Tell me who I am."

He looked confused. It was convincing. He said some garbage to the effect of, *Only you know who you are.*

This patch of land — ground, trees, sky, and water — felt utterly and completely different from only moments ago, when Aaron wasn't there. There was a violence to his passivity. A cold, bitter cruelty. Her hands gripped his shoulders and she dug her fingers in, as hard as she could. She tried to stop herself from shaking, from feeling as frightened as she did. "Look at me," she said.

"You're crying," he said. "Please," he whispered, "please."

"Please *what?* Why did you follow me?" she yelled. She could barely catch her breath.

"Because I knew you were upset. Please," he said again. "Because I feel something when I'm around you. Some kind of — I don't know — something good. I don't know how to explain it."

"Something *good?*" she said, not recognizing her life by her memories or by anything she'd been told. It may well be, she realized, that there were no reliable sources. Even Aaron, himself, might not choose to tell her, or even remember who he was and what he was doing ten years ago. Life might just have to start over right now.

Aaron came near her awkwardly, even by her standards, stroked her nest of hair. She looked at him, tears pouring from her eyes. She could barely feel herself crying. It didn't feel like crying. It didn't feel like she was actually here.

"Who are you?" was what he eventually said. It sounded like a line from a television show, an empty, mindless refrain.

She kissed him then, firm on the mouth, nothing soft about it. She was sobbing now, as she whispered it: "Aaron," she said. Then she stood up, and, feeling nothing but the need to move away, she whipped off her shirt and sweater, and dove into the lake. She swam underwater for a very long time, until her ears hurt, and she was profoundly disoriented, and there was no breath left at all.

Lila broke the lake's surface with a yell, with an acute fear of being lost, of drowning from her own panic. She could not see her brother and she was frozen with fear until she heard him call her name. She heard as he struggled to get the sound out, and he kept on saying it, loudly and relentlessly.

The word *Lila* was cried over and over to the dark night, to the trees, to the water, the moon. And to her.

CHAPTER TWENTY-FIVE

Coming out of the water was far more difficult than it had been diving in. Lila swam hard in Aaron's direction, but stopped when her feet touched the bottom, when she heard him crying out in a voice that she remembered — a gut-wrenching sob that continued much longer than would have seemed humanly possible. It was a cry that had infected her dreams for years. It was the sound of Jack's limbs spread over jagged rocks, the sound of Suzanne's naked body.

Lila wasn't naked, but she was close enough, and what heat she'd felt toward Aaron was transforming, if only slightly, into pity. But if it was pity, it was still urgent, still beyond control. She couldn't help but focus on the lingering shock of his lips, how his strong hands had turned awkward and daunted. Now, in the water, she was utterly awake, slightly revolted, and amazed he hadn't known. There was little of the stranger left in him now; but he was somehow more than simply her tearful older brother. She wanted to slap him, to do him damage. She also wanted to kiss him again, to curl up snug inside of him and tune out the rest of the world.

Lila was far enough away that she couldn't see Aaron's exact expression, yet she was close enough to see his arm literally reaching out to her. The lake's bottom was sickening to the touch, and she made no effort to lift her feet. She dug her toes down deep in the muck, making herself feel it, and the cold water too, the serious chill that was good and numbing. The party was probably still going strong, but she would never remember hearing any sounds of it when she tried, in the future, to put this moment together in her mind. There were no sounds but Aaron's sounds — the amorphous sobs and the two syllables of her name.

"Lila," he called, ruthlessly. "Lila!"

She didn't call back to him.

"Come here," he called.

"You killed him," she was yelling, and maybe had been yelling for some time now. "I know everything."

"What do you know?" he surprised her by yelling back. There was loathing in his voice and a frustration that scared her. She was cold in the water but she couldn't get near him like this; she felt far too exposed.

And her rationale was long gone. Her only manageable response was what she heard herself yelling over and over again. She yelled right over his questions that she couldn't hear, with her weak and hysterical voice, "You killed him and ran away."

"Lila," he yelled, "Lila, let me talk to you. Just shut up for a second!"

She turned from him and swam again, in the opposite direction of the shore. She swam the crawlstroke fast and tried to imagine how the world would go on, how she could be part of the world. She grappled with the ideas of daylight, food, the city of New York, her parents. And mostly she grappled with Ben. Lila pushed the water with her arms and legs, came up for air as little as possible, and imagined herself describing this night to him: *It was as if, for a moment, neither of us knew who we were. And then we did. Aaron was crying and sobbing. He had a terrible cough and a low . . . a pitiful . . . moan.* Describing it was the only way she knew how to remain conscious, alert, how not to toy with drowning — simply swimming until it would just be over without a confrontation. The confrontation — the one she'd thought she'd wanted — was now only horrifying. Her anger and frustration were only a very small part of it, as there was longing for Aaron and pity too. There was kindness, Aaron's kindness, alongside Jack's death; there was altogether too much in the mix. Lila tried to swim faster but she couldn't, and ended up paddling something between a breaststroke and a dog paddle, blowing bubbles for air.

When she looked back he wasn't there, and Lila became so panicked at the idea of his actually leaving again that she began calling his name so loudly that she almost choked.

"I'm right here," he told her.

She swung her head around to the nearest trees. He'd been following her, walking the lip of the shore. She could see him standing between two trees. Lila floated and watched him until she couldn't stand it any longer, and then she swam back in view of the clearing where her clothes were. He got there before she did. He wasn't going anywhere.

When the water grew finally unbearably cold (she wished it were a better reason, some kind of final resolve), Lila trudged back to where her brother stood, both of them somewhat quieted down. He stood with his sweatshirt between his hands like a towel, ready to help her get warm. She stepped into the sweatshirt and she let him try. It was impossible to deny such brief physical comfort, and a wave of exhaustion overcame her. He rubbed her hair between his hands like a magician before a new trick. Then he handed over her T-shirt, her pants, and favorite blue sweater — all of which were dirty but very welcome. Getting dressed gave her something to do.

He was still crying a little; every so often he'd wipe his nose on the back of his hand. "I didn't know," he repeated. "I didn't know it was you."

"Well, it is," she finally said, when she was dressed and standing still. "How could you not have known me?"

"You're right," he said, standing rooted before her. "Even though you look so different. I didn't want to see it. I must have suspected something, but I just thought . . ."

"What?"

"I thought what I was feeling — the recognition when I spoke to you, the wanting to look at you, everything — I thought it was . . . I don't know. I liked the sound of your voice. I haven't felt anything beyond compassion for someone in a very, very long time. You made me feel selfish." He reached out and grabbed her shoulders lightly. He gave an abrupt laugh. "And Lila," he said, "you're beautiful."

"I'm not beautiful," she said. "Give me a break."

"You take compliments well, too."

"Stop," she said, her face burning red; she was annoyingly, horribly dizzy. "This is a little too much for me. I brought it on, I know. But this is not what I imagined."

"What did you imagine?"

"Yelling," she said. "I imagined feeling nothing but anger and I thought I would punish you. I imagined feeling a lot more comfortable about making you tell me the truth."

"But you don't need to make me," he said. "I'll tell you anything you want to know."

"Do you know how I found you?" she asked, her voice on the rise, thinking of all the doubting and anxiety connected to his name.

Aaron shook his head. "You can tell me that some other time. Or now. If you want."

"Are you afraid to know?"

"Maybe," he said. "You know, I've been someone else for a long time."

"You've been lying for a very long time," she said.

"I don't lie about anything but my past. I am actually scrupulous about telling the truth day to day. But the past, yeah. I lie a lot."

"Does it get easier with time?"

"No," he said, "it gets harder. The place inside of me that knows the truth becomes smaller and more confined."

The wind was picking up a bit; the stars and trees seemed to shake from it. Lila wondered about Aaron's friends at the party, if they all had gone home long ago.

"I saw Suzanne," Lila said.

Aaron took a breath, and didn't say a thing.

"I spoke to her at length. More than once. I spoke to Pria Dajani." As Lila put out these names in the air, she felt an amorphous anger returning. "Did you think I just wouldn't care about this? That I would just grow up and move on?"

His expression was so painful to watch. She was glad for the cloak of darkness that limited exactly what she saw. His face was the face of a child or a very old man.

She said, "You didn't give much thought to me at all."

"That's not true," he said quietly. "I have. I've always wondered. I missed out on your life, everything that happened to you. It's already happened, and I missed it. How can I possibly explain?"

"I don't know, but I'm wide awake," she said.

Aaron sat down on a rock, and Lila settled herself on the ground, leaning back against a tree. Time was irrelevant. It might have been hours since the friends and the party — minutes or days gone by.

Finally he spoke up: "I've spent the past ten years imagining one night, over and over

525

again. I have literally traveled around the world and met people who've told me their stories of amazing regret. I sought them out for the first few years; no doubt I was looking to feel better about what happened. Because, yes, Lila," he said, in that unearthly rich voice, that thought-out speech pattern that seemed to come straight out of a brain consumed with doubt, "I blame myself for Jack's death," he said, and then fell prey to a spasm of tears as extravagant as his voice was restrained.

Lila waited for him to stop, and he did stop, much sooner than she would have imagined possible. The quick change in demeanor was absurd and painful.

"So at first, I was looking to feel better, to feel something besides horror and guilt. But of course I soon realized that what happened could never really fade. So I began to examine every second of that night. I began to document it in my mind over and over again. And I also wrote it down on paper. How I imagined it, I mean."

"You've helped people," Lila muttered. "That's what everyone here says about you." Her voice was almost free of defensiveness — almost, but not quite.

He stared blankly. "So," he said, timidly, "you saw Suzanne?"

Lila nodded. "She is not an easy woman."

Aaron laughed too loud.

"That was how I found you. Finally. At first she told me nothing. I actually saw her on the street; can you believe it? She was having dinner in a restaurant, leaning up against the window. She told me about the letters."

"So she receives the letters," he said neutrally. "Does she think I'm insane?"

"I don't think she gets that far. She said she's never read any of them. She's a terrified kind of person."

"Suzanne?"

"She seems afraid of a great many things. And she's afraid of how much you hate her."

Aaron put his head in his hands and kept it there for a while. He seemed to forget about the conversation.

"Do you?" Lila asked.

"I love her," he said, his voice riddled with confusion. "Somehow I *have* to love her. I mean I'm not really sure how I really feel about Suzanne, but for some reason I need to write her about once a month. I need to ask for her forgiveness."

"But didn't you — didn't you catch them together?"

"Who told you that?"

"Suzanne. Basically."

"I basically did. Jack told me that she had,

you know, come on to him, which I didn't believe. I didn't believe it for a long time. I'll never know what happened. But I think — and maybe I've just decided to think this — but I think that she probably *did* come on to him. I was so possessive, so . . ." His voice trailed off into the darkness.

Lila fought herself not to urge him to continue, not to push too hard, too soon.

Aaron cleared his throat and resumed. "I loved her but had no idea what she was thinking, and to tell you the truth that is still kind of how I feel. I know how crazy that must sound to you, but I feel some kind of need to hold on to her. Maybe I need to keep her important in order to assign some reason to what I did. Or maybe it's more mysterious. But I can't blame her alone. Even if I had reason to punch Jack, even if brothers punch each other all the time, *I* know it was more than that. I unleashed something that should never have ever been unleashed. People need to practice self-restraint. It's a crucial element to being human. That, by the way, is why I am celibate. I'm trying to learn something." He cleared his throat, as if he were, in fact, embarrassed.

"How long have you been on *that* kick?"

He looked at her disapprovingly and it made her feel better. "Since the last time I saw you," he said. "Ten years," he added, as if he were right now feeling just how very long that was, and it was something of which he was proud.

"Jesus," Lila said.

"There is something to be said for it," he said. Then he continued. "Jack was very complicated. I don't know what you remember, my God, you were so little." He burst into those sudden tears again, and again, he reined them in. "And I don't know what you heard from Suzanne, or from Pria for that matter, but he was someone who needed help. I'll never know what Jack was all about. He had been acting strangely toward me for some time. That night I thought he hated me, and maybe he did, but maybe he would have let go of all that in time. The sickness I feel," Aaron said calmly, almost as if he had practiced this speech, "is the fact that I ended so much possibility."

"You pushed him onto those rocks?" Lila asked, much more meekly than she'd intended. She tried to picture it, and couldn't.

"I punched him hard, harder than I would have ever thought possible. I wanted to kill him." He was looking right at her. "I could lie, and believe me I have tried to lie to myself and tell myself that I never really intended that, but it is not true. I wanted him dead."

Aaron covered his face with his hands.

There was an unexpected calm here. A sense of no great relief or surprise. His voice told the truth, which was as cold and useless as a dull blade.

For about an hour they sat and watched the night move slowly on, how the moon went in and out of gauzy clouds, how the lake remained the same. Once in a while Aaron would cry, but essentially they sat in silence, waiting for the right words.

Lila thought about the Jack she remembered. *That* Jack had taken her to the bird sanctuary and pointed out details as if they were secrets. He didn't ask her too many questions or make her feel like he was in charge. Jack acted as if she were his own good luck. He'd never said so, but Lila had thought she'd made him feel happier than he would have been by himself, alone with all those birds. The Jack she remembered was such a whole lot of fun, it was sad, somehow, to imagine him sleeping, let alone to imagine him dead. Lila pretended that he was swimming in the lake right now and making long strokes toward them. She pictured him at home, an adult with her parents, drinking a bottle of wine. And then — she couldn't stop it — she imagined Jack's body, the one he left behind, now eroded by earth and hungry bugs, the overall greediness of time.

"Do Mom and Jeb know where you are?" Aaron finally asked.

She shook her head, and he only nodded. He didn't seem surprised. "Do Mom and Jeb know where *you* are?" she asked.

"Not that I know about," he said, shaking his head. "I've talked to Mom," he admitted.

"You have?"

"I call her now and then, about three times a year. If she doesn't answer, I hang up."

"You hang up?" She almost smiled.

"What?"

"Nothing, go on," she said. "Please."

"It was always Jeb who couldn't forgive me. He called me a murderer before I left, and that was what it all came down to. When I first took off, I called them. You were staying with Nana and Grandpa, that summer after it happened. Mom, Jeb, and I had a number of overseas conversations, and no matter what he tried to say, it would come out eventually that he did not think he could forgive me. He told me it was too difficult to talk to me, and that I should make my own way for a while." Aaron paused and took a breath. "He was stubborn. Once, a year or so later, he told me that he was actually sorry, that he knew it was his failing but that he could not come to terms with what happened at all. Mom hoped he'd come around, but he didn't, and he wouldn't let her talk about it, or at least that's what she told me. Jeb had decided they should tell you that I was off traveling, still broken up by Jack's death, which I was."

"But what about later? Couldn't they have told me later?"

"After they'd made up a story about what happened, and made me tell the story to the hospital, after they outright lied about the cause of their son's death, they thought it was best for everyone's security to let you believe the cover-up and let it just fade with time. As a few years went by, Mom was torn about telling you more, but she was also very weak. She would do whatever Jeb thought he could live with. And I wasn't going to force myself back in."

"But what about Mom? Didn't she come and see you?"

"I didn't want her to," he said quietly. "I never let her know where I was."

"Why?"

"I don't know; I couldn't face anyone. And the longer I was gone, the harder it became."

"But didn't Mom want to know?"

"She did — at least she said she did — but if she knew, then she would have had to try to see me, and that would have caused everyone a whole new set of problems. As long as she didn't know where I was, I could stay in control of when I spoke to her, and she didn't have the pressure of having to make a choice between Jeb and me. Each year I sensed her becoming more comfortable with the situation."

"But it's so selfish," Lila said. "At least they had a choice in the matter of losing you."

"They don't see it that way. They're proud that they protected you. They made it clean — sad and mysterious — but clean."

"Didn't you have any feeling whatsoever about what *I* thought of you? Did it ever cross your mind that while you were reaching out to strangers, extending your *compassion,* that your own sister was left with a ridiculous amount to sort through with not one single resource?"

"I thought about showing up hundreds, thousands of times. I still think of it every day. I thought about driving home, seeing how you were. And then I'd think about the woods, and the same rocks and water. At some point it just didn't seem possible anymore."

Lila flinched. "That's cruel. And it's lazy. I'm one person who has been very much alive and considerably obsessed with you."

"I asked Mom about you every time. I did."

"I'm not dead," she said coldly. "I'm not dead. What did I ever do to you?"

"My God, Lila, nothing. I didn't know what they'd told you. I didn't know —"

"So I just got killed off? With Jack? It seems, from what I can see, you're playing God —"

"No," Aaron interrupted, "It is *not* that. I'm —"

"You're in control of every little thing!"

"I'm in control of nothing," he said. "I didn't kill you off. I always think of you."

"You don't even know me. You didn't even recognize me."

"I want to, believe me. I want to know right now what you've been doing with yourself, if you're in college or working or what. I want to know where you live, if you have some good friends, if you love someone. I think about you, I'm telling you. You are always, *always* with me."

Lila only looked at him. She waited for more.

"I have all these ideas about what I thought you might do. You were such a confident kid; I remember everything. I do." Aaron cracked his knuckles, and ran his hands through his hair. "So *are* you in school?"

Lila asked herself why she was digging her nails into her hand, why she felt increasingly angry. "Am I in school?"

He nodded.

"Am I in school?"

"What?"

"You can't just ask me questions. You can't just do that!"

"Why not?"

"How about you? Who the hell are you — David Silver. My God, is it legal? Do you pay taxes with this new identity? Did you sell your smuggled *artwork* with this name?" Her voice was so nasty she didn't recognize it; its sound cut into the cool air and the tranquil water. "This is ridiculous," she said.

He looked at her a moment; she could see the whites of his eyes. "Look what you've been doing for a couple of days. You've lied like a natural. It's easier than you'd think, isn't it?"

She didn't answer. It was, though. It was easier, a lot easier, than this.

"I got to Israel two days after Jack's funeral. I'd met a guy at Columbia who'd done a summer on a seaside kibbutz, and he'd made it sound easy to get into a routine, and that was all I wanted. Besides killing myself or going backward in time, I just wanted to go far away and be someone else with a task. So anyway, I called the guy up and somehow made my way very quickly to a kibbutz near Natanya —

that's in the north. By the beginning of June I was in an orange grove high up in a crane, but I wasn't eating or sleeping and I got so skinny that I was only capable of basic kitchen duty. I lost nearly sixty pounds and got very sick. That's when I met Sylvie."

Lila nodded her head and let him go on.

"Well," Aaron said, "she was cooking and I was doing prep work, and she asked me about myself and when I didn't answer, because I never answered for a while — I was just like that, silent — she started telling me how she was part of a Baptist church in Idaho, and that she'd had a dream telling her to come to Israel, that the Israeli children needed her and that Jesus had sent her here. She told me that after having the dream, she burnt all of her belongings in her family's front yard."

"Wow," Lila said.

"Well, yeah, I thought she was pretty much a Holy Roller, and I must have nodded and said something like, 'Is this enough garlic?' and then I guess she asked me more questions that I didn't answer. But then she came around at night to my room, and asked me to take a walk with her. She stood out to me among the other North Americans and Europeans there — she didn't belong to any group, and like me, she never socialized, so I suppose I paid attention."

Lila wondered if he'd ever told this story. He wasn't stumbling, but he seemed almost too excited to be talking — like a person who'd just learned a new language and was amazed how the words fit together so well.

"Sylvie talked a blue streak. She told me she was actually in Israel only because her boyfriend, who had recently been killed, had expressed interest in going there, and she was trying to do something right by him, and she was very lonely and recently suicidal, and decided to pick me to talk to." Aaron sped up his words and they acquired some bite. His tone held a dose or two of regret. "And so I finally responded. I guess I tried to comfort her. We talked for weeks. There was a period of intense hugs and me rejecting her affection and then there was me explaining why I didn't want to touch her. Why I didn't want to touch anyone again, and then I told her why I was there."

Aaron gave a sigh and muttered an apology, something to the effect of rolling his eyes. "I almost can't believe any of this when I say it," he said. "Fuck," he spit out angrily. "This is hard," he said. "This is really hard."

"I know," Lila said, uncomfortable with him, with his awkwardness, with his long and foreign story. She was uncomfortable, strangely enough, with his language. It was the first time he'd cursed in two days, or — for all Lila knew — ten years.

"We exchanged possessions," he continued, embarrassed. "I gave her my possessions, and she gave me hers. Her pictures and letters and odds and ends. And she gave me this strange freedom."

"I don't even know if you're telling me the truth."

"But I am. I needed guidance. I know that sounds dramatic, but I'd just been basically disowned by my family, and —"

"Not by me."

"I just needed someone."

"And she tried to get you to love her."

"Sylvie? Yes. She tried. I'd lie if I said I didn't try to love her back. I tried to lose myself completely and get rid of all my memories, but, as you probably know, that's not possible."

"Was she with you in Russia?"

Aaron shook his head, and didn't question Lila's knowledge of his travels. "I left Israel and traveled for a few years," Aaron said, "and during that time, I met an old painter in a bookstore. I was invited to his studio, where, at that point in his life, he mainly drank and played cards with his friends. And I saw his work. I had a very vague understanding that his work could be worth something, but I had no idea how much." He shook his head and looked angry with himself. "Why I should have had this luck makes no sense. It makes no sense at all. But the fact that I felt I had little to lose was an enormous help. I sent the old painter more money after the sale was made, and planned on doing so for longer, but he died shortly after I went back to Israel, where I had thought I was going to buy some land. When I returned to the kibbutz, those three years later, Sylvie was still there. She had an idea to go back to the States but she needed money. In the few years I was gone, a woman who'd just finished at the University of Michigan had passed through the kibbutz, and she'd befriended Sylvie. Sylvie had so little real contact with people that it really made quite an impression. And so, with our mutual — albeit strange — trust in each other, we decided to give it a try."

At this point, Aaron stood up and paced a little, before rooting himself squarely in one spot. He began again, but gentler: "We decided, Sylvie and I, to make a new start. I — we — decided to create a home. I wanted to help people who needed a place to figure things out. There are a lot of people who need new families, people a lot less screwed up than me."

"But she obviously has a slightly different

agenda from you, wouldn't you say?"

Aaron shrugged. "Sylvie's helped me; she's kept my secrets. And I've kept hers, and that means a lot. It's meant enough. We've been at each other's side for almost ten years."

Lila watched in astonishment as Aaron sat down again on a low rock, leaning forward like a younger, ganglier man — his old self after basketball. This was it. There was his story, the basics, anyway. There was so much more that Lila wanted to ask him — everything from the same question — *how could you have done it?* — to finding out what Israel was like, if he believed in God, if he liked movies, if he missed sex like crazy, if he thought she had turned out okay. "Aaron?" she tested out his name, testing how he'd respond.

"Yes?"

"I found the pictures of me, the ones in Sylvie's room."

Aaron nodded and then he smiled. "I sneak into Sylvie's room to look at those pictures too," he said. "When we exchanged our possessions, the idea was that we both found it too painful to look at our own stuff, so we made each other promise to keep everything hidden until the other person was ready to keep their possessions again. I haven't been ready but I couldn't help looking now and then."

Lila felt as small as a bird, one of the baby birds that Jack pointed out in the sanctuary, high up in a nest. Her little eyes could barely open and she thought her heart would burst. She was too far gone and probably too tired to be embarrassed anymore. He was her brother. He'd spent ten miserably guilty years taking small comfort from pictures of her. "I remember when you took them," she said.

"Is it," Aaron asked, "is it a good memory?" He seemed afraid of her response, afraid that she'd reject this part of his past, the part that gave him solace.

Lila nodded, her insides knotted into gently twisted knots. "You made me feel so safe," she said. "I just don't get it. It seems impossible that you could have ever become so violent that . . ."

"I know," Aaron said, and came over to where she sat. He was close enough that she could smell his same scent, now mixing with the soil and the damp of the lake. "It still seems impossible to me too."

"I don't know if it can ever subside," Lila said.

"What?"

She hesitated, but finally said, "That you killed him." She let the words hang in the air and she listened to their fading sound. She listened to the silence after the words were gone and how it was just her and Aaron and the lake. "It doesn't feel like you killed him," she finally said.

"I miss Jack," Aaron said through an onslaught of tears. His tears were not hysterical anymore, only steady. The sight of him so close and weeping was the sight of bottomless grief. Lila felt desire again, but the desire was to comfort him, and to place herself on his side. What she did was fall into him, and it was like diving into the lake, into the pond of their past — the change in atmosphere was no less than astonishing. She was shedding herself like clothing, one piece at a time. And then she was swimming. He was at her side; he was everywhere. Aaron surrounded her like water, like the quiet and simplicity of floating.

By sunrise, they were both asleep, their arms around one another like years before this morning, but not like years to come. They would never sleep like this again. After this night they would try to catch up to who they were now. Or at least that was what they each thought as they lay there, gripping skin and hair and hearing each other's heartbeats too fast and too loud.

Sometime after daybreak, Lila opened her

eyes and found Aaron sitting up beside her, watching the brightness of the world. To him it was a different place from just hours ago. The water was blue and the sky was pink and the trees flourishing green.

"Are you okay?" she said.

He said he was full of awe.

CHAPTER TWENTY-SIX

"One thing about airports," Ben said, "one really nice thing, is that they are, for the most part, very neutral."

"That's true," Lila said, smiling at him, smiling at everyone passing by. She tried to figure out what felt specifically different about this moment. "Everything feels a little less weird here. No matter what one's personal saga is, there are the same dependable tasks at hand — snacks, magazines, gum, bathroom —"

Ben was laughing, and Lila continued in the voice of an English nanny: "There is plenty to be done and the selection is generic and everyone moves along!"

Lila realized what was different, what was causing her to question every second. She was in an airport, a public space, and she wasn't looking for anyone. The attractive thirty-something women were compilations of good handbags and smooth skin. They weren't Suzanne anymore. Her brother Aaron was not in the face of each attractive man who walked by, because Lila now knew where he was. She was waiting for him to return from the bathroom, and she was sitting and talking with Ben. Jack — rest his soul — was dead. He would always be nineteen and exciting. He would always live on, but only in her heart, only in her mind. She wasn't *looking*.

There in the Detroit airport, a week after the trip to the lake, Ben and Lila watched Aaron's carry-on duffel, and each other. There were ten minutes left until her brother had to board his plane. He was leaving Ann Arbor as Aaron Wheeler, to the shock of his puzzled friends, and in order to be Aaron, to reclaim that name, her brother was headed back home.

Lila had made the phone call. On the Tuesday morning following the night of the lake, Lila walked with Aaron to a pay phone, after a mutual decision over large quantities of coffee in a big white café. "Hello," Lila had told her mother. "Tell Jeb to pick up the phone." She refused to answer any questions until they were both on the line. "I am standing here with my brother," she told them, "and I am sending him home."

As Lila fidgeted with a duffel-bag strap, she thought of all the places the bag had been, all the belongings he'd disposed of in only a couple of days. Besides the few things Lila claimed for herself, his books had been divvied up among friends and colleagues, some clothes were dropped off at the Salvation Army, and assorted treasures were given to Jacob and Keith.

Aaron was giving the house to Sylvie and he wanted nothing in return. She intended to go on taking care of everybody, maintaining the home they'd made. Sylvie hadn't so much as taken a break from cooking meals and making lists, maintaining the business of housekeeping. She'd kept her head up when Aaron told her he was leaving, and she had wished him a firm good luck. If she was saddened by his departure, she also wasn't shocked. According to Aaron, Sylvie confessed that his leaving was in some ways a great relief.

Ben took the bag's strap from her grasp. "I don't trust him," Ben said half seriously, as he nibbled on Twizzlers and took Lila's hand.

"I know, you've already said so."

"He's —"

"He's my brother," she said with that same uncontrollable smile, because she knew that what bothered Ben most about her brother, what seemed most suspect of all, was that he thought Aaron was too good-looking not to have had sex in ten whole years. Ben had brought it up repeatedly, mostly out of the blue. *Ten years?* he whispered to Lila during brunch with Aaron earlier in the day — *but ten?*

Her brother had quirks just like anyone's brother. He seemed a little pious, definitely anal, and he held anyone's gaze just a little too long. As far as she was concerned the clearer the quirks were, the better. She was so tired of imagining and projecting that anything Aaron did, however annoying, was basically fascinating. She wondered how long *that* would last.

Ben had asked her, only a week ago, to come with him to L.A. He had told her, resolutely, that he was driving out to get her, and she could, if she wanted to, keep driving west with him. Since then, she had, in fact, not been able to stop smiling. She was sure, at some point, she would be anxious again. But for now, everything seemed just fine, at least more so than she could have ever honestly imagined. To be with Ben in the Detroit airport saying a temporary farewell to her brother, to have her hand held by Ben as he made sarcastic and nervous remarks — everything felt as it should have.

It would be a while before she'd see her parents again, but she knew she would eventually, and that certain conversations would come with time. For now though, she was through with focusing on her family's various shortcomings; they were no longer enough of a reason on which to base her life. This wasn't a conscious choice, but when she saw Ben pull up to the church house in a decidedly used blue Buick — the car was so big, and Ben looked just right — she knew she had arrived somewhere on the other side of her brothers and her parents and Suzanne.

"I can't quite believe we're doing this," Ben said.

"I can," Lila told him. She kissed him and kissed him, and then Aaron came out of the bathroom and Ben pulled away so fast it was comical.

"Don't mind me," Aaron said. He grinned, but Lila could tell he felt awkward. Everything with Aaron felt awkward, at least a little bit. They had spent a week together on various walks, eating plenty of meals and losing track of time. She was used to his awkwardness; it was almost as familiar as her own.

Ben stood up, and Lila followed suit. "Aaron," he said, sticking out his hand, which Aaron gripped agreeably. Ben shook Aaron's hand too hard and said, "Good-bye. I'm going to give you some room." Then to Lila, "I'll bring the car 'round, all right?"

Lila nodded thanks, and Ben gave her brother a second enthusiastic good-bye, taking off in the direction of the garage.

Her love walked half like a tough guy, half like a child. His jeans were too short and his feet were too big, but his shoulders and arms were as graceful as those of a prince. Ben's orange bowling shirt looked strangely regal, and his hair was good and disheveled. Lila watched him for a moment, until she felt Aaron notice.

"You must be freaking out," Lila said, looking at her brother the way she looked at no one else. She had learned to match his intent gaze when she'd figured out that this made him feel better, that it signaled, to him, that she trusted him enough to really look. Aaron told her that he often felt invisible, and that he thought his sins could be known just by glancing at his face. It was a great relief to him when Lila looked and began to see more than what fate, in the form of a fatal punch, had laid out for them. She began to see a gentle man, a man afraid of his strengths, and when she'd told him so during a big breakfast of French toast at a crowded Ann Arbor breakfast spot he'd let his tears fall all over their food. It had been a week of public tears, of people staring and offering both puzzled and consoling looks. There had also been anger, both bottled up and let loose. She had seen the arboretum, where they'd frightened a strolling family of four and a few Frisbee players with their sudden loud outbursts.

"I don't know if I'm freaking out," Aaron finally replied, and then he nonchalantly cracked his back, which emitted a particularly loud release. He gave a small, apologetic grin to no one in particular. "All I can think of right now is that they both agreed to come meet me at the airport. I keep thinking of how Jeb said so little, only that he'd come. I just hope he doesn't change his mind."

"I sincerely doubt it," Lila said. "Once he's said something, that's generally what goes."

Aaron nodded. "I should get going." He cleared his throat. "There's way too much to say."

"Let's not say any of it," Lila suggested, as a formidable knot was being cinched in her throat. "I wonder what you'll do after this."

"I do too," Aaron said. "I'll let you know something soon. I will never lose touch with you," he said, his face particularly sober. "Even if you're lazy about it, I won't be. I can promise you that."

"Well," Lila said.

"Please be careful," he said shyly.

"It's in my nature," she said. "I'll drive off into the sunset wearing a seat belt."

They embraced finally, each of them releasing an excess breath and the extra set of arms at their sides with which they'd always been reaching.

As he picked up his duffel and slung it over his shoulder, it occurred to Lila just how young Aaron was. He approached the flight attendant checking tickets, a petite brunette, who, for at least one moment of this workday — when she looked up to see Aaron, beaming with a future — was somehow, whether she knew it or not, squarely in the realm of the blessed.

Lila was not quite panicked when he was gone, when she was again alone in a crowd. It might have been because crowds no longer held the imminent possibility of Aaron, or it might have been because she was not so alone anymore. Lila suspected it was a little of both. For the first time in her life, for the first time *really*, she felt she had somewhere to be.

Ben had a carful of belongings. He wanted to share everything with her, from books to showers to bright ideas, and she was shocked by how appealing it all was, how she longed to borrow his nubby cashmere sweaters. Lila realized how thoroughly bored she had become with her secretive behavior and selfish approach to her stories and her time. Now there were maps for her to navigate and sights that needed her attention. Ben wanted to be a movie star, and that seemed like a perfectly sound idea. He was larger than life already, larger than her past at least, and she was quickly becoming a fan. As for her, traveling was as good a start as any. She wanted to amble down the Venice boardwalk, watch the sun go down in lurid colors, and get used to the idea of heat. She wanted to drive far into the desert, where there was undoubtedly a different kind of quiet, where there were no lakes or ponds.

She was finally going forward, now walking through the airport, now running. She followed exit signs and emerged in the daylight, among the crowds where she did not search for the faces of her brothers. Horns blared and people were wonderful and terrible, and there was the Englishman from Washington Square, in a funny-looking car, honking his horn with what seemed like dire enthusiasm, ready to hit the road.